Mothers in a Million

Celebrate Mother's Day with Harlequin® Romance!

Enjoy four very different aspects of motherhood and celebrate that very special bond between mother and child with four extra-special Harlequin® Romances this month!

Whether it's the pitter-patter of tiny feet for the first time, or finding love the second time around, these four Romances offer tears, laughter and emotion and are guaranteed to celebrate those mothers in a million!

For the ultimate indulgent treat, don't miss:

A FATHER FOR HER TRIPLETS by Susan Meier

THE MATCHMAKER'S HAPPY ENDING by Shirley Jump

SECOND CHANCE WITH THE REBEL by Cara Colter

FIRST COMES BABY… by Michelle Douglas

Praise for Michelle Douglas

"Douglas' story is romantic, humorous and paced just right."

—*RT Book Reviews* on

Bella's Impossible Boss

"Laughter, holiday charm and characters with depth make this an exceptional story."
—*RT Book Reviews* on

The Nanny Who Saved Christmas

"Moving, heartwarming and absolutely impossible to put down, *The Man Who Saw Her Beauty* is another stunning Michelle Douglas romance that's going straight onto my keeper shelf!"

—*CataRomance* on

The Man Who Saw Her Beauty

MICHELLE DOUGLAS

First Comes Baby...

&

The Loner's Guarded Heart

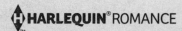
HARLEQUIN®ROMANCE

Recycling programs for this product may not exist in your area.

ISBN-13: 978-0-373-74243-1

FIRST COMES BABY...

First North American Publication 2013

Copyright © 2013 by Michelle Douglas

THE LONER'S GUARDED HEART

Copyright © 2008 by Michelle Douglas

All rights reserved. Except for use in any review, the reproduction or utilization of this work in whole or in part in any form by any electronic, mechanical or other means, now known or hereafter invented, including xerography, photocopying and recording, or in any information storage or retrieval system, is forbidden without the written permission of the publisher, Harlequin Enterprises Limited, 225 Duncan Mill Road, Don Mills, Ontario M3B 3K9, Canada.

This is a work of fiction. Names, characters, places and incidents are either the product of the author's imagination or are used fictitiously, and any resemblance to actual persons, living or dead, business establishments, events or locales is entirely coincidental.

This edition published by arrangement with Harlequin Books S.A.

For questions and comments about the quality of this book, please contact us at CustomerService@Harlequin.com.

® and TM are trademarks of Harlequin Enterprises Limited or its corporate affiliates. Trademarks indicated with ® are registered in the United States Patent and Trademark Office, the Canadian Trade Marks Office and in other countries.

Printed in U.S.A.

www.Harlequin.com

CONTENTS

At the age of eight **Michelle Douglas** was asked what she wanted to be when she grew up. She answered, "A writer." Years later she read an article about romance writing and thought, *Ooh, that'll be fun.* She was right. When she's not writing she can usually be found with her nose buried in a book. She is currently enrolled in an English master's program for the sole purpose of indulging her reading and writing habits further. She lives in a leafy suburb of Newcastle, on Australia's east coast, with her own romantic hero—husband Greg, who is the inspiration behind all her happy endings.

Michelle would love you to visit her at her website, www.michelle-douglas.com.

Books by Michelle Douglas

THE NANNY WHO SAVED CHRISTMAS
BELLA'S IMPOSSIBLE BOSS
THE MAN WHO SAW HER BEAUTY
THE SECRETARY'S SECRET
CHRISTMAS AT CANDLEBARK FARM
THE CATTLEMAN, THE BABY AND ME

Other titles by this author available in ebook format.

First Comes Baby...

To my editor, Sally Williamson, for her keen
editorial eye and all her support.

Many, many thanks.

CHAPTER ONE

'BEN, WOULD YOU consider being my sperm donor?'

Ben Sullivan's head rocked back at his best friend's question. He thrust his glass of wine to the coffee table before he spilled its contents all over the floor, and spun to face her. Meg held up her hand as if she expected him to interrupt her.

Interrupt her?

He coughed. Choked. He couldn't breathe, let alone interrupt her! When he'd demanded to know what was on her mind this wasn't what he'd been expecting. Not by a long shot. He'd thought it would be something to do Elsie or her father, but...

He collapsed onto the sofa and wedged himself in tight against the arm. Briefly, cravenly, he wished himself back in Mexico instead of here in Fingal Bay.

A sperm donor? Him?

A giant hand reached out to seize him around the chest, squeezing every last atom of air out of his lungs. A loud buzzing roared in his ears.

'Let me tell you first why I'd like you as my donor, and then what I see as your role in the baby's life.'

Her no-nonsense tone helped alleviate the pressure in his chest. The buzzing started to recede. He shot forward and stabbed a finger at her. 'Why in God's name do you need a sperm donor? Why are you pursuing IVF at all? You're not even thirty!' She was twenty-eight, like him. 'There's loads of time.'

'No, there's not.'

Everything inside him stilled.

She took a seat at the other end of the sofa and swallowed. He watched the bob of her throat and his hands clenched. She tried to smile but the effort it cost her hurt him.

'My doctor has told me I'm in danger of becoming infertile.'

Bile burned his throat. Meg had always wanted kids. She owned a childcare centre, for heaven's sake. She'd be a great mum. It took an enormous force of will to bite back the angry torrent that burned his throat. Railing at fate wouldn't help her.

'I'm booking in to have IVF so I can fall pregnant asap.'

Hence the reason she was asking him if he'd be her sperm donor. *Him*? He still couldn't get his head around it. But… 'You'll make a brilliant mum, Meg.'

'Thank you.' Her smile was a touch shy. It was

the kind of smile that could turn the screws on a guy. 'Not everyone will be as understanding, I fear, but...' She leaned towards him, her blonde hair brushing her shoulders. 'I'm not scared of being a single mum, and financially I'm doing very well. I have no doubt of my ability to look after not only myself but whoever else should come along.'

Neither did he. He'd meant it when he'd said she'd be a great mother. She wouldn't be cold and aloof. She'd love her child. She'd fill his or her days with love and laughter, and it would never have a moment's doubt about how much it was cherished.

His chest burned. An ache started up behind his eyes. She'd give her child the kind of childhood they had both craved.

Meg straightened. 'Now, listen. For the record, if you hate the idea, if it makes you the slightest bit uncomfortable, then we just drop the subject, okay?'

His heart started to thud.

'Ben?'

She had her bossy-boots voice on and it almost made him smile. He gave a hard nod. 'Right.'

'Right.' Her hands twisted together and she dragged in a deep breath. Her knuckles turned white. Ben's heart thumped harder.

'Ben, you're my dearest friend. I trust you with my life. So it somehow only seems right to trust you with another life—a life that will be so important to me.'

He closed his eyes and hauled in more air.

'You're healthy, fit and intelligent—everything I want for my child.'

He opened his eyes again.

She grinned. 'And, while you will never, ever get me to admit this in front of another living soul, there isn't another man whose genes I admire more.'

Behind the grin he sensed her sincerity. And, just like every other time he visited, Meg managed to melt the hardness that had grown in him while he'd been away jetting around the world.

'I want a baby so badly I ache with it.' Her smile faded. 'But having a baby like this—through IVF—there really isn't anyone else to share the journey with me. And an anonymous donor...' She glanced down at her hands. 'I don't know—it just seems a bit cold-blooded, that's all. But if that donor were you, knowing you were a part of it...'

She met his gaze. He read in her face how much this meant to her.

'Well, that wouldn't be so bad, you know? I mean, when my child eventually asks about its father I'll at least be able to answer his or her questions.'

Yeah, but *he'd* be that father. He ran a finger around the collar of his tee shirt. 'What kind of questions?'

'Hair colour, eye colour. If you were fun, if you were kind.' She pulled in a breath. 'Look, let me make it clear that I know you have absolutely no desire to settle down, and I know you've never wanted kids. That's not what I'm asking of you. I'm not asking you for any kind of commitment. I see your role as favourite uncle and nothing more.'

She stared at him for a moment. 'I know you, Ben. I promise your name won't appear on the birth certificate unless you want to. I promise the child will never know your identity. Also,' she added, 'I would absolutely die if you were to offer me any kind of financial assistance.'

That made him smile. Meg was darn independent—he'd give her that. Independent *and* bossy. He suspected she probably thought she made more money than him too.

The fact was neither one of them was crying poor.

'I know that whether you agree to my proposition or not you'll love and support any child of mine the way you love and support me.'

That was true.

She stared at him in a way that suddenly made him want to fidget.

She curled her legs beneath her. 'I can see there's something you want to say. Please, I know this is a big ask so don't hold back.'

Her words didn't surprise him. There'd never

been any games between him and Meg. Ben didn't rate family—not his mother, not his father and not his grandmother. Oh, he understood he owed his grandmother. Meg lectured him about it every time he was home, and she was right. Elsie had fed, clothed and housed him, had made sure he'd gone to school and visited the doctor when he was sick, but she'd done it all without any visible signs of pleasure. His visits now didn't seem to give her any pleasure either. They were merely a duty on both sides.

He'd make sure she never wanted for anything in her old age, but as far as he was concerned that was where his responsibility to her ended. He only visited her to make Meg happy.

He mightn't rate family, but he rated friendship—and Meg was the best friend he had. Megan Parrish had saved him. She'd taken one look at his ten-year-old self, newly abandoned on Elsie's doorstep, and had announced that from that day forth they were to be best friends for ever. She'd given his starved heart all the companionship, loyalty and love it had needed. She'd nurtured them both with fairytales about families who loved one another; and with the things they'd do, the adventures they'd have, when they grew up.

She'd jogged beside him when nothing else would ease the burn in his soul. He'd swum beside her when nothing else would do for her but to immerse herself in an underwater world—where she would swim for as long as she could before coming up for air.

And he'd watched more than once as she'd suffered the crippling agony of endometriosis. Nothing in all his life had ever made him feel so helpless as to witness her pain and be unable to ease it. His hands clenched. He hadn't realised she still suffered from it.

'Ben?'

'I'm concerned about your health.' Wouldn't her getting pregnant be an unnecessary risk at this point? 'That's what I want to talk about.'

He shifted on the sofa to survey her more fully. She held her glass out and he topped it up from the bottle of Chardonnay they'd opened during dinner. Her hand shook and something inside him clenched. He slammed the bottle to the coffee table. 'Are you okay?' he barked without preamble.

She eyed him over the glass as she took a sip. 'Yes.'

His tension eased. She wouldn't lie to him. 'But?'

'But it's a monthly problem.' She shrugged. 'You know that.'

But he'd thought she'd grown out of it!

Because that's what you wanted to think.

His hands fisted. 'Is there anything I can do?'

Her face softened in the dim light and he wanted to reach across and pull her into his arms and just hold her…breathe her in, press all of his good health and vitality into her body so she would never be sick again. 'No doubt Elsie's told you that I've had a couple of severe bouts of endometriosis over the last few months?'

His stomach rolled and roiled. He nodded. When he'd roared into town on his bike earlier in the day Meg had immediately sent him next door to duty-visit his grandmother, even though they all knew he only returned to Fingal Bay to visit Meg. Elsie's two topics of conversation had been Meg's health and Meg's father's health. The news had been chafing at him ever since.

'Is the endometriosis the reason you're in danger of becoming infertile?'

'Yes.' She sat back, but her knuckles had turned white again. 'Which is why I'm lusting after your genes and…'

'And?' His voice came out hoarse. How could fate do this to his best friend?

'I don't know what to call it. Maybe there isn't actually a term for it, but it seems somehow wrong to create a child with an anonymous person. So, I want your in-their-prime genes and your lack of anonymity.'

Holding her gaze, he rested his elbows on his knees. 'No fathering responsibilities at all?'

'God, no! If I thought for one moment you felt pressured in that direction I'd end this discussion now.'

And have a baby with an anonymous donor? He could see she would, but he could also see there'd always be a worry at the back of her mind. A fear of the unknown and what it could bring.

There was one very simple reason why Meg had turned to him—she trusted him. And he trusted her. She knew him, and knew how deftly he avoided commitment of any kind. She knew precisely what she was asking. And what she'd be getting if he went along with this scheme of hers.

If he agreed to be her sperm donor it would be him helping her become a mother. End of story. It wouldn't be his child. It would be Meg's.

Still, he knew Meg. He knew she'd risk her own health in an attempt to fall pregnant and then carry the child full term and give birth to it. Everything inside him wanted to weep at the thought of her never becoming a mother, but he couldn't be party to her risking her health further. He dragged a hand back through his hair and tried to find the words he needed.

'I will tell you something, though, that is far less admirable.' She sank back against the arm of the sofa and stretched her legs out until one of them touched his knee. 'I'm seriously looking forward to not having endometriosis.'

It took a moment for her words to reach him. He'd been too intent on studying the shape of her leg. And just like that he found himself transported to that moment ten years ago when he'd realised just how beautiful Meg had become. A moment that had started out as an attempt at comfort and turned passionate. In the blink of an eye.

The memory made him go cold all over. He'd thought he'd banished that memory from his mind for ever. That night he'd almost made the biggest mistake of his whole sorry life and risked destroying the only thing that meant anything to him— Meg's friendship. He shook his head, his heart suddenly pounding. It was stupid to remember it now. *Forget it!*

And then her words reached him. He leaned forward, careful not to touch her. 'What did you just say about the endometriosis?'

'You can't get endometriosis while you're pregnant. Pregnancy may even cure me of it.'

If he did what she asked, if he helped her get pregnant, she might never get endometriosis again.

He almost hollered out his assent before self-preservation kicked in. Not that he needed protecting from Meg, but he wanted them on the same page before he agreed to her plan.

'Let me just get this straight. I want to make sure we're working on the same assumptions here. If I agree to be your sperm donor I'd want to be completely anonymous. I wouldn't want anyone to know. I wouldn't want the child to ever know. Just like it wouldn't if you'd gone through a sperm bank.'

'Not all sperm banks are anonymous.' She shrugged. 'But I figured you'd want anonymity.'

She had that right. If the child knew who its father was it would have expectations. He didn't *do* expectations.

'And this is *your* baby, Meg. The only thing I'd be doing is donating sperm, right?'

'Absolutely.'

'I'd be Uncle Ben, nothing more?'

'Nothing more.'

He opened and closed his hands. Meg would be a brilliant mother and she deserved every opportunity of making that dream come true. She wasn't asking for more than he could give.

He stood. 'Yes,' he said. 'I'll help out any way I can.'

Meg leapt to her feet. Her heart pounded so hard and grew so big in her chest she thought she might take off into the air.

When she didn't, she leapt forward and threw her arms around all six-feet-three-inches of honed male muscle that was her dearest friend in the world. 'Thank you, Ben! Thank you!'

Dear, *dear* Ben.

She pulled back when his heat slammed into her, immediately reminded of the vitality and utter life contained by all that honed muscle and hot flesh. A reminder that hit her afresh during each and every one of Ben's brief visits.

Her pulse gave a funny little skip and she hugged herself. A baby!

Nevertheless, she made herself step back and swallow the excess of her excitement. 'Are you sure you don't want to take some time to think it over?' She had no intention of railroading him into a decision as important as this. She wanted— needed—him to be comfortable and at peace with this decision.

He shook his head. 'I know everything I need to. Plus I know you'll be a great mum. And you know everything you need to about me. If you're happy to be a single parent, then I'm happy to help you out.'

She hugged herself again. She knew her grin must be stupidly broad, but she couldn't help it. 'You don't know what this means to me.'

'Yes, I do.'

Yes, he probably did. His answering grin made her stomach soften, and the memory of their one illicit kiss stole through her—as it usually did when emotions ran high between the two of them.

She bit back a sigh. She'd done her best to forget that kiss, but ten years had passed and still she remembered it.

She stiffened. Not that she wanted to repeat it!

Good Lord! If things had got out of control that night, as they'd almost threatened to, they'd—

She suppressed a shudder. Well, for one thing they wouldn't be having this conversation now. In fact she'd probably never have clapped eyes on Ben again.

She swallowed her sudden nausea. 'How's the jet lag?' She made her voice deliberately brisk.

He folded his arms and hitched up his chin. It emphasised the shadow on his jaw. Emphasised the disreputable bad-boy languor—the cocky swing to his shoulders and the loose-limbed ease of his hips. 'I keep telling you, I don't get jet lag. One day you'll believe me.'

He grinned the slow grin that had knocked more women than she could count off their feet.

But not her.

She shook her head. She had no idea how he managed to slip in and out of different time zones so easily. 'I made a cheese and fruit platter, if you're interested, and I know it's only spring, and still cool, but as it's nearly a full moon I thought we could sit out on the veranda and admire the view.'

He shrugged with lazy ease. 'Sounds good to me.'

They moved to the padded chairs on the veranda. In the moonlight the arc of the bay glowed silver and the lights on the water winked and shimmered. Meg drew a breath of salt-laced air into her lungs. The night air cooled the overheated skin of her cheeks and neck, and eventually helped to slow the crazy racing of her pulse.

But her heart remained large and swollen in her chest. A baby!

'Elsie said your father's been ill?'

That brought her back to earth with a thump. She sliced off a piece of Camembert and nodded.

He frowned. The moonlight was brighter than the lamp-only light of the living room they'd just retired from, and she could see each and every one of his emotions clearly—primarily frustration and concern for her.

'Elsie said he'd had a kidney infection.'

Both she and Ben called his grandmother by her given name. Not Grandma, or Nanna, or even an honorary Aunt Elsie. It was what she preferred.

Meg bit back a sigh. 'It was awful.' It was pointless being anything other than honest with Ben, even as she tried to shield him from the worst of her father and Elsie. 'He became frail overnight. I moved back home to look after him for a bit.' She'd given up her apartment in Nelson Bay, but not her job as director of the childcare centre she owned, even if her second-in-command *had* had to step in and take charge for a week. Moving back home had only ever been meant as a temporary measure.

And it hadn't proved a very successful one. It hadn't drawn father and daughter closer. If anything her father had only retreated further. However, it had ensured he'd received three square meals a day and taken his medication.

'How is he now?'

'It took him a couple of months, but he's fit as a fiddle again. He's moved into a small apartment in Nelson Bay. He said he wanted to be closer to the amenities—the doctor, the shops, the bowling club.'

Nelson Bay was ten minutes away and the main metropolitan centre of Port Stephens. Fingal Bay crouched at Port Stephens' south-eastern edge— a small seaside community that was pretty and unspoilt. It was where she and Ben had grown up.

She loved it.

Ben didn't.

'Though I have a feeling that was just an excuse and he simply couldn't stand being in the same house as his only daughter any longer.'

Ben's glass halted halfway to his mouth and he swore at whatever he saw in her face. 'Hell,

Meg, why do you have to take this stuff so much to heart?'

After all this time. She heard his unspoken rider. She rubbed her chest and stared out at the bay and waited for the ache to recede.

'Anyway—' his frown grew ferocious '—I bet he just didn't want you sacrificing your life to look after him.'

She laughed. Dear Ben. 'You're sure about that, are you?' Ever since Meg's mother had died when she was eight years old her father had... What? Gone missing in action? Given up? Forgotten he had a daughter? Oh, he'd been there physically. He'd continued to work hard and rake in the money. But he'd shut himself off emotionally—even from her, his only child.

When she glanced back at Ben she found him staring out at the bay, lips tight and eyes narrowed to slits. She had a feeling he wasn't taking in the view at all. The ache in her chest didn't go away. 'I don't get them, you know.'

'Me neither.' He didn't turn. 'The difference between you and me, Meg, is that I've given up trying to work them out. I've given up caring.'

She believed the first statement, but not the second. Not for a moment.

He swung to glare at her. 'I think it's time you

stopped trying to understand them and caring so much about it all too.'

If only it were that easy. She shrugged and changed the topic. 'How was it today, with Elsie?'

His lip curled. 'The usual garrulous barrel of laughs.'

She winced. When she and Ben had been ten, his mother had dumped him with his grandmother. She'd never returned. She'd never phoned. Not once. Elsie, who had never exactly been lively, had become even less so. Meg couldn't never remember a single instance when Elsie had hugged Ben or showed him the smallest sign of affection. 'Something's going on with the both of them. They've become as thick as thieves.'

'Yeah, I got that feeling too.'

Her father had come to fatherhood late, Elsie had come to motherhood early, and her daughter— Ben's mother—had fallen pregnant young too. All of which made her father and Elsie contemporaries. She shook her head. They still seemed unlikely allies to her.

'But…' Ben shifted on his chair. 'Do we really care?'

Yes, unfortunately she did. Unlike her father, she couldn't turn her feelings off so easily. Unlike Ben, she couldn't bury them so deep they'd never see the light of day again.

Ben clenched a fist. 'You know what gets me? That you're now stuck looking after this monstrosity of a white elephant of a house.'

She stilled. Ben didn't know? 'I'm not precisely stuck with it, Ben. The house is now mine—he gifted it to me. He had the deeds transferred into my name before he left.'

His jaw slackened. 'He what? Why?'

She cut another slice of Camembert, popped it in her mouth and then shrugged. 'Search me.'

He leaned forward. 'And you accepted it?'

She had. And she refused to flinch at the incredulity in his voice. Some sixth sense had told her to, had warned her that something important hinged on her accepting this 'monstrosity of a white elephant of a house', as Ben called it.

'Why?'

She wasn't sure she'd be able to explain it to Ben, though. 'It seemed important to him.'

Dark blue eyes glared into hers. She knew their precise colour, even if she couldn't make it out in the moonlight.

'You're setting yourself up for more disappointment,' he growled.

'Maybe, but now nobody can argue that I don't have enough room to bring up a baby, because I most certainly do.'

He laughed. Just as she'd meant him to. 'Not

when you're living in a five-bedroom mansion with a formal living room, a family room, a rumpus and a three car garage,' he agreed.

'But?'

'Hell, it must be a nightmare to clean.'

'It's not so bad.' She grinned. 'Confession time—I have a cleaning lady.'

'Give me a tent any day.'

A tent was definitely more Ben's style.

She straightened. 'You're home for a week, right?' Ben never stayed longer than a week. 'Do you mind if I make us an appointment with my doctor for Wednesday or Thursday?'

'While I'm in Fingal Bay, Meg, I'm yours to command.'

The thing was, he meant it. Her heart swelled even more. 'Thank you.' She stared at him and something inside her stirred. She shook it away and helped herself to more cheese, forced herself to stare out at the bay. 'Now, you've told me how you ended up in Mexico when I thought you were leading a tour group to Machu Picchu, but where are you heading to next?'

Ben led adventure tours all around the world. He worked on a contract basis for multiple tour companies. He was in demand too, which meant he got to pick and choose where he went and what he did.

'The ski fields of Canada.'

He outlined his upcoming travel plans and his face lit up. Meg wondered what he'd do once he'd seen everything. Start at the beginning again? 'Have you crewed on a yacht sailing around the world yet?'

'Not yet.'

It was the goal on his bucket list he most wanted to achieve. And she didn't doubt that he eventually would. 'It must take a while to sail around the world. You sure you could go that long without female company?'

'Haven't you heard of a girl in every port?'

She laughed. She couldn't help it. The problem was with Ben it probably wasn't a joke.

Ben never dated a woman for longer than two weeks. He was careful not to date any woman long enough for her to become bossy or possessive. She doubted he ever would. Ben injected brand-new life into the word footloose. She'd never met anyone so jealous of his freedom, who fought ties and commitment so fiercely—and not just in his love-life either.

Her stomach clenched, and then she smiled. It was the reason he was the perfect candidate.

She gripped her hands together. A baby!

CHAPTER TWO

I'M PREGNANT!!!

The words appeared in large type on Ben's computer screen and a grin wider than the Great St Bernard Pass spread across his face.

Brilliant news, he typed back. *Congratulations!!!*

He signed off as *Uncle Ben*. He frowned at that for a moment, and then hit 'send' with a shake of his head and another grin. It had been a month since his visit home, and now... Meg—a mum-to-be! He slumped in his chair and ran a hand back through his hair. He'd toast her in the bar tonight with the rest of the crew.

He went to switch off his computer but a new e-mail had hit his inbox: *FAVOURITE Uncle Ben! Love, M xxx*

He tried the words out loud. 'Favourite Uncle Ben.' He shook his head again, and with a grin set off into the ice and snow of a Canadian ski slope.

* * *

Over the next two months Ben started seeing pregnant women everywhere—in Whistler ski lodges, lazing on the beaches of the Pacific islands, where he'd led a diving expedition, on a layover in Singapore, and in New Zealand before *and* after he led a small team on a six day hike from the Bay of Islands down to Trounson Kauri Park.

Pregnant women were suddenly everywhere, and they filled his line of vision. A maternal baby bulge had taken on the same fascination for him as the deep-sea pearls he collected for himself, the rare species of coral he hunted for research purposes, and his rare sightings of Tasmanian devils in the ancient Tasmanian rainforest. He started striking up conversations with pregnant women— congratulating them on the upcoming addition to their family.

To a woman, each and every one of them beamed back at him, their excitement and the love they already felt for their unborn child a mirror of how he knew Meg would be feeling. Damn it! He needed to find a window in his schedule to get home and see her, to share in her excitement.

In the third month he started hearing horror stories.

He shot off to Africa to lead a three-week safari tour, clapping his hands over his ears and doing all he could to put those stories out of his mind. Meg was healthy. And she was strong too—both emotionally and physically. Not to mention smart. His hand clenched. She'd be fine. Nothing bad would happen to her or the baby.

It wouldn't!

'You want to tell me what's eating you?' Stefan, the director of the tour company Ben was contracted to, demanded of Ben on his second night in Lusaka, Zambia. 'You're as snarly as a lion with a thorn in its paw.'

Ben had worked for Stefan for over five years. They'd formed a friendship based on their shared love of adventure and the great outdoors, but it suddenly struck Ben that he knew nothing about the other man's personal life. 'Do you have any kids, Stefan?'

He hadn't known he'd meant to ask the question until it had shot out of his mouth. Stefan gave him plenty of opportunity to retract it, but Ben merely shoved his shoulders back and waited. That was when Stefan shifted on his bar stool.

'You got some girl knocked up, Ben?'

He hadn't. He rolled his shoulders. At least not in the way Stefan meant. 'My best friend at home is pregnant. She's ecstatic about it, and I've been thrilled for her, but I've started hearing ugly stories.'

'What kind of stories?'

Ben took a gulp of his beer. 'Stories involving morning sickness and how debilitating it can be. Fatigue.' Bile filled his mouth and he slammed his glass down. 'Miscarriages. High blood pressure. Diabetes. Sixty-hour labours!' He spat each word out with all the venom that gnawed at his soul.

His hand clenched. So help him God, if any of those things happened to Meg…

'Being a father is the best thing I've ever done with my life.'

Ben's head rocked up to meet Stefan's gaze. What he saw there made his blood start to pump faster. A crack opened up in his chest. 'How many?' he croaked.

Stefan held up three fingers and Ben's jaw dropped.

Stefan clapped him on the shoulder. 'Sure, mate, there are risks, but I bet you a hundred bucks your friend will be fine. If she's a friend of yours she won't be an airhead, so I bet you'll find she's gone into all this with her eyes wide open.'

Meg had, he suddenly realised. But had he? For a moment the roaring in his ears drowned out the noise of the rowdy bar. It downed out everything. Stefan's lips moved. It took an effort of will to focus on the words emerging from them.

'…and she'll have the hubby and the rest of her

family to help her out and give her the support she'll need.'

Ben pinched the bridge of his nose and focused on his breathing. 'She's going to be a single mum.' She had no partner to help her, and as far as family went... Well, that had all gone to hell in a hand basket years ago. Meg's father and Elsie? Fat lot of good they'd be. Meg had no one to help her out, to offer her support. No one. Not even him—the man who'd helped get her pregnant.

A breath whistled out of Stefan. 'Man, that's tough.'

All the same, he found himself bristling on Meg's behalf. 'She'll cope just fine. She's smart and independent and—'

'I'm not talking about the mum-to-be, mate. I'm talking about the baby. I mean it's tough on the baby. A kid deserves to have a mother *and* a father.'

Ben found it suddenly hard to swallow. And breathe. Or speak. 'Why?' he croaked.

'Jeez, Ben, parenting is hard work. When one person hits the wall the other one can take over. When one gets sick, the other one's there. Besides, it means the kid gets exposed to two different views of the world—two different ways of doing things and two different ways of solving a problem. Having two parents opens up the world more for a child. From where I'm sitting, every kid deserves that.'

Ben's throat went desert-dry. He wanted to moisten it, to down the rest of his beer in one glorious gulp, but his hands had started to shake. He dragged them off the table and into his lap, clenched them. All he could see in his mind's eye was Meg, heavily pregnant with a child that had half his DNA.

When he'd agreed to help her out he hadn't known he'd feel this…*responsible.*

'But all that aside,' Stefan continued, 'a baby deserves to be loved unconditionally by the two people who created it. I know I'm talking about an ideal world, here, Ben, but…I just think every kid deserves that love.'

The kind of love he and Meg hadn't received.

The kind of love he was denying his child.

He swiped a hand in front of his face. No! *Her* child!

'You'll understand one day, when you have your own kids, mate.'

'I'm never—'

He couldn't finish the sentence. Because he *was*, wasn't he? He was about to become a father. And he knew in his bones with a clarity that stole his breath that Uncle Ben would never make up for the lack of a father in his child's life.

His child.

He turned back to Stefan. 'You're going to have to find someone to replace me. I can't lead Thursday's safari.' Three weeks in the heart of Africa? He shook his head. He didn't have that kind of time to spare. He had to get home and make sure Meg was all right.

He had to get home and make sure the baby was all right.

CHAPTER THREE

A MOTORBIKE TURNED in at the end of the street. Meg glanced up from weeding the garden and listened. That motorbike sounded just like Ben's, though it couldn't be. He wasn't due back in the country for another seven weeks.

She pressed her hands into the small of her back and stretched as well as she could while still on her knees. This house that her father had given her took a lot of maintenance—more than her little apartment ever had. She'd blocked out Saturday mornings for gardening, but something was going to have to give before the baby came. She just wouldn't have time for the upkeep on this kind of garden then.

She glanced down at her very small baby bump and a thrill shot through her. She rested a hand against it—*her baby*—and all felt right with the world.

And then the motorbike stopped. Right outside her house.

She leapt up and charged around to the front of the house, a different kind of grin building inside her. Ben? One glance at the rangy broad-shouldered frame confirmed it.

Still straddling his bike, he pulled off his helmet and shook out his too-long blond-streaked hair. He stretched his neck first to the left and then to the right before catching sight of her. He stilled, and then the slow grin that hooked up one side of his face lit him up from the inside out and hit her with its impact.

Good Lord. She stumbled. No wonder so many women had fallen for him over the years—he was gorgeous! She knew him so well that his physical appearance barely registered with her these days.

Except…

Except when his smile slipped and she read the uncertainty in his face. Her heart flooded with warmth. This was the first time he'd seen her since she'd become pregnant. Was he worried she wouldn't keep her word? That she'd expect more from him than he was willing or able to give?

She stifled a snort. *As if!*

While she normally delighted in teasing him— and this was an opportunity almost too good to pass up—he had made this dream of hers possible. It was only fair to lay his fears to rest as soon as she could.

With mock-seductive slowness she pulled off her gardening gloves one finger at a time and tossed them over her shoulder, and then she sashayed down the garden path and out the gate to where he still straddled his bike. She pulled her T-shirt tight across her belly and turned side-on so he could view it in all its glory.

'Hello, *Uncle Ben*. I'd like you to meet *my baby* bump—affectionately known as the Munchkin.'

She emphasised the words 'Uncle Ben' and 'my', so he'd know everything remained the same—that she hadn't changed her mind and was now expecting more from him than he could give. He should have more faith in her. She knew him. *Really* knew him. But she forgave him his fears. Ben and family? That'd be the day.

He stared at her, frozen. He didn't say anything. She straightened and folded her arms. 'What you're supposed to say, *Uncle Ben*, is that you're very pleased to meet said baby bump. And then you should enquire after my health.'

His head jerked up at her words. 'How are—?' He blinked. His brows drew together until he was practically glaring at her. 'Hell, Meg, you look great! As in *really* great.'

'I feel great too.' Pregnancy agreed with her. Ben wasn't the only one to notice. She'd received a lot of compliments over the last couple of months.

She stuck out a hip. 'What? Are you saying I was a right hag before?'

'Of course not, I—'

'Ha! Got you.'

But he didn't laugh. She leaned forward to peer into his face, took in the two days' worth of stubble and the dark circles under his eyes. Where on earth had he flown in from? 'How long since you had any sleep?' She shuddered at the thought of him riding on the freeway from Sydney on that bike of his. Ben took risks. He always had. But some of those risks were unnecessary.

His eyes had lowered to her abdomen again.

She tugged on his arm. 'C'mon, Ben. Shower and then sleep.'

'No.'

He didn't move. Beneath his leathers his arm flexed in rock-hardness. She let it go and stepped back. 'But you look a wreck.'

'I need to talk to you.'

His eyes hadn't lifted from her abdomen and she suddenly wanted to cover herself from his gaze. She brushed a hand across her eyes. *Get a grip. This is Ben.* The pregnancy hormones might have given her skin a lovely glow, but she was discovering they could make her emotionally weird at times too.

'Then surely talking over a cup of coffee makes

more sense than standing out here and giving the neighbours something to talk about.'

Frankly, Meg didn't care what any of the neighbours thought, and she doubted any of them, except perhaps for Elsie, gave two hoots about her and Ben. She just wanted him off that bike.

'You look as if you could do with a hot breakfast,' she added as a tempter. A glance at the sun told her it would be a late breakfast.

Finally Ben lifted one leg over the bike and came to stand beside her. She slipped her arm through his and led him towards the front door. She quickly assessed her schedule for the following week—there was nothing she couldn't cancel. 'How long are you home for this time, Uncle Ben?' She kept her voice light because she could feel the tension in him.

'No!' The word growled out of him as he pulled out of her grasp.

She blinked. What had she said wrong?

'I can't do this, Meg.'

Couldn't do what?

He leaned down until his face was level with hers. The light in his eyes blazed out at her. 'Not Uncle Ben, Meg, but Dad. I'm that baby's father.' He reached out and laid a hand across her stomach. '*Its father*. That's what I've got to talk to you about, because father is the role I want to take in its life.'

The heat from his hand burned like a brand. She shoved it away. Stepped back.

He straightened. 'I'm sorry. I know it's not what I agreed to. But—'

'Its father?' she hissed at him, her back rigid and her heart surging and crashing in her chest. The ground beneath her feet was buckling like dangerous surf. 'Damn it, Ben, you collected some sperm in a cup. That doesn't make you a father!'

She reefed open the door and stormed inside. Ben followed hot on her heels. Hot. Heat. His heat beat at her like a living, breathing thing. She pressed a hand to her forehead and kept walking until she reached the kitchen. Sun poured in at all the windows and an ache started up behind her eyes.

She whirled around to him. 'A father? *You?*' She didn't laugh. She didn't want to hurt him. But Ben—a father? She'd never heard anything more ridiculous. She pressed one hand to her stomach and the other to her forehead again. 'Since when have you ever wanted to be a father?'

He stared back at her, his skin pallid and his gaze stony.

Damn it! How long since he'd slept?

She pushed the thought away. 'Ben, you don't

have a single committed bone in your body.' What did he mean to do—hang around long enough to make the baby love him before dashing off to some far-flung corner of the globe? He would build her baby's hopes up just to dash them. He would do that again and again for all of its life—breezing in when it suited him and breezing back out when the idea of family started to suffocate him.

She pressed both hands to her stomach. It was her duty to protect this child. Even against her dearest friend. 'No.' Her voice rang clear in the sunny silence.

He shook his head, his mouth a determined line. 'This is one of the things you can't boss me about. I'm not giving way. I'm the father of the baby you're carrying. There's nothing you can do about that.'

Just for a moment wild hope lifted through her. Maybe they could make this work. In the next moment she shook it off. She'd thought that exact same thing once before—ten years ago, when they'd kissed. *Maybe they could make this work. Maybe she'd be the girl who'd make him stay. Maybe she'd be the girl to defeat his restlessness.* All silly schoolgirl nonsense, of course.

And so was this.

But the longer she stared at him the less she recognised the man in front of her. Her Ben was gone.

Replaced by a lean, dark stranger with a hunger in his eyes. An answering hunger started to build through her. She snapped it away, breathing hard, her chest clenching and unclenching like a fist. A storm raged in her throat, blocking it.

'I am going to be a part of this baby's life.'

She whirled back. She would fight him with everything she had.

He leant towards her, his face twisted and dark. 'Don't make me fight you on this. Don't make me fight you for custody, Meg, because I will.'

She froze. For a moment it felt as if even her heart had stopped.

The last of the colour leached from Ben's face. 'Hell.' He backed up a step, and then he turned and bolted.

Meg sprang after him and grabbed his arm just before he reached the back door. She held on for dear life. 'Ben, don't.' She rested her forehead against his shoulder and tried to block a sob. 'Don't look like that. You are not your father.' The father who had—

She couldn't bear to finish that thought. She might not think Ben decent father material, but he wasn't his father either.

'And stop trying to shake me off like that.' She did her best to make her voice crisp and cross. 'If I fall I could hurt the baby.'

He glared. 'That's emotional blackmail.'

'Of the worst kind,' she agreed.

He rolled his eyes, but beneath her hands she felt some of the tension seep out of him. She patted his arm and then backed up a step, uncomfortably aware of his proximity.

'I panicked. You just landed me with a scenario I wouldn't have foreseen in a million years. And you... You don't look like you've slept in days. Neither one of us is precisely firing on all cylinders at the moment.'

He hesitated, but then he nodded, his eyes hooded. 'Okay.'

This wasn't the first time she and Ben had fought. Not by a long shot. One of their biggest had been seven years ago, when Ben had seduced her friend Suzie. Meg had begged him not to. She'd begged Suzie not to fall for Ben's charm. They'd both ignored her.

And, predictably, as soon as Ben had slept with Suzie he'd lost all interest and had been off chasing his next adventure. Suzie had been heartbroken. Suzie had blamed Meg. Man, had Meg bawled him out over *that* one. He'd stayed away from her girlfriends after that.

This fight felt bigger than that one.

Worse still, just like that moment ten years ago—when they'd kissed—it had the potential to destroy their friendship. Instinct told her that. And Ben's friendship meant the world to her.

'So?'

She glanced up to find him studying her intently. 'So…' She straightened. 'You go catch up on some Zs and I'll—'

'Go for a walk along the spit.'

It was where she always went to clear her head. At low tide it was safe to walk all the way along Fingal Beach and across the sand spit to Fingal Island. It would take about sixty minutes there and back, and she had a feeling she would need every single one of those minutes plus more to get her head around Ben's bombshell.

Her hands opened and closed. She had to find out what had spooked him, and then she needed to un-spook him as quickly as she could. Then life could get back to normal and she could focus on her impending single motherhood.

Single. Solo. She'd sorted it all straight in her mind. She knew what she was doing and how she was going to do it. She would *not* let Ben mess with that.

'Take a water bottle and some fruit. You need to keep hydrated.'

'And you need to eat something halfway healthy before you hit the sack.'

'And we'll meet back here…?'

She glanced at her watch. 'Three o'clock.' That was five hours from now. Enough time for Ben to grab something to eat and catch up on some sleep.

He nodded and then shifted his feet. 'Are you going to make me go to Elsie's?'

She didn't have the energy for another fight. Not even a minor one. 'There are four guest bedrooms upstairs. Help yourself.'

They'd both started for their figurative separate corners when the doorbell rang. Meg could feel her shoulders literally sag.

Ben shot her a glance. 'I'll deal with it. I'll say you're not available and get rid of whoever it is asap.'

'Thanks.'

She half considered slipping out through the back door while he was gone and making her way down to the bay, but that seemed rude so she made herself remain in the kitchen, her fingers drumming against their opposite numbers.

Her mind whirled. *What on earth was Ben thinking*? She closed her eyes and swallowed. *How on earth was she going to make him see sense*?

'Uh, Meg?'

Her eyes sprang open as Ben returned, his eyes trying to send her some message.

And then Elsie and her father appeared behind him. It took an effort of will to check her surprise. Her father hadn't been in this house since he'd handed her the deeds. And Elsie? Had Elsie *ever* been inside?

Her father thrust out his jaw. 'We want to talk to you.'

She had to bite her lip to stop herself adding please. Her father would resent being corrected. She thrust her jaw out. Well, bad luck, because she resented being spoken to that way and—

'We brought morning tea,' Elsie offered, proffering a bakery bag.

It was so out of character—the whole idea of morning tea, let alone an offering of cake—that all coherent thought momentarily fled.

She hauled her jaw back into place. 'Thank you. Umm…lovely.' And she kicked herself forward to take the proffered bag.

She peeked inside to discover the most amazing sponge and cream concoction topped with rich pink icing. *Yum!* It was the last kind of cake she'd have expected Elsie to choose. It was so frivolous. She'd have pegged Elsie as more of a date roll kind of person, or a plain buttered scone. Not that Meg was complaining. No sirree. This cake was the bee's knees. Her mouth watered. Double *yum*.

She shook herself. 'I'll…um…go and put the percolator on.'

Ben moved towards the doorway. 'I'll make myself scarce.'

'No, Benjamin, it's fortunate you're here,' her father said. 'Elsie rang me when she heard you arrive. That's why we're here. What we have to say will affect you too.'

Ben glanced at Meg. She shrugged. All four of them in the kitchen made everything suddenly awkward. She thought fast. Her father would expect her to serve coffee in the formal lounge room. It was where he'd feel most comfortable.

It was the one room where Ben would feel least comfortable.

'Dad, why don't you and Elsie make yourselves comfortable in the family room? It's so lovely and sunny in there. I'll bring coffee and cake through in a moment.' Before her father could protest she turned to Ben. Getting stuck making small talk with her father and Elsie would be his worst nightmare. 'I'd appreciate it if you could set a tray for me.'

He immediately leapt into action. She turned away to set the percolator going. When she turned back her father and Elsie had moved into the family room.

'What's with them?' Ben murmured.

'I don't know, but I told you last time you were here that something was going down with them.'

They took the coffee and cake into the family room. Meg poured coffee, sliced cake and handed it around.

She took a sip of her decaf and lifted a morsel of cake to her mouth. 'This is *very* good.'

Her father and Elsie sat side by side on the sofa, stiff and formal. They didn't touch their coffee or their cake. They didn't appear to have a slouchy, comfortable bone between them. With a sigh, Meg set her fork on the side of her plate. If she'd been hoping the family room would loosen them up she was sorely disappointed.

She suddenly wanted to shake them! Neither one of them had asked Ben how he was doing, where he'd been, or how long he'd been back. Her hand clenched around her mug. They gave off nothing but a great big blank.

She glanced at Ben. He lounged in the armchair opposite, staring at his cake and gulping coffee. She wanted to shake him too.

She thumped her mug and cake plate down on the coffee table and pasted her brightest smile to her face. She utterly refused to do *blank*. 'While it's lovely to see you both, I get the impression this isn't a social visit. You said there's something you wanted to tell us?'

'That's correct, Megan.'

Her father's name was Lawrence Samuel Parrish. If they didn't call him Mr Parrish—people, that was, colleagues and acquaintances—they called him Laurie. She stared at him and couldn't find even a glimpse of the happy-go-lucky ease that 'Laurie' suggested. Did he resent the familiarity of that casual moniker?

It wasn't the kind of question she could ever ask. They didn't have that kind of a relationship. In fact, when you got right down to brass tacks, she and her father didn't have any kind of relationship worth speaking of.

Her father didn't continue. Elsie didn't take up where he left off. In fact the older woman seemed to be studying the ceiling light fixture. Meg glanced up too, but as far as she could tell there didn't seem to be anything amiss—no ancient cobwebs or dust, and it didn't appear to be in imminent danger of dropping on their heads.

'Well!' She clapped her hands and then rubbed them together. 'We're positively agog with excitement—aren't we, Ben?'

He started. 'We are?'

If she'd been closer she'd have kicked him. 'Yes, of course we are.'

Not.

Hmm... Actually, maybe a bit. This visit really was unprecedented. It was just that this ritual of her doing her best to brisk them up and them steadfastly resisting had become old hat. And suddenly she felt too tired for it.

She stared at *Laurie* and Elsie. They stared back, but said nothing. With a shrug she picked up her mug again, settled back in her *easy* chair and took a sip. She turned to Ben to start a conversation. *Any* conversation.

'Which part of the world have you been jaunting around this time?'

He turned so his body was angled towards her, effectively excluding the older couple. 'On safari in Africa.'

'Lions and elephants?'

'More than you could count.'

'Elsie and I are getting married.'

Meg sprayed the space between her and Ben with coffee. Ben returned the favour. Elsie promptly rose and took their mugs from them as they coughed and coughed. Her father handed them paper napkins. It was the most animated she'd ever seen them. But then they sat side-by-side on the sofa again, as stiff and formal as before.

Meg's coughing eased. She knew she should excuse herself for such disgusting manners, but she didn't. For once she asked what was uppermost in her mind. 'Are you serious?'

Her father remained wooden. 'Yes.'

That was it. A single yes. No explanation. No declaration of love. Nothing.

She glanced at Ben. He was staring at them as if he'd never seen them before. He was staring at them with a kind of fascinated horror, as if they were a car wreck he couldn't drag his gaze from.

She inched forward on her seat, doing all she could to catch first her father's and then Elsie's eyes. 'I don't mean to be impertinent, but...*why*?'

'That *is* impertinent.' Her father's chin lifted. 'And none of your business.'

'If it's not my business then I don't know who else's it is,' she shot back, surprising herself. Normally she was the keeper of the peace, the smoother-over of awkward moments, doing all she could to make things easy for this pair who, it suddenly occurred to her, had never exactly made things easy for either her or Ben.

'I told you they wouldn't approve!' Elsie said.

'Oh, it's not that I don't approve,' Meg managed.

'I don't,' Ben growled.

She stared at him. 'Yeah, but you don't approve of marriage on principle.' She rolled her eyes. Did he seriously think he wanted to be a father?

Think about that later.

She turned back to the older couple. 'The thing is, I didn't even know you were dating. Why the secrecy? And...and... I mean...'

Her father glanced at Elsie and then at Meg. 'What?' he rapped out.

'Do you love each other?'

Elsie glanced away. Her father's mouth opened and closed but no sound came out.

'I mean, surely that's the only good reason to marry, isn't it?'

Nobody said anything. Her lips twisted. *Have a banana, Meg.* Was she the only person in this room who believed in love—good, old-fashioned, rumpy-pumpy love?

'Elsie and I have decided that we'll rub along quite nicely together.'

She started to roll her eyes at her father's pomposity, but then he did something extraordinary— he reached out and clasped Elsie's hand. Elsie held his hand on her lap and it didn't look odd or alien or wrong.

Meg stared at those linked hands and had to fight down a sudden lump in her throat. 'In that case, congratulations.' She rose and kissed them both on the cheek.

Ben didn't join her.

She took her seat and sent him an uneasy glance. 'Ben?'

He shrugged. 'It's no business of mine.' He lolled in his chair with almost deliberate insolence. 'They're old enough to know what they want.'

'Precisely,' her father snapped.

She rubbed her forehead. No amount of smoothing would ease this awkward moment. She decided to move the moment forward instead. 'So, where will you live?'

'We'll live in my apartment at Nelson Bay.'

She turned to Elsie. 'What will you do with your house?'

Before he'd retired Meg's father had been a property developer. He still had a lot of contacts in the industry. Maybe they'd sell it. Maybe she'd end up with cheerful neighbours who'd wave whenever they saw her and have young children who'd develop lifelong friendships with her child.

'I'm going to give it to Ben.'

Ben shot upright to tower over all of them. 'I don't want it!'

Her father rose. 'That's an ungracious way to respond to such a generous gift.'

Ben glared at his grandmother. 'Is he railroading you into this?'

'Most certainly not!' She stood too. 'Meg's right. She's seen what you haven't—or what you can't. Not that I can blame you for that. But...but Laurie and I love each other. I understand how hard you might find that to believe after the way the two of us have been over the years, but I spent a lot of time with him when he was recuperating.'

She shot Meg an almost apologetic glance that made Meg fidget. 'When you were at work, that is. We talked a lot. And we're hoping it's not too late for all of us to become a family,' she finished falteringly, her cheeks pink with self-consciousness.

It was one of the longest speeches Meg had ever heard her utter, but one glance at Ben and she winced.

'A family?' he bellowed.

'Sit!' Meg hollered.

Everyone sat, and then stared at her in varying degrees of astonishment. She marvelled at her own daring, and decided to bluff it out. 'Have you set a date for the wedding?'

Elsie darted a glance at Meg's father. 'We thought the thirtieth of next month.'

Next month? The end of March?

That was only six weeks away!

'We'll be married by a celebrant at the registry office. We'd like you both to be there.' Her father didn't look at her as he spoke.

'Of course.' Though heaven only knew how she'd get Ben there. He avoided weddings like the plague—as if he thought they might somehow be catching.

'And where have you settled on for your honeymoon?'

'I...' He frowned. 'We're too old for a honeymoon.'

She caught his eye. 'Dad, do you love Elsie?'

He swallowed and nodded. She'd never seen him look more vulnerable in his life.

She blinked and swallowed. 'Then you're not too old for a honeymoon.' She hauled in a breath. 'And, like Elsie, are you hoping to rebuild family ties?'

'I sincerely hope so, Megan. I mean, you have a baby on the way now.'

Correction—she'd never seen him look more vulnerable until *now*. He was proffering the olive branch she'd been praying for ever since she was eight years old, and she found all she wanted to do was run from the room. A great ball of hardness lodged in her stomach. Her father was willing to change for a grandchild, but not for *her*.

'Meg.'

She understood the implicit warning Ben sent her. He didn't want her hurt or disappointed. *Again*. She understood then that the chasm between them all might be too wide ever to be breached.

She folded her arms, her brain whirling. Very slowly, out of the mists of confusion and befuddlement—and resentment—a plan started to form. She glanced at the happy couple. A plan perfect in its simplicity. She glanced at Ben. A plan devious in design. *A family, huh?* They'd see about that. All of them. Laurie and Elsie, and Ben too.

She stood and moved across to Ben's chair. 'You must allow Ben and I to throw you a wedding—a proper celebration to honour your public commitment to each other.'

'What the—?'

Ben broke off with a barely smothered curse when she surreptitiously pulled his hair.

'Oh, that's not necessary—' Elsie started.

'Of course it is!' Meg beamed at her. 'It will be our gift to you.'

Her father lumbered to his feet, panic racing across his face. Meg winked at Elsie before he could speak. 'Every woman deserves a wedding day, and my father knows the value of accepting generosity in the spirit it's given. Don't you, Dad?' *Family, huh?* Well, he'd have to prove it.

He stared at her, dumbfounded and just a little… afraid? That was when it hit her that all his pomposity and stiffness stemmed from nervousness. He was afraid that she'd reject him. The thought made her flinch. She pushed it away.

'We'll hold the wedding here,' she told them, lifting her chin. 'It'll be a quiet affair, but classy and elegant.'

'I…' Her father blinked.

Ben slouched down further in his chair.

Elsie studied the floor at her feet.

Meg met her father's gaze. 'I believe thank you is the phrase you're looking for.' She sat and lifted the knife. 'More cake, anyone?' She cut Ben another generous slice. 'Eat up, Ben. You're looking a bit peaky. I need you to keep your strength up.'

He glowered at her. But he demolished the cake. After the smallest hesitation, Elsie forked a sliver of cake into her mouth. Her eyes widened. Her head came up. She ate another tiny morsel. Watching her, Laurie did the same.

'What the hell do you think you're doing?' Ben rounded on her the instant the older couple left.

She folded her arms and nodded towards the staircase. 'You want to go take that nap?'

He thrust a finger under her nose. 'What kind of patsy do you take me for? I am *not* helping you organise some godforsaken wedding. You got that?'

Loud and clear.

'The day after tomorrow I'm out of here, and I won't be back for a good three months.'

Exactly what she'd expected.

'Do you hear me, Meg? Can I make myself any clearer?'

'The day after tomorrow, huh?'

'Yes.'

'And you won't be back until around May?'

'Precisely.' He set off towards the stairs.

She folded her arms even tighter. She waited until he'd placed his foot on the first riser. 'So you've given up on the idea of fatherhood, then?'

He froze. And then he swung around and let forth with a word so rude she clapped her hands across her stomach in an attempt to block her unborn baby's ears. *'Ben!'*

'You…' The finger he pointed at her shook.

'I *nothing*,' she shot back at him, her anger rising to match his. 'You can't just storm in here and demand all the rights and privileges of fatherhood unless you're prepared to put in the hard yards. Domesticity and commitment includes dealing with my father and your grandmother. It includes helping out at the odd wedding, attending baptisms and neighbourhood pool parties and all those other things you loathe.'

She strode across to stand directly in front of him. 'Nobody is asking you to put in those hard yards—least of all me.'

His eyes narrowed. 'I know exactly what you're up to.'

He probably did. That was what happened when someone knew you so well.

'You think the idea of helping out at this wedding is going to scare me off.'

She raised an eyebrow. Hadn't it?

'It won't work, Meg.'

They'd see about that. 'Believe me, Ben, a baby is a much scarier proposition than a wedding. Even this wedding.'

'You don't think I'll stick it out?'

Not for a moment. 'If you can't stick the wedding out then I can't see how you'll stick fatherhood out.' And she'd do everything she could to protect her child from that particular heartache. 'End of story.'

The pulse at the base of his jaw thumped and his eyes flashed blue fire. It was sexy as hell.

She blinked and then took a step back. Stupid pregnancy hormones!

He thrust out his hand. 'You have yourself a deal, Meg, and may the best man win.'

She refused to shake it. Her eyes stung. She swallowed a lump the size of a Victorian sponge. 'This isn't some stupid bet, Ben. This is my baby's life!'

His face softened but the fire in his eyes didn't dim. 'Wrong, Meg. Our baby. It's *our* baby's life.'

He reached out and touched the backs of his fingers to her cheek. And then he was gone.

'Oh, Ben,' she whispered after him, reaching up to touch the spot on her cheek that burned from his touch. He had no idea what he'd just let himself in for.

CHAPTER FOUR

BEN SLEPT IN one of Meg's spare bedrooms instead of next door at Elsie's.

He slept the sleep of the dead.

He slept for twenty straight hours.

When he finally woke and traipsed into the kitchen, the first thing he saw was Meg hunched over her laptop at the kitchen table. The sun poured in at the windows, haloing her in gold. She glanced up. She smiled. But it wasn't her regular wide, unguarded smile.

'I wondered when you'd surface.'

He rubbed the back of his neck. 'I can't remember the last time I slept that long.' Or that well.

'Where were you?'

He frowned and pointed. 'Your back bedroom.'

Her grin lit her entire face. 'I meant where exactly in Africa were you before you flew home to Australia?'

Oh, right. 'Zambia, to be exact.' He was supposed to be leading a safari.

She stared at him, but he couldn't tell what she was thinking. He remembered that conversation with Stefan, and the look of fulfilment that had spread across his friend's face when he'd spoken about his children. It had filled Ben with awe, and the sudden recognition of his responsibilities had changed everything.

He had to be a better father than his own had been. He had to or—

His stomach churned and he cut the thought off. It was too early in the day for such grim thoughts.

'Exciting,' she murmured.

He shifted his weight to the balls of his feet. 'Meg, are we okay—you and me?'

'Of course we are.' But she'd gone back to her laptop and she didn't look up as she spoke. When he didn't move she waved a hand towards the pantry. 'Look, we need to talk, but have something to eat first while I finish up these accounts. Then we'll do precisely that.'

He'd stormed in here yesterday and upended all of her plans. Meg liked her ducks in neat straight rows. She liked to know exactly where she was going and what she was working towards. He'd put paid to all of that, and he knew how much it rattled her when her plans went awry.

Awry? His lips twisted. He'd blown them to

smithereens. The least he could do was submit to her request with grace, but…

'You're working on a Sunday?'

'I run my own business, Ben. I work when I have to work.'

He shut up after that. It struck him how much Meg stuck to things, and how much *he* never had. As soon as he grew bored with a job or a place he moved on to the next one, abuzz with the novelty and promise of a new experience. His restlessness had become legendary amongst his friends and colleagues. No wonder she didn't have any faith in his potential as a father.

All you did was collect sperm in a cup.

He flinched, spilling cereal all over the bench. With a muffled curse he cleaned it up and then stood, staring out of the kitchen window at the garden beyond while he ate.

You never planned to have a child.

He hadn't. He'd done everything in his power to avoid that kind of commitment. Bile rose in his throat. So what the hell was he doing here?

He stared at the bowl he held and Stefan's face, words, rose in his mind. *A baby deserves both a mother and a father.* He pushed his shoulders back and rinsed his bowl. He might not have planned this, but he had no intention of walking away from his child. He couldn't.

He swung to Meg, but she didn't look up from her computer. He wasn't hungry but he made toast. He ate because he wanted his body clock to adjust to the time zone. He ate to stop himself from demanding that Meg stop what she was doing and talk to him right now.

After he'd washed and dried the dishes Meg turned off her computer and pushed it to one side. He poured two glasses of orange juice and sat down. 'You said we have to talk.' He pushed one of the glasses towards her.

She blinked. 'And you don't think that's necessary?'

'I said what I needed to say yesterday.' He eyed her for a moment. 'And I don't want to fight.'

She stared at him, as if waiting for more. When he remained silent she blew out a breath and shook her head.

He rolled his shoulders and fought a scowl. 'What?'

'You said yesterday that you want to be acknowledged as the baby's father.'

'I do.'

'And that you want to be a part of its life.'

He thrust out his jaw. 'That's right.'

'Then would you kindly outline the practicalities of that for me, please? What precisely are your intentions?'

He stared at her blankly. What was she talking about?

She shook her head again, her lips twisting. 'Does that mean you want to drop in and visit the baby once a week? Or does it mean you want the baby to live with you for two nights a week and every second weekend? Or are you after week-about parenting?' Her eyes suddenly blazed with scorn. 'Or do you mean to flit in and out of its life as you do now, only instead of calling you Uncle Ben the child gets the privilege of calling you Daddy?'

Her scorn almost burned the skin from his face.

She leaned towards him. 'Do you actually mean to settle down and help care for this baby?'

Settle down? His mouth went dry. He hadn't thought...

She drew back and folded her arms. 'Or do you mean to keep going on as you've always done?'

She stared at him, her blazing eyes and the tension in her folded arms demanding an answer. He had to say something. 'I...I haven't thought the nuts and bolts of the arrangements through.' It wasn't much to give her, but at least it was the truth.

'You can't have it both ways, Ben. You're either globe-trotting Uncle Ben or one hundred per cent involved Daddy. I won't settle for anything but the best for my child.'

He leapt out of his chair. 'You can't demand I change my entire life!'

She stared at him, her eyes shadowed. 'I'm not. I've never had any expectations of you. You're the one who stormed in here yesterday and said you wanted to be a father. And a true father is—'

'More than sperm in a cup.' He fell back into his seat.

She pressed her fingers to her eyes. 'I'm sorry. I put that very crudely yesterday.'

Her guilt raked at him. She hadn't done anything wrong. He was the one who'd waltzed in and overturned her carefully laid plans.

She lifted her head. 'A father is so much more than an uncle, Ben. Being a true father demands more commitment than your current lifestyle allows for. A father isn't just for fun and games. Being a father means staying up all night when your child is sick, running around to soccer and netball games, attending parent and teacher nights.'

His hands clenched. His stomach clenched tighter. He'd stormed in here without really knowing what he was demanding. He still didn't know what he was demanding. He just knew he couldn't walk away.

'Ben, what do you even know about babies?'

Zilch. Other than the fact that they were miracles. And that they deserved all the best life had to give.

'Have you ever held one?'

Nope. Not even once.

'Do you even know how to nurture someone?'

He stiffened. *What the hell...?*

'I don't mean do you know how to lead a group safely and successfully down the Amazon, or to base camp at Everest, or make sure someone attaches the safety harness on their climbing equipment correctly. Do you know how to care for someone who is sick or who's just feeling a bit depressed?'

What kind of selfish sod did she think him?

His mouth dried. What kind of selfish sod *was* he?

'I'm not criticising you. Those things have probably never passed across your radar before.' Her brow furrowed. 'You have this amazing and exciting life. Do you really want to give it up for nappies, teething, car pools and trips to the dentist?'

He couldn't answer that.

'Do you *really* want to be a father, Ben?'

He stared at his hands. He curled his fingers against his palms, forming them into fists. 'I don't know what to do.' He searched Meg's eyes—eyes that had given him answers in the past. 'What should I do?' Did she think he had it in him to become a good father?

'No way!' She shot back in her chair. 'I am not going to tell you what to do. I am not going to make this decision for you. It's too important. This is something you have to work out for yourself, Ben.'

His mouth went drier than the Kalahari Desert. Meg meant to desert him?

Her face softened. 'If you don't want that level of involvement I will understand. You won't be letting me down. We'll carry on as we've always done and there'll be no hard feelings. At least not on my side.'

Or his!

'But if you do want to be a proper father it only seems fair to warn you that my expectations will be high.'

He swallowed. He didn't *do* expectations.

She reached out and touched his hand. He stared at it and suddenly realised how small it was.

'I'm so grateful to you, Ben. I can't tell you how much I'm looking forward to becoming a mother—how happy I am that I'm pregnant. You helped make that possible for me. If you do want to be a fully involved father I would never deny that to you.'

It was a tiny hand, and as he stared at it he suddenly remembered the fairytales she'd once spun about families—perfect mothers and fathers, beautiful children, loving homes—when the two of them had been nothing but children themselves. She'd had big dreams.

He couldn't walk away. She was carrying *his* child. But could he live up to her expectations of what a father should be? Could he live up to his own expectations? Could he do a better job than his father had done?

His heart thumped against his ribcage. It might be better for all concerned if he got up from this table right now and just walked away.

'I realise this isn't the kind of decision you can make overnight.'

Her voice hauled him back from the brink of an abyss.

'But, Ben, for the baby's sake…and for mine… could you please make your decision by the time the wedding rolls around?'

His head lifted. Six weeks? She was giving him six weeks? If he could cope with six weeks living in Fingal Bay, that was.

He swallowed. If he couldn't he supposed they'd have their answer.

'And speaking of weddings…' She rose and hitched her head towards the back door.

Weddings? He scowled.

'C'mon. I need your help measuring the back yard.'

'What the hell for—?'

He broke off on an expletive to catch the industrial tape measure she tossed him—an old one of her father's, no doubt—before it brained him. She disappeared outside.

Glowering, he slouched after her. 'What for?' he repeated.

'For the marquee. Elsie and my father can be married in the side garden by the rose bushes, weather permitting, and we'll set up a marquee out the back here for the meal and speeches and dancing.'

'Why the hell can't they get married in the registry office?'

She spun around, hands on hips. The sun hit her hair, her eyes, the shine on her lips. With her baby bump, she looked like a golden goddess of fertility. A *desirable* goddess. He blinked and took a step back.

'This is a wedding. It should be celebrated.'

'I have never met two people less likely to want to celebrate.'

'Precisely.'

He narrowed his eyes. 'What are you up to?'

'Shut up, Ben, and measure.'

They measured.

The sun shone, the sky was clear and salt scented the air, mingling with the myriad scents from Meg's garden. Given the sobering discussion they'd just had, he'd have thought it impossible to relax, but as he jotted down the measurements that was exactly what he found himself doing.

To his relief, Meg did too. He knew he'd freaked her out with his announcement yesterday—that he'd shocked and stressed her. He paused. And then stiffened. He'd *stressed* her. She was pregnant and he'd stressed her. He was an idiot! Couldn't he have found a less threatening and shocking way of blurting his intentions out?

His hands clenched. He was a tenfold idiot for not actually working out the nuts and bolts of those intentions prior to bursting in on her the way he had—for not setting before her a carefully thought-out plan that she could work with. She'd spend the next six weeks in a state of uncertainty—which for Meg translated into stress and worry and an endless circling litany of 'what-ifs'—until he made a decision. He bit back a curse. She'd dealt with him with more grace than he deserved.

He shot a quick glance in her direction. She didn't look stressed or fragile or the worse for wear at the moment. Her skin glowed with a health and vigour he'd never noticed before. Her hair shone in the sun and…

He rolled his shoulders and tried to keep his attention above neck level.

It was just… Her baby bump was small, but it was unmistakable. And it fascinated him.

'Shouldn't you be taking it easy?' he blurted out in the middle of some soliloquy she was giving him about round tables versus rectangular.

She broke off to blink at him, and then she laughed. 'I'm pregnant, not ill. I can keep doing all the things I was doing before I became pregnant.'

Yeah, but she was doing a lot—perhaps more than was good for her. She ran her own childcare centre—worked there five days a week and heaven only knew how many other hours she put into it. She had to maintain this enormous house and garden. And now she was organising a wedding.

He folded his arms. It was just as well he had come home. He could at least shoulder some of the burden and make sure she looked after herself. Regardless of any other decision he came to, he could at least do that.

She started talking again and his gaze drifted back towards her baby bump. But on the way down the intriguing shadow of cleavage in the vee of her shirt snagged his attention. His breath jammed in his throat and a pulse pounded at his groin. The soft cotton of her blouse seemed to enhance the sweet fullness of her breasts.

That pulse pounded harder as he imagined the weight of those breasts in his hands and the way the nipples would harden if he were to run his thumbs over them—back and forth, over and over, until her head dropped back and her lips parted and her eyes glazed with desire.

His mouth dried as he imagined slipping the buttons free and easing that blouse from her shoulders, gazing at those magnificent breasts in the sun and dipping his head to—

He snapped away. *Oh, hell!* That was *Meg* he was staring at, lusting after.

He raked both hands back through his hair and paced, keeping his eyes firmly fixed on the ground in front of him. Jet lag—that had to be it. Plus his brain was addled and emotions were running high after the conversation they'd had.

And she was pregnant with *his* child. Surely it was only natural he'd see her differently? He swallowed and kept pacing. Once he'd sorted it all out in his head, worked out what he was going to do, things would return to normal again. His hands unclenched, his breathing eased. Of course it would.

He came back to himself to find her shaking

his arm. 'You haven't heard a word I've said, have you? What's wrong?'

Her lips looked plump and full and oh-so-kissable. He swallowed. 'I...uh...' They were measuring the back yard. That was right. 'Where are we going to find enough people to fill this tent of yours?'

'Marquee,' she corrected. 'And I'm going to need your help on that one.'

His help. *Focus on that—not on the way her bottom lip curves or the neckline of her shirt or—*

Keep your eyes above her neck!

'Help?' he croaked, suddenly parched.

'I want you to get the names of ten people Elsie would like to invite to the wedding.'

That snapped him to. 'Me?'

'I'll do the same for my father. I mean to invite some of my friends, along with the entire street. Let me know if there's anyone you'd like to invite too.'

'Dave Clements,' he said automatically. Dave had thrown Ben a lifeline when he'd most needed one. It would be great to catch up with him.

But then he focused on Meg's order again. Ten names from Elsie? She had to be joking right? 'Does she even *know* ten people?'

'She must do. She goes to Housie one afternoon a week.'

She did?

'Who knows? She might like to invite her chiropodist.'

Elsie had a chiropodist?

'But how am I going to get her to give me two names let alone ten?' He and his grandmother could barely manage a conversation about the weather, let alone anything more personal.

'That's your problem. You're supposed to be resourceful, aren't you? What do you do if wild hyenas invade your camp in Africa? Or if your rope starts to unravel when you're rock-climbing? Or your canoe overturns when you're white-water rafting? This should be a piece of cake in comparison.'

Piece of cake, his—

'Besides, I'm kicking you out of my spare room, so I expect you'll have plenty of time to work on her.'

He gaped at her. 'You're not going to let me stay?'

'Your place is over there.' She pointed across the fence. 'For heaven's sake, Ben, she's *giving* that house to you.'

'I don't want it.'

'Then you'd better find a more gracious way of refusing it than that.'

She stood there with hands on hips, eyes flashing, magnificent in the sunlight, and it suddenly occurred to him that moving out of her spare bedroom might be a very good plan. At least until his body clock adjusted.

She must have read the capitulation in his face because her shoulders lost their combativeness. She clasped her hands together and her gaze slid away. He wondered what she was up to now.

'I…um…' She glanced up at him again and swallowed. 'I want to ask you something, but I'm afraid it might offend you—which isn't my intention at all.'

He shrugged. 'Ask away, Meg.'

She bent down and pretended to study a nearby rosebush. He knew it was a pretence because he knew Meg. She glanced at him and then back at the rosebush. 'We're friends, right? Best friends. So that means it's okay to ask each other personal questions, don't you think?'

His curiosity grew. 'Sure.' For heaven's sake, they were having a baby together. How much more personal could it get?

'You really mean to stay in Fingal Bay for the next six weeks?'

'Yes.'

She straightened. 'Then I want to ask if you have enough money to see you through till then. Money isn't a problem for me, and if you need a loan…' She trailed off, swallowing. 'I've offended you, haven't I?'

He had to move away to sit on a nearby bench. Meg thought him some kind of freeloading loser? His stomach churned. He pinched the bridge of his nose. No wonder she questioned his ability to be any kind of decent father to their child.

'I'm not casting a slur on your life or your masculinity,' she mumbled, sitting beside him, 'but you live in the moment and go wherever the wind blows you. Financial security has never been important to you. Owning things has never been important to you.'

He lifted his head to survey the house behind her. 'And they are to you?' It wasn't the image he had of her in his mind. But her image of *him* was skewed. It was just possible they had each other completely wrong.

After all, how much time had they really spent in each other's company these last five to seven years?

She gave a tiny smile and an equally tiny shrug. 'With a baby on the way, financial security has become very important to me.'

'Is that why you let your father gift you this house?'

'No.'

'Then why?' He turned to face her more fully.

'I'd have thought you'd hate this place.' The same way he hated it.

She studied him for a long moment. 'Not all the associations are bad. This is where my mother came as a new bride. This is where I met my best friend.'

Him.

'Those memories are good. And look.' She grabbed his hand and tugged him around the side of the house to the front patio. 'Look at that view.'

She dropped his hand and a part of him wished she hadn't. The crazy mixed-up, jet lagged part.

'This has to be one of the most beautiful places in the world. Why wouldn't I want to wake up to that every day?'

He stared at the view.

'Besides, Fingal Bay is a nice little community. I think it's a great place to raise a child.'

He stared out at the view—at the roofs of the houses on the street below and the curving bay just beyond. The stretch of sand bordering the bay and leading out to the island gleamed gold in the sun. The water sparkled a magical green-blue. He stared at the boats on the water, listened to the cries of the seagulls, the laughter of children, and tried to see it all objectively.

He couldn't. Every rock and curve and bend was imbued with his childhood.

But…

He'd travelled all around the world and Meg was right. The picturesque bay in front of him rivalled any other sight he'd seen.

He turned to her. 'It's as simple as that? This is where you want to live so you accepted this house as a gift?'

A sigh whispered out of her, mingling with the sounds of the waves whooshing up onto the sand. 'It's a whole lot more complicated than that. It was as if…as if my father *needed* to give me this house.'

He leant towards her. 'Needed to?'

She shrugged, her teeth gnawing on her bottom teeth. 'I haven't got to the bottom of that yet, but…'

She gazed up at him, her hazel eyes steady and resolute, her chin at an angle, as if daring him to challenge her.

'I didn't have the heart to refuse him.'

'The same way you're hoping I won't refuse Elsie.'

'That's between you and her.'

'Don't you hold even the slightest grudge, Meg?'

'Don't you think it's time you let yours go?'

He swung away. Brilliant. Not only did she think him financially unsound, but she thought him irresponsible and immature on top of it.

At least he could answer one of those charges. 'Early in my working life I set up a financial security blanket, so to speak.' He'd invested in real estate. Quite a bit of it, actually.

Her eyes widened. 'You did?'

He had to grit his teeth at her incredulity. 'Yes.'

She pursed her lips and stared at him as if she'd never seen him before. 'That was very sensible of you.'

He ground his teeth harder. He'd watched Laurie Parrish for many years and, while he might not like the man, had learned a thing or two that he'd put into practice. Those wise investments had paid off.

'I have enough money to tide me over for the next six weeks.' And beyond. But he resisted the impulse to brag and tell her exactly how much money that financial security blanket of his held— that really would be immature.

'Okay.' She eyed him uncertainly. 'Good. I'm glad that's settled.'

'While we're on the subject of personal questions—' he rounded on her '—you want to tell me what you're trying to achieve with this godforsaken wedding?'

She hitched up her chin and stuck out a hip. 'I'm joying this "godforsaken wedding" up,' she told him. 'I'm going to *force* them to celebrate.'

He gaped at her. 'Why?'

'Because there was no joy when we were growing up.'

'They were never there for us, Meg. They don't deserve this—the effort you put in, the—'

'Everyone deserves the right to a little happiness. And if they truly want to mend bridges, then…'

'Then?'

'Then I only think it fair and right that we give them that opportunity.'

Ben's face closed up. Every single time he came home Meg cursed what his mother had done to him—abandoning him like she had with a woman who'd grown old before her time. Usually she would let a topic like this drop. Today she didn't. If Ben truly wanted to be a father, he needed to deal with his past.

She folded her arms, her heart pounding against the walls of her chest. 'When my mother died, my father just shut down, became a shell. Her death—it broke him. There was no room in his life for joy or celebration.'

Ben pushed his face in close to hers, his eyes flashing. 'He should've made an effort for you.'

Meg's hand slid across her stomach. She'd make every effort for *her* child, she couldn't imagine ever emotionally abandoning it, but maybe men were different—especially men of her father's generation.

She glanced at Ben. If a woman ever broke his heart, how would he react? She bit back a snigger. To break his heart a woman would have to get close to Ben, and he was never going to let that happen.

Ben's gaze lowered to where her hand rested against her stomach. His gaze had kept returning to her baby bump all morning. As if he couldn't get his fill. She swallowed. It was disconcerting, being the subject of his focus.

Not her, she corrected, the baby.

That didn't prevent the heat from rising in her cheeks or her breathing from becoming shallow and strained.

She tried to shake herself free from whatever weird and wacky pregnancy hormone currently gripped her. *Concentrate.*

'So,' she started, 'while my father went missing in action, your mother left you with Elsie and disappeared. She never rang or sent a letter or anything. Elsie must've been worried sick. She must've been afraid to love you.'

He snapped back. 'Afraid to—?'

'I mean, what if your mother came back and took you away and she never heard from either of you again? What if, when you grew up, you did exactly what your mother did and abandoned *her*?'

'My mother abandoned me, not Elsie.'

'She abandoned the both of you, Ben.'

His jaw dropped open.

Meg nodded. 'Yes, you're right. They both should've made a bigger effort for us. But at least we found each other. At least we both had one friend in the world we could totally depend upon. And whatever else you want to dispute, you can't deny that we didn't have fun together.'

He rolled his shoulders. 'I don't want to deny that.'

'Well, can't you see that my father and Elsie didn't even have that much? Life has left them crippled. But…' She swallowed. 'I demand joy in my life now, and I won't compromise on that. If they refuse to get into the swing of this wedding then I'll know those bridges—the distance between us—can never be mended. And I'll have my answer.'

She hauled in a breath. 'One last chance, Ben, that was what I'm giving them.' And that's what she wanted him to give them too.

Ben didn't say anything. She cast a sidelong glance at him and bit back a sigh. She wondered when Ben—*her* Ben, the Ben she knew, the Ben with an easy smile and a careless saunter, without a care in the world—would return. Ever since he'd pulled his bike to a halt out at the front of her house yesterday there'd been trouble in his eyes.

He turned to her, hands on hips. He had lean hips and a tall, rangy frame. With his blond-tipped hair he looked like a god. No wonder women fell for him left, right and centre.

Though if he'd had a little less in the charm and looks department maybe he'd have learned to treat those women with more sensitivity.

Then she considered his mother and thought maybe not.

'When was the last time *you* felt joyful?' she asked on impulse.

He scratched his chin. He still hadn't shaved. He should look scruffy, but the texture of his shadowed jaw spoke to some yearning deep inside her. The tips of her fingers tingled. She opened and closed her hands. If she reached out and—

She shook herself. Ben *did* look scruffy. Completely and utterly. He most certainly didn't look temptingly disreputable with all that bad-boy promise of his.

Her hands continued to open and close. She heaved back a sigh. Okay, we'll maybe he did. But that certainly wasn't the look she was into.

Normally.

She scowled. Darn pregnancy hormones. And

then the memory of that long ago kiss hit her and all the hairs on her arms stood to attention.

Stop it! She and Ben would never travel down that road again. There was simply too much at stake to risk it. *Ever.*

She folded her arms and swallowed. 'It can't be that hard, can it?' she demanded when he remained silent. Ben was the last person who'd need lessons in joy, surely?

'There are just so many to choose from,' he drawled, with that lazy hit-you-in-the-knees grin.

The grin was too slow coming to make her heart beat faster. Her heart had already started to sink. Ben was lying and it knocked her sideways. She'd always thought his exciting, devil-may-care life of freedom gave him endless pleasure and joy.

'The most recent instance that comes to mind is when I bungee-jumped over the Zambezi River from the Victoria Falls Bridge. Amazing rush of adrenaline. I felt like a superhero.'

She scratched a hand back through her hair. What was she thinking? Of *course* Ben's life gave him pleasure. He did so many exciting things. Did he really think he could give that all up for bottles and nappies?

'What about you? When was the last time you felt joyful?'

She didn't even need to think. She placed a hand

across her stomach. And even amid all her current confusion and, yes, fear a shaft of joy lifted her up. She smiled. 'The moment I found out I was pregnant.'

She was going to have a baby!

'And every single day after, just knowing I'm pregnant.' Ben had made that possible. She would never be able to thank him enough. Ever.

She set her shoulders. When he came to the conclusion she knew he would—that he wasn't cut out for domesticity—she would do everything in her power to make sure he felt neither guilty nor miserable about it.

Ben shaded his eyes and stared out at the perfect crescent of the bay. 'So you want to spread the joy, huh?'

'Absolutely.' Being pregnant had changed her perspective. In comparison to so many other people she was lucky. Very lucky. 'We know how to do joy, Ben, but my father and Elsie—well, they've either forgotten how or they never knew the secret in the first place.'

'It's not a secret, Meg.'

Tell her father and Elsie that.

'And if this scheme of yours doesn't work and they remain as sour and distant as ever?'

'I'm not going to break my heart over it, if that's

what you're worried about. But at least I'll know I tried.'

He shifted his weight and shoved his hands into the pockets of his jeans, making them ride even lower on his hips. The scent of leather slugged her in the stomach—which was odd, because Ben wasn't wearing his leather jacket.

'And what if it does work? Have you considered that?'

She dragged her gaze from his hips and tried to focus. 'That scenario could be the most challenging of all,' she agreed. 'The four of us…five,' she amended, glancing down at her stomach, 'all trying to become a family after all this time. It'll be tricky.'

She wanted to add, *but not impossible*, but her throat had closed over at the way he surveyed her stomach. Her chest tightened at the intensity of his focus. The light in his eyes made her thighs shake.

She cleared her throat and dragged in a breath. 'If it works I'll get a warm and fuzzy feeling,' she declared. Warm and fuzzy was preferable to hot and prickly. She rolled her shoulders. 'And perhaps you will too.'

Finally—*finally*—his gaze lifted to hers. 'More fairytales, Meg?'

Did he still hold that much resentment about

their less than ideal childhood? 'You still want to punish them?'

'No.' Very slowly he shook his head. 'But I don't think they deserve all your good efforts either. Especially when I'm far from convinced anything either one of us does will make a difference where they're concerned.'

'But what is it going to hurt to try?'

'I'm afraid it'll hurt *you*.'

He'd always looked out for her. She couldn't help but smile at him. 'I have a baby on the way. I'm on top of the world.'

He smiled suddenly too. A real smile—not one to trick or beguile. 'All right, Meg, I'm in. I'll do whatever I can to help.'

She let out a breath she hadn't even known she'd held.

'On one condition.'

She should've known. She folded her arms. 'Which is...?' She was *not* letting him sleep in her spare bedroom. He belonged next door. Besides... She swallowed. She needed her own space.

'You'll let me touch the baby.'

CHAPTER FIVE

MEG COULDN'T HELP her sudden grin. Lots of people had touched her baby bump—happy for her and awed by the miracle growing inside her. Why should Ben be any different?

Of course he'd be curious.

Of course he'd be invested.

He might never be Daddy but he'd always be Uncle Ben. *Favourite* Uncle Ben. Wanting to touch her baby bump was the most natural thing in the world.

She didn't try to temper her grin. 'Of course you can, Ben.'

She turned so she faced him front-on, offering her stomach to him, so to speak. His hands reached out, both of them strong and sure. They didn't waver. His hands curved around her abdomen—and just like that it stopped being the most natural thing in the world.

The pulse jammed in Meg's throat and she had to fight the urge to jolt away from him. Ben's hands suddenly didn't look like the hands of her best friend. They looked sensual and sure and knowing. They didn't feel like the hands of her best friend either.

Her breath hitched and her pulse skipped and spun like a kite-surfer in gale force winds. With excruciating thoroughness he explored every inch of her stomach through the thin cotton of her shirt. His fingers were hot and strong and surprisingly gentle.

And every part of her he touched he flooded with warmth and vigour.

She clenched her eyes shut. Her *best friend* had never looked at her with that possessive light in his eyes before. Not that it was aimed at her per se. Still, the baby was inside *her* abdomen.

He moved in closer and his heat swamped her. She opened her eyes and tried to focus on the quality of the light hitting the water of the bay below. But then his scent swirled around her—a mix of soap and leather and something darker and more illicit, like a fine Scotch whisky. She dragged in a shaky breath. Scotch wasn't Ben's drink. It was a crazy association. That thought, though, didn't make the scent go away.

Her heart all but stopped when he knelt down in front of her and pressed the left side of his face to her stomach, his arm going about her waist. She found her hand hovering above his head. She wanted to rest it there, but that would make them seem too much of a trio. Her throat thickened and tears stung her eyes. They weren't a trio. Even if by some miracle Ben stayed, they still wouldn't be a trio.

But he wouldn't stay.

And so her hand continued to hover awkwardly above his head.

'Hey, little baby,' he crooned. 'I'm your—'

'No!' She tried to move away but his grip about her tightened.

'I'm…I'm pleased to meet you,' he whispered against her stomach instead.

She closed her eyes and breathed hard.

When he climbed back to his feet their gazes clashed and locked. She'd never felt more confused in her entire life.

'Thank you.'

'You're welcome.'

Their gazes continued to battle until Ben finally took a step away and seemed to mentally shake himself. 'What's the plan for the rest of the day?'

The plan was to put as much distance between her and Ben as she could. Somewhere in the last day he'd become a stranger to her. A stranger who smelled good, who looked good, and who unnerved her.

This new Ben threatened more than her equilibrium. He threatened her unborn child's future and its happiness.

The Ben she knew would never do anything to hurt her. But this new Ben? She didn't trust him. She wanted to be away from him, to get her head back into some semblance of working order. She knew exactly how to accomplish that.

'I'm going into Nelson Bay to start on the wedding preparations.'

'Excellent plan. I'll come with you.'

She nearly choked. 'You'll what?'

'You said you wanted my help.' He lifted his arms. 'I'm yours to command.'

Why did that have to sound so suggestive?

'But—' She tried to think of something sensible to say. She couldn't, so she strode back around the side of the house.

'Time is a-wasting.' He kept perfect time beside her.

'It's really not necessary.' She tucked her hair back behind her ears, avoiding eye contact while she collected the tape measure along with the measurements he'd jotted down for her. 'You only got back from Africa yesterday. You are allowed a couple of days to catch your breath.'

'Are you trying to blow me off, Meg?'

Heat scorched her cheeks. 'Of course not.'

He grinned as if enjoying her discomfiture. 'Well, then...'

She blew out a breath. 'Have it your own way. But we're taking my car, not the bike, and I'm driving.'

'Whatever you say.'

He raised his hands in mock surrender, and suddenly he was her Ben again and it made her laugh. 'Be warned—I *will* make you buy me an ice cream cone. I cannot get enough of passionfruit ripple ice cream at the moment.'

He glanced at his watch. 'It's nearly lunchtime. I'll buy you a kilo of prawns from the co-op and we can stretch out on the beach and eat them.'

'You'll have to eat them on your own, then. And knowing how I feel about prawns, that'd be too cruel.'

He followed her into the house. 'They give you morning sickness?'

She patted her stomach. 'It has something to do with mercury levels in seafood. It could harm the baby. I'm afraid Camembert and salami are off the menu too.'

He stared at her, his jaw slack, and she could practically read his thoughts—shock that certain foods might harm the baby growing inside her—and his sudden confrontation with his own ignorance. Her natural impulse was to reassure him, but she stifled it. Ben was ignorant about babies and pregnancy, and it wasn't up to her to educate him. If he wanted to be a good father he would have to educate himself, exercising his own initiative, not because she prompted or nagged him to. But she didn't want the stranger back, so she kept her voice light and added, 'Not to mention wine and coffee. All of my favourite things. Still, I seem to be finding ample consolation in passion-fruit ripple ice cream.'

She washed her hands, dried them, stowed the measurements in her handbag and then lifted an eyebrow in Ben's direction. 'Ready?'

He still hadn't moved from his spot in the doorway, but at her words he strode across to the sink to pump the strawberry-scented hand-wash she kept on the window ledge into his hands. The scent only seemed to emphasise his masculinity. She watched him wash his hands and remembered the feel of them on her abdomen, their heat and their gentleness.

She jerked her gaze away.

'Ready.'

When she turned back he was drying his hands. And there was a new light in his eyes and a determined shape to his mouth. Normally she would take the time to dust a little powder on her nose and slick on a coat of lipstick, but she wanted to be out of the house and into the day. Right now!

She led the way to her car.

'Okay, the plan today is to hire a marquee for the big event—along with the associated paraphernalia. Tables chairs and whatnot,' she said as they drove the short distance to the neighbouring town. 'And then we'll reward ourselves with lunch.'

'Do you mind if we do a bit of shopping afterwards? I need to grab a few things.'

She glanced at him. Ben and shopping? She shook her head. 'Not at all.'

To Meg's utter surprise, Ben was a major help on the Great Marquee Hunt. He zeroed in immediately on the marquee that would best suit their purposes. The side panels could be rolled up to allow a breeze to filter through the interior if the evening proved warm. If the day was cool, however—and that wasn't unheard of in late March—the view of the bay could still be enjoyed through the clear panels that acted like windows in the marquee walls.

Ben insisted on putting down the deposit himself.

Given the expression on his face earlier, when she'd asked him about his financial circumstances, she decided it would be the better part of valour not to argue with him.

Furniture was next on the list, and Meg chose round tables and padded chairs. 'Round tables means the entire table can talk together with ease.' Hopefully it would promote conversation.

Ben's lips twisted. 'And they'll make the marquee look fuller, right?'

Exactly.

'What else?' he demanded.

'We need a long table for the wedding party.'

'There's only four of us. It won't need to be *that* long.'

'And tables for presents and the cake.'

Ben pointed out tables, the salesman made a note, and then they were done—all in under an hour.

Ben's hands went to his hips. 'What now?'

To see him so fully focused on the task made her smile. 'Now we congratulate ourselves on having made such excellent progress and reward ourselves with lunch.'

'That's it?'

She could tell he didn't believe her. 'It's one of the big things ticked off. It's all I had scheduled for today.'

'What are the other big things?'

'The catering, the cake, the invitations. And...' A grin tugged at her lips.

He leaned down to survey her face. His own lips twitched. 'And?'

'And shopping for Elsie's outfit.'

He shot away from her. 'Oh, no—no, no. You're *not* dragging me along on that.'

She choked back a laugh. 'Fat lot of use you'd be anyway. I'll let you off the hook if you buy me lunch.'

'Deal.'

They bought hot chips smothered in salt and vinegar, and dashed across the road to the beach.

School had gone back several weeks ago, but it was the weekend and the weather was divine. The long crescent of sand that bordered the bay was lined with families enjoying the sunshine, sand and water. Children's laughter, the sounds of waves whooshing up onto the beach and the cries of seagulls greeted them. *Divine!* She lifted her face to the sun and breathed it all in.

They found a spare patch of sand and Meg stretched out her legs, relishing the warmth of the sun on the bare skin of her arms and legs. She glanced at Ben as he hunkered down beside her. He must be hot.

'You should've changed into shorts.'

He unwrapped the chips. 'I'm good.'

Yeah, but he'd look great in shorts, and—

She blinked. What on earth…? And then the scent of salt and vinegar hit her and her stomach grumbled and her mouth watered. With a grin he held the packet towards her.

They ate, not saying much, just listening to the familiar sounds of children at play and the splashing of the tiny waves that broke onshore. Nearby a moored yacht's rigging clanged in the breeze, making a pelican lift out of the water and wheel up into the air. It was summer in the bay—her favourite time of year and her favourite patch of paradise.

She wasn't sure when they both started to observe the family—just that at some stage the nearby mother, father and two small girls snagged their attention. One of the little girls dashed down the beach towards them, screaming with delight when her father chased after her. Seizing her securely around the waist, he lifted her off her feet to swing her above his head.

'Higher, Daddy, higher!' she squealed, laughing down at him, her face alive with delight.

The other little girl, smaller than the first, lurched across the sand on chubby, unsteady legs to fling her arms around her father's thigh. She grinned and chortled up at him.

Meg swallowed and her chest started to cramp. Both of those little girls literally glowed with their love for their father.

She tore her gaze away to stare directly out in front of her, letting the sunlight that glinted off the water to dazzle and half-blind her.

'More?' Ben's voice came out hoarse and strained as he held the chips out to her.

She shook her head. Her appetite had fled.

He scrunched the remaining chips and she was aware of every crackle the paper made. And how white his knuckles had turned. She went back to staring directly out in front of her, tracking a speedboat as it zoomed past.

But it didn't drown out the laughter of the two little girls.

'Did you ever consider what you were depriving your child of when you decided to go it alone, Meg?'

His voice exploded at her—tight and barely controlled. She stiffened. And then she rounded on him. 'Don't take that high moral tone with me, Ben Sullivan! Since when in your entire adult life, have you *ever* put another person's needs or wants above your own?'

He blinked. 'I—'

'I didn't twist your arm. You had some say in the matter, you know.'

Her venom took him off guard. It took her off guard too, but his question had sliced right into the core of her. She'd thought she'd considered that question. She'd thought it wouldn't matter. But after seeing that family—the girls with their father, their love and sense of belonging—she felt the doubt demons rise to plague her.

'Families come in all shapes and sizes,' she hissed, more for her own benefit than his. Her baby would want for nothing! 'As for depriving my child of a father? Well, I don't rate my father very highly, and I sure as heck don't rate yours. There are worse things than not having a father.'

Ben's head rocked back in shock. Meg's sentiment didn't surprise him, but the way she expressed it did.

He clenched his jaw so hard he thought he might

break teeth. A weight pressed against his chest, making it difficult to breathe.

'Just like you don't rate me as a father, right?' he rasped out, acid burning his throat.

Eventually he turned to look at her. She immediately glanced away, but not before he recognised the scepticism stretching through her eyes. The weight in his chest grew heavier. If Meg didn't have any faith in him...

No, dammit! He clenched his hands. Meg didn't have all the answers.

He swore.

She flinched.

He kept his voice low. 'So I'm suitable as a sperm bank but not as anything more substantial?' Was *that* how she saw him?

She stared straight back out in front of her. 'That surprises you?'

'It does when that's your attitude, Meg.'

That made her turn to look at him.

Dammit it all to hell, she was supposed to *know* him!

A storm raged in the hazel depths of her eyes. He watched her swallow. She glanced down at her hands and then back up. 'How long have you wanted to be a father, Ben? A week?'

It was his turn to glance away.

'I've wanted to be a mother for as long as I can remember.'

'And you think that gives you more rights?'

'It means I know what to expect. It means I know I'm not going to change my mind next week. It means I know I'm committed to this child.' She slapped a hand to the sand. 'It means I know precisely what I'm getting into—that I've put plans into place in anticipation of the baby's arrival, and that I've adjusted my life so I can ensure my baby gets the very best care and has the very best life I can possibly give it. And now you turn up and think you have the right to tell me I'm selfish!'

She let out a harsh laugh that had his stomach churning.

'When have you ever committed to anybody or anything? You've never even taken a job on full-time. You've certainly never committed to a woman or what's left of your family. It's barely possible to get you to commit to dinner at the end of next week!'

'I'm committed to *you*.' The words burst out of him. 'If you'd ever needed me, Meg, I'd have come home.'

She smiled then, but there was an ache of sadness behind her eyes that he didn't understand. 'Yes, I believe you would've. But once I was back on my feet you'd have been off like a flash again, wouldn't you?'

He had no answer to that.

'The thing is, Ben, your trooping all over the world having adventures is fine in a best friend, but it's far from fine in a father.'

She had a point. He knew she did. And until he knew how involved he wanted to be he had no right to push her or judge her. 'I didn't mean to imply you were selfish. I think you'll be a great mum.'

But it didn't mean there wasn't room for him in the baby's life too.

She gestured to her right, to where that family now sat eating sandwiches, but she didn't look at them again. 'Is that what you really want?'

He stared at the picture of domestic bliss and had to repress a shudder. He wasn't doing marriage. Ever. He didn't believe in it. But... The way those little girls looked at their father—their faces so open and trusting. And loving. The thought of having someone look up to him like that both terrified and electrified him.

If he wanted to be a father—a proper father—his life would have to change. Drastically.

'Ben, I want a better father for my child than either one of us had.'

'Me too.' That at least was a no-brainer.

She eyed him for a moment. Whenever she was in the sun for any length of time the green flecks within the brown of her iris grew in intensity.

They flashed and sparkled now, complementing the aqua water only a few feet away.

Aqua eyes.

A smattering of freckles across her nose.

Blonde hair that brushed her shoulders.

And she smelled like pineapple and coconuts.

She was a golden goddess, encapsulating all he most loved about summer.

'Ben!'

He snapped to. 'What?'

Her nostrils flared, drawing his attention back to her freckles. She glanced away and then back again. 'I said, you *do* know that I'm not anti-commitment the way you are, right?'

'Yeah, sure.'

His attention remained on those cute freckles, their duskiness highlighting the golden glow of her skin. He'd never noticed how cute they were before—cute and kind of cheeky. They were new to him. This conversation wasn't. Commitment versus freedom. They'd thrashed it out endless time. To her credit, though, Meg had never tried to change his mind. They'd simply agreed to disagree. Even that one stupid time they had kissed.

Damn it! He'd promised never to think about that again.

'Then you should also be aware that I don't expect to "*deprive*"—' she made quotation marks in the air with her fingers '—my child of a father for ever.'

He frowned, still distracted by those freckles, and then by the shine on her lips when she moistened them. 'Right.'

She hauled in a breath and let it out again. The movement wafted a slug of coconut infused pineapple his way. He drew it into his lungs slowly, the way he would breathe in a finely aged Chardonnay before bringing the glass to his lips and sipping it.

'Just because I've decided to have a baby it doesn't mean I've given up on the idea of falling in love and getting married, maybe having more kids if I'm lucky.'

It took a moment for the significance of her words to connect, but when they did they smashed into him with the force of that imaginary bottle of Chardonnay wielded at his head. The beach tilted. The world turned black and white. He shoved his hands into the sand and clenched them.

'I might be doing things slightly out of order, but…' She let her words trail off.

He stabbed a finger at her, showering her with sand. 'You are *not* letting another man raise my child!'

He shot to his feet and paced down to the water's edge, tried to get his breathing back under control before he hyperventilated.

Another man would get the laughter…and the fun…and the love.

He dragged a hand back through his hair. Of course this schmuck would also be getting hog-tied into marriage and would have to deal with school runs, parent and teacher interviews and eat-your-greens arguments. But…

'No!'

He swung around to find Meg standing directly behind him. 'Keep your voice down,' she ordered, glancing around. 'There are small children about.'

Why the hell didn't she just bar him from all child-friendly zones? She obviously didn't rate his parenting abilities at all. His hands clenched. But giving his child—*his child*—to another man to raise? No way!

He must have said it out loud, because she arched an eyebrow at him. 'You think you can prevent me from marrying whoever I want?'

'Whomever,' he said, knowing that correcting her grammar would set her teeth on edge.

Which it did. 'You and whose army, Ben?'

'You can marry *whomever* you damn well please,' he growled, 'but this baby only has one father.' He pounded a fist to his chest. 'And that's me.'

She folded her arms. 'You're telling me that you're giving up your free and easy lifestyle to settle in Port Stephens, get a regular job and trade your motorbike for a station wagon?'

'That's exactly what I'm saying.'

'Why?'

It was a genuine question, not a challenge. He didn't know how to articulate the determination or sense of purpose that had overtaken him. He only knew that this decision was the most important of his life.

And he had no intention of getting it wrong.

He knew that walking away from their baby would be wrong.

But…

It left the rest of his life in tatters.

Meg sighed when he remained silent. She didn't believe he meant it. It was evident in her face, in her body language, in the way she turned away. Her lack of faith in him stung, but he had no one else to blame for that but himself.

He would prove himself to her. He would set all her fears to rest. And he would be the best father on the planet.

When she turned back he could see her nose had started to turn pink. Her nose always went pink before she cried. He stared at the pinkness. He glanced away. Meg hardly ever cried.

He glanced back. Swallowed. It could be sunburn. They'd been out in the sun for a while now.

He closed his eyes. He ached to wrap her in his arms and tell her he would not let either her or the baby down. Words, though, were cheap. Meg would need more than verbal assurances. She'd need action.

'We should make tracks.' She shaded her eyes against the sun. 'You said you needed to do some shopping?'

He did. But he needed a timeout from Meg more. He needed to get his head around the realisation that he was back in Port Stephens for good.

He feigned interest in a sultry brunette, wearing nothing but a bikini, who was ambling along the beach towards them.

'Ben?'

He lifted one shoulder in a lazy shrug. 'The shopping can wait.' He deliberately followed the brunette's progress instead of looking at Meg. 'Look, why don't you head off? I might hang around for a while. I'll find my own way home.'

He knew exactly what interpretation Meg would put on that.

The twist of her lips told her she had. Without another word, she turned and left.

Clenching his hands, he set off down the beach, not even noticing the brunette when he passed her.

A baby deserves to have the unconditional love of the two people who created it. If he left, who would his child have in its day-to-day life? Meg, who'd be wonderful, and Uncle Ben who'd never be there. His hands clenched. Meg's father and Elsie could hardly be relied on to provide the baby with emotional support.

He shook his head. He could at least make sure this child knew it was loved and wanted by its father. Things like that—they did matter.

And this baby deserved only good things.

When he reached the end of the beach he turned and walked back and then headed for the shops. Meg should be home by now, and he meant to buy every damn book about pregnancy and babies he could get his hands on. He wanted to be prepared for the baby's arrival. He wanted to help Meg out in any way he could.

What he didn't need was her damn superiority, or her looking over his shoulder and raising a sceptical eyebrow at the books he selected. He had enough doubt of his own to deal with.

He turned back to stare at the beach, the bay, and the water. Back in Port Stephens for good?

Him?

Hell.

CHAPTER SIX

MEG SANG ALONG to her Madonna CD in full voice. She'd turned the volume up loud to disguise the fact she couldn't reach the high notes and in an attempt to drown out the chorus of voices that plagued her—a litany of 'what ifs' and 'what the hells' and 'no ways'. All circular and pointless. But persistent. Singing helped to quiet them.

She broke off to complete a complicated manoeuvre with her crochet needle. At least as far as she was concerned it was complicated. Her friend Ally assured her that by the time she finished this baby shawl she'd have this particular stitch combination down pat.

She caressed the delicate white wool and surveyed her work so far. It didn't seem like much, considering how long it had taken her, but she didn't begrudge a moment of that time. She'd have this finished in time for the baby's arrival. Maybe only just, but it would be finished. And then she could wrap her baby in this lovely soft shawl, its wool so delicate it wouldn't irritate newborn skin. She'd wrap her baby in this shawl and it would know how much it was loved.

She lifted it to her cheek and savoured its softness.

The song came to an end. She lowered the crocheting back to her lap and was about to resume when some sixth sense had her glancing towards the doorway.

Ben.

Her throat tightened. She swallowed once, twice. 'Hey,' she finally managed.

'I knocked.' He pointed back behind him.

She grabbed the remote, turned the music down and motioned for him to take a seat. 'With the music blaring like that there's not a chance I'd have heard you.'

He stood awkwardly in the doorway. She gripped the crochet needle until the metal bit into her fingers.

'Madonna, huh?' He grinned but it didn't hide his discomfort.

'Yup.' She grinned back but she doubted it hid her tension, her uneasiness either.

He glanced around. 'We never sat in here when we were growing up.'

'No.' When they'd been growing up this had definitely been adult territory. When indoors, they'd stuck to the kitchen and the family room. 'But this is my house now and I can sit where I please.'

He didn't look convinced. Tension kept his spine straight and his shoulders tight. Last week she'd have risen and led him through to the family room, where he'd feel more comfortable. This week...?

She lifted her chin. This week making Ben comfortable was the last thing on her agenda. That knowledge made her stomach churn and bile rise in her throat. It didn't mean she wanted to make him *un*comfortable, though.

She cleared her throat. 'Have a look out of the front window.'

After a momentary hesitation he did as she ordered.

'It has the most divine view of the bay. I find that peaceful. When the wind is up you can hear the waves breaking on shore.'

'And that's a sound you've always loved.' He settled on the pristine white leather sofa. 'And you can hear it best in here.'

And in the front bedroom. She didn't mention that, though. Mentioning bedrooms to Ben didn't seem wise. Which was crazy. But...

She glanced at him and her pulse sped up and her skin prickled. *That* was what was crazy. He sprawled against the sofa with that easy, long-limbed grace of his, one arm resting along the back of the sofa as if in invitation. Her crochet needle trembled.

She dragged her gaze away and set her crochet work to one side. Her life was in turmoil. That was all this was—a reaction to all the changes happening in her life. The fact she had a baby on the way. The fact her father was marrying Elsie. The fact Ben claimed he wanted to be a father.

Ben nodded towards the wool. 'What are you doing?'

She had to moisten her lips before she could speak. 'I'm making a shawl for the baby.'

She laid the work out for him to see and he stared at it as if fascinated. When he glanced up at her, the warmth in those blue eyes caressed her.

'You can knit?'

She pretended to preen. 'Why, yes, I can, now that you mention it. Knitting clubs were more popular than book clubs around here for a while. But this isn't knitting—it's crochet, and I'm in the process of mastering the art.'

He frowned. And then he straightened. 'Why? Are you trying to save money?'

She folded her arms. That didn't deserve an answer.

His eyes narrowed. 'Or is this what your social life had descended to?'

If she could have kept a straight face she'd have let him go on believing that. It would be one seriously scary picture of life here in Fingal Bay for him to chew over. One he'd probably run from kicking and screaming. But she couldn't keep a straight face.

He leant back, his shoulders loosening, his grin hooking up one side of his face in that slow, melt-a-woman-to-her-core way he had. 'Okay, just call me an idiot.'

If she's had any breath left in her lungs she might have done exactly that. Only that grin of his had knocked all the spare oxygen out of her body.

'Your social life is obviously full. I've barely clapped eyes on you these last few days.'

Had he wanted to? The thought made her heart skip and stutter a little faster.

Stop being stupid! 'It's full enough for me.' She didn't tell him that Monday night had been an antenatal class, or that last night she'd cooked dinner for Ally, who was recovering from knee surgery. Ben's social life consisted of partying hard and having a good time, not preparing for babies or looking after friends.

Ben's life revolved around adrenaline junkie thrills, drinking hard and chasing women. She wondered why he wasn't out with that sexy brunette this evening—the one he'd obviously had every intention of playing kiss chase with the other day—and then kicked herself. Sunday to Wednesday? Ben would count that a long-term relationship. And they both knew what he thought about those.

'So why?' He gestured to the wool.

He really didn't get it, did he? An ache pressed behind her eyes. What the hell was he doing here? She closed her eyes, dragged in a breath and then opened them again. She settled more comfortably in her chair.

'Once upon a time...' she started.

Ben eased back in his seat too, slouching slightly, his eyes alive with interest.

'Once upon a time,' she repeated, 'the Queen announced she was going to have a baby. There was much rejoicing in the kingdom.'

He grinned that grin of his. 'Of course there was.'

'To celebrate and honour the impending arrival of the royal heir, the Queen fashioned a special shawl for the child to be wrapped in. It took an entire nine months to make, and every stitch was a marvel of delicate skill, awe-inspiring craftsmanship and love. All who saw it bowed down in awe.'

He snorted. 'Laying it on a bit thick, Meg. A shawl is never going to be a holy grail.'

She tossed her head. 'All who saw it bowed

down in awe, recognising it as the symbol of maternal love that it was.'

The teasing in Ben's face vanished. He stared at her with an intensity that made her swallow.

'When the last stitch was finished, the Queen promptly gave birth. And it was said that whenever the royal child was wrapped in that shawl its crying stopped and it was immediately comforted.' She lifted her chin. 'The shawl became a valued family heirloom, passed down throughout the generations.'

He eyed the work spread in her lap. Was it her imagination or did he fully check her chest out on the way down? Her pulse pounded. Wind rushed in her ears.

'You want to give your baby something special.'

His words pulled her back from her ridiculous imaginings. 'Yes.' She wanted to fill her baby's life with love and all manner of special things. The one thing she didn't want to give it was a father who would let it down. She didn't say that out loud, though. Ben knew her feelings on the subject. Harping on it would only get his back up. He had to come to the conclusion that he wasn't father material in his own time.

She didn't want to talk about the baby with Ben any longer. She didn't have the heart for it.

'So, how's your week been so far?'

His lips twisted. 'How the hell do you deal with Elsie?'

Ah.

'The woman is a goddamn clam—a locked box. I'm never going to get those names for you Meg.'

She'd known it would be a tough test. But if Ben couldn't pass it he had no business hanging around in Fingal Bay.

His eyes flashed. 'Is it against the rules to help me out?'

She guessed not. He'd still have to do the hard work, but...

She didn't want to help him. She stared down at her hands. She wanted him to leave Fingal Bay and not come back for seven, eight...ten months.

He's your best friend!

And he was turning her whole life upside down. Not to mention her baby's.

She remembered the way she'd ached for her father to show some interest in her life, to be there for her. And she remembered the soul-deep disappointment, the crushing emptiness, the disillusionment and the shame when he'd continued to turn away from her. Nausea swirled in her stomach. She didn't want that for her child.

Did her baby need protecting from Ben? She closed her eyes. If she knew the answer to that...

'Why didn't you come over for dinner tonight?

Elsie says you come to dinner every Wednesday night.'

She opened her eyes to find him leaning towards her. She shrugged. 'Except when you're home.'

His lips, which were normally relaxed and full of wicked promise, pressed into a thin line. 'And why's that?'

'I like to give you guys some space when you're home.'

'Is that all?'

Her automatic response was to open her mouth to tell him of course that was all. She stamped on it. Ben had changed everything when he'd burst in on Saturday. She wasn't sure she wanted to shield him any more. 'Precisely how much honesty do you want, Ben?'

His jaw slackened. 'I thought we were always honest.'

She pursed her lips. 'I'm about as honest as I can be when I see you for a total of three weeks in a year. Four if I'm lucky.'

His jaw clenched. His nostrils flared. 'Why didn't you come over to Elsie's tonight?'

Fine. She folded her arms. 'There are a couple of reasons. The first: Elsie is hard work. You're home so you can deal with her. It's nice to have a night off.'

He sagged back as if she'd slugged him on the jaw.

'I make her cook dinner for me every Wednesday night. It's a bargain we struck up. I do her groceries and she cooks me dinner on Wednesday nights. But really it's so I can make sure she's still functioning—keep an eye on her fine motor skills and whatnot. See if I can pick up any early signs of illness or dementia.'

Which proved difficult as Elsie had absolutely no conversation in her. Until one night about a month ago, when Elsie had suddenly started chatting and Meg had fled. It shamed her now—her panic and sense of resentment and her cowardice. She could see now that Elsie had tried to open a door, and Meg had slammed it shut in her face.

Ben stared at her. He didn't say a word. It was probably why Elsie had reverted to being a clam around Ben now.

Still, it wasn't beyond Ben to make an overture too, was it? Meg bit her lip. If he truly wanted to be a father.

'Look, when you breeze in for an odd week here and a few days there, I do my best to make it fun and not to bore you with tedious domestic details. But if you mean to move back to Port Stephens for good then you can jolly well share some of the load.'

He'd gone pale, as if he might throw up on her

pristine white carpet. 'What's the other reason you didn't come to dinner?' he finally asked.

She swallowed. Carpets could be cleaned. It was much harder to mend a child's broken heart. But...

'Meg?'

She lifted her chin and met his gaze head-on. 'I don't like seeing you and Elsie together. It's when I like you both least.'

He stared at her, his eyes dark. In one swift movement he rose. 'I should go.'

'Sit down, Ben.' She bit back a sigh. 'Do you mean to run away every time we have a difficult conversation? What about if that difficult conversation is about the baby? Are you going to run away then too?'

The pulse at the base of his jaw pounded. 'Couldn't you at least offer a guy a beer before tearing his character to shreds?'

She stood. 'You're right. But not a beer. You drink too much.'

'Hell, Meg, don't hold back!'

She managed a smile. Somehow. 'I'm having a hot chocolate. I'm trying to make sure I get enough calcium. Would you like one too, or would you prefer tea or coffee?'

He didn't answer, and she led the way to the kitchen and set about making hot chocolate. She was aware of how closely Ben watched her—she'd have had to be blind not to. It should have made her clumsy, but it didn't. It made her feel powerful and…and beautiful.

Which didn't make sense.

She shook the thought off and handed Ben one of the steaming mugs. 'Besides,' she started, as if there hadn't been a long, silent pause in their conversation, 'I'm not shredding your character. You're my best friend and I love you.'

She pulled a stool out at the breakfast bar and sat. 'But c'mon, Ben, what's to like about hanging out with you and Elsie? She barely speaks and you turn back into a sullen ten-year-old. All the conversation is left to me. You don't help me out, and Elsie answers any questions directed to her in words of two syllables. Preferably one if she can get away with it. Great night out for a girl.' She said it all with a grin, wanting to chase the shadows from his eyes.

'I…' Ben slammed his mug down, pulled out the stool beside her and wrapped an arm about her shoulders in a rough hug. 'Hell, Meg, I'm sorry. I never looked at it that way before.'

'That's okay.' He smelled of leather and Scotch and her senses greedily drank him in. 'I didn't mind when your visits were so fleeting—they were like moments stolen from reality. They never seemed part of the real world.'

'Which will change if I become a permanent fixture in the area?'

Exactly. She reached for her mug again. Ben removed his arm. Even though it was a warm night she missed its weight and its strength.

'I deal with Elsie by telling her stories.'

He swung around so quickly he almost spilled his drink. 'Like our fairytales?'

She shook her head. No, not like those. They were just for her and Ben. 'I talk at her—telling her what I've been up to for the week, what child did what to another child at work, what I saw someone wearing on the boardwalk in Nelson Bay, what wonderful new dish I've recently tried cooking, what book I'm reading. Just…monologues.'

It should be a tedious, monotonous rendition—a chore—but in between enquiring if Elsie had won anything at Housie or the raffles and if she'd made her shopping list yet, to amuse herself Meg dramatised everything to the nth degree. It made the time pass more quickly.

'So I should tell her what I've been up to?'

She shrugged.

'But I haven't been doing anything since I got back.'

She made her voice tart. 'Then I suggest you start doing something before you turn into a vegetable.'

A laugh shot out of him. 'Like I said earlier, don't hold back.'

She had no intention of doing so, but… She glanced at the handsome profile beside her and an icy hand clamped around her heart and squeezed. Her chest constricted painfully. She didn't want to make Ben miserable. She didn't want him feeling bad about himself. She wanted him to be happy.

And living in Fingal Bay would never make him happy.

She dragged her gaze back to the mug she cradled in her hands. 'I already have the names of ten guests from my father.'

'How'd you manage that?'

'Deceit and emotional blackmail.'

He grinned. And then he threw his head back and laughed. Captured in the moment like that he looked so alive it momentarily robbed her of breath, of speech, and of coherent thought. She never felt so alive as when Ben was home. Yearning rose inside her. Yearning for…

He glanced at her, stilled, and his eyes darkened. It seemed as if the very air between them shimmered. They swayed towards each other.

And then they both snapped away. Meg grabbed their now empty mugs and bolted for the sink, desperately working on getting her breathing back under control. They'd promised one another that they would never go *there* again. They'd agreed their friendship was too important to risk. And that still held true.

In the reflection of the window she could see Ben pacing on the other side of the breakfast bar, his hands clenched. Eventually she wouldn't be able to pretend to be washing the cups any more.

Ben coughed and then stared up at the ceiling. 'Deceit and emotional blackmail?'

She closed her eyes, counted to three and turned off the tap. She turned back to him, praying—very hard—that she looked casual and unconcerned. 'I told him that Elsie would love a small party for a reception and that if he cared about Elsie's needs then he'd give me the names of ten people I could invite to the wedding.'

'It obviously worked.'

Like a charm. Her father and Elsie might not be particularly demonstrative, but Meg didn't doubt they cared deeply for each other. She remembered their linked hands, the fire in Elsie's eyes when she'd defended Laurie to Ben, and her father's vulnerability.

She glanced at Ben. He seemed completely unfazed by that 'moment'. The hot chocolate in her stomach curdled. Maybe she'd been the only one caught up in it.

She cleared her throat. 'It worked so well he actually gave me a dozen names.'

Ben rubbed his chin. 'If I did it in reverse...'

'Worth a try,' she agreed.

'Brilliant!' He slapped a hand down on the breakfast bar. 'Thanks, Meg.'

'Any time.'

But the words sounded wooden, even to her own ears. He opened the back door, hesitated, and then turned back. 'I didn't come back to make your life chaotic on purpose, Meg.'

She managed a smile. 'I know.'

'What night do you check up on your father?'

She should have known he'd make that connection. 'Tomorrow night. He refuses to cook, or to let me cook, so we have dinner at the RSL club.'

'Would it be all right if Elsie and I came along with you tomorrow night?'

What? Like a family? She frowned and scratched the back of her neck. Eventually she managed to clear her throat again. 'The more the merrier.'

'What time should we be ready?'

'He likes to eat early these days, so I'll be leaving here at six.'

With a nod, he was gone.

Ben stood in the dark garden, adrift between Meg's house and Elsie's.

He'd wandered over to Meg's tonight because he couldn't have stood another ten minutes in Elsie's company, but…

He scratched a hand back through his hair. He hadn't expected to be confronted with his own inadequacies. With his selfishness.

He threw his head back to glare at the stars. He dragged cleansing breaths into his lungs. No wonder Meg didn't believe he'd see this fatherhood gig through.

He rested his hands against his knees and swore. He had to start pulling his weight. Meg was pregnant. She should be focussing on things like getting ready for the baby. Resting.

While he'd been off seeing the world Meg had been taking care of everyone. He straightened. Well, her days of being a drudge were over. He'd see to that.

He glanced at his grandmother's house. Shoving his shoulders back, he set off towards it.

He found Elsie at the kitchen table, playing Solitaire—just as she'd been doing when he'd left. The radio crooned songs from the 1950s.

'Drink?' he offered, going to the fridge.

'No, thank you.'

She didn't so much as glance at him. He grabbed a beer…stopped…set it back down again and seized a can of soda instead. The silence pressed down like a blanket of cold snow. He shot a glance towards the living room and the promised distraction of the television.

You turn back into a sullen ten-year-old.

He pulled out a chair and sat at the table with Elsie—something he hadn't done since he'd returned home—and watched as she finished her game. She glanced at him and then in the wink of an eye, almost as if she were afraid he'd change his mind, she dealt them both out seven cards each.

'Can you play rummy?'

'Sure I can.'

'Laurie taught me.'

His skin tightened. He rolled his shoulders. So far this was the longest conversation they'd had all week. 'I…uh…when he was recuperating and you visited?'

'That's right.'

He wanted to get up from the table and flee. It all felt so wrong. But he remembered Meg's crack about him reverting to a sullen ten-year-old and swallowed. 'When I was in Alaska I played a form of rummy with the guys off the fishing trawlers. Those guys were ruthless.'

But Elsie, it seemed, had clammed up again, and Ben wondered if it was something he'd said.

They played cards for a bit. Finally he broke

the silence. 'Meg's looking great. Pregnancy obviously agrees with her.'

Nothing.

'She's crocheting this thing—a baby shawl, I think she said. Looks hard, and progress is looking slow.' He picked up the three of spades Elsie had discarded. She still didn't say anything. He ground back a sigh. 'Can you crochet?'

'Yep.'

She could? He stared at her for a moment, trying not to rock back on his chair. 'You should ask her to bring this shawl over to show you. In fact, you should make something for the baby too.'

She didn't look up from her cards. 'Me?'

He frowned. 'And so should I.'

'You?' A snort accompanied the single syllable.

He cracked his knuckles. 'I might not be able to knit or sew, but travelling in the remote parts of the world forces a guy to become pretty handy.'

Handy? *Ha!* He could fashion a makeshift compass, build a temporary shelter and sterilise water, but what on earth could he make for the baby that would be useful? And beautiful. Because he'd want it to be beautiful too. An heirloom.

'A crib.' As the idea occurred to him he said it out loud. He knew a bit about carpentry. 'I'll build a crib for the baby.' He laid out his trio of threes, a trio of jacks and placed his final card on Elsie's sevens. 'Gin.'

Elsie threw her cards down with a sniff.

'Best of three,' Ben announced. 'You're rusty. You need the practice. Though it's got to be said those Alaskan fisherman took no prisoners.'

Elsie picked up her second hand without a word. Ben mentally rolled his eyes. Meg was right. This was hard work. But he found a certain grim enjoyment in needling Elsie too.

As they played he found himself taking note of Elsie's movements. Her hands were steady and she held herself stiffly erect. No signs of a debilitating disease there as far as he could see. When she won the game in three moves he had to conclude that, while she didn't say much, her mind was razor-sharp.

'Gin!' There was no mistaking her triumph, but she still didn't crack a smile.

He snorted. 'I went easy on you.'

Her chin came up a notch. Her eyes narrowed.

'Oh, and by the way, we're having dinner with Meg and her father tomorrow evening at the club. I said we'd be ready at six.'

'Right.'

They played in silence for several moments, and then all in a rush it suddenly occurred to Ben that he might be cramping the older couple's style. He cleared his throat. It wasn't easy imagining Elsie and Mr Parrish wanting—needing—privacy. But that didn't change the fact that they were engaged.

'Do you mind me staying here while I'm in town?'

'No.'

'Look, if it's not convenient I can arrange alternative accommodation. I might be staying a bit longer than usual.'

'How long?'

'I'm not sure yet.'

Oh, he was sure, all right. He was staying for good. Meg should be the first to know that, though. 'I'd certainly understand it if you'd like me to find somewhere else to stay.'

'No.'

He stared at her. She didn't say any more. 'Did my mother really never contact you, not even once, after she left me here?'

The question shocked him as much as it probably shocked Elsie. He hadn't known it had been hovering on his lips, waiting to pounce. He hadn't known he still even cared what the answer to the damn question might be.

Elsie folded her cards up as tight as her face and dropped them to the table. 'No.'

Without another word she rose and left the room.

'Goodnight, Ben,' he muttered under his breath.

'Goodnight, Elsie,' he forced himself to call out. 'Thanks for the card game.'

Ben and Elsie strolled across to Meg's the next evening at six on the dot. At least Ben strolled. Elsie never did anything quite so relaxed as stroll. Her gait was midway between a trudge and a march.

They waited while Meg reversed her car—a perky blue station wagon—out of the garage, and then Ben leant forward and opened the front passenger door for Elsie.

'I insist,' he said with a sweep of his arm when she started to back away. He blocked her path. Her choices were to plough through him or to subside into the front seat. She chose the latter.

'Hey, Meg.' He settled into the back seat.

'Hey, Ben.' She glanced at Elsie. 'Hello, Elsie.'

'Hello.'

He didn't need to see Elsie to know the precise way she'd just folded her hands in her lap.

'How was work?' he asked Meg as she turned the car in the direction of Nelson Bay. He was determined to hold up his end of the conversation this evening.

'Hectic… Fun.' She told them a silly story about one of the children there and then flicked a glance at Elsie. 'How was your day?'

'Fine.'

'What did you get up to?'

'Nothing new.'

In the rear vision mirror she caught Ben's glance and rolled her eyes.

'Though I did come across a recipe that I thought I might try. It's Indian. I've not tried Indian before.'

Silence—a stunned and at a loss silence—filled the car. Meg cleared her throat. 'Sounds…uh… great.' She glanced in the mirror again and Ben could almost see her mental shrug. She swallowed. 'What did *you* do today, Ben?'

'I bought some wood.'

She blinked as she stared at the road in front of her. 'Wood?'

'That's right. But don't ask me what it's for. It's a surprise.'

She glanced at Elsie. 'What's he up to? Is he building you a veggie patch?'

'Unlikely. But if he does it'll be *his* veggie patch.'

In the mirror Meg raised an eyebrow at him and he could read her mind. They were having a conversation like normal people—him, her and Elsie. He couldn't blame her for wondering if the sky was falling in.

'I'll tell you something that's surprised the pants off of me,' he said, as smoothly as he could.

In the mirror he watched her swallow. 'Don't keep me in suspense.'

'Elsie plays a mean hand of rummy.'

Meg glanced at her. 'You play rummy?'

'Yes, your father taught me.'

Just for a moment Meg's shoulders tightened, but then she rolled them and shrugged. 'Rummy is fun, but I prefer poker. Dad plays a mean hand of poker too.'

Did he? Ben wondered if he'd ever played a hand or two with his daughter.

'So Elsie kicked your butt, huh?'

'We're a game apiece. The tie-break's tonight.'

'Well, now.' Meg pulled the car to a halt in the RSL Club's parking lot. 'I expect to hear all about it tomorrow.'

'If she beats me, I'm making it the best of five.'

Elsie snorted. 'If you come to dinner next Wednesday, Meg, you can join in the fun.'

He wasn't sure who was more stunned by that offer—him, Meg or Elsie.

'Uh, right,' Meg managed. 'I'll look forward to it.'

Elsie's efforts at hospitality and conversation had thrown him as much as they'd obviously thrown Meg, but as Ben climbed out of the car he couldn't help wondering when he'd fallen into being so monosyllabic around his grandmother. Especially as he prided himself on being good company everywhere else.

He frowned and shook his head. He'd *never* been anything but monosyllabic around Elsie. It was a habit. One he hadn't even considered breaking until Meg had sent out the challenge.

He glanced at the older woman. When had she got into the habit? Maybe nobody had ever challenged her, and—

Holy crap!

Ben's jaw dropped and his skin tightened when Meg rounded the car to join them. His chest expanded. It was as if he didn't fit his body properly any more.

Holy mackerel!

She wore a short blue skirt that stopped a good three inches above her knees and swished and danced about flirty thighs.

Man, Meg had great legs!

He managed to lift a hand to swipe it across his chin. No drool. He didn't do drool. Though, that said, until this week he'd have said he didn't do ogling Meg either.

Now it seemed he couldn't do anything else.

She had legs that went on for ever. The illusion was aided and abetted by the four-inch wedge heels she wore, the same caramel colour as her blouse. He toenails were painted a sparkly dark brown.

She nudged him in the ribs. 'What's with you?'

'I…um…' He coughed. Elsie raised an eyebrow and for the first time in his life he saw her actually smile. Oh, brilliant! She'd seen the lot and knew the effect Meg was having on him.

'I…um…' He cleared his throat and pointed to Meg's feet. 'Those shoes should come with a warning sign. Are you sure pregnant women are allowed to wear those things?'

She snorted. 'Just watch me, buster.'

He didn't have any other choice.

'I've given up caffeine, alcohol, salami and Camembert, but I'm not giving up my sexy sandals.'

She and Elsie set off for the club's entrance. He trailed after, mesmerised by the way Meg's hips swayed with hypnotic temptation.

How had he never noticed *that* before?

He swallowed. He had a feeling he was in for a long night.

CHAPTER SEVEN

MEG GLANCED AT Ben sitting at the table next to her in the club, and then away again before anyone could accuse her of having an unhealthy fixation with her best friend.

But tonight he'd amazed her. He not only made an effort to take part in the conversation, he actively promoted it. He quizzed her father on the key differences between five-card draw poker, stud poker and Texas hold 'em. She hadn't seen her father so animated in a long time. And Elsie listened in with a greedy avidity that made Meg blink.

The more she watched, the more she realised how good the older couple were for each other.

She bit her lip and glanced around the crowded dining room. She wanted to be happy for her father and Elsie. She gritted her teeth. She *was* happy for them. But their newfound vim made her chafe and burn. It made her hands clench.

Ben trailed a finger across one of her fists, leaving a burning path of awareness in his wake. She promptly unclenched it. He sent her a smile filled with so much understanding she wanted to lay her head on his shoulder and bawl her eyes out.

Pregnancy hormones.

Do you mean to use that as an excuse for every uncomfortable emotion that pummels you at the moment?

It might not explain her unexpected resentment towards the older couple, but it was absolutely positively the reason her pulse quickened and her skin prickled at the mere sight of Ben. It had to be. And it was absolutely positively the reason her stomach clenched when his scent slugged into her—that peculiar but evocative mixture of leather and Scotch whisky.

For pity's sake, he wasn't even wearing leather or drinking whisky.

Her lips twisted. He couldn't help it. He smelled like a bad boy—all illicit temptation and promises he wouldn't keep. That grin and his free and easy swagger promised heaven. For one night. She didn't doubt for a moment that he'd deliver on *that* particular promise either.

And darn it all if she didn't want a piece of that!

She swallowed. She didn't just want it. She craved it. Her skin, her lungs, even her fingers ached with it.

Pregnancy hormones. *It had to be.*

Just her luck. Why couldn't she be like other women who became nauseous at the smell of frying bacon? That would be far preferable to feeling like *this* when Ben's scent hit her.

Her fingers curled into her palms. She had to find a way to resist all that seductive bad-boyness. For the sake of their friendship. And for the sake of her baby.

She dragged in a breath. She'd seen smart, sensible women make absolute fools of themselves over Ben and she had no intention of joining their ranks. She could *not* let lust deflect her from the important issue—ensuring her baby had the best possible life that she could give it. She could do that and save her friendship with Ben.

But not if she slept with him.

She ground her teeth together. Why had nobody warned her that being pregnant would make her…horny?

She shifted on her chair. Horny was the perfect description. There was nothing dignified and elegant or slow and easy in what she felt for Ben.

She risked a glance at him. Her blood Mexican-waved in her veins. Heat pounded through her and she squeezed her thighs tightly together. What she felt for Ben—*her best friend*—was hot and carnal, primal and urgent.

And it had to be denied.

She dragged her gaze away and fiddled with her cutlery.

Ben nudged her and she could have groaned out loud as a fresh wave of leather and whisky slammed into her. But it occurred to her then that she'd left the entire running of the conversation up to him so far. He probably thought she was doing it to punish him, or to prove some stupid point, when the real reason was she simply couldn't string two thoughts let alone two sentences together in a coherent fashion.

'Sorry, I was a million miles away.' She made herself smile around the table. 'My girlfriends have warned me about baby brain.'

Ben cocked an eyebrow. He grinned that slow and easy grin that could reduce a woman to the consistency of warm honey, inch by delicious inch.

She swallowed and forced her spine to straighten. 'Basically it means my brain will turn to mush and I won't be able to verbalise anything but nonsense for days at a time.'

She glanced at Elsie. 'Do you remember that when you were pregnant?'

Elsie drew back, paled, and Meg tried not to wince. She'd never asked Elsie about pregnancy or motherhood before and it was obviously a touchy subject. She hadn't meant to be insensitive.

In an effort to remove attention from Elsie, she swung to her father. 'Or can *you* remember Mum having baby brain when she was pregnant with me?'

An ugly red flushed his cheeks. As if she'd reached across and slapped him across the face. Twice.

Oh, great. Another no-go zone, huh?

She wanted nothing more than to lay her head on the table, close her eyes and rest for a while.

'And what a sterling example of baby brain in action,' Ben murmured in her ear, and she found herself coughing back a laugh instead.

'I guess that's a no on both counts,' she managed, deciding to brazen it out, hoping it would make it less awkward all round. She glanced around the crowded dining room. 'There's a good crowd in but, man, I'm hungry. I wonder when our food will be ready?'

On cue, their table buzzer rang. Ben and her father shot to their feet. 'I'll get yours,' Ben told her, placing a hand on her shoulder to keep her in her seat.

Elsie watched as the two men walked towards the bistro counter where their plates waited. Meg made herself smile. 'Well, this is nice, isn't it?'

'You shouldn't have mentioned your mother.'

Meg blinked. 'Why ever not?'

Elsie pressed her lips primly together. 'He doesn't like to talk about her.'

Wasn't that the truth? 'And yet she was *my* mother and I do. Why should my needs be subordinate to his?'

'That's a selfish way to look at it.'

Interesting...Elsie was prepared to go into battle for her father. Something in Meg's heart lifted.

But something else didn't. 'Maybe I'm tired of stepping on eggshells and being self-sacrificing.'

Elsie paled. 'Meg, I—'

The men chose that moment to return with the food and Elsie broke off. Meg couldn't help but be relieved.

Ben glanced at Elsie and then whispered to Meg, 'More baby brain?'

'"Curiouser and curiouser," said Alice,' she returned.

He grinned. She grinned back. And for a moment everything was right again—she and Ben against the world...or at least against Elsie and Laurie, who'd been the world when she and Ben had been ten-year-olds.

They ate, and her father and Elsie reverted to their customary silence. Between them Meg and Ben managed to keep up a steady flow of chatter, but Meg couldn't help wondering if the older couple heard a word they said.

When they were finished, their plates removed and drinks replenished, Meg clapped her hands. 'Okay, I want to talk about the wedding for a moment.'

Her father scowled. 'I don't want a damn circus, Megan.'

'It's not going to be a circus. It's going to be a simple celebration. A celebration of the love you and Elsie share.' She folded her arms. 'And if you can't muster the courtesy to give each other that much respect then you shouldn't be getting married in the first place.'

Elsie and Laurie stared at her in shock. Ben let forth with a low whistle.

'Elsie—not this Saturday but the one after you and I are going shopping for your outfit.'

'Oh, but I don't need anything new.'

'Yes, you do. And so do I.' Her father had multiple suits, but… She turned to Ben. 'You'll need a suit.'

He saluted. 'I'm onto it.'

She turned back to the older couple. 'And you will both need an attendant. Who would you like as your bridesmaid and best man?'

Nobody said anything for a moment. She heaved back a sigh. 'Who were you going to have as your witnesses?'

'You and Ben,' her father muttered.

'Fine. I'll be your best man, but I'll be wearing a dress.'

'And I'll be bridesmaid in a suit,' Ben said to Elsie.

He said it without rancour and without wincing. He even said it with a grin on his face. Meg could have hugged him.

'Now, Elsie, do you want someone to give you away?'

'Of course not! Who on earth would I ask to do that?'

Meg leant back. She stared at the ceiling and counted to three. 'I'd have thought Ben would be the logical choice.'

The other woman's chin shot up. 'Ben? Do you really expect him to still be here in six weeks' time?'

'If he says he will, then, yes.'

'Give me away?' Her face darkened as she glared at Ben. 'Oh, you'd like that, wouldn't you? You'd love to give me away and be done with me for ever.'

Meg took one look at her best friend's ashen face and a scorching red-hot savagery shook through her. She leant forward, acid burning her throat and a rank taste filling her mouth. 'And who could blame him? I don't know why he even bothers with you at all. What the hell have you ever given him that he couldn't have got from strangers? You never show the slightest interest in his life, never show him the slightest affection—not even a tiny bit of warmth. You have no right to criticise him. *None!*'

'Meg.'

Ben's voice burned low but she couldn't stop. Even if she'd wanted to, she couldn't have. And she didn't want to. 'It was your job to show him love and security when he was just a little boy, but did you ever once hug him or tell him you were glad he'd come to stay with you? No, not once. Why not? He was a great kid and you...you're nothing but a—'

'Megan, that's enough! You will *not* speak to my intended like that.'

'Or what?' she shot straight back at her father. 'You'll never speak to me again? Well, seeing as you barely speak to me now, I can hardly see that'd be any great loss.'

Even as the words ripped out of her she couldn't believe she was uttering them. But she meant them. Every single one of them. And the red mist held her too much in its sway for her to regret them.

She might never regret them, but if she remained here she would say things she *would* regret—mean, bitter things just for the sake of it. She pushed out of her seat and walked away, walked right out of the club. She tramped the two blocks down to the water's edge to sit on a bench overlooking the bay as the sun sank in the west.

The walking had helped work off some of her anger. The warm air caressed the bare skin of her neck and legs, and the late evening light was as soothing as the ebb and flow of the water.

'Are you okay?'

Ben. And his voice was as soothing as the water too. But it made her eyes prickle and sting. She nodded.

'Do you mind if I join you?'

She shook her head and gestured for him to take the seat beside her.

'What happened back there?' he finally asked. 'Baby brain?'

She didn't know if he was trying to make her laugh or if he was as honest-to-God puzzled as he sounded. She dragged in a breath that made her whole body shudder. 'That was honest, true-blue emotion, not baby brain. I've never told either one of them how I feel about our childhoods.'

'Well, you left them in no doubt about your feelings on the subject tonight.'

She glanced at him. 'I don't particularly feel bad about it.' Did that make her an awful person? 'I don't want revenge, and I don't want to ruin their happiness, but neither one of them has the right to criticise you or me for being unsupportive. Especially when we're bending over backwards for them.'

He rested his elbows on his knees and then glanced up at her. 'You've bottled that up for a long time. Why spill it now?'

She stared out at the water. The sky was quickly darkening now that the sun had gone down. The burning started behind her eyes again. 'Now that I'm pregnant and expecting a child of my own, their emotional abandonment of us seems so much more unforgivable to me.'

He straightened and she turned to him.

'Ben, I can't imagine not making every effort for my child, regardless of what else is happening in my life. I love it so much already and it makes me see…'

'What?'

She had to swallow. 'It makes me see that neither one of them loved us enough.'

'Oh, sweetheart.' He slipped an arm about her shoulders and she leant against him, soaking up his strength and his familiarity, his *Ben*-ness.

'You've never blown your top like that,' she murmured into his chest. And he had so much more to breathe fire about than her—not just Elsie, but his mother and father too. 'Why not?' It obviously hadn't been healthy for *her* to bottle her anger and hurt up for so long. If he was bottling it up—

'Meg, honey.' He gave a low laugh. 'I did it with actions rather than words. Don't you remember?'

She thought about it for a while and then nodded. 'You rebelled big-time.' He'd started teenage binge-drinking at sixteen, and staying out until the wee small hours, getting into the occasional fight—and, she suspected, making himself at home in older women's beds.

The police had brought him home on more than one occasion. He'd had a couple of fathers and one husband warn him off—violently. Yes. She nodded again. Ben had gone off the rails in a big way, and she could see it now for the thumbing of his nose at his family that it had been.

Still, he'd had the strength and the sense to pull out of that downward spiral. Dave Clements—a local tour operator—had offered him a part-time job and had taken him under his wing, had encouraged Ben to finish school. And Ben had, and now he led the kind of life most people could only dream of.

But was he happy?

She'd thought so, but... She glanced up into his face and recognised the shadows there. She straightened and slipped her hand into his, held it tight. 'I'm sorry if my outburst brought up bad stuff for you. I didn't mean—'

'For me?' He swung to her. 'Hell, Meg, you were magnificent! I just...'

She swallowed. 'What?'

He released her to rest his elbows on his knees again and drag both hands back through his hair. She wanted his arm resting back across her shoulders. She wanted not to have hurt him.

'Is it my coming home and turning your nicely ordered plans on their head? Did that have a bearing on your outburst tonight? I don't mean to be causing you stress.'

'No! That had nothing to do with it. That—' she waved back behind her '—was about me and them. Not about me and you.' She moistened her lips. 'It was about me and my father.' And about her anger at Elsie for not having shown Ben any love or affection. 'You had nothing to do with that except in...'

'What?'

'When I was busy doing what you were mostly doing tonight,' she started slowly, 'making sure the conversation flowed and that there weren't any awkward moments, I didn't have the time to feel those old hurts and resentments.'

'While I, at least whenever I've been home,' he

said with a delicious twist of his lips, 'have been far too busy stewing on them.'

'But when you took on my role tonight I started to wonder why I was always so careful around them, and I realised what a lie it all seemed.'

'So you exploded.'

She slouched back against the bench. 'Why can't I just make it all go away and not matter any more? It all seems so pointless and self-defeating.' She couldn't change the past any more than she could change her father or Elsie. Her hands clenched. 'I should be able to just get over it.' She wasn't ten years old any more.

'It doesn't work like that.'

She knew he was right. She lifted her chin. 'It doesn't mean I have to let it blight the future, though. I don't have to continue mollycoddling my father or Elsie. At least not at the expense of myself.'

'No, you don't.'

He'd been telling her that for years. She'd never really seen what he meant till now.

'And I have a baby on the way.' She hugged herself. 'And that's incredibly exciting and it makes me happier than I have words for.'

He stared at her. He didn't smile. *They* had a baby on the way. *They.* She could read that in his face, but he didn't correct her.

She stared back out at the bay. The last scrap of light in the sky had faded and house lights and boat lights and street lights danced on the undulating water, turning it into a kind of fairyland.

Only this wasn't a fairytale. Ben said he wanted to be involved in their baby's life, but so far he hadn't shown any joy or excitement—only agitation and unease.

'So…?'

His word hung in the air. She didn't know what it referred to. She hauled in a breath and raised one shoulder. 'I don't much feel like going back to the club and dealing with my father and Elsie.'

'You don't have to. I asked your father if he'd see Elsie home.'

She swung back to him. 'I could kiss you!'

He grinned. A grin full of a slow burn that melted her insides and sent need hurtling through her. She started to reach for him, realised what she was doing, and turned the questing touch into a slap to his thigh before leaping to her feet.

'Feel like going for a walk?' She couldn't keep sitting here next to him and not give in to temptation.

Which was crazy.

Truly crazy.

Nonetheless, walking was a much safer option. With a shrug he rose and they set off along the boardwalk in the direction of the Nelson Bay marina, where there was a lot of distraction—lights and people and noise. Meg swallowed. Down at this end of the beach it was dark and almost deserted. It would take ten minutes to reach the marina. And then they'd have to walk back this way. In the dark and the quiet.

Her feet slowed.

But by then—after all that distraction and the exercise of walking—she'd have found a way to get her stupid hormones back under control, right?

She went to speed up again, but Ben took her arm and led her across a strip of grass and down to the sand. He kicked off his shoes, and after a moment's hesitation she eased her feet out of her wedges.

They paddled without talking very much. The water was warm. She needed icy cold rather than this beguiling warmth that brought all her senses dancing to life. Paddling with Ben in all the warmth of a late summer evening, with the scent of a nearby frangipani drenching the air, was far too intimate. Even though they'd done this a thousand times and it had never felt intimate before.

Except that one time after her high school graduation, when he'd been her white knight and taken her to the prom.

Don't think about that!

She cleared her throat. 'Tell me again how magnificent I was.' Maybe teasing and banter would help her find her way back to a more comfortable place.

Ben turned and moved back towards her. He inadvertently flicked up a few drops of water that hit her mid-calf…and higher. They beaded and rolled down her legs with delicious promise.

He halted in front of her, reaching out and cupping her cheek. 'Meg, nobody has ever stood up for me the way you did tonight. Not ever.'

In the moonlight his eyes shimmered. 'Oh, Ben,' she whispered, reaching up to cover his hand with hers. He deserved to have so many more people in his life willing to go out on a limb for him.

'You made me feel as if I could fly.'

She smiled. 'You mean you can't?'

He laughed softly and pulled her in close for a hug. She clenched her eyes shut and gritted her teeth as she forced her arms around him to squeeze him back for a moment. She started to release him, but he didn't release her. She rested her cheek on his shoulder and bit her lip until she tasted blood. It took all her concentration to keep her hands where they ought to be.

And then his hand slid down her back and it wasn't a between-friends gesture. It was…

She drew back to glance into his face. The hunger and the need reflected in his eyes made her sway towards him. She planted her hands against his chest to keep her balance, to keep from falling against him. As soon as she regained her footing she meant to push him away.

Only, her hands, it seemed, had a different idea altogether. They slid across his shirt, completely ignoring the pleasant sensation of soft cotton to revel in the honed male flesh beneath it. Ben's chest had so much *definition*. And he was hot! His heat branded her through his shirt and his heart beat against her palm like a dark throbbing promise. The pulse in her throat quivered.

She swallowed and tried to catch her breath. She should move away.

But the longer she remained in the circle of Ben's arms, the more the strength and the will drained from her body and the harder it became to think clearly and logically.

And beneath her hands his body continued to beat at her like a wild thing—a tempting and tempestuous primal force, urging her to connect with something wild and elemental within herself.

She lifted her gaze to his. A light blazed from his eyes, revealing his need, an unchecked recklessness and his exaltation.

'I've been fighting this all night,' he rasped, 'but I'm not going to fight it any more.'

He tangled his hand in her hair and pulled it back until her lips lifted, angled just so to give him maximum access, and then his mouth came down on hers—hot, hungry, unchecked.

His lips laid waste to all her preconceptions. She'd thought he'd taste wickedly illicit and forbidden, but he didn't taste like whisky or leather or midnight. He tasted like summer and ripe strawberries and the tang of the ocean breeze. He tasted like freedom.

It was more intoxicating than anything she'd ever experienced.

Kissing Ben was like flying.

A swooping, swirling, tumbling-in-the-surf kind of flying.

He pulled her closer, positioned his body in such a way that it pressed against all the parts of her she most wanted touched—but it didn't appease her, only inflamed. His name ripped from her throat and he took advantage of it to deepen the kiss further. She followed his lead, drinking him in greedily. Her head swam. She fisted her hands in his shirt and dragged him closer. His strength was the only thing keeping them both upright.

She needed him *now*. Her body screamed for him. She pressed herself against him in the most shameless way she could—pelvis to pelvis, making it clear what she wanted. Demanding fulfilment.

His mouth lifted from hers. He dragged in air and then his teeth grazed her throat. She arched against him. 'Please, Ben. Please.' she sobbed.

With a growl, he scrunched her skirt in his hand. He traced the line of her panty elastic with one finger and she thought she might explode then and there.

His finger shifted, slid beneath the elastic.

Oh, please. Please.

A car horn blared, renting the air with discord, and Ben leapt away from her so fast she'd have fallen if he hadn't shot out an arm to steady her. When she regained her balance he released her with an oath that burned her ears.

'What the *hell* were you thinking?' His finger shook as he pointed it at her.

Same as you. Only she couldn't get her tongue to work properly and utter that remark out loud.

He wheeled away, dragging both hands back through his hair.

No, no, no, she wanted to wail. *Don't turn knight on me now—you're a bad boy!*

But when he swung back his face was tense and drawn, and she was grateful she hadn't said it out loud.

Because it would have been stupid.

And wrong.

Her flesh chilled. Trembling set in. She walked

away from him and up the beach a little way to sit. She needed to think. And she couldn't think and walk at the same time because her limbs were boneless and it took all her concentration to remain upright. She pulled her skirt down as far as it would go and kept her legs flat out in front of her to reveal as little thigh as possible.

He strode up to her and punched a finger at her again. 'This is not on, Meg. You and me. It's never going to happen.'

'Don't use that tone with me.' She glared at him. 'You started it.'

'You could've said no!'

'You could've not kissed me in the first place!'

She expected him to stride away into the night, but he didn't. He paced for a bit and then eventually came back and sat beside her. But not too close.

'Are we still okay?' he growled.

'Sure we are.' But her throat was tight.

'I don't know what came over me.'

'It's been an emotional evening.' She swallowed. 'And when emotions run high you always seek a physical outlet.'

He nodded. There was a pause. 'It's not usually your style, though.'

She shifted, rolled her shoulders. 'Yeah, well, it seems that being pregnant has made me…itchy.'

He stared. And then he leaned slightly away from her. 'You're joking?'

'I wish I were.'

She had to stop looking at him. She forced her gaze back to the front—to the gently lapping water of the bay. Which wasn't precisely the mood she was after. She forced her gaze upwards. Stars. She heaved out a sigh and gave up.

'So you're feeling...? Umm...? All of the time?'

She pressed her hands to her cheeks and stared doggedly out at the water, desperately wishing for some of its calm to enter her soul. 'I expected to feel all maternal and Mother Earthy. Not sexy.'

'You know, it kind of makes sense,' he said after a bit. 'All those pregnancy hormones are making you look great.'

At the moment she'd take the haggard morning sickness look if it would get things between her and Ben on an even keel again.

'You sure we're okay?' he said again.

She bit back a sigh. 'I'm not going to fall for you, Ben, if that's what you're worried about.'

'No, I—'

'For a start, I don't like the way you treat women, and I'm sure as hell not going to let any man treat me like that.'

'I do not treat women badly,' he growled.

'Wham, bam, thank you, ma'am. That's your style.'

And as far as she was concerned it was appalling. She grimaced. Even if a short time ago she'd been begging for exactly that. She massaged her temples. She found her own behaviour this evening appalling too. She'd never acted like that before—so heedless and mindless. Not with any man.

'I haven't had any complaints.'

She snorted. 'Because you don't stick around long enough to hear them.'

'Hell, Meg.' He scowled. 'I show a woman a good time. I don't make promises.'

But he didn't care if a woman did read more into their encounter. He'd used that to his advantage on more than one occasion.

'Yeah, well, I want more than that from a relationship, and that's something I know you're not in the market for.' He grabbed her arm when she went to rise. She fell back to the sand, her shoulder jostling his. 'What?'

He let her go again. 'I'm glad we're on the same page, because…'

An ache started up behind her eyes. 'Because?'

'I've made a decision and we need to talk about it.'

She smoothed her skirt down towards her knees

again. Ben was going to leave right after the wedding. That was what he wanted to tell her, wasn't it?

She pulled in a breath and readied herself for his news. It was good news, she told herself, straightening her spine and setting her shoulders. Things could get back to normal again.

'I've made the decision to stay in Port Stephens. I'll find work here and I'll find a place to live. I want to be a father to our baby, Meg. A *proper* father.'

CHAPTER EIGHT

THE WORLD TILTED to one side. Meg planted a hand against shifting sand. 'Staying?' Her voice wobbled.

Living here in Port Stephens, so close to Elsie and his childhood, would make Ben miserable. She closed her eyes. In less than six months he'd go stir crazy and flee in a trail of dust.

And where would that leave her baby and their friendship?

Depending on how much under the six-month mark Ben managed to hold on for, her baby might not even have been born. She opened her eyes. In which case it wouldn't have come to rely on Ben or to love him.

It wouldn't be hurt by his desertion.

But Ben would be. His failure to do this would destroy something essential in him.

And she didn't want to bear witness to that.

She turned to find him studying her. His shoulders were hitched in a way that told her he was waiting for her to say something hard and cruel.

And the memory of their kiss—that bone-crushing kiss—throbbed in all the spaces between them.

She moistened her lips. 'You haven't been back here a full week yet. This is a big decision—huge. It's life-changing. You don't have to rush it, or make a hasty choice, or—'

'When it comes down to brass tacks, Meg, the decision itself is remarkably simple.'

It was?

'Being a parent—a father—is the most important job in the world.'

Her heart pounded. He would hate himself—*hate*—when he found out he wasn't up to the task. Her heart burned, her eyes ached and her temples throbbed.

And at the back of her mind all she could think about was kissing him again. Kissing him had been a mistake. But that didn't stop her from wanting to repeat it.

And repeat it.

Over and over again.

But if they did it would destroy their friendship. She clenched her hands in her lap and battled the need to reach out and touch him again, kiss him again, as she hungered to do.

'Coming back home this time…' He glanced down at his hands. 'I've started to realise how shallow my life really is.'

Her jaw dropped.

'I know it looks exciting, and I guess it is. But it's shallow too. I've spent my whole life running away from responsibility. I'm starting to see I haven't achieved anything of real value at all.'

She straightened. 'That's not true. You help people achieve their dreams. You give them once-in-a-lifetime experiences—stories they can tell their children.'

'And who am I going to tell *my* stories to?'

Her heart started to thud.

'I've steered clear of any thoughts of children in my future, afraid I'd turn out like my parents.' His face grew grim but his chin lifted. 'That will only happen if I let it.'

He turned to her. *Stop thinking about kissing him!*

'What I really want to know is what you're scared of, Meg. Why does the thought of my coming home for good and being a father to our child freak you out?'

Because what if I never do manage to get my hormones back under control?

She snapped away at that thought. It was ludicrous. And unworthy. This should have nothing to do with her feelings and everything to do with her baby's. She couldn't let how she felt colour that reality.

'Meg?'

The notion of Ben coming home for good *did* freak her out. It scared her to the soles of her feet. He knew her too well for her to deny it. 'I don't want to hurt you,' she whispered.

He set his shoulders in a rigid line. 'Give it to me straight.'

She glanced at her hands. She hauled in a breath. 'I'm afraid you'll hang around just long enough for the baby to love you. I'm afraid the baby will come to love and rely on you but you won't be able to hack the monotony of domesticity. I'm afraid your restlessness will get the better of you and you'll leave. And if you do that, Ben, you will break my baby's heart.'

He flinched. The throbbing behind her eyes intensified.

'And if you do that, Ben...' she forced herself to continue '...I don't know if I could ever forgive you.'

And they would both lose the most important friendship of their lives.

He shot to his feet and strode down to the water's edge.

'And what's more,' she called after him, doing

what she could to keep her voice strong, 'if that's the way this all plays out, I think you will hate yourself.'

There was so much to lose if he stayed.

He strode back to where she sat, planted his feet in front of her. 'I can't do anything about your fears, Meg. I'm sorry you feel the way you do. I know I have no one to blame but myself, and that only time will put your fears to rest.' He dragged a hand back through his hair. 'But when *our* baby is born I'm going to be there for it every step of the way. I want it to love me. I want it to rely on me. I'll be doing everything to make that happen.'

She shrank from him. 'But—'

'I mean to be the best father I can be. I mean to be the kind of father to my son or daughter that my father wasn't to me. I want our baby to have everything good in life, and I mean to stick around to make sure that happens.'

Meg covered her face with her hands. 'Oh, Ben, I'm sorry. I'm so, so sorry.'

Ben stared at Meg, with her head bowed and her shoulders slumped, and knelt down on the sand beside her, his heart burning. He pulled her hands from her face. 'What on earth are you sorry for?' She didn't have anything to be sorry about.

'I'm sorry I asked you to donate sperm. I'm

sorry I've created such an upheaval in your life. I didn't mean for that to happen. I didn't mean to turn your life upside down.'

The darkness in her eyes, the guilt and sorrow swirling in their depths, speared into him. 'I know that.' He sat beside her again. 'When I agreed to be your sperm donor I had no idea I'd feel this way, and I'm sorry that's turned all your plans on their head.'

She pulled in a breath that made her whole body shudder. He wanted to wrap her in his arms. She moved away as if she'd read that thought in his face. It was only an inch, but it was enough. *All because of that stupid kiss.*

Why the hell had he kissed her? He clenched a hand. Ten years ago he'd promised he would never do that again. Ten years ago, when that jerk she'd been dating had dumped her. She'd been vulnerable then. She'd been vulnerable tonight too. And he'd taken advantage of that fact.

Meg wasn't the kind of girl a guy kissed and then walked away from. He might be staying in Port Stephens for good, but he wasn't changing his life *that* much. He had to stop sending her such mixed signals. They were friends. *Just* friends. *Best friends.*

He closed his eyes and gritted his teeth. Control—he needed to find control.

And he needed to forget how divine she'd felt in his arms and how that kiss had made him feel like a superhero, shooting off into the sky.

She cleared her throat, snagging his attention again. 'Obviously neither one of us foresaw what would happen.'

Her sigh cut him to the quick. 'I know this is hard for you, Meg, but I do mean to be a true father to our child.'

She still didn't believe him. It was in her face. In the way she opened her hands and let the sand trickle out of them. In the way she turned to stare out at the water.

'And because I do want to be a better father than my own, I need to clear the air about that kiss.'

His body heated up in an instant as the impact of their kiss surged through him again. That kiss had been—

He fisted his hands and tried to cut the memory from his mind. He was not going to dwell on that kiss again. *Ever.* He couldn't. Not if he wanted to maintain his sanity. Not if he wanted to save their friendship.

Meg slapped her hands to the sides of her knees. 'You are nothing like your father.'

How could she be so sure of that?

'You would never, *ever* put a gun to anyone's head—let alone your own child's.'

Bile rose in his throat. That had happened nearly twenty years ago, but the day and all its horror was etched on his memory as if with indelible ink. His mother and father had undergone one of the most acrimonious divorces in the history of man. In the custody battle that had ensued they had used their only son to score as many points off one another as they could. At every available opportunity.

Their bitterness and their hate had turned them into people Ben hadn't been able to recognise. They'd pushed and pushed and pushed each other, until one day his father had shown up on the front doorstep with a shotgun.

Ben's heart pounded. He could still taste the fear in his mouth when he'd first caught sight of the gun—could still feel the grip of a hard hand on the back of his neck when he'd turned to run. He'd been convinced his father would kill them.

Ben pressed a hand to his forehead and drew oxygen into his lungs. Meg wrapped her arm through his. It helped anchor him back in the present moment, drawing him out of that awful one twenty years ago.

'My parents must've cared for each other once—maybe even loved each other—but marriage for them resulted in my father being in prison and my mother dumping me with Elsie and never being heard from again.'

'Not all marriages end like that, Ben.'

'True.'

But he had the same raging passions inside him that his parents had. He had no intention of setting them free. That was why he kept his interludes with women light and brief. It was safer all round.

Gently, he detached his arm from Meg's. 'Whatever else I do, though, marriage is something I'm never going to risk.'

She shook her head and went back to lifting sand and letting it trickle through her hand. 'This is one of those circular arguments that just go round and round without ending. We agreed to disagree about this years ago.'

He heard her unspoken question. *So why bring it up now?*

'Regardless of what you think, Meg, I do mean to be a good father. But that doesn't mean I've changed my mind about marriage.'

She stopped playing with the sand. 'And you think because I'm feeling a little sexy that I'm going to weave you into my fantasies and cast you in the role of handsome prince?' She snorted. 'Court jester, more like. It'd take more than a kiss for me to fall in love with you, Ben Sullivan. I may have baby brain, but that doesn't mean I've turned into a moron. Especially—' she shot to her feet '—when I don't believe you'll hang around long enough for anyone to fall in love with you anyway.'

He didn't argue the point any further. Only time would prove to her that he really did mean to stick around.

He scrambled to his feet. He just had to make sure he didn't kiss her again. Meg didn't do one-night stands—it wasn't how she was built inside. She got emotionally involved. He knew that. He'd always known that. He pushed his shoulders back and shoved his hands into the pockets of his shorts. He'd made a lot of mistakes in his sorry life, but he wasn't making that one.

He set off after Meg. 'What would you like me to do in relation to the wedding this week?'

She'd walked back to where they'd kicked off their shoes. He held her arm as she slid hers back on. He gritted his teeth in an effort to counter the warm temptation of her skin.

She blinked up at him as she slid a finger around the back of one of her sandals. She righted herself and moved out of his grasp. 'There's still a lot to do.' She glanced at him again. 'How busy are you this coming week?'

He'd be hard at work, casting around for employment opportunities, putting out feelers and sifting through a few preliminary ideas he'd had, but he'd find time to help her out with this blasted wedding. The days of leaving everything up to her were through. 'I have loads of time.'

'Well, for a start, I need those names from Elsie.'

'Right.'

They set off back towards the club and Meg's car. 'I don't suppose you'd organise the invitations, would you? I wasn't going to worry with anything too fancy. I was just going to grab a few packets of nice invitations from the newsagents and write them out myself. Calligraphy is unnecessary—they just need to be legible.'

'Leave it to me.'

'Thank you. That'll be a big help.'

'Anything else?'

'I would be very, very grateful if you could find me a gardener. I just don't have the spare time to keep on top of it at the moment. This wedding will be that garden's last hurrah, because I'm having all those high-maintenance annuals ripped out and replaced with easy-care natives.'

He nodded. 'Not a problem.'

They drove home in silence. When Meg turned in at her driveway and turned off the ignition she didn't invite him in for a drink and he didn't suggest it either. Instead, with a quick goodnight, he headed next door.

The first thing he saw when he entered the kitchen was Elsie, sitting at the table shuffling a deck of cards. Without a word, she dealt out a hand for rummy. Ben hesitated and then sat.

'How's Meg?'

'She's fine.'

'Good.'

He shifted. 'She'd feel a whole lot happier, though, if you'd give her a list of ten people she can invite to the wedding.'

Elsie snorted. He blinked again. Had that been a *laugh*?

'She said that although her father won't admit it, he'd like more than a registry office wedding.'

Elsie snorted again, and this time there was no mistaking it—it was definitely a laugh. 'I'll make a deal with you, Ben.'

Good Lord. The woman was practically garrulous. 'A deal?'

'For every hand you win, I'll give you a name.'

He straightened on his chair. 'You're on.'

Meg glanced around at a tap on the back door. And then froze. Ben stood there, looking devastatingly delicious, and a traitorous tremor weakened her knees.

With a gulp, she waved him in. Other than a couple of rushed conversations about the wedding, she hadn't seen much of him during the last two weeks. Work had been crazy, with two of her staff down with the flu, and whenever she had seen Ben and asked what he'd been up to he'd simply answered with a cryptic, 'I've been busy.' Long, leisurely conversations obviously hadn't been on either of their agendas.

Her gaze lowered to his lips. Lips that had caressed hers. Lips that had transported her to a place beyond herself and made her yearn for more. So much more. Lips that were moving now.

'Whatever it is you're cooking, Meg, no known man would be able to resist it.'

She snapped away and forced a smile.

'Cookies?'

Her smile became almost genuine at the hope in his voice. 'Chocolate chip,' she confirmed.

'Even better.' He glanced at her baking companions. 'Sounds like you guys have been having fun in here.'

Loss suddenly opened up inside her. He was her best friend. They had to find a way to overcome this horrid awkwardness.

She swallowed and hauled in a breath, gestured to the two children. 'This is Laura, who is ten, and Lochie, who is eight.'

'We're brother and sister,' Laura announced importantly.

'And Auntie Meg used to go to school with Mummy.'

'Felicity Strickland,' Meg said at his raised eyebrow. 'Laura and Lochie—this is my friend Ben from next door. He went to school with your mummy too. What do you think? Will we let him share our cookies?'

Lochie nodded immediately. 'That means there'll be another boy.'

In Lochie's mind another boy meant an ally, and Meg had a feeling he was heartily sick of being bossed by his sister.

Laura folded her arms. 'He'll have to work for them. It's only fair, because we've all worked.'

Meg choked back a laugh. She half expected Ben to make some excuse and back out through the door.

'What would I have to do?' he asked Laura instead. 'I'll do just about anything for choc-chip cookies. Especially ones that smell this good.'

Laura glanced up at Meg.

'How about Ben sets the table?'

'And pours the milk?'

She nodded. 'Sounds fair.'

Ben tackled setting the table and pouring out four glasses of milk while Meg pulled a second tray of cookies from the oven and set them to cool on the counter. She'd hoped that baking cookies would make her feel super-maternal, but one glance at Ben threw that theory out of the water.

She still felt—

Don't think about it!

Her hands shook as she placed the first batch of cookies on a plate and handed them to Laura, who took them over to the table.

They ate cookies and drank milk.

But even over the home-baked goodness of choc-chip cookies Meg caught a hint of leather and whisky. She tried to block it from her mind, tried to ignore the longing that burned through her veins.

The children regaled Ben with stories of their Christmas trip to Bali. Meg glanced at Ben and then glanced away again, biting her lip. It was no use telling herself this was just Ben. There was no *just* Ben about it—only a hard, persistent throb in her blood and an ache in her body.

When the phone rang she leapt to her feet, eager for distraction.

Ben's eyes zeroed in on her face the moment she returned to the kitchen. 'Problem?'

She clenched and unclenched her hands. 'The caterers I had lined up for the wedding have cancelled on me, the rotten—' she glanced at the children '—so-and-sos.'

She pressed her fingers to her temples and paced up and down on the other side of the breakfast bar. The wedding was three weeks away. Less than that. Two weeks and six days. Not that she was counting or anything.

Ben stood. 'What can I do?'

She glanced at him. She glanced at the children. A plan—devious, and perhaps a little unfair—slid beneath her guard. No, she couldn't.

Two weeks and six days.

She folded her arms. 'Are you up for a challenge, Ben Sullivan?'

He rocked back on his heels. 'What kind of challenge?'

She glanced at the children and then back at him, with enough meaning in her face that he couldn't possibly mistake her message.

He folded his arms too. 'Bring it on.'

'If you keep Laura and Lochie amused for an hour or two, it'll give me a chance to ring around and find a replacement caterer.'

He glanced at the television. 'Not a problem.'

She shook her head and glanced out of the kitchen window towards the back yard. There was no mistaking the panic that momentarily filled his eyes. 'I'll need peace and quiet.'

Did he even know the first thing about children and how much work they could sometimes be? Laura truly was the kind of child designed to test Ben's patience to the limit too. And when he found out the truth that being a father wasn't all beer and skittles—all fun and laughter at the beach and I-love-you-Daddy cuddles—how long before he left?

She did what she could to harden her heart, to stop it from sinking, to cut off its protests.

Lochie's face lit up. 'Can we go to the beach? Can we go swimming?'

Relief lit Ben's face too, but Meg shook her head. 'Your mum said no swimming.' Besides, she wanted them all here, right under her nose, where she could keep an eye on them.

Ben glared at her. 'Why not?'

She reached out and brushed a hand through Lochie's hair, pulled him against her in a hug. 'Lochie's recovering from an ear infection.'

Ben shuffled his feet. 'I'm sorry to hear that, mate.'

Lochie straightened. 'We could play Uno. Laura remembered to bring it.'

'Because you *didn't*.' She rolled her eyes. 'You never do. Do you know how to play?' she demanded of Ben.

'No idea.'

'Then I'll teach you.' She took Ben's hand. 'Get the game, Lochie.'

'Please,' Ben corrected.

Laura blinked. So did Meg. 'Get the game, *please*, Lochie,' Laura amended, leading both males outside as she waxed lyrical about the importance of good manners.

Meg grimaced. Poor Ben. Laura was ten going on eighty. It hardly seemed fair to expect him to cope with her. She glanced down at her baby bump, rested her hand on it before glancing back out of the window. It was an hour. Two hours tops. She'd be nearby, and if he couldn't deal with Laura for that length of time then he had no right remaining here in Port Stephens at all.

Still, even with that decided Meg couldn't move from the window. She watched as the trio settled on the outdoor furniture, and as Ben listened while Laura explained the rules of the game in exhaustive detail. His patience touched her. Once the game started he kept both children giggling so hard she found herself wishing she could go outside and join them.

She shook her head. Two weeks and six days. She had a caterer to find.

It took Meg forty minutes' worth of phone calls before she found a replacement caterer. She glanced at her watch and winced. How on earth was Ben surviving? She raced into the family room to peer out through the glass sliding door that afforded an excellent view of the back yard and started to laugh.

Ben had set up an old slip 'n' slide of hers—one

they'd played on when they were children—and the three of them were having the time of their lives. Laura giggled, Lochie chortled, and Ben's whole face had come alive. It shone.

She took a step towards the door, transfixed, her hand reaching out to rest against the glass as if reaching for...

Ben's face shone.

Her other hand moved to cover her stomach. What if Ben *did* stay? What if he kept his word and found fatherhood satisfying? What if he didn't run away?

Her heart thudded as she allowed the idea truly to sink in. The blood vessels in her hand pulsed against the glass. If Ben kept his word then her baby would have a father.

A real father.

She snatched her hand away. She backed up to the sofa. But she couldn't drag her gaze away from the happy trio in her back yard, watching in amazement as Ben effortlessly stepped in to prevent a spat between the children. He had them laughing again in no time. The man was a natural.

And he had a butt that—

She waved a hand in front of her face to shoo the thought away. She didn't have time for butts— not even butts as sublime as Ben's.

Or chests. She blinked and leaned forward. He

really did have the most amazing body. He'd kept his shirt on, but it was now so wet it stuck to him like a second skin, outlining every delicious muscle and—

She promptly changed seats and placed her back to the door. She dragged in a breath and tried to control the crazy beating of her heart.

If Ben *did* overcome his wanderlust…

She swallowed. He'd never lied to her before. Why would he lie to her now? Especially about something as important as their child's happiness.

No! She shot to her feet. *Her* child!

She raced to the refrigerator to pour herself an ice-cold glass of water, but when she tipped her head back to drink it her eyes caught on the vivid blue of the water slide and the children's laughter filled her ears.

Slowly she righted her glass. This was their child. *Theirs.* She'd let fear cloud her judgement. Not fear for the baby, but fear for herself. Fear that this child might somehow damage her friendship with Ben. Fear that she might come to rely on him too heavily. Fear at having to share her child.

She abandoned her water to grip her hands together. She hadn't expected to share this baby. In her possessiveness, was she sabotaging Ben's efforts?

She moistened suddenly dry lips. It would be

hard, relinquishing complete control and having to consider someone else's opinions and ideas about the baby, but behind that there would be a sense of relief too, and comfort. To know she wasn't in this on her own, that someone else would have her and the baby's backs.

She'd fully expected to be a single mum—had been prepared for it. But if she didn't have to go it alone…

If her baby could have a father…

Barely aware of what she was doing, Meg walked back to the double glass doors. Ben had a child under each arm and he was swinging them round and round until they shrieked with laughter. Laura broke away to grab the hose and aimed it directly at his chest. He clutched at the spot as if shot and fell down, feigning injury. Both children immediately pounced on him.

The longer Meg watched them the clearer the picture in her mind became. Her baby could have a mother *and* a father. Her baby could have it all!

Pictures formed in her mind—pictures of family picnics and trips to the beach, of happy rollicking Christmases, of shared meals and quiet times when the baby was put down and—

She snapped away. Heat rushed through her. *Get a grip!* Her baby might have a father, but that didn't mean she and Ben would form a cosy ro-

mantic bond and become the ideal picture-perfect
family. That would never happen.

Her heart pounded so hard it almost hurt, and
she had to close her eyes briefly until she could
draw much needed breath into straining lungs.

Ben would never do family in the way she
wanted or needed. That stupid kiss ten years ago
and the way Ben had bolted from town afterwards
had only reinforced what she'd always known—
that he would never surrender to the unpredict-
ability and raw emotion of romantic love, with
all its attendant highs and lows. She might have
baby brain and crazy hormones at the moment, but
she'd better not forget that fact—not for a single,
solitary moment.

Best friends.

She opened her eyes and nodded. They were
best friends who happened to have a child together
and they'd remain friends. They *could* make this
work.

She rested her forehead against the glass, her
breath fogging it so she saw the trio dimly, through
a haze. If only she knew for certain that Ben
wouldn't leave, that he wouldn't let them down.
That he'd stay. She wanted a guarantee, but there
weren't—

She froze.

She turned to press her back against the door.

What did Ben want more than anything else in the world?

To be on the crew of a yacht that was sailing around the world.

Did he want that more than he wanted to be a father?

Her heart pounded. Her stomach churned. She pushed away from the door and made for the phone, dialling the number for Dave Clements' travel agency. 'Dave? Hi, it's Meg.'

'Hey, Meg. Winnie and I are really looking forward to the wedding. How are the preparations coming along?'

'Oh, God, don't ask.'

He laughed. 'If there's anything I can do?'

'Actually, I do need to come in and talk to you about organising a honeymoon trip for the happy couple.'

'Drop in any time and we'll put together something fabulous for them.'

'Thank you.' She swallowed. 'But that's not the reason I called.' Her mouth went dry. She had to swallow again. 'I've been racking my brain, trying to come up with a way to thank Ben. He's been such a help with the preparations and everything.'

'And?'

'Look,' she started in a rush, 'you know he's always wanted to crew on a round-the-world yacht expedition? I wondered if there was a way you could help me make that happen?'

A whistle travelled down the line. She picked up a pen and doodled furiously on the pad by the phone, concentrating on everything but her desire to retract her request.

'Are you sure that's what you want, Meg? When I spoke to him through the week it sounded like he was pretty set on staying in Port Stephens.'

She glanced out of the window at Ben and the children. Still laughing. Still having the time of their lives. 'It's something he's always wanted. I want him to at least have the opportunity to turn it down.'

But would he?

'Okay, leave it with me. I'll see what I can do.'

'Thanks, Dave.'

She replaced the receiver. If Ben turned the opportunity down she'd have her guarantee.

If he didn't?

She swallowed. Well, at least that would be an answer too.

CHAPTER NINE

BEN CRUISED THE road between Nelson Bay and Fingal Bay with the driver's window down, letting the breeze dance through the car and ruffle his hair. He put his foot down a centimetre and then grinned in satisfaction. This baby, unlike his motorbike, barely responded.

Perfect.

The coastal forest and salt-hardy scrubland retreated as the road curved into the small township. On impulse he parked the car and considered the view.

As a kid, he'd loved the beach. He and Meg had spent more time down there than they had in their own homes. Maybe he'd taken it for granted. Or maybe he'd needed to leave it for a time to see some of the world's other beautiful places before he could come back and truly appreciate it.

Because Meg was right—for sheer beauty, Fingal Bay was hard to beat. The line of the beach, the rocky outcrop of Fingal Island directly opposite and the sand spit leading out to it formed a cradle that enclosed the bay on three of its sides. The unbelievably clear water revealed the sandy bottom of the bay, and the bottle-nosed dolphins that were almost daily visitors.

He'd fled this place as soon as he was of a legal age. Staring at it now, he felt as if it welcomed him back. He dragged in a breath of late-afternoon air—salt-scented and warm—then glanced at his watch and grinned. Meg should be home by now.

He drove to her house, pulled the car into her driveway and blared the horn. He counted to five before her front door swung open.

Meg stood silhouetted in the light with the darkness of the house behind her and every skin cell he possessed tightened. Her baby bump had grown in the month he'd been home. He gazed at it hungrily. He gazed at *her* hungrily.

He gave himself a mental slap upside the head. He'd promised to stop thinking about Meg that way. He'd promised not to send her any more mixed messages. He would never be able to give her all the things a woman like her wanted and needed, and he valued their friendship too much to pretend otherwise.

If only it were as easy as it sounded.

With a twist of his lips, he vaulted out of the car. When she saw him, her jaw dropped. She stumbled down the driveway to where he stood, her mouth opening and closing, her eyes widening. 'What on earth is that?'

He grinned and puffed out his chest. 'This—' he slapped the bonnet '—is my new car.' This would prove to her that he was a changed man, that he was capable of responsibility and stability. That he was capable of fatherhood.

He pushed his hands into the pockets of his jeans, his shoulders free and easy, while he waited for her to finish her survey of the car and then pat him on the back and meet his gaze with new respect in her eyes.

'You…' She swallowed. 'You've bought a station wagon?'

'I have.' His grin widened. He'd need room for kid stuff now. And this baby had plenty of room.

'You've gone and bought an ugly, boxy *white* station wagon?'

She stared at him as if he'd just broken out in green and purple spots. His shoulders froze in place. So did his grin. She planted her hands on her hips and glared. The sun picked out the golden highlights in her hair. Her eyes blazed, but her lips were the sweetest pink he'd ever seen.

Meg was hot. He shifted, adjusting his jeans. Not just pretty, but smokin' hot. Knock-a-man-off-his-feet hot. He needed something ice-cold to slake the heat rising through him or he'd—

'Where's your bike?' she demanded.

He moistened his lips. 'I traded it.' The icy sting of the cold current that visited the bay at this time of year might do the trick.

'You. Did. *What?*' Her voice rose on the last word. Her nostrils flared. She poked him in the shoulder. 'Have you gone mad? What on earth were you thinking?'

He leant towards her, all his easy self-satisfaction slaughtered. 'I was trying to prove to you that I've changed,' he ground out. 'This car is a symbol that I can be a good father.'

'It shows you've lost your mind!'

She dragged both hands back through her hair. She stared at him for a moment, before transferring her gaze back to the station wagon.

'Inside—now,' she ordered. 'I don't want to have this conversation on the street.'

He planted his feet. 'I'm not some child you can order about. If you want to talk to me, then you can ask me like a civilised person. I'm tired of you treating me like a second-class citizen.' Like someone who couldn't get one damn thing right.

He knew she was stressed about the wedding, about the baby, about him—about that damn kiss!—but he was through with taking this kind of abuse from her. Meg had always been a control freak, but she was getting worse and it was time she eased up.

He welcomed the shock in her eyes, but not the pain that followed swiftly on its heels. Meg was a part of him. Hurting her was like hurting himself.

She swallowed and nodded. 'Sorry, that really was very rude of me. It's just…I think we need to talk about that.' She gestured to his car. 'Would you come inside for coffee so we can discuss it?' When he didn't say anything she added, 'Please?'

He nodded and followed her into the house.

She glanced at the kitchen clock. 'Coffee or a beer?'

'Coffee, thanks.' Meg had been right about the drinking. Somewhere along the line, when he hadn't been paying attention, it had become a habit. He'd made an effort to cut back.

She made coffee for him and decaf for herself. He took in the tired lines around her eyes and mouth and the pallor of her skin where previously there'd been a golden glow and something snagged in his chest. 'What's wrong with the car?' he said, accepting the mug she handed him. 'I thought it would show you I'm serious about sticking around and being involved with the baby.'

'I think I've been unfair to you on that, Ben.'

She gestured to the family room sofas and he followed her in a daze.

She sat. She didn't tuck her legs beneath her like she normally did. She didn't lean back against the sofa's cushioned softness. She perched on the edge of the seat, looking weary and pale. Her mug sat on the coffee table, untouched. He wanted to ease her back into that seat and massage her shoulders…or her feet. Whichever would most help her to relax.

Except he had a no-touching-Meg rule. And he wasn't confident enough in his own strength to break it.

She glanced up, the green in her eyes subdued. 'You said you wanted to be an involved father and I automatically assumed…'

'That I was lying.'

'Not on purpose, no.' She frowned. 'But I didn't think you really knew what you were talking about. I didn't think you understood the reality of what you were planning to do.'

And why should she? The truth was he hadn't understood the reality at all. Not at first.

She glanced back at him and her gaze settled on his mouth for a beat too long. Blood rushed in his ears. When she realised her preoccupation she jerked away.

'I didn't think you knew your own mind.' She

swallowed. 'That wasn't fair of me. I'm sorry for doubting you. And I'm sorry I haven't been more supportive of your decision.'

'Hell, don't apologise.' Coffee sloshed over the side of his mug and he mopped it up with the sleeve of his shirt. 'I needed your challenges to make me analyse what I was doing and what it is I want. I should be thanking you for forcing me to face facts.' For forcing him to grow up.

When he glanced back up he found her making a detailed inventory of his chest and shoulders. Her lips parted and fire licked along his veins.

Don't betray yourself, he tutored himself. *Don't!*

Her eyes searched his, and then the light in them dulled and she glanced away, biting her lip.

He had to close his eyes. 'You don't need to apologise about anything.'

He opened his eyes and almost groaned at the strain in her face. He made himself grin, wanting to wipe the tension away, wanting desperately for things to return to normal between them again.

'Though I have to say if I'd known that calling you on the way you've been treating me would change your thinking I'd have done it days ago.'

'Oh, it wasn't that.' She offered him a weak smile that didn't reach her eyes. 'It was watching you with Laura and Lochie last Saturday.'

He'd sensed that had been a test. He just hadn't known if he'd passed it or not.

'I had a ball.'

'I know. And so did they.'

'They're great kids.'

Just for a moment her eyes danced. 'Laura can be a challenge at times.'

'She just needs to loosen up a bit, that's all.' In the same way Meg needed to loosen up.

Who made sure Meg had fun these days? Who made sure she didn't take herself too seriously? She'd said that the baby gave her joy, but it wasn't here yet. What else gave her joy? It seemed to him that at the moment Meg was too busy for joy, and that was no way to live a life.

He'd need to ponder that a bit more, but in the meantime...

'What's your beef with the car?'

That brought the life back to her cheeks. He sat back, intrigued.

'Could you have picked a more boring car if you'd tried?'

'*You* have a station wagon,' he pointed out.

'But at least mine is a sporty version and it's useful for work. And it's blue!'

'The colour doesn't matter.'

'Of course it does.' She leant to towards him. 'I understand you want to prove you're good father material, but that doesn't mean you have to become *beige*!'

'Beige' had been their teenage term for all things boring.

'I agree that with a baby you'll need a car. But you're allowed to buy a car you'll enjoy. A two-seat convertible may not be practical, but you're an action man, Ben, and you like speed. You could've bought some powerful V6 thing that you could open up on the freeway, or a four-wheel drive you could take off-road and drive on the beach—or anything other than that boring beige box sitting in my driveway.'

He considered her words.

'Do you think fatherhood is going to be beige?' she demanded.

'No!'

She closed her eyes and let out a breath. 'That's something, at least.'

He saw it then—the reason for her outburst. She'd started to believe in him, in his sense of purpose and determination, and then he'd turned up in that most conservative of conservative cars and he'd freaked her out.

Again.

He was determined to get things back on an even footing between them again. And he'd suc-ceed. As long as he ignored the sweet temptation of her lips and the long clean line of her limbs. And the desire that flared in her green-flecked eyes.

'You don't have to change who you are, Ben. You might not be travelling around the globe any more, throwing yourself off mountains, negotiating the rapids of some huge river or trekking to base camp at Everest—but, for heaven's sake, it doesn't mean you have to give up your motorbike, does it?'

That—trading in his bike—had been darn hard. It was why it had taken him a full month of being back in Fingal Bay before he'd found the courage to do it. But he'd figured it was a symbol of his old life and therefore had to go. But if Meg was right…

'I want you to go back to that stupid car yard and buy it back.'

A weight lifted from his shoulders. He opened and closed his hands. 'You think I should?'

'Yes! Where else am I going to get my occasional pillion-passenger thrill? All that speed and power? And, while I know you can't literally feel the wind in your hair because of the helmet, that's exactly what it feels like. It's like flying.'

He had a vision of Meg on the back of his bike, her front pressed against his back and her arms wrapped around his waist. He shot to his feet. 'If

I race back now I might catch the manager before he leaves for the day.' He had to get his bike back. 'He had a nice-looking four wheel drive in stock. That could be a bit of fun.' He rubbed at his jaw. 'I could take it for a test drive.'

Meg trailed after him to the front door. 'Good luck.'

Halfway down the path, he swung back. 'What are you doing Saturday?'

'Elsie and I are shopping for wedding outfits in the morning.' She grimaced. 'It's not like we've left it to the last minute or anything, but that grandmother of yours can be darn slippery when she wants to be.'

The wedding was a fortnight this Saturday. 'And in the afternoon?'

She shook her head and shrugged.

'Keep it free,' he ordered. Then he strode back, slipped a hand around the back of her head and pressed a kiss to her brow. 'Thanks, Meg.'

And then he left before he did something stupid, like kiss her for real. That wouldn't be getting their friendship back on track.

Meg glanced up at the tap on the back door. 'How did the shopping go?' Ben asked, stepping into the family room with the kind of grin designed to bring a grown woman to her knees.

Her heart swelled at the sight of him. *Don't drool. Smile. Don't forget to smile.*

The smiling was easy. Holding back a groan of pure need wasn't. 'The shopping? Oh, it went surprisingly well,' she managed. Elsie had been remarkably amiable and co-operative. 'We both now have outfits.'

They'd found a lovely lavender suit in shot silk for Elsie. Though she'd protested that it was too young for her, her protests had subsided once Meg had pronounced it perfect. Meg had settled on a deep purple satin halter dress with a chiffon over-lay that hid her growing baby bulge. It made her feel like a princess.

'How are the wedding preparation coming along? What do you need me to do this week?'

Ben had, without murmur, executed to perfection whatever job she'd assigned to him. He'd been amazing.

She thought of the request she'd made of Dave and bit her lip. Perhaps she should call that off. Ben had settled into a routine here as if...almost as if he'd never been away. The thought of him leaving...

She shook herself. The wedding. They were talking about the wedding. 'You have a suit?'

'Yep.'

'Then there's not much else to be done. The

marquee is being erected on the Friday afternoon prior, and the tables and chairs will all be set up then too.'

'I'll make sure I'm here in case there are any hitches.'

'Thank you.' He eyed her for a moment. It made her skin prickle. 'What?'

He shook himself. 'Have you managed to keep this afternoon free?'

'Uh-huh.' Something in her stomach shifted—a dark, dangerous thrill at the thought of spending a whole afternoon in Ben's company. 'What do you have planned?' If both of them were sensible it would be something practical and beige boring.

Ben's eyes—the way they danced and the way that grin hooked up the right side of his face—told her this afternoon's adventure, whatever it might be, was not going to be beige.

'It's a surprise.'

Her blood quickened. She should make an excuse and cry off, but...

Damn it all, this was Ben—*her best friend*—and that grin of his was irresistible. She glanced down at her sundress. 'Is what I'm wearing okay?'

'Absolutely not.' His grin widened. 'You're going to need a pair of swimmers, and something to put on over them to protect you from sunburn.'

Her bones heated up. She really, truly should

make an excuse. 'And a hat, I suppose?' she said, moving in the direction of her bedroom to change.

'You get the picture,' he said.

Meg lifted her face into the breeze and let out a yell for the sheer fun of it. Ben had driven them into Nelson Bay in his brand new *red* four-wheel drive to hire a rubber dinghy with an outboard motor for the afternoon. They were zipping across the vast expanse of the bay as if they were flying.

Ben had given her the wind in her hair for real, and she couldn't remember the last time she'd had this much fun. She released the rope that ran around the dinghy's perimeter and flung her arms back, giving herself up to sheer exhilaration.

'Meg!'

She opened her eyes at Ben's shout, saw they were about to hit the wake from a speedboat, and grabbed the rope again for balance. They bounced over the waves, her knees cushioned by the buoyant softness of the rubber base.

Eventually Ben cut the motor and they drifted. She trailed her hand in the water, relishing its refreshing coolness as she dragged the scent of salt and summer into her lungs. Silver scales glittered in the sun when a fish jumped out of the water nearby. Three pelicans watched from a few metres away, and above them a flock of seagulls cried as they headed for the marina.

The pelicans set off after them, and Meg turned around and stretched her legs out. The dinghy was only small, but there was plenty of room for Meg and Ben to sit facing one another, with their legs stretched to the side. She savoured the way the dinghy rocked and swayed, making their legs press against each other's, the warm surge that shot through her at each contact.

Ever since that kiss she'd found herself craving to touch Ben—to test the firmness of his skin, to explore his muscled leanness and discover if it would unleash the heat that could rise in her without any warning.

It was dangerous, touching like this, but she couldn't stop herself. Besides, it was summer—the sun shone, the gulls wheeled and screeched, and water splashed against the sides of the dingy. For a moment it all made her feel young and reckless.

'This was a brilliant idea, Ben.'

He grinned. 'It's certainly had the desired effect.'

She reached up to adjust the brim of her sunhat. 'Which was?'

'To put the colour back in your cheeks.'

She stilled. It was strange to have someone looking out for her, looking after her. 'Thank you.' If Ben did stay—

She cut that thought off. Whether Ben stayed or not, it wasn't his job to look after her. He might fill her with heat, but that didn't mean they had any kind of future together.

Except as friends.

He shrugged. 'Besides, it's nice to have some buddy-time.'

She gritted her teeth. Buddy-time was excellent. It *was*!

She glanced at him and tried to decipher the emotions that tangled inside her, coiling her up tight.

She started to name them silently. One: desire. Her lips twisted. *Please God, let that pass*. Two: anger that he'd turned her nicely ordered world on its head. She shook her head. *Deal with it*. Three: love for her oldest, dearest friend, for all they'd been through together, for all they'd shared, and for all the support and friendship he'd given her over the years.

And there was another emotion there too— something that burned and chafed. A throbbing sore. It was...

Hurt.

That made her blink. Hurt? She swallowed and forced herself to examine the feeling. An ache started at her temples. Hurt that he'd stay in Port Stephens for their baby in a way he'd never have stayed for her.

Oh, that was petty. And nonsensical.

She rubbed her hands up and down her arms. She hadn't harboured hidden hopes that Ben would come back for her. *She hadn't!* But seeing him now on such a regular basis…not to mention that kiss on the beach…that devastating kiss…

'Cold?'

She shook her head and abruptly dropped her hands back to her lap. She dragged in a breath. She had to be careful. She couldn't go weaving Ben into her romantic fantasies. It would end in tears. It would wreck their friendship. And that would be the worst thing in the world. It was why she hadn't let herself get hooked on that kiss ten years ago. It was why she had to forget that kiss the other night.

A romantic relationship—even if Ben was willing—wasn't worth risking their friendship over.

Deep inside, a part of her started to weep. She swallowed. Hormones, that was all.

'I can still hardly believe that Elsie and your father are marrying.'

She nodded, prayed her voice would work properly, prayed she could hide her strain. 'It shows a remarkable optimism on both their parts.'

He surveyed her for a moment. 'How are you getting on with your father?'

'Same as usual.' She lifted her face to the sun to counter a sudden chill. 'Neither he nor Elsie have mentioned my outburst. It seems we're all back to pretending it never happened.' Not that she knew what else she'd been expecting. Or hoping for. 'It's the elephant in the room nobody mentions.'

'It's had a good effect on Elsie, though.'

She straightened from her slouch. 'No?'

'Yep.' He flicked water at her. 'She's less buttoned-up and more relaxed. She makes more of an effort at conversation too.'

'*No?*'

He flicked water at her again. 'Yep.'

'I'd say that's down to the effect of her romance with my father.'

'She's even knitting the baby some booties.'

Meg leant towards him, even though she was in danger of getting more water flicked at her. 'You're kidding me?'

He didn't flick more water at her, but she realised it had been a mistake to lean towards him when the scent of leather and whisky slugged into her, heating her up...tightening her up. Making her want forbidden things.

She sat back. Darn it all! How on earth could she be so aware of his scent out here in the vast expanse of the bay? Surely the salt water and the sun should erase it, dilute it?

She scooped up a whole handful of water and threw it at him.

And then they had the kind of water fight that drenched them both and had her squealing and him laughing and them both breathing heavily from the exertion.

'How long since you've been out on the bay like this?' he demanded, subsiding back into his corner.

'Like this?' She readjusted her sunhat. 'Probably not since the last time we did it.'

'That has to be two years ago!'

'I've been out on a couple of dinner cruises, and I've swum more times than I can count.'

'What about kayaking?'

That was one of her favourite things—to take a kayak out in the early evening, when the shadows were long, the light dusky and the water calm. Paddling around the bay left her feeling at one with nature and the world. But when had she'd actually last done that?

She cocked her head to one side. She'd gone out a few times in December, but...

She hadn't been out once this year! 'I...I guess I've been busy.'

'You need to stop and smell the roses.'

He was right. This afternoon—full of sun, bay and a beat-up rubber dinghy—had proved that to her. She wanted to set her child a good example. She had no intention of turning into a distracted workaholic mother. She thought about her father and Elsie, how easily they'd fallen into unhealthy routines and habits.

She swallowed and glanced at Ben. He always took the time to smell the roses. Her lips twisted. Sometimes he breathed them in a little too deeply, and for a little too long, but nobody could accuse him of not living life to the full.

Would he still feel life was full after he'd been living in Port Stephens for a couple of years?

She glanced around. It was beautiful here. He was having fun, wasn't he?

For today.

But what would happen tomorrow, the day after that, and next week, next month, or even next year? *Please, God, don't let Ben be miserable.*

There was still so much that had to be settled. She leant back and swallowed. 'I agree it's important to slow down and to enjoy all the best that life has to offer, but you've still got some big decisions ahead of you, Ben.' And she doubted she'd be able to relax fully until he'd made them.

'Like?'

'Like what are you going to do with Elsie's

house? Will you live there on your own after the wedding?'

'I haven't thought about it.'

'And what about a job? I'm not meaning to be nosy or pushy or anything, but…'

His lips twitched. 'But?'

'I figure you don't want to live off your savings for ever.'

'I have a couple of irons in the fire.'

He did? She opened her mouth but he held up a hand to forestall her.

'Once I have something concrete to report you'll be the first to know. I promise.'

She wanted to demand a timeframe on his promise, but she knew he'd scoff at that. And probably rightly so.

'Do you think I should move into Elsie's house?'

Her mouth dried. 'I…'

'If I do, I'll be paying her rent.' He scowled. 'I don't want her to give the darn thing to me. It's hers.'

She eyed him for a moment. 'What if she gifts it to the baby?'

His mouth opened and closed but no sound came out. It obviously wasn't a scenario he'd envisaged. 'I…' He didn't go on.

She glanced away, her stomach shrinking. The

two of them had to have a serious conversation. But not today. They could save it for some other time.

'You better spit it out, Meg.'

She glared at the water. Ben knowing her so well could be darn inconvenient at times. She blew out a breath and turned to him. 'There are a few things I think we need to discuss in relation to the baby, but they can wait until after the wedding. It's such a glorious afternoon.'

And she didn't want to spoil it. Or ruin this easy-going camaraderie that should have been familiar to them but had been elusive these last few weeks.

'It could be the perfect afternoon for such a discussion,' he countered, gesturing to the sun, the bay and the holiday atmosphere of these last dog days of summer. 'When we're both relaxed.'

If she uttered the C-word he wouldn't remain relaxed. Still, she knew him well enough to know he wouldn't let it drop. She glanced around. Maybe he was right. Maybe she *should* lay a few things out there for him to mull over before Dave presented him with that dream offer. It only seemed fair.

She shivered, suddenly chilled, as if a cloud had passed over the sun. 'You won't like it,' she warned.

'I'm a big boy, Meg. I have broad shoulders.'

'You want to know if I think you should live in Elsie's house? That depends on…' She swallowed.

'On?'

'On what kind of access you want to have to the baby.'

He frowned. 'What do you mean?'

She wasn't going to be able to get away with not using the C-word. Dancing around it would only make matters worse.

'What I'm talking about, Ben, are our custody arrangements.'

Custody?

Ben flinched as the word ripped beneath his guard. His head was filled with the sound of shouting and screaming and abuse.

Custody?

'No!' He stabbed a finger at her. He swore. Once. Hard. Tried to quieten the racket in his head. He swore again, the storm raging inside him growing in strength. 'What the bloody hell are you talking about? *Custody?*' He spat the word out. 'No way! We don't need *custody* arrangements. We aren't like that. You and I can work it out like civilised people.'

Meg had gone white.

He realised he was shouting. Just like his mother

had shouted. Just like his father had shouted. He couldn't stop. 'We're supposed to be friends.'

She swallowed and bile filled his mouth. Was she afraid of him? Wind rushed through his ears. No! She knew him well enough to know he'd never hut her. Didn't she?

His hands clenched. If she knew him well enough, she'd have never raised this issue in the first place.

'We're friends who are having a baby,' she said, her voice low. 'We need certain safeguards in place to ensure—'

'Garbage!' He slashed a hand through the air. 'We can keep going the way we have been—the way we've always done things. When you've had the baby I can come over any time and help, maybe take care of it some days while you're at work, and help you in the evenings with feeding and baths and—'

'So basically we'd live like a married couple but without the benefits?'

Her scorn almost blasted the flesh from his bones.

'No, Ben, that's *not* how it's going to be. Living like that—don't you think it would do our child's head in?' She stabbed a finger at him. 'Besides, I still believe in love and marriage. I am *so* not going to have you cramp my style like that.'

The storm inside him built to fever-pitch. 'You really mean to let another man help raise *my* child?'

'That's something you're going to have to learn to live with. Just like I will if you ever become serious about a woman.'

He went ice-cold then. 'You never wanted me as part of this picture, did you? I've ruined your pretty fantasy of domestic bliss and now you're trying to punish me.' He leaned towards her. 'You're hoping this will drive me away.'

The last of the colour bled from her face. 'That's not true.'

Wasn't it? His harsh laugh told her better than words could what he thought about that.

Her colour didn't return. She gripped her hands together in her lap. 'I want you to decide what you want the custody arrangements to be. Do you want fifty-fifty custody? A night through the week and every second weekend? Or…whatever? This is something we need to settle.'

Custody. The word stabbed through him, leaving a great gaping hole at the centre of his being. He wanted to cover his ears and hide under his bed as he had as a ten-year-old. The sense of helplessness, of his life spinning out of control, made him suddenly ferocious.

'What if I want full custody?' he snarled.

He wanted to frighten her. He wanted her to back down, to admit that this was all a mistake, that she was sorry and she didn't mean it.

He wanted her to acknowledge that he wasn't like his father!

Her chin shot up. 'You wouldn't get it.'

A savage laugh ripped from his throat. He should have known better. Meg would be well versed in her rights. She'd have made sure of them before bringing this subject up.

'I want the custody arrangements settled in black and white before the baby is born.'

That ice-cold remoteness settled over him again. She didn't trust him. 'Do you have to live your entire life by rules?'

Her throat bobbed as she swallowed. 'I'm sorry, Ben, but in this instance I'm going to choose what's best for the baby, not what's best for you.'

She was choosing what was best for *her*. End of story. Acid burned his throat. Meg didn't even know who he was any more, and he sure as hell didn't know her. The pedestal he'd had her on for all these years had toppled and smashed.

'And as for you living next door in Elsie's house...' She shook her head. 'I think that's a very bad idea.'

He didn't say another word. He just started the dinghy's motor and headed for shore.

* * *

'How's Meg?'

Ben scowled as he reached for a beer. With a muttered oath he put it back and chose a can of lemon squash instead. He swung back to Elsie, the habit of a lifetime's loyalty preventing him from saying what he wanted to say—from howling out his rage.

'She's fine.'

Elsie sat at the kitchen table, knitting. It reminded him of Meg's baby shawl, and the almost completed crib he'd been working on in Elsie's garden shed.

'Is she okay with me taking her mother's place?'

Whoa! He reached out a hand to steady himself against the counter. Where on earth had that come from? He shook his head and counted to three. 'Let's get a couple of things straight. First of all, you won't be taking her mother's place. Meg is all grown-up.'

She might be grown-up, but she was also pedantic, anal and cruel.

He hauled in a breath. 'She doesn't need a mother any more. For heaven's sake, she's going to be a mother herself soon.'

He added controlling, jealous and possessive to his list. He adjusted his stance.

'Secondly, she won't be doing anything daft like calling you Mum.'

Elsie stared back at him. 'I meant taking her mother's place in her father's affections,' she finally said.

Oh. He frowned.

'Do you think she minds us marrying?'

Meg might be a lot of things he hadn't counted on, but she wasn't petty. 'She's throwing you a wedding. Doesn't that say it all?'

Elsie paused in her knitting. 'The thing is, she always was the kind of girl to put on a brave front.' She tapped a knitting needle against the table. 'You both were.'

He pulled out a chair and sat before he fell.

'Do *you* mind Laurie and I marrying?'

He shook his head. 'No.' And he realised he meant it.

'Good.' She nodded. 'Yes, that's good.' She stared at him for a bit, and then leaned towards him a fraction. 'Do you think Meg will let the baby call me Grandma?'

He didn't know what to say. 'I expect so. If that's what you want. You'll have to tell her that's what you'd prefer, though, rather than Elsie,' he couldn't resist adding.

Elsie set her knitting down. She took off her glasses and rubbed her eyes. Finally she looked at him again. 'After she left, I never heard from your mother, Ben. Not once.'

Ben's mouth went dry.

Elsie's hands shook. 'I waited and waited.'

Just for a moment the room, the table and Elsie receded. And then they came rushing back. 'But...?' he croaked.

Elsie shook her head, looking suddenly old. 'But...nothing. I can't tell you anything, though I wish to heaven I could. I don't know where she went. I don't know if she's alive or not. All I do know is it's been eighteen years.' A breath shuddered out of her. 'And that she knows how to get in contact with us, but to the best of my knowledge she's never tried to.'

He stared at her, trying to process what she'd said and how he felt about it.

'Your father broke something in her.'

He shook his head at that. 'No. The way they acted—they let hate and bitterness destroy them. She had a chance to pull back. They both did. But they chose not to. She was as much to blame as him.'

Elsie clenched her hand. 'All I know is that she left and I grieved. My only child...'

Ben thought about the child Meg carried and closed his eyes.

'When I came out of that fog I...we...me and

you were set in our ways, our routines, our way of dealing with each other.'

Was it that simple? Elsie had been grief-stricken and just hadn't known how to deal with a young boy whose whole world had imploded.

'Your mother always said I suffocated her and that's why she went with your father. I failed her somehow—I still don't know how, can't find any explanation for it—and I just didn't want to go through all that again.'

He pulled in a breath. 'So you kept me at arm's length?'

'It was wrong of me, Ben, and I'm sorry.'

So much pain and misery. If his and Meg's child ever disappeared the way his mother had, could he honestly say he'd deal with it any better than Elsie had? He didn't know.

In the end he swallowed and nodded. 'Thank you for explaining it to me.'

'It was long overdue.'

He didn't know what to do, what to say.

'I'm grateful you had Meg.'

Meg. Her name burned through him. What would Meg want him to do now?

From somewhere he found a smile, and it didn't feel forced. 'I'm sure she'll be happy for the baby to call you Grandma.'

CHAPTER TEN

ON THE MORNING of the wedding Meg woke early. She leapt out of bed, pulled on a robe and raced downstairs, her mind throbbing with the million things that must need doing. And then she pulled to a halt in the kitchen and turned on the spot. Actually, what *was* there to do? Everything was pretty much done. She and Elsie had hair and make-up appointments later in the day, and her father was coming over mid-afternoon to get ready for the wedding, but till then her time was her own.

She made a cup of tea and let herself out through the glass sliding door. The garden looked lovely, and the marquee sat in the midst of it like a joyful jewel.

And then she saw Ben.

He stood a few feet away, a steaming mug of his own in hand, surveying the marquee too. He looked deliciously dishevelled and rumpled, as if he'd only just climbed out of bed. He didn't do designer stubble. Ben didn't do designer anything. There was nothing designed in the way he looked, but...

Her hand tightened about her mug. An ache burned in her abdomen. She'd barely seen him these last two weeks. He'd rung a few times, to check if there was anything she'd needed him to do, but he'd kept the calls brief and businesslike. He'd overseen the assembly of the marquee yesterday afternoon, but he'd disappeared back next door as soon as the workmen had left. He'd avoided her ever since she'd mentioned the C word.

'Morning, Meg.'

He didn't turn his head to look at her now either.

A cold fist closed about her heart. He was her best friend. He'd been an integral part of her life for eighteen years. She couldn't lose him. If she lost his friendship she would lose a part of herself.

The same way her father had lost a part of himself the day her mother had died.

The pressure in her chest grew until she thought it might split her in two.

'Lovely day for a wedding.'

He was talking to her about the weather. Everything in the garden blurred. She lifted her face to the sky and blinked, tried to draw breath into lungs that had cramped.

When she didn't speak, he turned to look at her.

His eyes darkened and his face paled at whatever he saw in her face.

He shook his head. 'Don't look at me like that.'

She couldn't help it. 'Do you mean to resent me for ever? Do you mean to keep avoiding me? All because I want to do what's right for our baby?' The words tumbled out, tripping and falling over each other. 'Don't you trust me any more, Ben?'

His head snapped back. 'This is about your trust, not mine!' He stabbed a finger at her. 'You wouldn't need some third party to come in and organise custody arrangements if you trusted me.'

She flinched, but she held her ground. 'Have you considered the fact that it might be myself I don't trust?' She poured the rest of her now tepid tea onto the nearest rosebush. 'I already feel crazily possessive about this baby.'

She rested a hand against her rounded stomach. He followed the movement. She moistened her lips when he met her gaze again. 'I'm going to find it hard to share this child with anyone— even with you, Ben. It wasn't part of my grand plan.' As he well knew. 'I know that's far from noble, but I can't help the way I feel. I also know that you're this baby's father and you have a right to be a part of its life.'

But the first time their baby spent twenty-four full hours with Ben—twenty-four hours away from her—she'd cry her eyes out. She'd wander from room to room in her huge house, lost.

'Having everything down in black and white will protect your rights. Have you not considered that?'

One glance at his face told her he hadn't.

'I don't see why making everything clear—what we expect from each other and what our child can expect from us—is such a bad thing.'

He didn't say anything. He didn't even move.

'I understand that down the track things might change. We can discuss and adapt to those changes as and when we need to. I'm not locking us into a for ever contract. We can include a clause that says we'll renegotiate every two years, if you want.'

But she knew they needed something on paper that would set out their responsibilities and expectations and how they'd move forward.

For the sake of the baby.

And for the sake of their friendship.

'I know you love this baby, Ben.'

Dark eyes surveyed her.

'You wouldn't turn your whole life on its head for no good reason. You want to be a good father.'

He'd stay for the baby in a way he'd never have stayed for her, but she wanted him to stay. She wanted it so badly she could almost taste it.

'And you think agreeing to legalise our custody arrangements will prove I'll be a good father?'

She tried not to flinch at the scorn in his voice. She was asking him to face his greatest fear. Nobody did that without putting up a fight. And when he wanted to Ben could put up a hell of a fight.

She tipped up her chin. 'It'll make us better co-parents. So, yes—I think it *will* make me a better mother and you a better father.'

His jaw slackened.

She stared at him and then shook her head. Her throat tightened. She'd really started to believe that he'd stay, but now...

'I'm sorry,' she whispered. 'If I'd known five months ago what would come of asking you to be my sperm donor I'd never have asked.' She'd have left well alone and not put him through all this.

He stiffened. 'But I want this baby.'

Something inside her snapped then. 'Well, then, suck it up.' She tossed her mug to the soft grass at her feet and planted her hands on her hips. 'If you want this baby then man up to your responsibilities. If you can't do that—if they intimidate you that much—then run off back to Africa and go bungee-jump off a high bridge, or rappel down a cliff, or go deep-sea diving in the Atlantic, or any of those other things that aren't half as scary as fatherhood!'

He folded his arms and nodded. 'That's better. That meek and mild act doesn't suit you.'

Her hand clenched. She stared at her fist and then at his jaw.

'You're right. I do need to man up and face my responsibilities.'

Her hand promptly unclenched.

He ran a hand through his hair. 'Especially when they intimidate me, I expect.'

She stared, and then shook herself. 'Exactly at what point in the conversation did you come to that conclusion?'

'When you said how possessive you feel about the baby.'

Her nose started to curl. 'When you realised a custody agreement would protect your interests?'

'When I realised you weren't my mother.'

Everything inside her stilled.

'When I realised that, regardless of what happens, you will *never* become my mother. I know you will always put the baby's best interests first. That's when I realised I was fighting shadows— because regardless of what differences we might have in the future, Meg, we will never re-enact my parents' drama.'

She folded her arms.

'Are you going to tell me off now, for taking so long to come to that conclusion?'

'I'm going to tell you off for not telling me you'd already come to that conclusion. For letting me rabbit on and...' And abuse him.

'I needed a few moments to process the discovery.' He shifted his weight. 'And I wanted to razz you a bit until you stopped looking so damn fragile and depressed. That's not like you, Meg. What the hell is that all about?'

She glanced away.

'I want the truth.'

That made her smile. 'Have we ever been less than honest with each other?' They knew each other too well to lie effectively to the other. 'I've been feeling sick this past fortnight, worried that I've hurt our friendship. I want to do what's right for the baby. But hurting you kills me.'

He tossed his now-empty mug to the grass, as she had earlier. It rolled towards her mug, the two handles almost touching. At his sides, his hands clenched.

'The thing is, Ben, after this baby your friendship is the most important thing in the world to me. If I lost it...'

With a smothered oath, he closed the distance between them and pulled her in close, hugged her tightly. 'That's not going to happen, Meg. It will never happen.'

He held her tight, and yet she felt as if she was

falling and falling without an end in sight. Even first thing in the morning he smelled of leather and whisky. She tried to focus on that instead of falling.

Eventually she disengaged herself. 'There's something else that's been bothering me.'

'What's that?'

'You keep saying you have no intention of forming a serious relationship with any woman.'

'I don't.'

'Well, I think you need to seriously rethink that philosophy of yours, because quite frankly it sucks.'

He gaped at her.

'You think fatherhood will be fulfilling, don't you?'

'Yes, but—'

'So can committing to one person and building a life with them.'

He glared. 'For you, perhaps.'

'And for you too. You're not exempt from the rest of the human race. No matter how much you'd like to think you are.'

He adjusted his stance, slammed his hands to his hips. 'What is it with you? You've never tried to change my mind on this before.'

That was true, but... 'I never thought you'd want fatherhood either, but I was obviously wrong about that. And I think *you're* wrong to discount a long-term romantic relationship.'

He shook his head. 'I'm not risking it.'

'You just admitted I'm not like your mother. There are other women—' the words tasted like acid on her tongue but she forced them out '—who aren't like your mother either.' She'd hate to see him with another woman, which didn't make a whole lot of sense. She closed her mind to the pictures that bombarded her.

'But I know you, Meg. I've known you for most of my life.'

'Then take the time to get to know someone else.'

His face shuttered closed. 'No.'

She refused to give up. 'I think you'll be a brilliant father. I think you deserve to have lots more children. Wouldn't you like that?'

He didn't say anything, and she couldn't read his face.

'I think you'd make a wonderful husband too.' She could see it more clearly than she'd ever thought possible and it made her heart beat harder and faster. 'I think any woman would be lucky to have you in her life. And, Ben, I think it would make you happy.' And she wanted him happy with every fibre of her being.

He thrust out his jaw. 'I'm perfectly happy as I am.'

She wanted to call him a liar, except…

Except maybe he was right. The beguiling picture of Ben as a loving husband and doting father faded. Maybe the things that would make her happy would only make him miserable. The thought cut at her with a ferocity she couldn't account for.

She swallowed. 'I just want you to be happy,' she whispered.

He blew out a breath. 'I know.'

She wanted Ben to stay in Port Stephens. She *really* wanted that. If he fell in love with some woman… She shied away from the thought.

Her heart burned. She twisted her hands together. This evening Dave meant to offer Ben the chance to fulfil his dream—to offer him a place on that yacht.

'Can I hit you with another scary proposition?'

He squared his shoulders. 'You bet.'

Would it translate into emotional blackmail? Was it an attempt to make sure he did stay?

He leant down to peer into her face. 'Meg?'

She shook herself. It wasn't blackmail. It was her making sure Ben had all the options, knew his choices, that was all.

She swallowed. 'Would you like to be my birth

partner? Would you like to be present at the birth of our child?'

He stilled.

'If you want to think about it—'

'I don't need to think about it.' Wonder filled his face. 'Yes, Meg. Yes. A thousand times yes.'

Finally she found she could smile again. What was a round-the-world yacht voyage compared to seeing his own child born? Behind her back, she crossed her fingers.

'Megan, I'm marrying Elsie because I care about her.' Laurie Parrish lifted his chin. 'Because I love her.'

Meg glanced up from fussing with her dress. In ten minutes he and she would walk out into the garden to meet Elsie and Ben and the ceremony would begin.

'I never doubted it for a moment.' She hesitated, and then leant across and took the liberty of straightening his tie.

He took her hand before she could move away again. 'Before I embark on my new life I want to apologise to you and acknowledge that I haven't been much of a father to you. I can't...' His voice grew gruff. 'I can't tell you how much I regret that.'

She stared at him and finally nodded. It was

why he'd given her the house. She'd always sensed that. But it was nice to hear him acknowledge it out loud too. 'Okay, Dad, apology accepted.'

She tried to disengage her hand, but he refused to release it. 'I'm also aware that an apology and an expression of regret doesn't mean that we're suddenly going to have a great relationship.'

She blinked. *Wow!*

'But if it would be okay with you, if it won't make you uncomfortable or unhappy, I would like to try and build a relationship—a good, solid relationship—with you.'

Her initial scepticism turned to all-out shock.

'Would you have a problem with that?'

Slowly, she shook her head. She had absolutely no problem with that. It would be wonderful for her child to have grandparents who loved it, who wanted to be involved. Only...

She straightened. 'I'll need you to be a bit more enthusiastic and engaged. Not just in my life but in your own too.' She would need him to make some of the running instead of leaving it all up to her. But if he truly meant it...

Her heart lifted and the resentment that had built inside her these last few months started to abate. Unlike Ben, bitterness and anger hadn't crippled her during her teenage years. Sadness and yearning had. She couldn't erase that sadness and yearning now, and nor could her father. Nobody could. They would never get back those lost years, but she was willing to put effort into the future.

'Giving me the house was your way of saying sorry and trying to make amends, wasn't it?'

He nodded. 'I wanted your future secure. It seemed the least I could do.'

His admission touched her.

'But moving out of this house brought me to my senses about Elsie too. Missing her made me realise what she'd come to mean to me.'

So that had been the trigger—an illness, a recuperation, and then a change of address. Evidently romance worked in mysterious ways.

'I know this isn't going to change anything, Megan, but when you were growing up I thought you were spending so much time at Elsie's because she'd become a kind of surrogate mother to you. When I was recovering from my illness and Elsie was coming over to sit with me, I found out she'd thought Ben was spending that time here because I was providing the role of surrogate father. With each of us thinking that…' He pressed his fingers to his eyes. 'We just let things slide along the way they were.'

If they'd known differently, would he and Elsie

have roused themselves from their depression? It was something they'd never know now.

She squeezed his hand. 'I think it's time to put the past behind us.' And as she said the words she realised she meant them. She had a baby on the way. She wanted to look towards the future, not back to the past.

'C'mon, I think it's time.'

'Is Ben going to do the right thing by you and the baby?'

She and Ben hadn't told a soul that he was the baby's father. But her father and Elsie weren't stupid or blind. She pulled in a breath. 'Yes, he will. He always does what's best for me.'

She just wished she knew if that meant he was staying or if he was going. 'You have to understand, though, that what you think is best and what Ben and I think is best may be two very different things.' She didn't want the older couple hassling Ben, pressuring him.

'I understand.' Her father nodded heavily. 'I have no right to interfere. I just want to see you happy, Megan.'

'No,' she agreed, 'you're *not* allowed to interfere.' She took his arm and squeezed it. 'But you are allowed to care.'

She smiled up at him. He smiled back. 'C'mon—let's go get you married and then celebrate in style.'

* * *

The moment Meg stepped into the rose garden with her father Ben couldn't take his eyes from her.

'Are they there yet?' Elsie asked, her voice fretful, her fingers tapping against the kitchen table. 'They're late.'

He snapped to. 'They're exactly on time.' He kept his eyes on Meg for as long as he could as he backed away from the window. Swallowing, he turned to find Elsie alternately plucking at her skirt, her flowers and her hair. It was good to know she wasn't as cool and calm as she appeared or wanted everyone to think. 'Ready?'

She nodded. She looked lovelier than he'd ever seen her. He thought about what Meg would want him to say at this moment. 'Elsie?'

She glanced up at him.

'Mr Parrish is a very lucky man.'

'Oh!' Her cheeks turned pink.

He suddenly grinned. 'I expect he's going to take one look at you and want to drag you away from the celebrations at an indecently early hour.'

Her cheeks turned even redder and she pressed her hands to them. The she reached out and swatted him with her bouquet. 'Don't talk such nonsense, Ben!'

He tucked her hand into the crock of his arm

and led her through the house and out through the front door. 'It's not nonsense. Just you wait.'

Ben had meant to watch for the expression on Laurie's face the first moment he glimpsed Elsie, but one sidelong glance at Meg and Ben's attention was lost. Perspiration prickled his nape. He couldn't drag his gaze away.

Meg wore a deep purplish-blue dress, and in the sun it gleamed like a jewel. She stood there erect and proud, with her gently rounded stomach, looking out-of-this-world desirable. Like a Grecian goddess. He stared at her bare shoulders and all he could think of was pressing kisses to the beckoning golden skin. He could imagine their satin sun-kissed warmth. He sucked air into oxygen-starved lungs. A raging thirst built inside him.

A diamante brooch gathered the material of the dress between her breasts. Filmy material floated in the breeze and drifted down to her ankles. She'd be wearing sexy sandals and he wanted to look, really he did, but he found it impossible to drag his gaze from the lush curves of her breasts.

He moistened his lips. His heart thumped against his ribcage. His skin started to burn. Meg's dress did nothing to hide her new curves. Curves he could imagine in intimate detail—their softness, their weight in his hands, the way her nipples would peak under his hungry gaze as they were doing now. He imagined how they'd tauten further as he ran a thumb back and forth across them, the taste of them and their texture as he—

For Pete's sake!

He wrenched his gaze away, his mouth dry. A halfway decent guy did *not* turn his best friend into an object of lust. A halfway decent guy would not let her think even for a single second that there could ever be anything more between them than friendship.

He did his best to keep his gaze averted from all her golden promise, tried to focus on the ceremony. He wasn't equal to the task—not even when Elsie and Laurie surprised everyone by revealing they'd written their own vows. He was too busy concentrating on not staring at Meg, on not lusting after her, to catch what those vows were.

A quick glance at Meg—a super-quick glance— told him they'd been touching. Her eyes had grown bright with unshed tears, her smile soft, and her lips—

He dragged his gaze away again, his pulse thundering in his ears.

It seemed to take a hundred years, but finally Elsie and Laurie were pronounced husband and wife. And then Laurie kissed Elsie in a way that didn't help the pressure building in Ben's gut. There were cheers and congratulations all round.

Four of Meg's girlfriends threw glittery confetti in the air. Gold and silver spangles settled in Meg's hair, on her cheek and shoulders, and one landed on the skin of her chest just above her—

He jerked his gaze heavenward.

Meg broke away from the group surrounding the newlyweds to slip her arm through his. 'We're going to have a ten-minute photoshoot with the photographer, and then it'll be party time.'

There was a photographer? He glanced around. He hadn't captured the way Ben had been ogling Meg, had he? Please, God.

'You scrub up real nice, Ben Sullivan.' She squeezed his arm. 'I don't think I've seen you in a suit since you stepped in to take me to my high school formal when Jason Prior dumped me to partner Rochelle Collins instead.'

He'd stepped in as a friend back then. He needed to find that same frame of mind, that same outlook, quick-smart.

Minus the kiss that had happened that night!

He dragged in a breath.

Don't think about it.

He'd been a sex-starved teenager back then, that's all.

And Meg had been beautiful.

She's more beautiful now.

'But I don't remember you filling out a suit half so well back then.'

He closed his eyes. Not just at her words, but at the husky tone in which they were uttered. The last thing he needed right now was for Meg to start feeling sexy. At least she had an excuse—pregnancy hormones. Him? He was just low life scum.

If he kissed Meg again it wouldn't stop at kisses. They both knew that. But one night would never be enough for Meg. And two nights was one night too many as far as he was concerned.

It would wreck their friendship. He couldn't risk that—not now they had a child to consider.

'You okay?'

He steeled himself and then glanced down. Her brow had creased, her eyes were wary. He swallowed and nodded.

She gestured towards the newlyweds. 'The service was lovely.'

'Yep.'

His tie tightened about his throat. Please God, don't let her ask him anything specific. He couldn't remember a damn thing about the ceremony.

She smiled, wide and broad. 'I have a good feeling about all of this.'

Just for a moment that made him smile too. 'Pollyanna,' he teased.

Her eyes danced, her lips shone, and hunger stretched through him.

If I lost your friendship, I don't know what I would do.

He swallowed the bile that burned his throat. He couldn't think of anything worse than losing Meg's friendship.

And yet…

He clenched his hands. Yet it wasn't enough to dampen his rising desire to seduce her.

Something in his face must have betrayed him because she snapped away from him, pulling her arm from his. 'Stop looking at me like that!'

The colour had grown high in her cheeks. Her eyes blazed. Neither of those things dampened his libido. That said, he wasn't sure a slap to the face or a cold shower would have much of an effect either.

'Darn it, Ben. I should have known this was how you'd react to the wedding.'

She kept her voice low—bedroom-low—and—

He cut the thought off and tried to focus on her words. 'What are you talking about?'

'All this hearts and flowers stuff has made you want to beat your chest and revert to your usual caveman tactics just to prove you're not affected. That you're immune.'

'Caveman?' he spluttered. 'I'll have you know I have more finesse than that.'

They glared at each other.

'Besides, you're underestimating yourself.' He scowled. 'You look great in that dress.' With a superhuman effort he managed to maintain eye contact and slowly the tension between them lessened. 'Can we get these photos underway?' he growled.

He needed to be away from Meg asap with an ice-cold beer in his hand.

The reception went without a hitch.

The food was great. The music was great. The company was great. The speech Laurie made thanking Meg and Ben for the wedding and admitting what a lucky man he was, admitting that he'd found a new lease of life, touched even Ben.

The reception went without a hitch except throughout it all Ben was far too aware of Meg. Of the way she moved, the sound of her laughter, the warmth she gave out to all those around her. Of the sultry way she moved on the dance floor. He scowled. She certainly hadn't lacked for dance partners.

He'd made sure that he'd danced too. There were several beautiful women here, and three months ago he'd have done his best to hook up with one of them—go for a drink somewhere and then back to her place afterwards. It seemed like a damn fine plan except...

I don't like the way you treat women.

He'd stopped dancing after that.

His gaze lowered to the rounded curve of Meg's stomach and his throat tightened.

'Hey, buddy!' A clap on the shoulder brought him back.

Ben turned and then stood to shake hands. 'Dave, mate—great to see you here. Meg said you were coming. Have a seat.'

They sat and Dave surveyed him. 'It's been a great night.'

'Yeah.'

'Meg's told me what a help you've been with the wedding prep.'

She had? He shrugged. 'It was nothing.'

Dave glanced at Meg on the dance floor. 'That's not how she sees it.'

He bit back a groan. The last thing he needed was someone admiring Meg when he was doing his damnedest to concentrate on doing anything but.

Dave shifted on his chair to face him more fully. 'Something has popped up in my portfolio that I think will interest you.'

Anything that could keep his mind off Meg for

any length of time was a welcome distraction. 'Tell me more.'

'If you want it, I can get you on the crew for a yacht that's setting off around the world. It leaves the week after next and expects to be gone five months.' He shrugged and sat back. 'I know it's something you've always wanted to do.'

Ben stared at the other man and waited for the rush of anticipation to hit him. This was something he'd always wanted—the last challenge on his adventure list. It would kill him to turn it down, but...

He waited and waited.

And kept right on waiting.

The anticipation didn't come. In fact he could barely manage a flicker of interest. He frowned and straightened.

'Mate, I appreciate the offer but...' His eyes sought out Meg on the dance floor, lowered to her baby bump. 'I have bigger fish to fry at the moment.'

Dave shrugged. 'Fair enough. I just wanted to run it by you.'

'And I appreciate it.' But what he wanted and who he was had crystallised in his mind in sharp relief. He was going to be a father and he wanted to be a *good* father—the best.

Dave clapped him on the back. 'I'll catch you

later, Ben. It's time to drag that gorgeous wife of mine onto the dance floor.'

Ben waved in absent acknowledgment. A smile grew inside him. He was going to be a father. Nothing could shake him from wanting to be the best one he could be. His new sense of purpose held far more power than his old dreams ever had.

Her father and Elsie left at a relatively early hour, but the party in Meg's garden continued into the night. She danced with her girlfriends and made sure she spoke to everyone.

Everyone, that was, except Ben.

She stayed away from Ben. Tonight he was just too potent. He wore some gorgeous subtle aftershave that made her think of Omar Sharif and harems, but it didn't completely mask the scent of leather and whisky either, and the combination made her head whirl.

Some instinct warned her that if she gave in to the temptation he represented tonight she'd be lost.

'Meg?' Dave touched her arm and she blinked herself back inside the marquee. 'Winnie and I are heading off, but thanks for a great party. We had a ball.'

'I'm glad you enjoyed yourselves. I'll see you out.'

'No need.'

'Believe me, the fresh air will do me good.'

Keeping busy was the answer. Not remembering the way Ben's eyes had practically devoured her earlier was key too. She swallowed. When he looked at her the way a man looked at a woman he found desirable he skyrocketed her temperature and had her pulse racing off the chart. He made her want to do wild reckless things.

She couldn't do wild and reckless things. She was about to become a mother.

And when he didn't look at her like that, when he gazed at her baby bump with his heart in his eyes—oh, it made her wish for other things. It made her wish they could be a family—a proper family.

But of course that way madness lay. And a broken heart.

She led Dave and Winnie through the rose garden, concentrating on keeping both her temperature and her pulse at even, moderate levels.

Just before they reached the front yard Dave said, 'I made Ben that offer you and I spoke about a while back.'

She stumbled to a halt. Her heart lurched. She had to lock her knees to stop herself from dropping to the ground. 'And…?' Her heart beat against her ribs.

'And I turned it down,' a voice drawled from behind her.

She swung around. *Ben!* And the way his eyes glittered dangerously in the moonlight told her he was less than impressed. She swallowed. In fact he looked downright furious.

'Have I caused any trouble?' Dave murmured.

'Not at all,' she denied, unable to keep the strain from her voice.

Winnie took her husband's arm. 'Thank you both for a lovely evening.' With a quick goodnight, the other couple beat a hasty retreat.

Meg swallowed and turned back to Ben. 'I...'

He raised an eyebrow and folded his arms. 'You can explain, right?'

Could she?

'Another test?' he spat out.

She nodded.

'My word wasn't good enough?'

'It should've been, but...' She moistened suddenly parched lips. 'I wanted a guarantee,' she whispered.

He stabbed a finger at her. 'You of all people should know there's no such thing.'

Her heart beat like a panicked animal when he wheeled away from her. 'Please, Ben—'

He swung back. 'What exactly are you most afraid of, Meg? That I'll leave or that I'll stay?'

Then it hit her.

'Oh!'

She took a step away from him. The lock on her knees gave out and she plumped down to the soft grass in a tangle of satin and chiffon. She covered her mouth with one hand as she stared up at him.

Leaving. She was afraid of him leaving. Deathly afraid. Deep-down-in-her-bones afraid.

Break-her-heart afraid.

Because she'd gone and done the unthinkable— she'd fallen in love with Ben.

She'd fallen in love with her best friend. A man who didn't believe in love and marriage or commitment to any woman. She'd fallen in love with him and she didn't want him to leave. And yet by staying he would break her heart afresh every single day of her life to come.

And she would have to bear it.

Because Ben staying was what would be best for their baby.

CHAPTER ELEVEN

WITH HER DRESS mushroomed around her, her hair done up in a pretty knot and her golden shoulders drooping, Meg reminded Ben of a delicate orchid he'd once seen in a rainforest far from civilisation.

He swooped down and drew her back to her feet, his heart clenching at her expression. 'Don't look like that, Meg. We'll sort it out. I didn't mean to yell.'

He'd do anything to stop her from looking like that—as if the world had come to an end, as if there was no joy and laughter, dancing and champagne, warm summer nights and lazy kisses left in the world. As if all those things had been taken away from her.

'Meg?'

Finally she glanced up. He had to suck in a breath. Her pain burned a hole though his chest and thickened his throat. He dragged in a breath and blinked hard.

She lifted her chin and very gently moved out of his grasp. The abyss inside him grew.

'I'm sorry, Ben. What I asked Dave to do was unfair. I thought it would prove one way or the other whether you were ready for fatherhood.'

'I know you're worried. I can repeat over and over that I'm committed to all of this, but I know that won't allay your fears.' And he was sorrier than he could say about that.

'No.' She twisted her hands together. 'You've never lied to me before. It shows an ungenerosity of spirit to keep testing you as I've done. Your word should be good enough for me. And it is. I do believe you. I do believe you'll stay.'

He eyed her for a moment. He wanted her to stop whipping herself into such a frenzy of guilt. This situation was so new to both of them. 'You don't need to apologise. You're trying to do what's best for the baby. There's no shame in that. Let's forget all about it— move forward and—'

'Forget about it? Ben, I *hurt* you! I can't tell you how sorry I am.'

She didn't have to. He could see it in her face.

'I let you down and I'm sorry.'

And how many times had he let *her* down over the years? Leaving her to deal with Laurie and Elsie on her own, expecting her to drop everything when he came home for a few days here and there, not ringing for her birthday.

'Although I don't think it's necessary, apology accepted.'

'Thank you.'

She smiled, but it didn't dispel the shadows in her eyes or the lines of strain about her mouth. His stomach dropped. *If I ever lost your friendship.* His hands clenched. It wouldn't happen. He wouldn't let it happen.

Music and laughter drifted down to them from the marquee. The lights spilling from it were festive and cheerful. Out here where he and Meg stood cloaked in the shadows of the garden, it was cool and the festivities seemed almost out of reach.

He swallowed and shifted his weight. 'You want to tell me what else is wrong?'

She glanced at him; took a step back. 'There's nothing.'

Acid filled his mouth. 'Don't lie to me, Meg.'

She glanced away. With her face in profile, her loveliness made his jaw ache. He stared at her, willing her to trust him, to share what troubled her so he could make it better. She was so lovely…and hurting so badly. He wanted—*needed*—to make things right for her.

She took another step away from him. 'Some things are better left unspoken.'

He wasn't having that. He took her arm and led her to a garden bench in the front yard. 'No more secrets, Meg. Full disclosure. We need to be completely open about anything that will affect our dealings with each other and the baby.' He leaned towards her. 'We're friends. Best friends. We can sort this out.'

She closed her eyes, her brow wrinkling and her breath catching.

'I promise we can get through anything.' He tried to impart his certainty to her, wanting it to buck her up and bring the colour back to her cheeks, the sparkle to her eyes. 'We really can.'

She opened her eyes and gazed out at the bay spread below them. 'If I share this particular truth with you, Ben, it will freak you out. It will freak you out more than anything I've ever said to you before. If I tell you, you will get up and walk out into the night without letting me finish, and I don't think I could stand that.'

She turned and met his gaze then and his stomach lurched. Some innate sense of self-preservation warned him to get up now and leave. Not just to walk away, but to run. He ignored it. This was Meg. She needed him. He would not let her down.

'I promise you I will not leave until the conversation has run its course.' His voice came out hoarse. 'I promise.'

Her face softened. 'You don't know how hard that promise will be to keep.'

'Another test, Meg?'

'No.'

She shook her head and he believed her.

Her hands twisted together in her lap. She glanced at him, glanced away, glanced down at her hands. 'I love you, Ben.'

'I love you too.' She had to know how much she meant to him.

She closed her eyes briefly before meeting his gaze again. She shook her head gently. 'I mean I've fallen in love with you.'

The words didn't make sense. He stared, unable to move.

'Actually, fallen is a rather apt description, because the sensation is far from comfortable.'

He snapped back, away from her. *I've fallen in love with you*. No! She—

'I didn't mean for it to happen. If I could make it unhappen I would. But I can't.'

'No!' He shot to his feet. He paced away from her, then remembered his promise and strode back. He thrust a finger at her. *'No!'*

She stared back at him with big, wounded eyes. She chafed her arms. He slipped his jacket off and settled it around her shoulders before falling back on the seat beside her.

'Why?' he finally croaked. He'd done his best to maintain a civilised distance ever since that kiss.

'I know.' She sighed. 'It should never have happened.'

Except…that kiss! That damn kiss on the beach. In the moonlight, no less. A moment of magic that neither one of them could forget, but…

'Maybe it's just pregnancy hormones?'

She pulled his jacket about her more tightly. 'That's what I've been telling myself, trying to will myself to believe. But I can't hide behind that as an excuse any longer.'

'Maybe it's just lust?'

She was silent for a long moment. 'Despite what you think, Ben, you have a lot more to offer a woman than just sex. I've been almost the sole focus of your attention this last month and a half and it's been addictive. But it's not just that. You've risen to every challenge I've thrown your way. You've been patient, understanding and kind. You've tried to make things easier for me. And I can see how much you already care for our child. You have amazed me, Ben, and I think you're amazing.'

His heart thumped against his ribs. If this were a movie he'd take her in his arms right now and declare his undying love. But this wasn't a movie.

It was him and Meg on a garden bench. It was a nightmare!

His tie tightened about his throat. His mouth dried. He swallowed with difficulty. He might not be able to declare his undying love to her, but he could do the right thing by her.

'Would you like us to get married?'

'No!'

Ordinarily her horror would have made him laugh. He rolled his shoulders and frowned. 'Why not? I thought you said you love me?' Wasn't marriage and babies what women wanted?

'Too much to trap you into marriage! God, Ben, I know how you feel about marriage. The crazy thing is I would turn my nice, safe world upside down if it would make any difference. I'd follow you on your round-the-world yacht voyage, wait in some small village in Bhutan while you scaled a mountain, go with you on safari into deepest darkest Africa. But I know none of those things will make a difference. And, honestly, how happy do you think either one of us would be—you feeling trapped and suffocated and me knowing I'd made you feel that way?' She shook her head. 'A thousand times no.'

He rested his elbows on his knees and his head in his hands. His heart thudded in a sickening slow-quick rhythm in his chest. 'Would you like me to leave town? It'll be easier if you don't have to see me every day.'

'I expect you're right.'

He closed his eyes.

'But while that might be best for me, it's not what's best for the baby. Our baby's life will be significantly richer for having you as its father. So, no, Ben, I don't want you to leave.'

He stared. She'd told him he was amazing, but she was the amazing one. For a moment he couldn't speak. Eventually he managed to clear his throat. 'I don't know how to make things better or easier for you.'

She glanced down at her hands. 'For a start you can promise not to hate me for having made a hash of this, for changing things between us so significantly.'

He thrust his shoulders back. 'I will never hate you.' He and Meg were different from his parents. He lifted his chin. They would get their friendship back on track eventually.

'I expect I'll get over it sooner or later. I mean, people do, don't they?'

It had taken her father twenty years. He swallowed and nodded.

She turned to him. 'It's four months before the baby is due. Can we...? Can we have a time-out till then?'

She wanted him to stop coming round? She didn't want to see him for four months? He swallowed. It would be no different from setting off on one of his adventure tours. So why did darkness descend all around him? He wanted to rail and yell. But not at Meg.

He rose to his feet. 'I'll go play host for the rest of the evening. I'll help with the clean-up tomorrow and then I'll lock Elsie's house up and go.'

'I'm sorry,' she whispered.

'No need.'

'Thank you.'

He tried to say *you're welcome*, but he couldn't push the words out. 'If you want to retire for the night I'll take care of everything out here.'

'I'll take you up on that.'

She handed him back his jacket, not meeting his eyes, and his heart burned. She turned and strode towards the house. He watched her walk away and it felt as if all the lights had gone out in his world.

Ben moved into a unit in Nelson Bay. He should have moved further away—to the metropolis of Newcastle, an hour away and an easy enough commute—but he couldn't stand the thought of being that far from Meg. What if she needed help? What if she needed something done before the baby came? She knew he was only a phone call or an e-mail away.

When he'd told her as much the day after the wedding she'd nodded and thanked him. And then she'd made him promise neither to ring nor e-mail her—not to contact her at all. He'd barely recognised the woman who'd asked that of him.

'It shouldn't be that hard,' she'd chided at whatever she'd seen in his face. 'In the past you've disappeared for months on end without so much as a phone call between visits.'

It was true.

But this time he didn't have the distraction of the next great adventure between him and home. Was this how Meg had felt when he'd left for each new trip? Worried about his safety and concerned for his health?

Always wondering if he were happy or not?

He threw himself into preparations for the big things he had planned for his future—things he'd only hinted to Meg about. Plans that would cement his financial future, and his child's, and integrate him into the community in Port Stephens.

But somewhere along the way his buzz and excitement had waned. When he couldn't share them with Meg, those plans didn't seem so big, or so bright and shining. He'd never realised how much he'd counted on her or how her friendship had kept him anchored.

Damn it all! She'd gone and wrecked everything—changed the rules and ruined a perfectly good friendship for something as stupid and ephemeral as love.

On the weekends he went out to nightclubs. He drank too much and searched for a woman to take his mind off Meg—a temporary respite, an attempt to get some balance back in his life. It didn't work.

I don't like the way you treat women.

Whenever he looked at a woman now, instead of good-time sass all he saw was vulnerability. He left the clubs early and returned home alone.

'Oh, you have it bad all right.' Dave laughed as they shared a beer one afternoon, a month after Ben had moved into his apartment in Nelson Bay.

Ben scowled. 'What are you talking about?' He'd hoped a beer with his friend would drag his mind from its worry about Meg and move it to more sensible and constructive areas, like fishing and boating.

'Mate, you can't be that clueless.'

He took a swig of his beer. 'I have no idea what you're talking about.' Did Dave think he was pining for greener pastures and new adventures? He shook his head. 'You've got it wrong. I'm happy to be back in Port Stephens, and I appreciate all your help over these last couple of months.'

Dave had tipped Ben off about a local eco-tourism adventure company that had come up for tender. There'd been several companies Ben had considered, but this one had ticked all the boxes. Contracts would be exchanged this coming week.

'This new direction I'm moving in is really exciting. I want to expand the range of tours offered, which means hiring new people.' He shrugged. 'But I've a lot of connections in the industry.' He meant to make his company the best. 'These are exciting times.'

Dave leant back. 'Then why aren't you erupting with enthusiasm? Why aren't you detailing every tour you mean to offer in minute detail to me this very minute and telling me how brilliant it's all going to be?'

Ben rolled his shoulders. 'I don't want to bore you.'

'Oh? And sitting there with a scowl on your face barely grunting at anything I say is designed to be entertaining, is it?'

His jaw dropped. 'I…' Was that what he'd been doing?

Dave leaned towards him. 'Listen, ever since you and Meg had that falling-out you've been moping around as if the world has come to an end.'

'I have not.'

Dave raised an eyebrow.

He thrust out his jaw. 'How many times do I have to tell you? We did not have a falling out.'

Dave eyed him over his beer. 'The two of you can't keep going on like this, you know? You have a baby on the way.'

Ben's head snapped back.

'It *is* yours, isn't it?' Dave said, his eyes serious.

Ben hesitated and then nodded.

'You need to sort it out.'

Ben stared down into his beer. The problem was they had sorted it out and this was the solution. He'd do what Meg needed him to do. Even if it killed him.

'Look, why don't you take the lady flowers and chocolates and just tell her you love her?'

Liquid sloshed over the sides of Ben's glass. 'I don't love her!' He slammed his glass to the table.

'Really?' Dave drawled. 'You're doing a damn fine impression of it, moping around like a love-sick idiot.'

'Remind me,' he growled. 'We *are* supposed to be mates, right?'

Dave ignored him. 'I saw the way you looked at her at the wedding. You could barely drag your eyes from her.'

'That's just lust.' Even now her image fevered

his dreams, had him waking in tangled sheets with an ache pulsing at his groin. It made him feel guilty, thinking about Meg that way, but it didn't make the ache go away.

Dave sat back. 'If it were any other woman I'd agree with you, but this is Meg we're talking about. Meg has never been just another woman to you.'

Ben slumped back.

'Tell me—when have you ever obsessed about a woman the way you've been obsessing about Meg?'

She was the mother of his child. She was his best friend. Of course he was concerned about her.

'Never, right?'

Bingo. But...

The beer garden spun.

And then everything stilled.

Bingo.

He stared at Dave, unable to utter a word. Dave drained the rest of his beer and clapped him on the shoulder. 'I'm off home to the wife and kiddies. You take care, Ben. We'll catch up again soon.'

Ben lifted a hand in acknowledgement, but all the time his mind whirled.

In love with Meg? *Him?*

It all finally fell into place.

Piece by glorious piece.

Him and Meg.

He shoved away from the table and raced out into the mid-afternoon sunshine. He powered down the arcade and marched into the nearest gourmet food shop.

'Can I help you, sir?'

'I'm after a box of chocolates. Your best chocolates.'

The sales assistant picked up a box. 'One can't go past Belgian, sir.'

He surveyed it. 'Do you have something bigger?'

'We have three sizes and—'

'I'll take the biggest box you have.'

It was huge. Tucking it under his arm, he strode into the florist across the way. He stared in bewilderment at bucket upon bucket of choice. So many different kinds of flowers…

'Good afternoon, son, what can I get for you?'

'Uh…I want some flowers.'

'What kind of flowers, laddie? You'll need to be more specific.'

'Something bright and cheerful. And beautiful.' Just like Meg.

'These gerberas are in their prime.'

The florist pointed to a bucket. The flowers were stunning in their vibrancy. Ben nodded. 'Perfect.'

He frowned, though, when the florist extracted a bunch. They seemed a little paltry. The florist eyed him for a moment. 'Perhaps you'd prefer two bunches?'

Ben's face unclouded. 'I'll take all of them.'

'All six bunches, laddie?'

He nodded and thrust money at the man—impatient to be away, impatient to be with Meg. He caught sight of a purple orchid by the till that brought him up short. A perfectly formed orchid that was beautiful in its fragility—its form, its colour and even its shape. It reminded him vividly of Meg on the night of the wedding.

He'd been such an idiot. He'd offered to marry her when he'd thought marriage was the last thing he wanted. He'd acknowledged that he and she were not his mother and father—their relationship would never descend to that kind of hatred and bitterness. He'd faced two of his biggest demons— for Meg—and still he hadn't made the connection.

Idiot!

Meg brought out the best in him, not the worst. She made him want to be a better man. All he could do was pray he hadn't left it too late.

The florist handed him the orchid, a gentle smile lighting his weathered face. 'On the house, sonny.'

Ben thanked him, collected up the armful of

flowers and strode back in the direction of his car. His feet slowed as he passed an ice cream shop. Meg couldn't eat prawns or Camembert or salami, but she could have ice cream.

He strode inside and ordered a family-size tub of their finest. His arms were so full he had to ask the salesgirl to fish the money out of his jacket pocket. She put the tub of ice cream in a carrier bag and carefully hooked it around his free fingers.

She placed his change into his jacket pocket. 'She's a lucky lady.'

He shook his head. 'If I can pull this off, I'll be the lucky one.' He strode to his car, his stomach churning.

If he could pull this off. *If.*

He closed his eyes. *Please, God.*

CHAPTER TWELVE

MEG HEAVED A sigh and pulled yet more lids from the back of her kitchen cupboard. From her spot on the floor she could see there were still more in there. She had an assortment of lids that just didn't seem to belong to anything else she owned. She'd tossed another lid on the 'to-be-identified-and-hopefully-partnered-up' pile when the doorbell rang.

She considered ignoring it, but with a quick shake of her head she rolled to her knees and lumbered upright. She would not turn into her father. She would not let heartbreak turn her into a hermit.

Pushing her hands into the small of her back, she started for the door. Sorting cupboards hadn't induced an early nesting instinct in her as she'd hoped—hadn't distracted her from the hole that had opened up in her world. A hole once filled by Ben.

Stop it!

Company—perhaps that would do the trick?

She opened the door with a ready smile, more

than willing to be distracted by whoever might be on the other side, and then blinked at the blaze of colour that greeted her. Flowers almost completely obscured the person holding them. Flowers in every colour. Beautiful flowers.

Then she recognised the legs beneath all those flowers. And the scent of leather and whisky hit her, playing havoc with her senses.

That was definitely distracting.

Her pulse kicked. Her skin tingled. She swallowed. This kind of distraction had to be bad for her. *Very* bad.

She swallowed again. 'Ben?'

'Hey, Meg.'

And she couldn't help it. Her lips started to twitch. It probably had something to do with the surge of giddy joy the very sight of him sent spinning through her.

'Let me guess—you're opening a florist shop?'

'They're for you.'

For *her*? Her smile faded. An awkward pause opened up between them. Ben shuffled his feet. 'Take pity on a guy, won't you, Meg, and grab an armful?'

It was better than standing there like a landed fish. She moved forward and took several bunches of flowers out of his arms, burying her face in them in an attempt to drown out the much more beguiling scent of her best friend.

She led the way through to the kitchen and set the flowers in the sink, before taking the rest of the flowers from Ben and setting them in the sink too.

'Careful,' she murmured, pointing to the stacks of plastic containers littering the floor.

Every skin cell she possessed ached, screaming for her to throw herself into his arms. Her fingers tingled with the need to touch him. Ben had hugged her more times than she could count. He wouldn't protest if she hugged him now.

Her mouth dried. Her throat ached. The pulse points in her neck, her wrists, her ankles all throbbed.

She couldn't hug him. She wouldn't be hugging him as her best friend. She'd be hugging him as her dearest, darling Ben—the man she was in love with, the man she wanted to get downright dirty and naked with.

And he'd...

She closed her eyes. 'What are you doing here, Ben?'

When she opened them again she found him holding out a box of chocolates. 'For you.'

His voice came out low. The air between them crackled and sparked.

Or was that just her?

She took the chocolates in a daze. 'I...' She moistened her lips. 'Thank you.'

A silence stretched between them. She wanted to stare and stare at him, drink in her fill, but she wouldn't be able to keep the hunger from her eyes if she did. And she didn't want him to witness that. She didn't want his pity.

He started, and then held out a bag. 'I remembered you said you'd had a craving for ice cream.'

She set the chocolates on the bench and reached for the ice cream with both hands, her mouth watering at the label on the carrier bag—it bore the name of her favourite ice cream shop.

'What flavour?'

'Passionfruit ripple.'

He'd remembered.

She seized two spoons from the cutlery drawer, pulled off the lid and tucked straight in. She closed her eyes in bliss at the first mouthful. 'Oh, man, this is good.'

When she opened her eyes again she found him eyeing her hungrily, as if he wanted to devour her in exactly the same way she was devouring the ice cream.

She shook herself and swallowed. Maybe he did, but that didn't change anything between them. Sleeping with Ben wouldn't make him miraculously fall in love with her. Worst luck.

She pushed a spoon towards him. 'Tuck in.'

He didn't move. Standing so close to him was too much torture. She picked up the ice cream tub and moved to the kitchen table.

He'd brought her flowers. He'd brought her chocolates. And he'd brought her ice cream.

She sat. 'So, what's the sting in the tail?'

He started. 'What do you mean?'

She gestured. 'You've brought me the sweeteners, so what is it that needs sweetening?'

Her appetite promptly fled. She laid her spoon down. Was he leaving? Had he come to say goodbye?

She entertained that thought for all of five seconds before dismissing it. Ben wanted to be a part of their baby's life. He had no intention of running away.

She went to pick her spoon up again and then stopped. There was still another three months before the baby was due. Maybe he was leaving Port Stephens until then.

It shouldn't matter. After all, she hadn't clapped eyes on him for almost a month.

She deliberately unclenched her hands. *Get over yourself.* He'd only be a phone call away if she should need him.

Need him? She ached for him with every fibre of her being. And seeing him like this was too hard. She wanted to yell at him to go away, but the shadows beneath his eyes and the gaunt line of his cheeks stopped her.

She picked up her spoon and hoed back into her ice cream. She gestured with what she dearly hoped was a semblance of nonchalance to the chair opposite and drawled, 'Any time you'd like to join the party...'

He sat.

He fidgeted.

He jumped back up and put all the flowers into vases. She doggedly kept eating ice cream. It was delicious. At least she was pretty sure it was delicious. When he came back to the table, though, it was impossible to eat. The tension rose between them with every breath.

She set her spoon down, stared at all the flowers lined up on the kitchen bench, at the enormous box of chocolates—Belgian, no less—and then at the tub of ice cream. Her shoulders slumped. What did he have to tell her that could be so bad he needed to give her all these gifts first?

Flowers and chocolates—gifts for lovers. She brushed a hand across her eyes. Didn't he know what he was doing to her?

'I've missed you, Meg.'

And his voice...

'I needed to see you.'

She shoved her shoulders back. 'I thought we had an agreement?' He was supposed to stay away.

Was this a fight she would ever win? Her fingers shook as she pressed them to her temples. Would she ever stop needing to breathe him in, to feast her eyes on him, to wipe those haunted shadows from his eyes?

I love you!

Why couldn't that be enough?

She dragged her hands down into her lap and clenched them. 'Why?'

She might not be able to harden her heart against him, but she could make sure they didn't draw this interview out any longer than necessary.

'I realised something this afternoon.' The pulse at the base of his jaw pounded. 'And once I did I had to see you as soon as I could.'

Her heart slammed against her ribs. Just looking at him made a pulse start to throb inside her. She folded her arms. 'Are you going to enlighten me?'

He stared at her as if at an utter loss. 'I…uh…' He moistened his lips. 'I realised that I love you. That I'm *in love* with you.'

Three beats passed. Bam. Bam. Bam.

And then what he'd said collided with her grey matter. She shoved her chair back and wheeled away from him.

Typical! Ben had missed her and panicked. She got that. But in love with her? Fat chance!

She spun back and folded her arms. 'The Ben I know wouldn't have stopped to get flowers and chocolates if he'd had an epiphany like that. He'd have raced straight over here and blurted it out on the front doorstep the moment I opened the door.'

'Yeah, well, the guy I thought I was wouldn't have believed any of this possible.' He shot to his feet, his chair crashing to the floor behind him. 'The guy I thought I was didn't believe in love. The guy I thought I was would never have thought he could feel so awkward and at a loss around you, Meg!'

Her jaw dropped. She hitched it back up. 'None of that means you're in love with me. I accept that you miss me, but—'

'Then how about this?'

He strode around the table and shoved a finger under her nose. His scent slugged into her, swirling around her, playing havoc with her senses, playing havoc with her ability to remain upright.

'For the last month all I've been able to think about is you. I'm worried that you're hurting. I'm worried you're not eating properly and that you're working too hard. I'm worried there's no one around to make you laugh and to stop you from taking the world and yourself too seriously. Every waking moment,' he growled.

He planted his hands on his hips and started to pace. 'And then I worry that you might've found someone who makes you laugh and forget your troubles.' He wheeled back to her. 'Are you dating anyone?'

He all but shouted the question at her. For the first time a tiny ray broke through all her doubts. She tried to dispel it. This was about the baby, not her.

'Ben, no other man will ever take your place in our child's affections.'

'This isn't about the baby!' He paced harder. 'Every waking moment,' he growled. He spun and glared at her. 'And then, when I try to go to sleep, you plague my dreams. And, Meg—' He broke off with a low, mirthless laugh. 'The things I dream of doing to you—well, you don't want to know.'

Ooh, yes, she did.

'For these last two and a half months—eleven weeks—however long it's been—I've been feeling like some kind of sick pervert for thinking of you the way I have been. For having you star in my X-rated fantasies. I've struggled against it because you deserve better than that. So much better. It was only today that my brain finally caught up with my body. This is not just a case of out-and-out lust.'

He moved in close, crowding her with his heat and his scent.

'I want to make love to you until you are begging me for release.'

Her knees trembled at his low voice, rich with sin and promise. Heat pooled low in her abdomen. She couldn't have moved away from him if she'd wanted to.

'Because I love you.'

He hooked a hand behind her head and drew her mouth up to his, his lips crashing against hers in a hard kiss, as if trying to burn the truth of his words against her lips.

He broke away before she could respond, before she'd had enough...anywhere near enough.

He grabbed her hand and dragged her towards the back door. 'Where are we going?'

'There's something I want to show you.'

He pulled her all the way across to Elsie's yard, not stopping till they reached the garden shed. Flinging the door open, he bundled her inside.

In the middle of the floor sat a baby's crib. A wooden, hand-turned baby's crib. She sucked in a breath, marvelling at the beauty and craftsmanship in the simple lines. She knelt down to touch it. The wood was smooth against her palm.

'I've been coming here every day to finish it. I wait until you leave for work. I make sure I'm gone again before you get home.'

Her hand stilled. 'You made this?'

Drawing her back to her feet, he led her outside

again. He gestured across to her garden. 'Who do you think is taking care of all that?'

For the first time in a month she suddenly realised how well kept the garden looked. She swallowed. It certainly wasn't her doing. She swung to him. 'You?'

'Tending your garden, making that crib for our baby—nothing has filled me with more satisfaction in my life before. Meg, you make me want to be a better man.'

He cradled her face in his hands. She'd never seen him more earnest or more determined.

'I want to build a life with you and our children—marriage, domesticity and a lifetime commitment. That's what I want.' His hands tightened about her face. 'But only with you. It's only ever been you. You're my destiny, Meg. You're the girl I always come home to. I just never saw it till now.'

For a moment everything blurred—Ben, the garden shed, the sky behind it.

'And if you don't believe me I mean to seduce you until you don't have a doubt left. And if you utter any doubts tomorrow I'll seduce you again, until you can't think straight and all you can think about is me. And I'll do that again and again until you do believe me.'

She lifted her hand to his mouth. 'And if I tell you that I *do* believe you?' She smiled. A smile that became a grin. She had to grin or the happiness swelling inside her might make her burst. 'Will you still seduce me?'

That slow, sinfully wicked grin of his hooked up the right side of his mouth. He traced a finger along her jaw and down her neck, making her breath hitch. 'Again and again and again,' he vowed, his fingers trailing a teasing path along the neckline of her shirt back and forth with delicious promise.

'Oh!' She caught his hand before he addled her brain completely.

'*Do* you believe me, Meg?' His lips travelled the same path his finger had, his tongue lapping at her skin and making her tremble.

'Yes.' She breathed the word into his mouth as his lips claimed hers.

The kiss transported her to a place she'd never been before—to a kingdom where all her fairytales had come true. She wrapped her arms about his neck, revelling in the lean hardness of his body, and kissed him back with everything she had.

It was a long time before they surfaced. Eventually they broke off to drag oxygen into starved lungs. She smiled up at him.

He grinned down at her. 'You love me, huh?'

'Yep, and you love me.'

Was it possible to die from happiness? She

shifted against him, revelling in the way he sucked in a breath.

'You want to explain about the flowers and the chocolates?'

The fingers of his right hand walked down each vertebra of her spine to rest in the small of her back, raising gooseflesh on her arms. 'Dave said I should woo you with flowers and chocolates. I wanted to woo you right, Meg.'

She moved in closer. That hand splayed against her back. 'And the ice cream?'

'That was my own touch.'

'It was my favourite bit.'

His lips descended. 'Your favourite?'

'Second favourite,' she murmured, falling into his kiss, falling into Ben. *Her* Ben.

When he lifted his head again, many minutes later, she tried to catch her breath. 'Ben?'

'Hmm?'

'Do you think we can make our next baby the regular way?'

He grinned that grin. Her heart throbbed.

'You bet. And the one after that, and the one after that,' he promised.

* * * * *

The Loner's Guarded Heart

CHAPTER ONE

'HELLO?'

Josie Peterson bent down and called her greeting into the half-open window before knocking on the door again.

No movement. No sound. Nothing.

Chewing her lip, she stepped back and surveyed the front of the cottage—weatherboard, neatly painted white. A serviceable grey-checked gingham curtain hung at the windows.

Grey? A sigh rose up through her. She was tired of grey. She wanted frills. And colour. She wanted fun and fanciful.

She could feel the grey try to settle over her shoulders.

She shook herself and swung away, took in the view about her. The paths were swept, the lawns were cared for, but there wasn't a single garden bed to soften the uniformity. Not even a pot plant. At the moment, Josie would kill for the sight of a single cheerful gerbera, let alone a whole row of them.

Six wooden cabins marched down the slope away from the cottage. Nothing moved. No signs of habitation greeted her. No cars, no towels drying on verandas, no pushbikes or cricket bats leant against the walls.

No people.

Fun and fanciful weren't the first descriptions that came to mind. The grass around the cabins, though, was green and clipped short. Someone took the trouble to maintain it all.

If only she could find that person.

Or people. She prayed for people.

The view spread before her was a glorious patchwork of golden grasses, khaki gum trees and a flash of silver river, all haloed and in soft focus from the late-afternoon sunshine. Josie had to fight back the absurd desire to cry.

What on earth had Marty and Frank been thinking?

You were the one who said you wanted some peace and quiet, she reminded herself, collapsing on the top step and propping her chin in her hands.

Yes, but there was peace and quiet and then there was this.

From the front veranda of the cottage, there wasn't another habitation in sight. She hid her face in her hands. Marty and Frank knew her well enough to know she hadn't meant this, didn't they?

Her insides clenched and she pulled her hands away. She didn't want the kind of peace and quiet that landed a person so far from civilisation they couldn't get a signal on their cell-phone.

She wanted people. She wanted to lie back, close her eyes and hear people laughing and living. She wanted to watch people laughing and living. She wanted—

Enough already! This was the one nice thing Marty and Frank had done for her in...

She tried to remember, but her mind went blank. OK, so maybe they weren't the most demonstrative of brothers, but sending her on holiday was a nice thing. Did she intend spoiling it with criticisms and rank ingratitude?

Some people would kill to be in her position. Lots of people would love to spend a month in the gorgeous Upper Hunter Valley of rural New South Wales with nothing to do.

She gazed about her wistfully. She wished all those people were lining the hills of this valley right now.

She dusted off her hands and pushed to her feet. She'd make the best of it. According to her map there was a town a few kilometres further on. She could drive in there whenever she wanted. She'd make friends. She was tired. That was all. It had taken too long to get here, which was probably why her landlord had given up on her.

She wondered what kind of people would live out here all on their own. Hopefully the kind of people who took a solitary soul under their wing, introduced them around and enthusiastically outlined all the local activities available. Hopefully they'd love a chat over a cup of tea and a biscuit.

Josie would provide the biscuits.

Impatience shifted through her. She rolled her shoulders, stamped her feet and gulped in a breath of late-afternoon air. She didn't recognise the dry, dusty scents she pulled into her lungs, so different from the humid, salt-laden air of Buchanan's Point on the coast, her home. Her stomach clenched up again at the unfamiliarity.

She didn't belong here.

'Nonsense.' She tried to laugh away the fanciful notion, but a great yearning for home welled inside her. The greyness settled more securely around her. She hastened down the three steps and back along the gravel path, hoping movement would give her thoughts new direction. She swung one way then another. She could check around the back, she supposed. Her landlord could be working in a…shed or vegetable plot or something.

In her hunger to clap eyes on a friendly face,

Josie rushed around the side of the house to open the gate. Her fingers fumbled with the latch. Need ballooned inside her, a need for companionship, a need to connect with someone. The gate finally swung back to reveal a neat garden. Again, no flower beds or pots broke the austerity, but the lawn here too was clipped and short, the edges so precise they looked as if they'd been trimmed using a set square.

The fence was painted white to match the house and the obligatory rotary clothes-line sat smack-bang in the middle of it all. An old-fashioned steel one like the one Josie had at home. Its prosaic familiarity reassured her. She stared at the faded jeans, blue chambray shirt and navy boxer shorts hanging from it and decided her landlord must be male.

Why hadn't she found out his name from Marty or Frank? Although everything had moved so fast. They'd popped this surprise on her last night and had insisted on seeing her off at the crack of dawn this morning. Mrs Pengilly's bad turn, though, had put paid to an early start. Josie bit her lip. Maybe she should've stayed and—

A low, vicious growl halted her in her tracks. Icy fingers shot down her back and across her scalp.

Please God, no.

There hadn't been a 'Beware of the Dog' sign

on the gate. She'd have seen it. She paid attention to those things. Close attention.

The growl came again, followed by the owner of the growl, and Josie's heart slugged so hard against her ribs she thought it might dash itself to pieces before the dog got anywhere near her. Her knees started to shake.

'Nice doggy,' she tried, but her tongue stuck to the roof of her mouth, slurring her words and making them unintelligible.

The dog growled in answer. Nuh-uh, it wasn't a nice doggy and, although it wasn't as large as a Rottweiler or a Dobermann, it was heavy-set and its teeth, when bared, looked as vicious as if it were. She could imagine how easily those teeth would tear flesh.

She took a step back. The dog took a step forward. She stopped. It stopped.

Her heart pounded so hard it hurt. She wanted to buckle over but she refused to drop her eyes from the dog's glare. It lowered its head and showed its teeth again. All the hackles on its back lifted.

Ooh. Not a good sign. Everything inside Josie strained towards the gate and freedom, but she knew she wouldn't make it. The dog would be on her before she was halfway there. And those teeth...

Swallowing, she took another step back. The dog stayed put.

Another step. The dog didn't move. Its hackles didn't lower.

With a half-sob, Josie flung herself sideways and somehow managed to half climb, half pull her way up until she was sitting on top of the rotary clothes-line.

'Help!' she hollered at the top of her voice.

Something tickled her face. She lifted a hand to brush it away. Spider web! She tried to claw it off but it stuck with clammy tentacles to her face and neck. It was the last straw. Josie burst into tears.

The dog took up position directly beneath her. Lifting its head, it howled. It made Josie cry harder.

'What the devil—?'

A person. 'Thank you, God.' Finally, a friendly face. She swung towards the voice, almost falling off the clothes-line in relief.

She stared.

Her heart all but stopped.

Then it dropped clean out of her chest to lie gasping and flailing on the ground like a dying fish. *This was her friendly face?*

No!

Fresh sobs shook her. The dog started up its mournful howl again.

'For the love of...'

The man glared at her, shifted his feet, hands on hips. Nice lean hips she couldn't help noticing.

'Why in the dickens are you crying?'

She'd give up the sight of those lean hips and taut male thighs for a single smile.

He didn't smile. She stared at the hard, rocky crags of his face and doubted this man could do friendly. He didn't have a single friendly feature on his face. Not one. Not even a tiny little one. The flint of his eyes didn't hold a speck of softness or warmth. She bet dickens wasn't the term he wanted to use either.

Heaven help her. This wasn't the kind of man who'd take her under his wing. A hysterical bubble rose in her throat. 'You're my landlord?'

His eyes narrowed. 'Are you Josephine Peterson?'

She nodded.

'Yes.' He scowled. 'I'm Kent Black.'

He didn't offer his hand, which she had to admit might be difficult considering she was stuck up his clothes-line.

'I asked why you were crying.'

Coming from another person the question would've been sympathetic, but not from Kent Black. Anyway, she'd have thought a more pressing question was 'What the dickens are you doing in my clothes-line?'

'Well?' He shifted again on those long, lean legs.

An hysterical bubble burst right out of her

mouth. 'Why am I crying?' She bet he thought she was a madwoman.

'Yes.' His lips cracked open to issue the one curt word then closed over again.

'Why am I crying?' Her voice rose an octave. 'I'll tell you why I'm crying. I'm crying because, well look at this place.' She lifted her hands. 'It's the end of the earth,' She fixed him with a glare. It was the only thing that stopped her from crying again. 'How could Marty and Frank think I'd want to come here, huh?'

'Look, Ms Peterson, I think you ought to calm—'

'Oh, no, you don't. You asked the question and demanded an answer so you can darn well listen to it.' She pointed her finger at him as if he was personally responsible for everything that had gone wrong today.

'Not only am I stuck here at the end of the earth but…but I'm stuck in a clothes-line at the end of the earth. And to rub salt into the wound, I got lost trying to find this rotten place and ended up in Timbuktu, where I got a flat tyre. Then your dog chased me up this rotten clothes-line and there's spider web everywhere!'

Her voice rose with each word in a way that appalled her, but she couldn't rein it back the way she normally did. 'And Mrs Pengilly took a bad turn this morning and I had to call an ambulance and…and I buried my father a fortnight ago and…'

Her anger ran out. Just like that. She closed her eyes and dropped her head. 'And I miss him,' she finished on a whisper so soft she hardly heard it herself.

Darn it. She reluctantly opened one eye and found him staring at her as if she was a mad-woman. She opened the other eye and straight-ened. Then smoothed down her hair. She wasn't a madwoman. And despite her outburst she didn't feel much like apologising either. He didn't have the kind of face that invited apologies. She pulled in a breath and met his gaze.

'You're afraid of my dog?'

She raised an eyebrow. Did he think she sat in clothes-lines for the fun of it? 'Even at the end of the earth you should put signs up on your gates warning people about vicious dogs.'

He continued to survey her with that flinty gaze and she felt herself redden beneath it. With a sigh, she lifted her T-shirt. She didn't need to glance down to see the jagged white scar that ran the length of her right side and across her stomach. She could trace it in her dreams. To do him credit, though, he hardly blinked.

'How old were you?'

'Twelve.'

'And you're afraid of Molly here?'

Wasn't that obvious?

She glanced at the dog. Molly? The name wasn't right up there with Killer or Slasher or Crusher, was it? And with Kent Black standing beside her the dog didn't look anywhere near as formidable as it had a moment ago. Josie gulped. 'She's a girl?'

'Yep.'

The dog that had attacked her had been a big male Dobermann. 'She growled at me.'

'You frightened her.'

'Me?' She nearly fell out of the clothes-line.

'If you'd clapped your hands and said boo she'd have run away.'

Now she really didn't believe him.

His lips twisted, but not into a smile. 'Moll.' The dog wagged her tail and shuffled across to him. He scratched her behind the ears. 'Roll over, girl.'

His voice was low and gentle and it snagged at Josie's insides. Molly rolled onto her back and a part of Josie didn't blame her. If he spoke to her like that she'd roll over too.

Oh, don't be so ridiculous, she ordered. She focused her attention back on Kent. He parted the fur on the dog's belly. He had large, weathered hands. Even from her perch in the clothes-line she could see the calluses that lined his fingers.

'Look,' he ordered.

She did, and saw a mirror image of her own scar etched in the dog's flesh. An ugly white raised scar that jagged across Molly's stomach and ribs.

'A man with a piece of four-by-two studded with nails did that to her.'

Sympathy and horror pounded through Josie in equal measure. How could someone hurt a defenceless animal like that? It was inhuman.

She scrambled down out of the clothes-line, dropped to her knees at its base and held out her arms. 'You poor thing.'

Molly walked straight into them.

Kent had never seen anything like it in all his thirty-two years. Molly hid from strangers. When someone surprised her, like Josephine Peterson here obviously had, she'd try and bluff her way out of it by growling and stalking off. Then she'd hide. The one thing she didn't do was let strangers pet her. She sure as hell didn't let them hug her.

For the first time in a long time Kent found himself wanting to smile. Then he remembered Josephine Peterson's blood-curdling cry for help and he went cold all over again. He didn't need a woman like her at Eagle Reach.

A woman who couldn't look after herself.

He'd bet each and every one of his grass-fed

steers that Josephine Peterson didn't have a self-sufficient bone in her body. And he'd be blowed if he'd take on the role of her protector.

His lip curled. She was a mouse. She had mousy brown hair, mousy brown eyes and a mouse-thin body that looked as if it'd bow under the weight of an armload of firewood. Even her smile was all mousiness—timid and tentative. She aimed it at him now, but he refused to return it.

It trembled right off her lips. Guilt slugged him in the guts. He bit back an oath.

She rose and cast a fearful glance at the back of the house. 'Do…do you have any other dogs?'

'No.' The memory of her scarred abdomen rushed on him again. His hands clenched to fists. When she'd lifted her shirt, shown him her scar, it wasn't tenderness or desire that had surged through him. He had a feeling, though, that it was something closely related, something part-way between the two, something he didn't have a name for.

What he did know was he didn't want Josephine Peterson here on his hill. She didn't belong here. She was a townie, a city girl. For Pete's sake, look at her fingernails. Long and perfectly painted in a shimmery pink. They were squared off at the tips with such uniformity he knew they had to be fake. This wasn't fake-fingernail country.

It was roughing-it country.

He hadn't seen anyone less likely to want to rough it than Josephine Peterson.

When he glanced at her again she tried another smile. 'Do you have a wife?'

Her soft question slammed into him with more force than it had any right to. She needn't look to him for that either!

He glanced into her hopeful face and despite his best intentions desire fired along his nerve-endings, quickening his blood, reminding him of everything he'd turned his back on. Now that she stood directly in front of him, rather than perched up in his clothes-line or on her knees with her face buried in Molly's fur, he could see the gold flecks inside the melt-in-your-mouth chocolate of her iris. That didn't look too mousy.

Get a grip! Whatever the colour of her eyes, it didn't change the fact she wasn't the kind of woman he went for. He'd been stuck up this hill too long. He liked tall, curvy blondes who were out for a good time and nothing more. Josephine Peterson wasn't tall, curvy or blonde. And she looked too earnest for the kind of no-strings affairs he occasionally indulged in.

She continued to gaze at him hopefully. 'No,' he bit out. 'I don't have a wife.' And he had no intention of landing himself with one either. The sooner this woman realised that the better.

Rather than light up with interest, with calculation, her face fell. Kent did a double take.

'That's a shame. It would've been nice to have a woman around to talk to.'

He'd have laughed out loud at his mistake only he'd lost his funny bone.

'Is there anyone else here besides you?'

'No.' He snapped the word out. 'I'll get the key to your cabin.'

She blinked at his abruptness. 'Which one is mine?'

'They're all empty.' He strode around to the back of his house. She had to run to keep up with him. With a supreme effort he slowed his stride. 'You can have your pick.'

'I'll take that one.'

She pointed to the nearest cabin and Kent found himself biting back another oath. Damn and blast. Why hadn't he put her in the furthest one and been done with it? He disappeared inside, seized the key then strode back outside and thrust it at her.

'Thank…thank you. Umm…' She shuffled from one foot to the other. 'Does the cabin have a phone?'

His lip curled. He despised city folk. They came here mouthing clichés proclaiming they wanted to get away from it all, get back to nature, but all hell broke loose when they discovered they had to do without their little luxuries. It made him sick.

Granted, though, Josephine Peterson looked as though she wanted to be at Eagle Reach about as much as he wanted her here. Her earlier words came back to him and a laugh scraped out of his throat. 'This is the end of the earth, remember? What do you think?'

She eyed him warily. The gold in her eyes glittered. 'I'm guessing that's a no.'

'You're guessing right.'

She wouldn't last a month. At this rate she'd be lucky to last two days. What on earth had possessed her to book a cabin for four whole weeks? The advertisement he'd placed in the local tourism rag made no false promises. It sure as hell wasn't the kind of advert designed to attract the attention of the likes of her.

'Look, Ms Peterson, this obviously isn't your cup of tea. Why don't you go on into Gloucester? It's only half an hour further on. You'll find accommodation more suited to your tastes there.' Behind his back he crossed his fingers. 'I'll even return your deposit.'

'Please, call me Josie.'

She paused as if waiting for him to return the favour and tell her to call him Kent, but he had no intention of making any friendly overtures. He wanted her out of here.

When he remained silent, she sighed. 'I have to stay. My brothers organised all this as a treat.'

He recalled her rant whilst she'd clung to his clothes-line. Marty and Frank, wasn't it? His eyes narrowed. 'Are they practical jokers?'

'Heavens, no.' For a moment she looked as if she might laugh. It faded quickly. 'Which is why I have to stay. I wouldn't hurt their feelings for the world. And they would be hurt if they found out I'd stayed somewhere else.'

Fabulous.

She smiled then. He recognised the effort behind it, and its simple courage did strange things to his insides. He wanted to resist it. Instinct warned him against befriending this woman.

'Is Gloucester where I'll find the nearest phone? It's just…I'm not getting a signal on my mobile.'

Which was one of the reasons he loved this hill.

'And I'd really like to check on my neighbour, Mrs Pengilly.'

For a mouse she could sure make him feel like a heel. 'There's a phone in there.' He hitched his head in the direction of the house.

Josie's face lit up. 'May I…?'

'It's in the kitchen.'

She raced inside as if afraid he'd take his offer

back. He collapsed onto the top step, shoulders sagging, and tried not to overhear her conversation, tried not to hear how she assured whoever answered the phone that the Gloucester Valley was beautiful, that the view from her cabin was glorious, that her cabin was wonderful.

He leapt up and started to pace. Two out of three wasn't bad. The Gloucester Valley *was* beautiful, and her view *was* glorious. He had a feeling she'd give up both for the wonderful cabin.

He blinked when she reappeared moments later. He'd expected her to be on the phone for hours. It was what women did, wasn't it?

She tripped down the back steps. 'Thank you, I…' She made as if to clasp his arm then stepped back as though she'd thought better of it. 'Thank you.'

His pulse quickened. 'How's your Mrs Pengilly?'

He couldn't believe he'd asked. Maybe it was time he had a holiday.

A smile lit her face. 'Her son Jacob came down from Brisbane and he says she's going to be OK. Apparently she has late-onset diabetes.'

'Once they've stabilised her blood sugar and organised her medication she'll be fine.' The words rolled out of him with an ease that was disconcerting.

'Yes.' The gold of her eyes glittered with curiosity. 'You sound like you know all about it.'

'I do.' But he wasn't volunteering any more information. He'd already given enough away. He reached across and plucked the key from her fingers. 'Let's get you settled.'

To Josie, Kent's words sounded more like 'Let's get you out of my hair'. Nope, not a friendly bone in his body.

He did have a nice body, though—broad-shouldered, lean-hipped, athletic. And he wasn't all bad. He had let her use his phone. And he'd asked after Mrs Pengilly.

She trotted to keep up with him. She glanced at him from the corner of her eye and noted the uncompromising line of his mouth. Maybe he was just out of practice. Living here all on his own, he wouldn't get much chance at personable conversation. Anyhow, she was determined to give him the benefit of the doubt because the alternative was too bleak for words—stuck out in the middle of nowhere with a man who wouldn't give her the time of day.

No. No. She bit back a rising tide of panic. Beneath his gruffness Kent had a kind heart.

On what proof are you basing such an assumption? a disbelieving voice at the back of her head demanded.

She swallowed. He'd asked after an old lady. And... And he had a dog.

Not much though, is it? the same voice pointed out with maddening logic.

No, she guessed not. The panic rose through her again. 'Did you nurse Molly back to health?'

'Yes.'

One uncompromising word, but it lifted the weight settling across her shoulders. See? He did have a kind heart. For dogs.

It was a start.

Kent leapt up onto the tiny veranda that fronted the cabin and pushed the key into the door. Josie started after him then swallowed. The cabins all looked really tiny. She'd hoped...

The door swung open and she gulped back a surge of disappointment. When Marty and Frank had said 'cabin' she'd thought... Well, she hadn't expected five-star luxury or anything, but she had hoped for three-star comfort.

She was landed with one-star basic. And that was being charitable.

Kent's shoulders stiffened as if he sensed her judgement and resented it. 'It has everything you need.' He pointed. 'The sofa pulls out into a bed.'

Uh-huh. She took a tentative step into the room

and glanced around. Where were the flowers? The bowl of fruit? The welcoming bottle of bubbly? There wasn't a single rug on the floor or print on the wall. No colourful throw on the sofa either. In fact, there wasn't a throw full stop, grey or otherwise.

Admittedly, everything looked clean, scrubbed to within an inch of its life. By the light of the single overhead bulb—no light shade—the table and two chairs gleamed dully. Would it really have been such an effort to toss over a tablecloth and tie on chair pads?

'The kitchen is fully equipped.'

It was. It had an oven and hotplates, a toaster and kettle. But it didn't have any complimentary sachets of tea or coffee. It didn't have a dishwasher. She hadn't wanted the world, but—

An awful thought struck her. 'Is there a bathroom?'

Without a word, Kent strode forward and opened a door she hadn't noticed in the far wall. She wasn't sure she wanted to look.

She ordered her legs forward, glanced through the door and released the breath she held. There was a flushable toilet. And a shower.

But no bathtub.

So much for the aromatherapy candles and scented bath oils she'd packed.

'What do you think?'

Josie gaped at him. The question seemed so out of character she found herself blurting out her first impression without restraint. 'It's awful.'

He stiffened as if she'd slapped him.

'I'm sorry, I don't mean to offend you, but it's a dog kennel.' In fact, she bet Molly's quarters surpassed this. 'It's... Do all the cabins have the same colour scheme?'

The pulse at the base of his jaw jerked. 'What's wrong with the colour scheme?'

'It's grey!' Couldn't he see that? Did he seriously think grey made for a homely, inspiring atmosphere? A holiday atmosphere?

He folded his arms. His eyes glittered. 'All the cabins are identical.'

So she was stuck with it, then.

'Look, I know this probably isn't up to your usual standard,' he unfolded his arms, 'but I only promised basic accommodation and—'

'It doesn't matter.' Tiredness surged through her. Was this all Marty and Frank thought she was worth? She gulped back the lump in her throat.

'Like you said, it has everything I need.' The greyness settled behind her eyelids.

CHAPTER TWO

KENT STRODE OFF into the lengthening shadows of the afternoon, his back stiff, his jaw clenched. For once he didn't notice the purple-green goldness of the approaching sunset. He skidded to a halt, spun around and slapped a hand to his thigh. 'C'mon, Moll.'

Molly pricked her ears forward, thumped her tail against the rough-hewn boards of the cabin's veranda, but she didn't move from her post by Josie's door.

Oh, great. Just great.

'See if I care,' he muttered, stalking back off. Solitude was his preferred state of affairs. Josie Peterson was welcome to his dog for all the good it would do her. Molly wouldn't say boo to a fly.

Birds of a feather…

Up on the ridge a kookaburra started its boisterous cry and in the next moment the hills were ringing with answering laughter. Kent ground to a halt. He swung back in frustration, hands on hips.

These cabins weren't meant for the likes of her. They were meant for men like him. And for men who lived in cities and hungered to get away occasionally, even if only for a long weekend. Men who wanted to leave the stench of car exhaust fumes and smog and crowds and endless traffic behind. Men who wanted nothing more than to see the sky above their heads, breathe fresh air into their lungs, and feel grass rather than concrete beneath their feet. Men happy to live on toast and tea and beer for three days.

Josie didn't want that. She'd want spa baths and waterbeds. She'd want seafood platters and racks of lamb and soft, woody chardonnays.

And he didn't blame her. If she'd just lost her father she probably deserved some pampering, a treat, not this rugged emptiness. Her brothers had to be certifiable idiots.

He kicked at a stone. He couldn't give her spa baths and seafood platters.

A vivid image of mousy Josie Peterson lying back in a bubble-filled spa rose up through him and his skin went tight. She didn't look too mousy in that fantasy.

He scratched a hand through his hair. Idiot. The kookaburras continued to laugh. Their derision itched through him. He surveyed the cabin, hands on hips. Not a sign of movement. His earlier vision gave way to one of her lying face down on the sofa, sobbing. He took a step towards the cabin.

He ground to a halt.

He didn't do crying women. Not any more.

A month. *A whole month.*

His gaze flicked to her car. He wasn't a blasted porter either, but that didn't stop him from stalking over to it and removing two suitcases and a box of groceries. Or from stalking back to the house, grabbing a bottle of chardonnay and shoving it in an ice bucket and adding that to the items piled up by her front door.

He bent down and scratched Molly's ears. 'Keep an eye on her, girl.' That would have to do. Common decency demanded he check on her in the morning, then his neighbourly duty was done.

If she hadn't already had a crying jag when perched in the clothes-line, Josie would've had one now. But she decided one a day was enough.

A whole month. She was stuck out here for a whole month. *On her own.*

She tried to repress a shudder. She tried to force herself to smile as she glanced around the interior of the cabin again. She'd read somewhere that if you smiled it actually helped lift your spirits.

Ha! Not working.

She scrubbed her hands down her face. Oh,

well, she supposed if nothing else she at least had plenty of time to sort out what she was going to do with the rest of her life. And that was the point of this holiday after all.

Things inside her cringed and burned. She wrapped her arms around her waist. She wasn't qualified to do anything other than look after sick people. And she didn't want to do that any more.

Familiar doubts and worries crowded in on her. She pushed them away. Later. She'd deal with them later.

With a sigh, she collapsed onto the sofa. Then groaned. It was as rock-hard as Kent Black. That didn't bode well. She twisted against it, trying to get comfortable. It didn't take a brain surgeon to work out Kent didn't want her here. As far as she could see, he didn't have an ounce of sympathy in that big, broad body of his for weakness of any kind.

She had to admit it was a nice, broad body though, with scrummy shoulders. If a girl disregarded that scowl she could get all sorts of ideas in her head and—

No, she couldn't! Besides, Josie could never disregard that scowl. Kent didn't think she belonged out here and he was one hundred per cent right.

A whole month.

'Stop it!'

Her voice echoed eerily in the cabin, reminding

her how alone she was. She suppressed another shudder. She was just tired, that was all, and sitting around wallowing in self-pity wasn't going to help. A shower, that was what she needed. That'd pep her up. Then she'd unpack the car and make a cup of tea. Things always looked better over a cup of tea.

The shower did help. She emerged into the main room of the cabin, vigorously drying her hair. Then froze.

Something was on her veranda!

There it was again. A scuffling, creaking, snorting noise right outside her front door. She hadn't locked it!

Josie's mouth went dry. She held the towel to her face. Oh, please. Whatever was out there she prayed it didn't have an opposable thumb, that it couldn't reach out and open door handles.

And that it didn't have the kind of bulk that barged through flimsy wooden doors.

Just clap your hands and say boo!

Kent's earlier advice almost made her laugh out loud. Not funny ha-ha, but losing it big-time ha-ha. She retreated to the bathroom door. She doubted she could manage much of a boo at the moment.

'Kent?' Maybe he was out there. Maybe he'd come back for... She couldn't think of any conceivable reason why he'd come back. He hadn't been able to get away fast enough, horrible, unfriendly man.

She'd give anything for it to be him out there now, though.

'Mr Black?'

A low whine answered her, followed by scratching at her door and a bark.

'Molly.' With her heart hammering in her throat, Josie stumbled forward, wrenched the door open and dropped to her knees to hug the dog. 'You scared me half out of my wits,' she scolded. Molly licked her face in response.

Thank heavens Kent hadn't been here to witness her panic. He'd have laughed his head off then curled his lip in scorn. She'd have died on the spot.

She glanced out into the darkness and gulped. Night had fallen in full force. She couldn't remember a night so dark. Not a single streetlight pierced the blackness. Her cabin faced away from Kent's house, so not a single house light penetrated it either. The moon hadn't risen yet, but a multitude of stars arced across the sky in a display that hitched the breath in her throat.

She should've unpacked her car whilst it was light. She didn't fancy stumbling around in the dark. Dragging her eyes from the glory of the night sky, she turned and found her suitcases lined up neatly on the end of her veranda. Her jaw dropped. Kent had unpacked her car for her?

That was nice. Friendly. In fact—she struggled to her feet—it was almost…sweet?

No, you couldn't describe Kent as sweet.

She reached for the nearest bag then stilled. She adjusted her reach to the right and picked up an ice bucket, complete with a bottle of wine.

She blinked madly and hugged it to her chest. Now, that *was* friendly.

And sweet. Most definitely sweet.

Josie groaned and pulled a pillow over her head in an effort to drown out the cacophony of noise. Molly whined and scratched to be let out. She'd spent the night sleeping on the end of the sofa bed, and Josie had welcomed the company. Molly's presence had made her feel less alone. Last night she'd needed that.

Now she needed sleep.

Molly whined again. Groaning, Josie reached for her watch. Six o'clock! She crawled out of bed and opened the door. Kookaburras laughed as if the sight of her filled them with hilarity and, overhead, white cockatoos screeched, three crows adding their raucous caws. And that wasn't counting all the other cheeps and peeps and twitters she didn't recognise in the general riot. Magpies started warbling in a nearby gum tree. For heaven's sake, what was this place—a bird sanctuary?

Flashes of red and green passed directly in front of her to settle in a row of nearby grevillias, twittering happily as they supped on red-flowered nectar. Rosellas. Ooh. She loved rosellas.

Racing back inside, she clicked on the kettle, pulled on her jeans, threw on a shirt then dashed back out to her veranda with a steaming mug of coffee to watch as the world woke up around her.

OK. So maybe Eagle Reach was at the end of the earth, but she couldn't deny its beauty. To her left, the row of grevillias, still covered in rosellas, merged into a forest of gums and banksias. To her right, the five other cabins stretched away down the slope. Directly in front of her the hill fell away in gentle folds, the grassy slopes golden in the early-morning sunlight, dazzled with dew.

She blinked at its brightness, the freshness. Moist earth and sun-warmed grasses and the faint tang of eucalyptus scented the air. She gulped it in greedily.

In the distance the River Gloucester, lined with river gums and weeping willows, wound its way along the base of the hill to disappear behind a neighbouring slope. Josie knew that if she followed the river she would eventually come to the little township of Martin's Gully, and then, further along, the larger township of Gloucester itself.

As one, the rosellas lifted from the bushes and took flight and, just like that, Josie found herself alone again. She swallowed. What would she find to do all day? Especially in light of the resolution she'd made last night.

She chafed her hands. She'd think of something. She'd stay at Eagle Reach for the whole day if it killed her. She would not drive into either Martin's Gully or Gloucester. Kent Black would expect her to do exactly that. And for some reason she found herself wanting to smash his expectations.

She found herself aching for just an ounce of his strength too.

By eight o'clock Josie wondered again at the sense of such a resolution. She'd breakfasted, tidied the cabin and now...

Nothing.

She made another coffee and sat back out on the veranda. She checked her watch. Five past eight. Even if she went to bed disgustingly early she still had at least twelve hours to kill. Her shoulders started to sag and her spine lost its early-morning buoyancy, the greyness of grief descending over her again.

She shouldn't have come here. It was too soon for a holiday. Any holiday. She'd buried her father a fortnight ago. She should be at home. She should be with her friends, her family. Maybe, right at this very minute, she could be forging closer bonds with Marty and Frank. Surely that was more important than—

'Good morning!'

Josie jumped out of her skin. Coffee sloshed over the side of her cup and onto her feet. Kent Black. Her heart hammered, though she told herself it was the effect of her fright. Not the fact that his big, broad body looked superb in a pair of faded jeans and a navy T-shirt that fitted him in a way that highlighted bulging arm muscles.

'Sorry. Didn't mean to startle you.'

He didn't look the least bit sorry. And if he didn't mean to startle people he shouldn't bark out good-mornings like a sergeant major springing a surprise inspection.

'Not a problem.' She tried to smile. 'Good morning.'

He didn't step any closer, he didn't come and sit with her on the veranda. She quelled her disappointment and tried to tell herself she didn't care.

'How'd you sleep?' The words scraped out of a throat that sounded rusty with disuse.

'Like a top,' she lied. She decided she'd been rude enough about the amenities—or lack of amenities—last night. She couldn't start back in on him today. Yesterday at least she could plead the excuse of tiredness. 'I'm sorry about my lack of enthusiasm last night. It had been a long day and, like you said, the cabin is perfectly adequate.'

He blinked. His eyes narrowed. Up close she could see they were the most startling shade of blue, almost navy. Still, it didn't mean she wanted them practically dissecting her.

'How was the wine?'

A smile spread through her. He could look as unfriendly and unapproachable as he liked, but actions spoke louder than words. Last night, over her first glass of wine, she'd decided Kent Black had a kind heart. He'd just forgotten how to show it, that was all. 'The wine was lovely.'

Really lovely. So lovely she'd drunk half the bottle before she'd realised it. Once she had, she'd hastily shoved the rest of the bottle in the tiny bar fridge. Quaffing copious quantities of wine when she was stuck out here all on her own might not be the wisest of ideas.

'It was a really thoughtful gesture. Thank you, Mr Black.' She waited for him to tell her to call him Kent. She bit back a sigh when he didn't.

He touched the brim of his hat in what she took to be a kind of farewell salute and panic spiked through her. She didn't want to be left all alone again. Not yet.

Molly nudged Josie's arm with her nose, forcing

her to lift it so she could sidle in close. 'I, umm…
Molly is a lovely dog. Really lovely. I was wrong
about her too.' Ugh, she should be ashamed of such
inane babble. 'I… She spent the night with me.'

He spun back, hands on hips. 'I noticed.'

Oh, dear. She should've let him leave. Her fingers curled into Molly's fur. She didn't want to
give Molly up. 'I… Do you want me to shoo her
home in future?'

'She's all yours.'

Relief chugged through her and she swore his
eyes softened. Then he turned away again and
she knew she must've imagined it. 'Are any of the
other cabins booked over the next few weeks?' She
crossed her fingers.

His impatience, when he turned back, made her
want to cringe.

'No.'

The single syllable rang a death knell through
her last forlorn hope. All alone. For a month.
'Then…what do people do out here?'

'Do?' One eyebrow lifted. 'Nothing. That's the
point.'

Dread fizzed through her. 'Would you like a cup
of tea?' Surely he'd like a cup of tea. Kind hearts
and cups of tea went together and—

'No.'

She gulped. Couldn't he have at least added a

thank-you to his refusal? She tried to dredge up indignation, but her loneliness overrode it.

'Some of us actually have work to do.'

Work? 'What kind of work?' Could she help? She knew she was grasping at straws, but she couldn't stop herself. She knew she'd die a thousand deaths when she went back over this conversation later.

'I run cattle on this hill, Ms Peterson.'

'Josie,' she whispered, a hand fluttering to her throat. 'Please call me Josie.'

He pulled the brim of his hat down low over his eyes. 'Bushwalking.'

'I beg your pardon?'

'People who come here. They like to bushwalk.'

'Oh. OK.' She liked walking. She walked on the beach back home. She didn't know her way around here, though. What if she got lost? Who'd know she was missing? She didn't trust Kent Black to notice.

'There are some pretty trails through there.' He pointed at the forest of gums. 'They lead down to the river.'

Trails? She brightened. She could follow a path without getting lost.

'Take Molly with you.'

'OK. Thank you,' she called out after him, but she doubted he'd heard. His long legs had already put an alarming amount of distance between them in a seriously short space of time.

She turned her gaze to the shadowed depths of the eucalypt forest and made out the beginnings of a path. A walk? She leapt up, glad to have a purpose.

Kent swung around as an almighty screech pierced the forest. Birds lifted from trees and fluttered away. He glanced at his watch and shook his head. Fifteen minutes. She'd lasted fifteen minutes. Not that he'd deliberately followed her, of course. He hadn't. He'd just taken note of when she'd set off and down which path, that was all.

He'd chosen a different path, an adjacent one, and it wasn't as if he was keeping an eye on her or anything. He had business down this way.

Yeah, but not until later this afternoon, a voice in his head jeered.

He ignored it.

No more screams or screeches or shrieks for help followed. She'd probably walked into a spider's web or something. But then Molly started up her low, mournful howl. Kent folded his arms and glared. With a muttered curse, he unfolded his arms, cut through the undergrowth and set off towards the noise.

He almost laughed out loud when he reached them. Josie clung to a branch of a nearby gum and a goanna clung to the main trunk of the same tree, effectively cutting off her escape. Molly sat beneath it all, howling for all she was worth. He chuckled then realised what he'd done.

'Enjoying your walk I hope, Ms Peterson?'

She swung her head around to glare at him over her shoulder. The branch swayed precariously. He readied himself to catch her if she overbalanced.

'What do you think?' she snapped.

'I think you enjoy scaring all the wildlife on my side of the hill.'

'Scaring? Me?' Her mouth opened and closed but no sound came out. She pointed an accusing finger at the goanna then clutched the branch again as it started to sway. 'Move it.'

He glanced at it. 'Nope, not touching it.'

'So, you're scared of it too?' she hissed.

'Let's just say I like to treat our native wildlife with a great deal of respect.'

'Oh, that's just great. Of all the wildlife in this God-forsaken place I had to get a…a dinosaur rather than a cute, cuddly koala, huh? Any wildlife wrestlers in the neighbourhood by any chance?'

'Not much call for them out here.'

'How am I going to get down?'

Behind her bluff he could see she was scared. He had a feeling she hadn't stopped being scared since she'd scrambled out of his clothes-line yesterday. 'Jump,' he ordered. 'I'll catch you.' She wasn't that high up. In fact, if she hung from that branch by her hands, she'd only be four or five feet from the ground. He knew it would look vastly different from her perspective, though.

He wished she wasn't so cute.

The thought flitted in and out of his head in the time it took to blink. 'Cut out the racket, Molly,' he growled. The dog had kept right on howling all this time. Like most of the females of his experience, Molly loved the sound of her own voice.

Josie bit her lip and glanced at the goanna. 'Is it going to jump too? Or chase me?'

'Nope. This is his tree. It's where he feels safe.'

She glared at him again. 'So, of all the trees in the forest I had to pick his?'

'Yep.'

'I'm so happy.'

He guessed from the way she gritted her teeth together as she said it, she didn't mean it.

Without any more prompting on his part, Josie shifted her weight from her behind to her stomach then tried to take her full weight with her arms to lower herself to the ground. Kent leapt forward and wrapped his arms around the tops of her thighs.

'I don't need—'

The rest of her words were lost when her hands slipped and she landed against him with a muffled, 'Oomph.'

Kent couldn't manage much either as the top half of her body slumped over him and he found his face mashed between her breasts. Then a long, delicious slide as her body slipped down his.

They were both breathing hard when her feet finally touched the ground.

They paused then sprang apart.

'Thank you,' Josie babbled, smoothing down her hair. 'I, umm… It probably wasn't necessary to jump to my rescue like that, but, umm…thank you all the same.'

'Are you going to make a habit of that?' he snapped. He darn well hoped not. His body wouldn't cope with it. Even now he had to fight down a rising tide of raw desire. He didn't need this.

'It's not part of my plans.'

He wanted her off his mountain. Fast. He flung his arms out. 'Doesn't this prove how unsuited you are to this place?'

Her chin shot up although her shoulders stayed hunched around her ears. 'Because I'm frightened of goannas?'

'Because you're frightened of everything.'

'I'm not afraid of Molly. Not now,' she pointed out reasonably enough. 'I just didn't know what to do when that thing started running at me.'

'Run away at right angles to it,' he answered automatically.

'I'll remember that.'

He didn't want her remembering. He wanted her gone. 'You don't know how to protect yourself out here.'

'Well…I'm not dead yet.'

'What would you do if some big, burly guy jumped out at you, huh?' To prove his point, he lunged at her.

The next moment he was lying on his back, and staring up through the leaves of the trees at the clear blue of the sky. With no idea how he had got there.

Josie's face hovered into view as she leaned over him. 'Does that answer your question?'

She'd thrown him? He deserved that smug little smile. For some reason he wanted to laugh again.

He scowled. No, he didn't. He wanted her off his mountain.

'I might be hopeless, but I'm not completely helpless, you know. Men I can defend myself against. It's the dogs and goannas that I have trouble with.'

He rolled over onto his stomach to watch her saunter away. He really wished he didn't notice how sweetly she filled out a pair of jeans. Molly licked his face, as if in sympathy, then trotted after her new-found friend.

CHAPTER THREE

JOSIE WAS BACK at her cabin by ten o'clock.

So, now she only had ten hours to kill.

She wished she'd learnt how to draw or paint. Or knit.

A craft project, that was what she needed. She made a mental note to hunt out a craft shop when she went into Gloucester. Tomorrow.

Still, what would it hurt if she went in today and—?

Kent's scornful lips flashed through her mind. No! She'd manage to stick it out here for a whole day. Somehow.

Books. She'd buy some books. And a radio. Tomorrow.

She rearranged her grocery supplies on the kitchen shelves. That took less than ten minutes. She made a shopping list. For tomorrow. That took another ten minutes, but only because she dallied over it. She glanced around, clapped her hands together and wondered what she could do next.

'Oh, for heaven's sake!' she growled out loud,

suddenly impatient. Seizing a pen and notepad, she plonked herself down at the table. If she'd just work out what she wanted to do with the rest of her life instead of putting it off, then she could get on with living that life and leave this awful place behind. Marty and Frank would forgive her for curtailing her holiday if she came up with a plan.

At the top of the page she wrote: 'What do I want to do with my life?' Her mind went blank, so she added an exclamation mark, in brackets.

Familiar doubts and worries flitted about her. She swallowed and tried not to panic. She was looking at this all wrong. She should break it down into smaller, more manageable bits. Skills. She should list her skills.

1—Assistant in Nursing certificate. 2—She could give bed baths. 3—She could measure out medicines. 4—She could coax a difficult patient to eat. 5—

No. No. No.

She slammed the pen to the table. She didn't want to do those things any more. There had to be other things she could do. She had to have at least one talent that could steer her towards a new vocation. Take her brothers. Frank had a great head for figures, which made him a successful accountant. Marty had great spatial abilities, which was why he was an architect. She had…?

Nothing.

Her shoulders sagged. She couldn't think of one single thing she had a talent for. Except looking after sick people, dying people. Fear clogged her throat. She couldn't do that. Not any more. She'd loved her father dearly, missed him terribly, and she didn't regret one single day she'd spent looking after him. But...

She couldn't take on another dementia patient. She couldn't watch another person die.

She leapt up and started to pace. The grey drabness of the cabin pressed in against her. The only splashes of colour were the labels on her groceries. Her gaze drifted across them, paused on the packet cake mix that, for some reason, she'd thrown in. What? Did she think she'd be giving tea parties? Her laugh held an edge that earned her a low bark from Molly.

She'd love to give a tea party. A sigh welled up inside her. She chewed her bottom lip and cast another glance at the cake mix. She could cook it up for Kent.

As a thank-you for last night's bottle of wine.

Maybe he'd even invite her to stay and share it. She chewed her bottom lip some more. She wanted to find out what made him tick, what made him so strong. She wanted to be more like that. She put her list away and reached for a mixing bowl.

* * *

Kent rubbed his hands together as he waited for the tea to brew. With his chores done, he could kick back and enjoy the fading golden light of the afternoon, his favourite time of day.

The cattle were fed and watered. He ran a herd small enough to manage on his own. And between them, the cattle and the cabins, they kept him busy enough through the days.

The nights, though…

The nights nothing!

A knock sounded on his back door. He swung around. Josie?

It had to be. He rarely had visitors out here, which was the way he liked it. He wasn't a sociable man. He thought he'd made that plain to her this morning.

Guilt wormed through him. He scowled at the teapot.

Maybe she'd come to return the key and tell him she was leaving? His jaw clenched. Good. She could drive off into the sunset. He didn't care. No skin off his nose.

'Kent?' She knocked again.

He bit back a string of curses and strode out to answer the door. The sharp remark on his lips died when he found her standing on the bottom step with a frosted chocolate cake in her hands and a hopeful expression in her gold-flecked eyes.

Damn.

'Hello.' She smiled, or at least her lips gave the tiniest of upward lifts.

He grunted in reply. Things inside him shuffled about and refused to settle into place.

She'd recently showered and damp hair curled around her shoulders. It gleamed in the last shaft of sunlight that touched his house for the afternoon, and he could pick out more shades of brown than he thought possible for one person to possess. Everything from light honeyed brown all the way through to rich walnut.

And not a mouse in sight.

She smelled fresh and fruity. Not run-of-the-mill apples and oranges either, but something more exotic. Like pineapple and…cucumber? She smelt like summer nights on the beach.

He couldn't remember the last time he'd sat on a beach. Or when he'd last wanted to. He couldn't remember the last time he'd eaten chocolate cake either. He tried to stop his mouth from watering.

She thrust the cake towards him. 'This is for you.'

He had no option but to take it. 'Why?' His eyes narrowed. He didn't trust the sensations pounding through him and he didn't trust her either.

Her gaze darted behind him into the house. She

moistened her lips when she met his gaze again. 'I, umm—'

'You want to use the phone again?' Typical woman. Couldn't be without—

'No.' She drew herself up. 'It's a thank-you for last night's bottle of wine.'

He'd known he'd end up regretting that bottle of wine. He stared at her. She had a pointy little chin that stuck out when indignant. He wanted to reach out a finger and trace the fine line of her jaw.

He darn well didn't! He shoved the cake back at her. 'I don't want it.'

She took a step back and blinked. Then amazingly she laughed. 'Wrong answer, Mr Black; you're supposed to say thank you.'

Shame bore down on him. There was a world of difference between unsociable and downright rude. Jeez. 'You're right.' He dragged his free hand down his face. 'I'm sorry.' He pulled in a breath and tried to gulp back hasty words clamouring for release. 'You better call me Kent.'

He couldn't grind back the rest of his words either. 'I've just made a pot of tea. Would you like to join me?'

The gold flecks in her eyes lit up. 'Yes, please.'

Josie wanted to run from Kent's scowl. Then she remembered the only place she could run to was her cabin. Her bleak, lonely cabin. She gulped back her trepidation and followed him into the kitchen.

She wrinkled her nose as she glanced around. Definitely a bachelor's pad—no frills, no colour, next to no comfort. A woman wouldn't put up with this.

She glanced at Kent. She had a feeling he wouldn't give two hoots what a woman thought.

A large wooden table dominated the room. That was about all she'd taken in yesterday when she'd made her quick phone call. She wondered if there was a separate dining room, then dismissed the idea. The house wasn't large enough.

She glanced through the doorway leading through to the rest of the house. It looked like a typical gun-barrel miner's cottage. The next room along would be the living room then a short hallway would lead to two bedrooms at the front of the house.

She also guessed she'd never make it past this kitchen.

Heat suddenly flamed through her. Not that she wanted to make it as far as the bedroom with Kent Black, of course. Good lord. She couldn't imagine him unbending his stiff upper lip long enough to kiss a woman, let alone—

Are you so sure? a wicked voice asked.

Umm…

She slammed a lid on that thought, swung away and found herself confronted with the hard, lean lines of Kent's back…and backside, as he reached into a cupboard above the sink for two mugs.

Oh, dear. She fanned her face and swung around another ninety degrees. She didn't want to ogle his, uh, assets. In fact, it probably wasn't a good idea to ogle any man's assets until she'd sorted out what she was going to do with the rest of her life.

The rest of her life? What was she going to do with the next ten minutes?

Arghh. She scanned the room, searching for distraction. Her eyes landed on a chess set. A beautiful hand-carved chess set.

At her indrawn breath, audible in the silence of the room, Kent spun to face her. 'What?' He glanced around as if searching for a spider or lizard, some creepy-crawly that may have frightened her.

'I…' She pointed. 'Did you make that?'

He grunted and shrugged.

'It's beautiful.' She stared at him, trying to recognise the creator of the work of art in the hard stern man in front of her. 'It's one of the most beautiful things I've ever seen.'

'Then you need to get out more.'

She'd have laughed at his response if she hadn't

been so engrossed in admiring the individual chess pieces. Each one was intricately carved into the shape of a tree. The skill and workmanship that had gone into each piece took her breath away. The kings were mighty oaks, the queens graceful weeping willows and the bishops upright poplars. Talk about a craft project!

She held her breath and reached out to pick up a pawn—a miniature banksia—and marvelled at the detail. She could see each cylindrical flower on the delicate branches. How on earth had he managed that?

'Do you play?'

She jumped, startled by his closeness. His breath disturbed the hair at her temple as he leant over to survey the piece she held. 'I...'

He took a step back and she found she could breathe again.

'Not really.' She placed the pawn back on the board and sadness pierced her. She tried to smile. 'My father was teaching me before he fell ill.'

The rest of Kent Black could look as hard as stone, but his eyes could soften from a winter gale to a spring breeze in the time it took to draw breath. Josie's heart started to pound.

'I'm sorry about your father, Josie.'

'Thank you.' *He'd called her Josie.*

'I'm sorry he never had a chance to finish teaching you how to play.'

'Me too.' She couldn't look away.

'I'll give you lessons if you like.'

She wondered if she looked as surprised by the offer as he did. She had no intention of letting him off the hook, though. 'I'd like that very much.'

He grunted and took a step back. With one blink his eyes became as carved-from-rock hard as the rest of him.

'When?' she persisted. 'Now?'

'No.' He strode back to the table. 'Monday afternoons,' he said after a pause. 'At about this time.'

It was Tuesday now. Monday was six whole days away. He'd done that on purpose, she was sure of it. She'd missed out one lesson already if you counted yesterday.

She wanted to stamp a foot in frustration. The glint in his eye told her he knew it too. She forced her lips into a smile instead. 'I'll look forward to it.' Beggars couldn't be choosers, and she now only had six afternoons a week to fill. She didn't want him retracting the offer.

She wondered if she could talk him into two afternoons a week? One look at his face told her to leave it for now.

'Why don't we have our tea outside?' He lifted a

tray holding their tea things and Josie had no choice but to follow him back out into the sunshine.

She cut large wedges of cake whilst he poured out mugs of tea. He made no attempt at conversation and, strangely, Josie didn't mind. She watched him instead. He devoured his slice of chocolate cake with the kind of hunger that did strange things to her insides.

Warm, fuzzy things.

She had to glance away when he licked the frosting from his fingers. She cut him another slice then cleared her throat. 'Did you grow up around here?'

'No.'

He physically drew back in his seat, his face shuttered, and disappointment filtered through her. He didn't want her prying into his background. Though at least she now knew his unique brand of strength wasn't something born and bred into him because he'd grown up out here on Eagle Reach. There was hope for her yet.

He eyed her warily. She smiled back. 'It's only a packet mix.' She motioned to the cake. 'I make a much better one from scratch.'

'It's good.'

His manners were improving, but the wariness didn't leave his eyes. It made her feel...wrong. She couldn't remember making anyone feel wary before. She didn't like the sensation. She searched for something deliberately inconsequential to say. She stared at the cake. Her lips twitched. 'I was sorry I didn't pack hundreds and thousands to sprinkle on top.'

Kent choked.

'But then I figured you probably weren't a hundreds and thousands kind of guy. A chocolate-sprinkle kind of guy maybe, but not hundreds and thousands.'

Kent stared at her. Then his wariness fled. He threw his head back and laughed. It changed him utterly, and it stole Josie's breath.

One thing became brilliantly and dazzlingly clear. She could certainly imagine this incarnation of Kent kissing a woman. She saw it in bright Technicolor vividness.

Seeing it, though, didn't mean she wanted it.

It didn't.

Kent rolled his shoulders, stretching out the aches in his muscles. He'd spent most of the day fixing a broken fence and he was dying for his afternoon cup of tea.

And the rest of that chocolate cake Josie had baked yesterday. He couldn't remember the last time he'd eaten anything quite so satisfying. His stomach grumbled low and long. His mouth watered. He reached out to unlatch the back gate then froze.

'Kent?'

Josie.

He peered over the palings and found her standing on the top step of his house, hand raised to knock on his back door. In her other hand she held a plate of what looked suspiciously like freshly baked biscuits.

His stomach growled again. His mouth watered some more. In the sunlight her hair glowed all the hues of a varnished piece of sandalwood and his stomach clenched. He couldn't believe he'd ever thought it mousy. Anticipation leapt to life in his chest. He reached out to unlatch the gate again when reality crashed around him.

This couldn't happen. He didn't do afternoon tea parties.

You don't do chess lessons either, a wry voice in his head pointed out.

Yeah, well, as soon as he found a way to get out of those you could bet your life he would.

'Kent?'

Her soft contralto voice tugged at him. She turned to survey the surrounding area and with a muffled oath he ducked down behind the fence.

Grown men don't hide behind fences, he told himself. For Pete's sake, what would it hurt to have another cup of tea with her? Yesterday's hadn't killed him.

A scowl shuffled through him. He knew exactly how it would hurt. He'd recognised the loneliness in her eyes. If he had a cup of tea again with her today it'd become a habit. A daily thing. She'd start to rely on him. He scowled down at his work-roughened hands. He wasn't going to let that happen.

He'd seen the flash of awareness in her eyes yesterday. He knew exactly where that would lead, because in the space of a heartbeat desire had thrummed through him in unequivocal response. He'd be an idiot to ignore it.

If he met with Josie Peterson for afternoon tea today, she'd be in his bed by the end of the week.

His skin went hard and tight at the thought.

But he knew women like Josie didn't indulge in affairs.

And men like him didn't offer anything more.

He edged away from the fence and stole back the way he'd come, throbbing with a mixture of guilt and desire. He tried to tell himself this was best for both of them. Somehow, though, the sentiment rang hollow.

A spurt of anger shot through him, lending speed to his feet. Darn her for invading his space. Darn her for invading his refuge.

CHAPTER FOUR

JOSIE WOKE ON Thursday morning to rain. She sat on her tiny veranda in the gaily patterned camp chair she'd bought on her trip into Gloucester yesterday, her hands curled around her morning coffee, and stared out into the greyness. Given half a chance she feared that greyness would invade her.

She dropped a hand to Molly's head. 'It doesn't look like we'll get a walk in today.' That had been the plan—a big hike. Especially since Kent had assured her goannas weren't ferocious carnivores.

The rain put paid to that.

She wondered if the rain affected Kent's work. She wondered if he'd be home if she knocked at his back door with muffins this afternoon.

Was he even OK? She hadn't clapped eyes on him since Tuesday afternoon. What if he'd fallen in some gully and broken his leg? What if a brown snake had bitten him? What if—?

Stop it! He'd lived at Eagle Reach for heaven only knew how many years. He wasn't going to start breaking legs or getting bitten by snakes because she'd shown up. Besides, Molly would know if something was wrong. Josie glanced down at the dog and bit her lip. She would, wouldn't she?

Face it. Kent just didn't need people the way she did. Yesterday she'd sat in two different cafés in Gloucester's main street, lapping up the noise and bustle along with her coffee. In a few days, when the isolation became too much, she'd do it again.

Not today, though. Today she'd start one of her craft projects—the embroidered cushion, or the latch-hook wall hanging, or the candle-making. Or she could finish reading the newspapers. She'd seized every available paper yesterday and wasn't halfway through them yet. Or she could start reading one of the novels she'd bought. She'd bought six.

She drained her coffee and strode inside, determined to make a decision, but the drab bleakness of the cabin's interior sucked all the energy out of her. It really was horrible. Ugly.

Yesterday, when she hadn't found Kent home, she'd come back here, collapsed into a chair and stared at a wall until the dark had gathered about her and she couldn't see her surroundings any more.

It had frightened her when she finally came back to herself. She didn't want that happening again.

'You know what, Molly?' Molly's tail thumped against the bare floorboards in instant response. 'If I want to stay sane for the next month we're going to have to spend today making this place fit to live in.'

She threw open her suitcase and rifled through its contents, searching for inspiration. Suddenly, she laughed. Sarongs! She'd packed her sarongs.

That was when she'd imagined cabins to mean pretty little cabanas set in lush gardens, encircling a lagoon-style swimming pool. Back when she'd pictured banana loungers and exotic drinks in coconut shells with colourful paper umbrellas sticking out of them at jaunty angles.

She'd pictured comfort and ease. Relaxation. Not bare, lonely landscapes that stretched as wide as the empty places inside her.

She pulled the sarongs out in a hasty rush then switched on her brand-new transistor radio. She tuned it to one of those ubiquitous radio stations that played cheerful, inane pop, twenty-four-seven. She'd push back the greyness. Somehow. And cheerful and inane would do very nicely at the moment, thank you.

'OK.' Josie pulled in a breath. 'Are you ready for the big test?'

Molly wagged her tail.

Josie drank the last of her tea, crossed her fingers and leapt to her feet. She'd worked on the interior of the cabin for hours. Now came the test—to walk through the door and see if it still sucked the lifeblood from her.

Without giving herself any more time to think, Josie strode across the threshold and into the cabin. She held her breath and completed a slow circle. With a sigh of relief, almost a sob, she dropped to her knees and hugged Molly hard. 'Now this is a place I can live in for the next month. What do you say?'

Molly's answer was a wet lick up the side of her face. Laughing, Josie jumped up. OK, what to do for the rest of the day?

Her eyes fell on the notepad on the table. The what-am-I-going-to-do-with-the-rest-of-my-life-and-what-skills-do-I-have? notepad. Her heart dropped, her shoulders sagged. She gulped back a hard ball of panic.

'Muffins.' Her voice held a high edge that stopped Molly's tail mid-wag. 'Which would your master prefer, do you think? Date and walnut or apple and cinnamon?'

Kent swore when the knock sounded on his back door. He set down the chess piece he was carving and glanced at his watch. Two o'clock.

Four o'clock on Tuesday. Three o'clock yesterday. She wouldn't last the week at this rate.

Good. He clenched his jaw. Josie Peterson was getting as pesky as a darn mosquito. And as persistent. He rubbed the back of his neck. He could always sneak out the front way. She'd never know.

No. She wasn't chasing him out of his house. Another knock sounded. He gritted his teeth. She wasn't worming her way into it either. The sooner he set the ground rules the easier the next month would be. He stormed to the back door and flung it open. As he expected, Josie stood there. The rain had stopped, the sun hadn't come out, but her hair still gleamed like burnished sandalwood, which for some reason irritated him.

'What?' he barked. No pretence at friendliness, no pretence at politeness.

Josie's face fell. He hardened his heart and hated himself for it.

'I, umm…' She moistened her lips. 'I've been baking and I've made too much for one. It seems a shame to waste it all, though. I thought you might like some.'

The aroma of freshly baked muffins mingled with her fresh, fruity fragrance and ploughed straight into his gut. He couldn't remember the last time he'd faced so much temptation. 'You thought wrong,' he snapped.

Strong. Hc had to stay strong.

Darn it! Those muffins looked good. Dangerously good. Just like her. He had a feeling he could get used to her cooking. If the truth be told, he had a feeling he could get used to her, and that couldn't happen. He'd let her down. The way he'd let—

The gold flecks in her eyes suddenly flashed. 'You didn't mind the chocolate cake the other day.' Her chin quivered when she stuck it out. 'We had a very pleasant half an hour over that cake.'

Precisely. Which was why it wasn't going to happen again. 'Look, Ms Peterson—'

'Josie.'

'I am not your nursemaid. I am not your friend. I am the man you've rented a cabin from for a month and that's as far as our association goes, got it?'

Her eyes widened at his bluntness. Her mouth worked. 'Don't you get lonely?' she finally blurted out.

'Nope.' Not any more. Not most of the time anyway.

'So how do you do it?' She lifted the plate of muffins as if they could provide an answer. 'How do you manage to live out here all on your own and not mind?'

He could see it wasn't idle curiosity. She wanted

to know. Needed to know, maybe. He supposed he'd started off much the same way she was now.

Not the searching out of human contact. He'd shunned that from the start. But he'd carved and whittled wood the way she baked. He'd kept himself busy with cattle and cabins and carving until the days had taken on a shape of their own.

So he didn't need the likes of her coming around here now and disrupting it. Making him ache for things that couldn't be.

She shook her head. 'You can't be human.'

He wished that were true.

'We all need people.'

'Believe me, some needy fly-by-night is not essential to my well-being.'

She paled at his words and he loathed himself all the more. His resolve started to waver and weaken. 'What do you see happening between us?' he snapped out. 'You'll be gone in a month.' Probably less. That thought steeled his determination again.

'Friends?' she whispered.

He laughed, a harsh sound that scraped out of his throat leaving it raw. He had to get rid of her. She could capture a man with those sad, gold-flecked eyes and the soft curve of her lips. It'd all end in tears. Her tears. Then he'd really hate himself.

She took one step back, then another, her face white. 'You are a piece of work, you know that?'

Yep. It wasn't news to him. But Josie wasn't cut out for all this. 'Try the general store in Martin's Gully.' He nodded at the plate in her hand. 'They might be interested in placing an order or two with you.'

Liz Perkins would take Josie under her ample, matronly wing. It'd do both of them the world of good. On that thought, he slammed the door in Josie's face before guilt got the better of him and he hauled her inside and tried to make amends.

Josie stalked back to her cabin, quivering all over with outrage. She ranted in incoherent half-sentences to Molly.

'Of all the arrogant assumptions! Needy fly-by-night? Who does he think he is?'

She slammed the plate to the kitchen bench and paced. Ha! At least she'd eradicated his grey presence from her cabin. Satisfaction shot through her when she surveyed the changes she'd made.

'And he needn't think I'm going to sit around here all afternoon and moon about it either.'

Molly whined and pushed her nose against Josie's hand. Josie dropped to her knees and scratched Molly's ears. 'I'm sorry, girl. It's not your fault. You're lovely and loyal and sweet and too good for the likes of him. It's not your fault you drew the short straw when it came to masters.'

Molly rolled onto her back and groaned with pleasure when Josie scratched her tummy. 'You're gorgeous and beautiful.'

Her fingers brushed the scar that zigzagged across Molly's abdomen and she stilled. 'I don't get him at all.' She meant to take his advice, though.

It took exactly twelve and a half minutes to reach the tiny township of Martin's Gully. It wasn't exactly a blink-and-miss town, but it wasn't far from it. It had, at the most, two-dozen houses, though it boasted its own tiny wooden church. Completing the picture was a post office that, according to the sign in its window, opened two and a half days a week, and Perkins' General Store.

Josie pushed through the door of the latter then waited for her eyes to adjust to the dimness. She blinked as the size of the interior came into focus. Bags of feed grain competed with tools for floor space on her left. Bolts of material lined the wall. On her right, shelves full of tinned food and every known grocery item arced away from her. Down the middle sat an old-fashioned freezer. The store smelt dry and dusty and good.

'Can I help you?' a thin, middle-aged woman hailed her from behind the counter at the rear of the room.

Someone with a smile. Josie hastened towards her. 'Hi, I'm Josie Peterson. I'm staying at Eagle Reach for the next few weeks.'

'Bridget Anderson.' Her eyes narrowed as she shook Josie's proffered hand. 'Ain't Eagle Reach Kent Black's place?'

Josie nodded. She'd have thought everyone in Martin's Gully would know everybody else's business. Maybe Kent Black maintained an unfriendly distance with the folk in town too?

As if reading her mind, the other woman leaned in closer. 'This is my sister's store. I'm helping out for a bit.'

Another newcomer? Fellow feeling rushed through Josie.

'Lizzie's husband, Ted, died back in November.'

'Oh, that's awful.'

'And she won't have a word said against Kent Black.'

Really? Josie tried to stop her eyebrows from shooting straight up into her hairline. So, Kent had at least one friend in town, did he?

Bridget's face darkened. 'Me, on the other hand…'

'He's very solitary,' Josie offered, she hoped tactfully.

Bridget snorted. 'Downright unfriendly if you ask me.'

She recalled Kent's black glare. Ooh, yes, she'd agree. Not that she had any intention of saying so, of course.

'Though a body can understand it, what with all that tragedy in his past and all.'

'Tragedy?' The word slipped out before she could help it.

'Aye. His father tried to murder the entire family in their beds as they slept. Set fire to the house in the wee hours of the morning. Kent was the only one that got out. It claimed his mother and sister, his father too.'

Josie's jaw dropped. The room spun. She gripped the counter top for support. 'That's…that's one of the most awful things I've ever heard.'

'Aye. The father was a violent man, from all accounts.'

What accounts?

'You wanna hear the worst of it?'

No, she didn't. She'd heard enough. But she couldn't move to shake her head. She'd frozen to a block of ice.

'Kent had taken the mother and sister to live with him, to protect them. Didn't work out, though, did it?'

Bile rose in Josie's throat. No wonder Kent scowled and growled and hid away as he did. To lose his entire family in such an awful way.

She promptly forgave him every unfriendly scowl, each clipped word and all the times he'd turned away without so much as a backward glance. But was burying yourself away from the entire human race the answer? She remembered the way he'd tucked into her chocolate cake. She bet he was hungry for a whole lot more than flour and sugar.

Bridget opened her mouth to add what Josie imagined would be more lurid details, so she quickly peeled the lid off her container and held it out, hastily changing the subject. 'I was wondering if there'd be a market for any home-baked goodies around here at all?'

Bridget's nose quivered appreciatively. She reached in, seized a muffin and greedily devoured it. 'Mmm… We can see how they go, love.' She brushed crumbs off her fingers. 'You never know what'll happen once word gets around.' Her eyes narrowed. 'But if you're only here on holiday, what you doing cookin'?'

Josie gulped. She didn't want to be the latest object of Bridget's gossip. 'It's a hobby,' she lied. 'I wanted to try out some new recipes while I had the time, that's all.'

Bridget helped herself to another muffin. 'What are your other specialities?'

'What do you think would sell well?'

'Caramel slice, homemade shortbread, lemon meringue pie.'

She wondered if Bridget was merely reciting her own list of favourites.

'The church fête is on Sunday. We're always looking for goodies to sell. Why don't you make up a few batches of whatever you like and see how they go over?'

If Josie had ears like Molly they'd have immediately pricked forward. A church fête? This Sunday? That gave her something to do over the weekend. Time suddenly didn't hang quite so heavily about her. 'That sounds like fun.'

'Lizzie and me, we're manning our own stall. Would you like to join us, love?'

Would she what? 'It sounds lovely.'

'Have you ever made a Mars-bar slice? Give it a go,' she advised when Josie shook her head. 'It'll be a real winner.'

Josie's lips twitched as Bridget reached for a third muffin. From where she was standing, the feedback was already pretty positive. At this rate there wouldn't be any muffins left for the rest of Martin's Gully to sample.

That was OK. She'd bake more for Sunday.

But as she drove back to Eagle's Reach it wasn't church fêtes or muffin and slice recipes that wove through her mind, but the awful history Bridget had related about Kent. More than anything, she found herself wishing she could do something for him. Something more than chocolate cake.

CHAPTER FIVE

FRIDAY MORNING JOSIE drove into Gloucester, stocked up on supplies and bought a recipe book.

Friday afternoon she and Molly went for a big walk. Kent was right. The trails leading down to the river really were very pretty. Not that she had a chance to tell him. She didn't clap eyes on him.

Friday night she made toffee and rum balls.

Saturday morning she made muffins, caramel slice, a Mars-bar slice and cooked chocolate cake from scratch.

Saturday afternoon she found a tick at her waist.

She promptly sat, took a deep breath and tried to remember her first aid. She was an AIN, for heaven's sake, an Assistant in Nursing. She gulped, but her mind went blank. Her kind of nursing hadn't involved ticks. It had involved watching her father die.

She peeled back the waistband of her shorts and stared at the tick again. She must've picked it up on her walk yesterday. It wriggled. Ugh. She hastily folded the waistband back into place. What if there were more? What if she was covered in ticks?

The entire surface of her skin started to itch.

'Don't be ridiculous,' she said out loud. But panic and adrenaline surged through her. Did adrenaline do anything to ticks? She gulped. It probably turned them into super-ticks or something.

'Oh, get a grip.'

Molly whined and rested her head on Josie's lap. Josie stared down at the trusting brown eyes and stiffened. What if Molly had ticks too? How did you get ticks off a dog? She surged to her feet. She'd have to ask Kent.

Josie was proud of herself for not racing as fast as she could for Kent's back door and pounding on it with both fists. She made herself walk at an even pace, a quick even pace, and when she reached his door she raised her hand and knocked twice. A quick rat-tat.

His frown was the first thing she registered. She raised her hand before he could say something sharp and cutting. 'I just want to ask a quick question, that's all. It won't take long, I swear.'

'Well?' he snapped when she paused.

'What…what is the treatment for ticks?'

Kent stared at her for a moment. The dark blue eyes did strange things to her insides as they roamed across her face. With a smothered oath, he seized her elbow and pulled her inside.

'Where?' he demanded, letting her go and planting his hands on his hips.

'Please check Molly first. She's smaller than me and I hear ticks can do nasty things to dogs.' Awful, terrible things like paralysis and…and worse.

'They can do nasty things to humans too.'

When Josie folded her hands flat against her stomach and said nothing, he raised his eyes to the ceiling. 'Molly will be fine. I give her a monthly tablet.'

Josie sagged. Relief pounded through her. 'Thank heavens. I'd thought…' The rest of her words dried up in her throat as Kent continued to stare at her.

'Where is this tick?'

She had a sudden vision of his strong, tanned fingers on her flesh and her pulse started to pound. 'If you, umm, just tell me what I should do I'll take care of it. I don't mean to put you out or anything.'

She didn't think she wanted Kent touching her. She had a feeling it'd be a whole lot safer for her peace of mind if he didn't. His lips twitched as if he knew exactly what she was thinking, and Josie's heart hammered all the way into her throat and back again.

'What you need to do, Josie, is point to the tick.'

Her name rolled off his tongue, thick and sweet like golden syrup. It turned her insides thick and syrupy too.

The twitch of his lips became a kind of half-grin. 'Trust me.' He waggled his fingers. 'I'm a doctor.'

'Yeah, right.' The one thing she did trust was that he wholly enjoyed her discomfort. She remembered what Bridget had said the day before yesterday and surrendered with a sigh. 'Here.' She peeled back the waistband of her shorts to show him.

He crouched down beside her, his fingers gentle on her skin as he turned her towards the light. Then he leapt up, grabbed a jar of Vaseline from beneath the sink, crouched down beside her again and swiped a generous glob of the ointment across the tick's body.

'Vaseline?' Her voice was breathy. She wondered if he felt the leap of her blood against his fingertips. Oh, boy. She'd known there were areas of her life she'd neglected in the last few months, but this was ridiculous.

'Ticks breathe through their rear-ends. It can't breathe through the Vaseline, so it'll work its way out. Then I'll pick it off with these.' He held up a pair of tweezers. 'It means there's little chance of the head breaking off.'

She gulped. 'Good.' She didn't want the tick

leaving any of its body parts behind, thank you. She didn't want to know what would happen if it did either.

'Do you have any more?'

His words cut through a fog that seemed to have descended around her brain. 'More ticks?'

His lips twitched again. 'Yes.'

'Oh, umm.' She shrugged. 'I don't know.'

'Spin for me.'

She did. His finger trailed across the bare flesh of her waist as she turned, making her suck in a breath.

'All clear there, now sit.' He pushed her into a kitchen chair. 'Ticks, like most other living creatures, choose warm, protected places to live.'

'Uh-huh.' It was about as much as she could manage.

'Like behind the ears and at the nape of the neck.'

He brushed her hair to one side and it was all she could do not to melt against him as his fingers moved across said areas. Up this close his heat buffeted her. As did his hot man scent, a combination of wood and wood smoke and freshly cut grass. She wanted to breathe him in and never stop.

Crazy thought. Nerves skittered through her. 'Thank you for the tip about taking my muffins into the general store.' She knew she was about to start babbling, but she needed to distract herself somehow and babbling seemed relatively innocuous, given the alternatives racing through her mind.

'Did you meet Liz Perkins?'

She seized the question as a verbal lifeline and tried for all she was worth to erect some kind of metaphorical wall between them. 'Umm, no.'

The metaphorical-wall thing wasn't working. It did nothing to assuage the sensations that pounded through her when he swept her hair across the other side of her neck. She closed her eyes and bit back a groan.

'Liz wasn't there.' Concentrate, she ordered herself. 'I met her sister, Bridget.'

Kent's humph told her exactly what he thought of Bridget.

She didn't blame him. Not when she recalled how eager Bridget had been to impart her information. Guilt squirmed through her. She'd listened, hadn't she?

'I'm going to the church fête on Sunday,' she rushed on quickly. 'Tomorrow.' Sunday was tomorrow, she reminded herself. Though, with Kent standing this close, she wouldn't swear to it. She wouldn't swear which way was up.

His fingers stilled. 'Is that why you're cooking up a storm?'

'Uh-huh.' How'd he know she was cooking up a storm?

'The smells have been wafting up the hill,' he said as if she'd asked the question out loud. His fingers moved across her neck again. 'It smells good.'

'What's your favourite sweet treat?' If he told her she'd make it for him. As a thank-you, nothing more. She certainly wouldn't make the mistake of expecting him to share it or anything.

'Why?'

She winced at the sudden harsh note in his voice. 'No reason, just looking for inspiration,' she lied. 'Bridget asked me to make a Mars-bar slice.'

He finished checking her neck and she breathed a sigh of relief when he moved away, but only for a moment, as he almost immediately crouched down beside her to check the tick at her waist again.

'It needs a couple more minutes.'

He moved off abruptly to a chair opposite, and, contrarily, Josie missed the warmth of his hands, the touch of his breath against her flesh.

His eyes narrowed on her face. 'You feel OK? Any nausea or wooziness?'

'No.' Unbalanced by his touch, maybe, but she had a feeling that was not what he meant.

'So, Bridget has roped you into all that baking?'

'No.' She lifted her chin. Not everyone found her company abhorrent. 'She and Liz are manning a stall and I'm going to help.'

He gave a short laugh. 'She's an opportunist, that one. I'll give her that.'

'I wanted to do it.' But then she recalled how Bridget had said more muffins would go down a treat, not to mention a chocolate cake. And that if Josie had time, maybe she could come by early and help them set up the trestle table for the stall too.

She shook her head impatiently. It didn't matter. She wanted to help. It'd be fun. The knowing twist of his lips, though, irked her. 'Are you going?'

'Me? You're joking, right?'

'Why not?' She lifted her hands. 'This is a tiny community. You should support it.'

'By letting the Bridgets of the town get their claws into me? No, thank you very much. I've far better things to do on a Sunday than be hounded into helping set up stalls and manning the chocolate wheel.'

Like what? she wanted to ask. She didn't, though. She didn't dare. 'I think it'll be fun. It's not like you'd have to do anything. Just…'

'Just what?' he mocked.

'Just take part,' she snapped back.

Then wished she hadn't as everything she'd found out about Kent yesterday rose up inside her. Her stomach burned acid. 'You're right. Bridget is a terrible gossip. But it doesn't necessarily follow that she's a bad person. And not everyone in Martin's Gully is like that, surely?'

His eyes darkened and narrowed in on her in the space of a heartbeat.

Josie flushed and twisted her hands together. She knew precisely how guilty she looked. 'Bridget told me what happened to your mother and sister,' she blurted out.

Kent reared back as if her words had slapped him. His face paled. Dark red slashed his cheekbones. 'She had no right—'

'No, she didn't,' Josie hastily agreed. 'No right at all.' She wanted to reach out and touch him, but was too afraid to. 'I'm sorry. What happened to them…' She lifted her hands again. 'It must've been the most awful thing in the world.' His eyes glittered dangerously. 'I'm sorry,' she repeated. She wanted to say so much more but didn't have the words for it.

He stared at her as if he didn't know what to say. She didn't know what to say either.

His gaze dropped to her waist. 'That tick should be ready to come out now.'

Before she was aware of it, he'd tweezered it out.

'Thank you.' Her breath hitched at his nearness. She rose and took a hasty step back. 'Would you like me to bring you anything from the fête?'

'Like?'

'I don't know.' She had an awful feeling she was babbling again. 'Maybe you have a secret yearning for Mrs Elwood's tomato chutney or Mr Smith's home-produced honey?'

'There aren't any Mrs Elwoods in Martin's Gully.'

'Any Mr Smiths?'

'Several, but none of them are beekeepers.'

She edged towards his back door. 'So, no tomato chutney or honey, then?'

'No, thank you.'

'OK.' She practically fell down the back steps. 'Goodnight, then.'

'Josie.'

She turned back, her heart thumping.

'I...'

She held her breath, but she hardly knew what she was waiting for.

'You need to shower. You need to check under your arms and behind your knees. Anywhere a tick might get.'

'OK.' She waited but when he didn't add anything else she gave a tiny wave then fled.

Josie left early the next morning. Kent knew because he watched. His lips drew back from his teeth in a grimace. So Bridget Anderson had roped Josie into setting up the stall, huh?

He remembered the way Josie had hugged Molly that first day. He remembered the feel of her curves pressed against him as she'd slid out of that tree and down his body. He shook his head and called himself every kind of idiot he could think of. Josie Peterson could look after herself. She wasn't his responsibility.

'Go check the cattle,' he growled out loud. At least they were something he was responsible for.

Not that checking the cattle required much effort. More a case of checking the levels in the water troughs, checking the fences, making sure the steers hadn't picked up an injury or were showing signs of disease.

Checking the cattle took less than an hour.

He wondered how Josie was finding the fête. He bet her goodies sold fast. He bet Bridget Anderson had her stuck behind that stall all day. He bet she wouldn't even get a chance to buy a ticket in the chocolate wheel.

Josie would like the chocolate wheel.

For Pete's sake! 'Go clean the cabins.'

He grabbed the bucket of cleaning supplies and an ancient wooden broom. He averted his gaze as he stalked past Josie's cabin. His nostrils flared, though, and he imagined, if he took a deep enough breath, her fresh, fruity fragrance would fill his lungs.

He held his breath and tried to banish her from his mind.

By lunchtime he'd finished cleaning the cabins. Every surface gleamed with fresh-scrubbed cleanliness. Just as they had before he'd started.

He averted his gaze as he stalked past her cabin again, but he remembered the way her eyes had filled with a soft light when she'd told him how sorry she was about his mother and sister. He couldn't doubt her sincerity. He'd wanted to rage and stamp and throw things, but that soft light in her eyes had held him still.

Nobody in Martin's Gully, not even Liz Perkins, had dared mention his past. He hadn't encouraged them to. He hadn't confided in a single soul. But they all knew what had happened and they skirted around the subject, skirted around him. Not Josie, though. He couldn't help but admire her honesty, her guts.

Her generosity.

A generosity he didn't doubt Bridget Anderson was taking advantage of right now.

He stowed away the broom and bucket then glanced around the kitchen. Darn it! He jammed his hat on his head and grabbed his car keys. He had a sudden craving for tomato chutney and honey. He refused to acknowledge any more than that.

Kent spotted Josie straight away, sitting all by

herself at the far end of a row of trestle tables. Her hair gleamed, but her shoulders sagged. The rest of the town congregated on the opposite side of the field around a flatbed truck for the traditional auction. He bit back an oath, adjusted the brim of his hat and headed towards her.

Her eyes widened when he strode up. 'Kent! What are you doing here? I mean…' She glanced away then back again as if trying to moderate her surprise. 'I didn't think this was your thing.'

'I'm all out of tomato chutney and honey,' he muttered.

She smiled then, and it kicked him right in the gut. With a flourish, she waved her arm across the table. 'Can I tempt you with any of our goodies?'

Our? He recognised Liz's gramma pies and choko pickles, but he'd bet Josie had contributed the rest. 'How long have you been stuck behind there?'

Her smile slipped. 'It doesn't matter. I'm sure once the auction is over Bridget will be back and—'

'You haven't moved from there all morning, have you? You haven't even had a chance to look around yet?'

'There's still plenty of time.'

'Have you had lunch?' he barked.

She started to laugh. 'I'm being punished for

skipping breakfast. Smell that,' she ordered. She pulled in a big breath and he practically saw her start to salivate. 'They've set up a sausage sizzle behind the church hall and all I can smell is frying onions. It's pure torture.'

He could tell she was only joking, but a surge of anger shot through him. Bloody Bridget. 'Where's Liz?'

'Sick.'

Sick of her sister, he'd bet.

Josie's skin was pale and he could see it starting to turn pink in the sun. She'd erected a canopy to shelter the food, but not one for herself.

'C'mon.' He waved a hand, practically ordering her out from behind the trestle table.

'I can't leave.'

'Why not? Everyone else has.'

'But…but I told Bridget I'd man the fort and… then there's the money tin and—'

'Give it to me.'

'But…'

He reached over and took it, placing it firmly in the middle of the table. 'Now seems to me you've done your share. If Bridget wants the stall manned, she'll come back when she sees it's empty. Right then, see that weeping willow down by the river?' He pointed and she nodded. 'Grab us something,' he nodded at the table, 'and meet me down there.'

'I can't just take something.'

'Why not? You cooked it.'

She drew herself up. 'It's for charity!'

He laughed at the outrage plastered across her face. Josie Peterson made him feel light years younger. He fished out a twenty-dollar note from his pocket, held it out for her to see then put it into the money tin.

Her jaw dropped. 'That's too much.'

'It's for charity, isn't it?'

She stared then laughed, and it throbbed through him in all the places he shouldn't be thinking about.

'So, you're pretty hungry, huh?'

'Starved.' And it'd take a whole lot more than sugar to satisfy his cravings.

'The weeping willow?'

'The weeping willow,' he agreed.

With that he turned and headed straight across the field before he could pull Josie over the trestle table and kiss her.

When she reached the tree, Josie had to admit Kent had chosen a pretty spot for a picnic. The river slid by, silver and silent, meditative. It soothed the sore, bruised places inside her. She wondered if it did the same for Kent. Maybe that was why he chose to bury himself out here.

Settling on the grass beneath the tree, she welcomed the shade and the almost hypnotic sway of fronds in the breeze, and wondered about her unusual rescue. And her even more unusual rescuer.

Kent, carrying sausage sandwiches and cans of lemonade, appeared and Josie's hunger momentarily overrode her other concerns. 'Mmm.' She closed her eyes and savoured her first bite. 'This is fabulous.' When she opened them again she found Kent staring at her strangely. She suddenly remembered her manners. 'Thank you.'

'You're welcome.'

The faded blue of his chambray shirt highlighted the brilliant blue of his eyes. The snug fit of his jeans highlighted the firmness of his thighs. The sudden shortness of Josie's breath highlighted her heretofore unknown partiality for firm thigh muscles encased in faded denim.

'I, umm…' She dragged her gaze upwards. 'Thank you for rescuing me…again.' That seemed to be becoming a habit.

'Not a problem.'

Oh, dear. She obviously had a partiality for firm lips and chiselled jaws too. She dragged her gaze to the river and tried to recreate the peace it had invoked in her only moments ago. She ate the rest of her sausage sandwich in silence.

Three ducks, small, brown and dappled, paddled by; bellbirds started up on the other bank. She pulled in a breath and her tension eased out of her, but her awareness for the man opposite didn't.

'When I look at all this,' she motioned to the river, 'I can see why you live out here. It's beautiful.'

'Yep.' A pause. 'You can't imagine living out here yourself?'

'No.' And she couldn't. Too much of it frightened her, even as she admired the starkness of its beauty.

'A city girl at heart?'

She glanced at him sharply, but no scorn or censure marred the perfect blue of his eyes. 'No, not a city girl.' Though she could more easily imagine living in a city than at Eagle Reach. 'I live in a sleepy little town on the coast about three hours north from here.' Her whole frame lightened when she thought of it. 'It's beautiful. Especially at this time of year.' When summer merged into autumn, the days still warm but the nights cool.

'If it's so pretty there, what are you doing here?'

Good question. Sadness and a thread of something harsher—anger?—trickled through her. She quashed it. 'My father died. He'd suffered from dementia for a few years. I was his full-time carer. I needed to get away for a bit.'

But somewhere nice. Somewhere she could

close her eyes and breathe more freely. Not somewhere that scared her half out of her wits in one instant then stole her breath with its beauty the next. And she hadn't wanted to be shipped off for a whole month. A week would've done.

She gulped. She was an ungrateful wretch.

Kent reached out and covered her hand with his. 'That must've been hard.'

She nodded, her throat thickening with unshed tears at the kindness reflected in the deep blue of his eyes. She could see he understood her grief.

Dear heavens above, of course he did!

She gazed back out at the river, determined not to cry, but as the warmth of his hand stole through her her heart started to pound. She glanced up at him and her mouth went dry. Did he feel it too?

As if in answer, his hand tightened over hers. Exhilaration sped through her when his eyes narrowed on her lips, then desire—hot and hard and relentless. Three feet separated them and she wanted that gap closed, fast. Needed it. She couldn't remember craving a man's touch so intently. She wanted to lose herself in him and not come up for air.

Gripped by forces greater than common sense, Josie swayed towards him, lips parted. Time freeze-framed and lost all meaning, except in the way it sharpened all her senses. Every single muscle ached to meld itself against him. Her fingers, her palm, hungered to caress the dark shading at his jaw. She wanted to breathe in his hot male scent, she wanted to wrap her arms around his neck and slide her fingers through the crisp darkness of his hair.

Hunger flared in his eyes. Her own blood quickened in response. Then, with a tiny shake of his head, he removed his hand and sat back, his mouth a grim line as he stared out at the river. Disappointment flooded her, filling her mouth with the acrid taste of its bitterness.

Embarrassment quickly followed. 'I, umm… Dessert?'

She seized the bag of goodies like a lifeline. 'I didn't know what you felt like so I grabbed a couple of pieces of caramel slice, half a dozen oatmeal biscuits and a slice each of lemon meringue pie and chocolate cake.'

As she named each item she pulled the appropriate paper plate out of the bag and lined them up between them. His twenty dollars deserved a whole lot more than this, but she couldn't have carried anything else. 'I mean, you could've had carrot cake or muffins,' she babbled on, scrunching the plastic carrier bag into a tiny ball and squeezing it. 'But if you'd prefer something else then I'm sure…'

He reached across and halted her movements. The rest of her words dried up in her throat. Her stupid pulse fluttered in her throat.

'It wouldn't have been a good idea.'

She knew he wasn't talking about cake. He was talking about kissing her. She nodded, her throat tight. 'I know.'

He drew back. 'What do you want?' He motioned to the plates.

She seized the oatmeal biscuits, more for something to do, than because she was hungry. Her hunger had fled.

Her hunger for food, that was.

Stop thinking about it!

She flung a glance over her shoulder, searching for something, anything, and her jaw dropped at the size of the crowd milling in the field behind her. 'Where did they all come from?'

Kent glanced up then shrugged and stretched out on his side. 'I'd heard the fête took off in the afternoon. The folk of Gloucester have caught wind of it in the last few years.'

She glanced at him and tried not to notice how the lean angles of his body stretched out like an invitation. 'Why?'

'A couple of the local specialities have started making names for themselves,' he said, peeling plastic wrap from around the chocolate cake.

Her ears pricked up. 'Like?' She shuffled around on her knees to watch the crowd. Lots of people, lots of laughter—it loosened the knots inside her.

'You mean besides tomato chutney and honey?'

She glanced at him then laughed. So, scowling-don't-get-too-close-to-me Kent could crack a joke...and grin while he did it. She could grow to like this Kent. A lot. 'So, I was on the money with my guess, huh?'

'If you substitute the chutney for Liz's choko pickles then yes.'

His smile crinkled the lines around his eyes. Her stomach flip-flopped.

'They're famous and with some cause. Nothing beats a silverside and choko pickle sandwich.'

She filed that for future reference.

'Except maybe this!' His eyes bugged as he chewed chocolate cake. 'Jeez, Josie.' He stared at her, half in admiration, half in consternation. 'This is...'

'Good?'

'Better than good.'

'I told you I made a better one from scratch.'

He chuckled at the smug toss of her head and her stomach flip-flopped more.

'What else should I be on the look-out for?'

'Chloe Isaac's homemade soap. Popular opinion is divided between the granulated strawberry bar and the smooth lemon myrtle.'

'Ooh, yum. I'm getting both.' She pointed an accusing finger at him, but kept her eyes on the crowd. 'That's the sort of thing you should put in the cabins. People would love it.' She sent him a sly glance. 'What about the honey? Famous too?'

He polished off the rest of the cake with a grin. 'I'll introduce you to our local beekeeper, old Fraser Todd. He'll sell you a pot of honey fresh from the hive with a piece of the honeycomb still in it. You'll never taste anything like it,' he promised.

Her mouth watered. She pushed the plate of biscuits towards him. She'd better save her appetite. 'You think I need fattening up or something?'

'You were the one who said you were hungry. You've still a slice of lemon meringue pie and a couple of pieces of caramel slice to go yet.'

'I'll save them for later.' He nodded towards the stalls with their crowds clustered around them. 'Besides, I'd have thought you'd be eager to get us out amongst them, fighting for all the goodies before they're gone.'

She loved the way he said 'us'; it meant he intended to hang around for a bit. Her blood did a funny little dance through her veins, which she tried to ignore. She lifted a hand that encompassed the scene before her. 'I'm enjoying all this first.'

'Enjoying what?'

'Watching the people having fun, hearing them laugh. It's what I meant when I told Marty and Frank I wanted a break.'

Kent stilled, mid-munch. Carefully, he chewed and swallowed the rest of his biscuit. 'Don't you want to be a part of it?'

'Eventually.' She didn't take her eyes off the crowd, lapping it all up like a starving dog. 'But I'm happy to savour it all first. Ooh, an artist is setting up.'

'She's one of our best-kept secrets.'

Kent collected up the uneaten goodies and placed them back in the bag, then, with his face gentle, offered Josie his hand. 'C'mon, why don't I show you the cream of the town's offerings?'

Josie was more than happy to place her hand in Kent's tanned, capable one and be pulled to her feet, more than ready to become one with the laughing, happy crowd.

CHAPTER SIX

'YOU SHOULD BE ashamed of yourself,' Josie chided a couple of hours later, collapsing at a picnic table.

'Ashamed of myself?'

What the…? He'd made a sterling effort to play the sociable companion to Josie over the afternoon. What was more, he thought he'd succeeded.

Not that it'd been an effort. No effort at all. It had earned him more than one speculative glance from more than one local, though. Not that he cared. Their gossip couldn't touch him and Josie would be gone in three weeks, so it couldn't hurt her either.

Three weeks. And don't you forget it, he warned himself. He eased his long legs beneath the table to sit opposite her when he had a feeling what he should be doing was getting to his feet and running in the opposite direction.

Fast.

He couldn't. When Josie had made her remarkable declaration about what she really wanted from her holiday—her eyes hungry on the crowd, those peculiarly restful hands of hers folded against her knees and a tendril of weeping willow playing across her shoulder and catching in her hair—he'd gained a sudden insight into all she'd given up when she'd taken on the role of carer to her father.

She didn't need a holiday stuck halfway up a mountain. She needed people, she needed to feel connected again. She needed images of life and laughter to help mitigate the recent images of sickness and death. He understood that. And he cursed her brothers for not seeing it.

He couldn't help that she was stuck halfway up a mountain, but he had taken it upon himself to make sure she enjoyed the fête today. And that no one, including that witch Bridget Anderson, took advantage of her generosity. Now here she was, telling him he should be ashamed of himself? So much for gratitude.

'Why?' he demanded, irked more than he wanted to admit.

She spread her arms wide and he found himself wanting to walk straight into them. He scowled. 'What?'

'Look at the wealth of all this local produce.'

He reckoned she'd bought just about every example of it too. That made him grin. Her delight in the smallest of things had touched him. 'And?'

'With all this available at your fingertips, how could you possibly make such a sorry job on those cabins?'

'Sorry job!' His jaw dropped. He jabbed the air between them with a finger. 'I know Eagle Reach isn't exactly the Ritz, but—'

Her snort cut him short. 'You can say that again.'

'Look, you're not my usual grade of clientele.'

She leaned forward. 'I know you keep saying the cabins attract the tough, rugged outdoor types, but really...' She leaned back, arms outspread again.

He wished she'd stop doing that. 'What?' He lifted a hand. 'What?' The cabins were perfectly... adequate.

'Would it really be such an effort to make them a little more inviting?'

She had to be joking, right?

'Even rough, rugged outdoor types like something nice to come home to after all that hiking and fishing or whatever it is rough, rugged outdoor types do.'

'So...so you want me to put strawberry-scented soap in the bathrooms,' he spluttered, 'and...and frangipani-scented candles in the living rooms?' It'd make him a laughing stock.

'Maybe not the strawberry soap,' she allowed. 'That might not be a big hit with your tough types, but what about the mint and eucalyptus soap, huh? It'd add a bit of local colour and wouldn't threaten anyone's masculinity. What's wrong with that? It's a nice touch.'

She folded her arms and glared at him. He folded his arms and glared back.

'A couple of Mrs Gower's rag rugs wouldn't go astray either.'

Rugs!

'Not to mention a painting or two.'

OK, so the cabins were bare. He'd admit that much.

'And I know you're not a fruit and flowers kind of guy—'

It was his turn to snort. 'You can say that again.'

'But,' she persisted, 'a jar of Mr Todd's honey and Liz's choko pickles would be a friendly gesture. To the town as well as the guests.'

He wished he could ignore the way the gold flecks in her eyes flashed when she got all fired up, or the way her pretty little chin pointed at him, angling her lips in a way that made his mouth water.

Not good. He shouldn't be thinking about kissing her. He clenched his hands beneath the table to stop from reaching out and grabbing that pretty little chin in his fingers and slanting his lips over hers. Heck, that'd get the gossips' tongues wagging.

'You know what?'

'What?' The word growled out of him from between teeth that were likewise clenched. Fortunately, or unfortunately, his gruffness didn't so much as make her blink any more.

'I think you're afraid of making those cabins too home-like.'

He jerked back.

'I think you're afraid to make any place too much like home.'

Something started to thud painfully in his chest. He tried to throw her words off, but found he couldn't. 'All this because I like simple and plain?' he snapped.

Not so much as a blink. 'Either that or you're afraid of making them so nice that you'll have to share your mountain with all of the repeat business you'd get.'

The thudding eased to an ache at her teasing.

'You could be on to something, lass. Our Kent here doesn't like to share his solitude.'

Kent jumped up, pleasure lighting through him at the sight of Clancy Whitehall's dancing dark eyes and thatch of white hair. He helped the elderly man to a seat. 'Clancy, this is Josie Peterson. She's staying at Eagle Reach for a few weeks.'

'A pleasure. Clancy Whitehall.' He introduced himself before Kent had a chance. His dark eyes danced across Josie's face as he shook her hand. 'I have the dubious distinction of being Martin's Gully's oldest resident.'

Josie broke into one of those grins that hit Kent square in the gut. 'Pleased to meet you, Mr Whitehall.'

'Call me Clancy, please. Mr Whitehall was my father.'

Josie laughed, her eyes darting to Kent's to share her delight. Kent could've groaned out loud when Clancy followed the movement. The old man was as sharp as all get out and Kent didn't like the speculation suddenly rife in the older man's eyes. Or the smile that curved his lips.

'Have you lived in Martin's Gully all your life, Clancy?'

'Aye, lass.'

'I bet you've some stories you could tell.'

Kent could see Josie would love to hear each and every one of them.

'That I could.' Clancy's gaze darted from Josie to Kent and back again. 'How are you finding the hospitality at Eagle Reach?'

Josie's lips twitched and her eyes met Kent's again. 'Improving.'

Great. Wonderful. He knew exactly what Clancy would make of that.

As expected, Clancy raised a telling eyebrow and Kent found himself leaping to his feet. He didn't care what the gossips like Bridget Anderson thought, but he did care what Clancy thought. And he wanted Clancy to unthink it right now.

'Kent?'

Josie's breathy whisper brought him back. 'It's time I was going.' He pulled the brim of his hat down low on his forehead. 'I want to check on Liz before I head back.'

'I hear she's poorly. Give her my love.'

Kent nodded then strode off, though he didn't know whose gaze burned through him the hotter—Clancy's or Josie's.

Josie pulled her gaze from Kent's rigid, rapidly retreating back and smiled at Clancy.

Clancy's eyes were knowing. He nodded after Kent. 'He's a good lad.'

Good? Lad? More like maddening man. Not that that did justice to the clamour Kent created inside her either, but she nodded all the same. Kent obviously looked out for Clancy and she had to give him credit for that. In fact, it was right neighbourly of him. 'He saved me from a day of servitude behind one of the stalls.' That was right neighbourly too.

Clancy chuckled. 'Bridget Anderson got her claws into you, did she? She's a managing kind of woman, that one. Likes to run things. She should've gone into politics.'

Josie laughed at the idea, but it was perfect. She wondered if Clancy could come up with a vocation as appropriate for her?

'How are you enjoying your holiday at Eagle Reach?'

Her hesitation betrayed her. 'I… It's a bit lonely.' She shrugged. 'I mean, it is beautiful—the bush, the river, and I've never seen night skies quite like it.' She didn't want Clancy thinking she didn't appreciate it. 'I just… I don't think I'm cut out for so much solitude.'

'Aye.' Clancy nodded. 'Neither is Kent.'

She sat back so fast she nearly fell off her seat. 'Are you serious?'

His eyes twinkled for a moment then they sobered. 'Aye, lass.'

'But…' She floundered with the idea. 'He's so rugged and strong and…hard. He doesn't look as if it bothers him at all.' She frowned. 'In fact, he seems jealous of it, doesn't want anything encroaching on it.' Especially her.

'Ahh…'

But Clancy didn't add anything and Josie refused to pry. The older man's eyes did watch her closely though, speculation rife in their depths, and she suddenly realised why Kent had left so abruptly. It made her want to laugh. Then it didn't.

Clancy was the one person she'd met in Martin's Gully who cared about Kent. Their mutual respect, their friendship, had been evident from the first moment. She reached across the table and touched the older man's hand. 'I'm only here for three more weeks. Kent thinks I'm a lame duck. Believe me, he'll be glad to see the back of me.'

Clancy chuckled. 'That's what he wants you to think.' He patted her hand. 'Now, why don't you come visit an old man next time you're in town?'

'I'd love to.'

'That's my place there.'

He nodded to a neat weatherboard house across the road and Josie beamed. The next three weeks were starting to look brighter and brighter.

Josie tried to slow her heart rate as she raised her hand and knocked on Kent's back door. 'Hi,' she said when he appeared. She tried to grin but found her lips had gone as rubbery as her knees.

He eyed her for a moment. 'Hi.'

No scowl, not even a frown, just a wary caution. Relief slugged through her. She hoped she'd seen the last of the prickly, unfriendly Kent. She much preferred the laughing, teasing one.

He glanced behind her. 'Is everything OK?'

'Yes, of course; I…'

He'd forgotten. She wanted to stamp her feet. She wanted to slap him. She wanted to cry with irrational disappointment. She'd looked forward to this all day, and…and he'd forgotten.

She didn't stamp her feet. She didn't slap him. She didn't cry. She kept right on trying to smile. 'It's Monday.'

His eyes narrowed and travelled over her face as if searching for signs of sunstroke. 'That's right,' he said slowly, as if agreeing with a child.

Which didn't help her eradicate those childish impulses. She pulled in a breath and counted to three. 'You said you'd give me a chess lesson.'

He slapped a hand to his forehead and scowled. Josie took two steps back. 'Don't do that,' she hollered, keeping a tight rein on feet that itched to stamp and hands that burned to slap.

His scowl deepened. 'Do what?'

'Look like that, turn back into Mr Hyde.' Pride lifted her chin. 'I know you're not my nursemaid, I know you're not even my friend, but we can at least be civil to each other and enjoy a game of chess, can't we?'

'Sure we can.'

'We had a nice time yesterday.'

'Yep.'

She wished he'd show a bit more enthusiasm.

He shuffled his feet. 'So, no chocolate cake?' He smiled, but it didn't reach his eyes.

'Umm, no.' She'd hummed and hawed over that for ages. Then she'd remembered his reaction the last time she'd brought afternoon tea. 'Didn't you have enough of it yesterday?'

'Not on your life.'

This time the smile made it all the way to his eyes and Josie found herself breathing easier. 'Next Monday,' she promised.

He should've found a way to get out of this.

Josie stood there in a pair of white cargo shorts and a jade-green tank-top and she looked better than chocolate cake. She looked better than anything he'd seen in a long, long time. He had the distinct feeling the less time he spent in her company, though, the better. She made him want things he'd forced himself to forget. But as he stared down into her half-hopeful, half-fearful face, he couldn't turn her away. He'd promised.

'Why don't we sit out here?' He nodded to the seating on his veranda. He didn't want to sit in the kitchen, didn't want her scent clogging up his senses and wafting through his house so the first thing he smelt when he woke in the morning was her.

With a shrug she took a seat, stared out at him from her gold-flecked eyes then crossed her legs. Jeez! She couldn't be more than a hundred and sixty centimetres, tops, but she had legs that went on forever. He turned and stumbled back into the house, tossed a critical glance around the kitchen then scowled. The real reason he didn't want her in here was so he didn't have to hear any more about his lack of homeliness. That still stung.

'Smile,' she ordered when he reappeared with the chess set, dimpling herself.

He did his best to tutor his face into a bland mask. Yesterday he'd found it too easy to smile with Josie, too easy to laugh. It wasn't a habit he intended to cultivate. Women like Josie were best protected from men like him.

Chess lesson. They'd concentrate on the chess lesson. 'How well can you play?' He sighed when she stared at him blankly. 'How much do you know?'

'I know how the pieces move.'

It was a starting point.

Forty minutes later, Kent came to the conclusion that Josie was a terrible chess player. She seemed to have a constitutional aversion to seizing her opponent's pieces. Or, for that matter, giving up any of her own. He attacked. She retreated, trying to find a way to save every single pawn. She didn't understand the concept of sacrificing a piece for the greater good. She didn't have an attacking bone in her body.

Nice body, though.

Stop it. Focus on the chess. Don't go noticing… other stuff.

Problem was, he'd spent the entire chess lesson noticing other stuff. Noticing how still her hands were between plays. How small and shapely they were. Noticing how she caught her bottom lip between her teeth as she attempted to decipher the complexities of the game. Noticing how her skin had started to take on a golden glow after a week of being out in the sun.

Her tank-top outlined a shape that had his hands clenching into fists beneath the table. He'd deliberately angled his chair so he couldn't see her legs. He knew they were there, though. He bet she'd feel like silk. Warm silk. He wondered if he could ask her to wear something long-sleeved and shapeless next time. And a bag over her head.

Get a grip. He'd lost his marbles. Too much time in her company had addled his brain.

He shifted in his chair. Fat lot of good it'd do him anyway. It wouldn't matter how many layers she wore, they couldn't hide the unconscious grace of her hand movements. Even when he closed his eyes against the tug of her body, he could still smell her.

She didn't even chatter away at him, which was a darn shame because inane chatter always got on his nerves. And if she got on his nerves it might distract him from her more…from other things. But no, he wasn't to be given even that salve. She sat there, hands folded on the table, eyes intent on the game, perfectly relaxed, perfectly at ease. Perfectly happy to keep her mouth-watering lips curved in a smile without offering up so much as one inane remark.

With something midway between a sigh of frustration and a groan of relief, Kent moved his queen in front of her king. 'Checkmate.'

Very gently, Josie laid her oak-tree king on its side then looked at all her pieces lined up on Kent's side of the table. 'I may not know a great deal about chess, but you just smashed me, didn't you?'

'Yep.'

'I'm pretty terrible, aren't I?'

'Yep.' If he was lucky she might give it up as a bad joke. Especially if he didn't encourage her.

'I'll get better with practice.'

Damn.

She angled her cute little chin at him. Double damn.

She motioned to the chessboard. 'Do you want any help packing up?'

'No.'

'Well, thanks for the game.' She leapt up and, with a little wave, sauntered off. If Kent didn't know better he'd swear pique rather than relief needled through him. He opened his mouth to call something after her then snapped it shut.

Seizing the game board, he stomped inside, his shoulders as stiff and wooden as one of his chess pieces.

'Which way, Molly?'

Molly panted and pushed herself against Josie's legs when Josie paused at the juncture of the path, but didn't indicate which direction she'd prefer.

Josie pursed her lips. They'd explored downriver last week. So, should they cross the river or explore upstream? She lifted her face to the sun, revelling in its warmth, noted the shade on the other side of the river and promptly made her decision. 'Upriver today, Molly. What do you say?'

Molly's tail wagged harder, making Josie laugh. If anyone heard the way she spoke to the dog they'd think she was certifiable. She'd begun to look forward to her daily walks, though. They might have started out as a way to kill time, but she could feel her body reaping the benefits of regular exercise.

Since she'd been practically housebound for the last few months, it felt good to work her muscles and drag fresh, clean air into her lungs. She'd continue the walks when she got home too.

And she'd get a dog.

She and Molly walked for about ten minutes before the trees started to thin and the river widened and grew shallow, creating a natural ford. Boulders dotted the river and both banks. The splashing of water and the glint of sun off mini-rapids and the pleasant browns and reds of the river stone created a scene that charmed her.

Until she heard a deeper splash immediately up ahead behind another group of boulders.

She didn't like big noises. That kind of splash indicated an animal at least as big as Molly. Were there wild pigs out here? She didn't know and didn't want to find out. She started to back up. 'C'mon, Molly, time to…'

She didn't get to finish her sentence because Molly, with a bark, charged ahead. Oh, lord. Josie groaned and took off after her. What on earth would she say to Kent if anything happened to Molly?

No way was she skirting around the boulders as Molly had, though. Josie scrambled on top of them, hoping for a height advantage, readying herself to wave her arms and holler her lungs out in an effort to appear as big and scary as possible to whatever was below.

She wound up for her first holler when... 'Hello, Josie.'

Josie nearly fell into the river. 'Kent!'

Below her, Kent trod water in a natural pool formed by the boulders. Something midway between a scowl and a grimace darted across his face. Water glistened off his hair and his tanned, broad shoulders, and Josie's heart started to pound. She had a startlingly erotic image of licking those water droplets from his body, and the breath hitched in her throat. The water was clear, but the lower portion of his body was hidden by the shadow cast by the boulders.

Good thing!

When Josie didn't answer him Kent shaded his eyes and stared up at her. He must've noticed the colour in her cheeks, the way her eyes bugged, because a slow smile tilted one corner of his mouth. 'Earth to Josie.'

She started and rushed to cover her confusion. 'I, umm, heard a splash.'

'And you decided to investigate?'

'Umm, no.' She scrambled down from the boulder before she fell off. From the bank she couldn't see any part of Kent below the water line, but if she moved a little to her left and took a step forward—

Arghh! She hauled herself back and promptly sat on a rock, and tried to quell the outrageous impulses coursing through her. She wrapped her arms around her knees to stop them trembling. 'No, umm...'

She grasped around for her train of thought, found it, and started to breathe easier once again. 'It sounded like a big splash, so I was going to slink back the way I'd come.' She sent him an apologetic grimace. 'Afraid I'm not interested in bumping into a hippopotamus or polar bear or anything.'

His smile became a grin. 'Last time I checked, they didn't do real well in the Australian wild.'

His grin was infectious. 'You know what I mean.' She grinned back. 'A wild pig or something.'

'You're pretty safe around here, but up a tree is a seriously good option if you ever do come across one. OK?'

'OK.' She filed the information away.

'So how come you decided to investigate?'

'Molly took off up here.'

'And you figured it was safe?'

She wanted to slap a hand to her forehead. Of course it was safe. Molly was a bigger scaredy cat than Josie. She must've smelt Kent or something. She wouldn't have gone racing off into danger. Josie suddenly felt like the biggest idiot on the planet. 'Umm,' she moistened her lips, 'that's right.'

Kent threw his head back and laughed. 'Liar. You thought Molly needed protecting, didn't you?'

She hitched up her chin. 'What's wrong with that?

He shook his head and grinned. 'Josie, you're a hopeless case, you know that?'

But he said it so nicely she didn't care. 'This is a lovely spot.' She lifted her face to the sun and glanced around with half-closed eyes, took in the clothes tossed on a nearby rock—shirt, jeans... underpants. Her eyes widened. 'Are you skinny-dipping, Mr Black?'

'I most certainly am, Ms Peterson.'

Warmth and wistfulness squirmed through her in equal measure. She bet it was lovely, the cool silk of water flowing over you without impediment. The freedom of it. 'I've never skinny-dipped in my life.'

He smiled challengingly and waggled his eyebrows. 'Wanna try it?'

He should do that more. Smile. It softened the craggy lines of his face and made him look like a man she could—

Nonsense! Crazy thought. She smiled and settled back on her sun-warmed rock. 'No, thank you.' Her smile widened. 'Though I might take it up as a spectator sport.'

Ooh, yes, definitely some ogling potential here. Not that she needed to see more than his shoulders and arms. He had biceps that could hurl a girl's heart rate right off the chart.

'If you don't stop looking at me like that I'm going to pull you in here to cool off.'

He practically growled the words at her and their former teasing banter vanished, replaced by a hot and heavy awareness. Heat surged through her...and not just in her cheeks. For one heart-stopping moment she was tempted to keep ogling and see what happened.

Another crazy thought. If he pulled her in there with him neither one of them would cool off. She tried to school her face. 'Sorry.'

'I'm going to get out now.'

Her mouth watered. 'Uh-huh.'

'Would you like to turn around?'

Her lips twitched at the gentleness of the question. 'Why, Kent Black, are you embarrassed?'

'No.' He held her gaze. 'But I thought you might be.'

He started to rise and with a squawk she leapt off her rock and spun around, heart pounding. His chuckle made it that much harder to keep from turning around. She could imagine what she'd see.

All too vividly. She forced herself to take several paces upstream. Away from temptation. Or, at least, another couple of big rocks from it.

If only she was the kind of woman who could indulge in a holiday romance, in transitory affairs.

Her heart slapped against her ribcage. Her mind suddenly whirled. Well, why couldn't she? She was on holiday, wasn't she? She wanted to change her life, didn't she? Maybe that meant taking a few risks.

And if it meant seeing Kent naked…

She didn't think twice, she swung back to face him. Ooh…jockey shorts—navy blue—plastered to—

Oh, God! She couldn't drag her eyes away from the evidence of his arousal.

'What do you think you're doing?' Kent shouted at her, his eyes starting from his head.

She tried to stop her heart from thudding right out of her chest. Oh, dear lord. The man was beautiful. The air in front of her eyes shimmered with heat. He wanted her. That much was obvious. And exhilarating. It gave her the courage to hitch up her chin and meet his gaze. 'I've changed my mind.'

'About?'

'Seeing you naked.'

'You what?'

'So couldn't we take it from the top?' She took a step towards him. 'I'd love to try skinny-dipping.'

He stabbed a finger at her. He glared. 'You stay right where you are.'

His eyes darkened when she ignored him, when she moved in so close she could watch the pulse pounding at the base of his throat. She wanted to touch her tongue to it.

'You don't know what you're doing.' His voice rasped out of his throat. His chest rose and fell.

'I know exactly what I'm doing.' She reached out and placed her hand over his heart. He stiffened, but he didn't step back. His skin was cool and firm. The blood pounded beneath her palm, making her tremble.

'Think, Josie, think!' The words rapped out of him like stone on tin. 'You're not a holiday-fling kind of person. You couldn't stop it from meaning too much. I've met women like you before.'

Still…he didn't step away.

'You'd smother me, I'd fight for space,' his voice grew ragged, 'we'd argue, you'd cry.' He pulled in a breath. 'It'd get complicated and I don't do complicated.'

'Complicated? How?'

'You said you couldn't live out here and I can't live anywhere else.'

Can't or won't? But she let it pass. Beneath her hand his heart pounded hard and fast.

'Too complicated,' he repeated, but she noted the way his jaw clenched, the way his eyes flared with desire.

'On the contrary, it's remarkably simple.' She reached out and took his right hand, placed it between her breasts so he could feel her heart racing too. 'I want to touch you, and I want you to touch me.' The warmth of his hand pressed into her. She arched against it. Her lips parted. 'What's complicated about that?'

The words had barely left her when, with a wild oath, Kent swung an arm around her waist and his mouth crashed down on hers. His urgency, the hardness of his arousal against her stomach, fired her with an answering urgency, with a hunger she hadn't known she possessed, hadn't even known existed.

His tongue swept across her inner lips, enticed her to tangle her tongue with his, and turned everything topsy-turvy. The shoulders, the rock-hard body she clung to, though, stayed upright and held her fast, one hand at her hip, the other tangled in her hair, urging her closer.

He broke off to press hot kisses to her throat before claiming her mouth again. Their desire swept her along like a swollen current of the river, like gale-force winds that bent the tops of trees. She felt wild, free…cherished. She—

'No!'

Kent jerked back and glared. Through the haze of her desire she saw the torment in his eyes. His fingers bit into her shoulders and he shook her, but she had a feeling it was himself he wanted to shake. She made a move to reach out to him, to try and wipe away the pain that raked his face, but he dropped his hands and stepped back out of her reach.

'This is not going to happen,' he ground out.

Her arms felt bereft, cold. She gulped. Need lapped at her. 'Don't you want me?' she whispered. What had she done wrong?

A laugh scraped out of Kent's throat. He shoved his hands into opposite armpits and gripped for dear life. 'Don't play the ingénue. You can't be blind to the effect you have on men.'

The effect she had on…

What? Her? A smile suddenly zipped through her. Kent backed up as if he'd seen and recognised the glint in her eyes. He seized his jeans and shoved his legs into them bending over as he pulled on his boots.

'Nice butt,' she offered.

He glared, pushed his arms into his chambray shirt.

'Ditto for the shoulders.'

He growled but she couldn't make out what he said. It sounded like 'crazy thinking' and something about a mouse, which didn't make any sense at all.

He seized his hat, slapped it against his thigh and strode off without saying another word. Josie watched him until he disappeared into the trees then she dropped to her knees and buried her face in Molly's fur. 'He wants me,' she whispered. She couldn't temper the jubilation that rushed through her, didn't try to.

He wanted her. He just needed some time to get used to the idea. That was all.

CHAPTER SEVEN

JOSIE DIDN'T CLAP eyes on Kent again till Friday. Three whole days since that kiss by the river. And it wasn't for lack of trying. She'd kept her eyes peeled for sight of him, whilst her imagination played any number of fantasies through her mind. Lovely, provocative fantasies.

Three days. She'd tried to keep a lid on her impatience, reminded herself he needed time.

Then on Friday, when she pulled up in her car after visiting Clancy, she glanced up to find Kent striding towards her cabin. He wore an expression of such single-minded determination that her heart started to hammer. Oh, man, had he finally come to his senses? She leapt out of her car, her knees barely holding her up.

Then she saw the bucket and broom in his hands and her heart plummeted. He wasn't looking for her. He wasn't heading for her cabin, but the one next door. He had no intention of sweeping her up in his arms and kissing her senseless.

Across a distance of twenty feet or so, they stopped and stared at each other like adversaries in an old-fashioned gun draw, each waiting for the other to make a move.

She swallowed back her disappointment...and impatience...brought their kiss to the forefront of her mind and grinned. Kent could act as aloof and distant as he wanted. She knew better. And she had no intention of making things easy for him. She sent him a cheery wave. 'Hey, Kent. Want a coffee?'

He tipped his hat in answer and bolted.

Her mouth dropped open and, unbidden, tears blurred her vision as a shaft of pain skewered her to the spot. In that moment she saw with startling clarity what she'd refused to see before. Kent had been right. If she couldn't stop a kiss from meaning too much, how would she cope with making love with him? She sagged against the bonnet of her car. How could she walk away at the end of her holiday if they made love?

She wouldn't, that was what. And Kent knew it. She'd cling; he'd rebel. She'd cry; he'd hate himself. A shudder racked through her. Dear lord, what had she been thinking?

Quite obviously she hadn't been thinking at all. But no matter how many times she listed all the reasons why it was a bad idea to make love with

Kent, her wayward body went right on trying to imagine it anyway.

The last three days had created a gentle rhythm to Josie's days. She'd wake early, have her first cup of coffee on the veranda with Molly and the birds, then she'd bake up a batch of muffins and a cake, or some biscuits and a tart, and drive into Martin's Gully to the general store.

She'd met Liz on Monday, recovered from the worst of her flu, and had immediately warmed to the other woman. She understood why Kent held her in such high esteem. Liz Perkins had a kind heart and not a bad word for anybody. So, naturally, Josie, Liz and Bridget breakfasted together over muffins and a pot of tea.

Then it was home again to wash her pots and pans, tidy her cabin, and to read the day's paper. As soon as any disquieting thought popped into her head she'd quickly push it aside. She'd decided the question of what to do with the rest of her life could wait until the middle of next week. She'd have a go at sorting it all out then, but she'd resolved on at least two weeks of complete relaxation first.

Then it was back into Martin's Gully for lunch with Clancy, a habit she was hardly aware of forming, but one she enjoyed all the same. Once home again, she and Molly would go for their walk.

Most of the time, throughout the day, Josie could push thoughts of Kent from her mind. Mostly. Sure, it required the occasional concerted effort, but she managed it. The nights, though, were a different matter.

As soon as evening fell another woman seemed to inhabit her body. A reckless, wanton woman who wanted nothing more than to stride up to Kent's back door in something skimpy and seductive and demand entry. No number of craft projects, no amount of postcard writing could drive the ensuing images out of her mind.

When sleep finally claimed her, she tossed and turned and groaned until Molly's whine or bark woke her. Then she'd surge upright, erotic images branded on her brain, her skin fevered with need.

Molly took to sleeping on the floor rather than the foot of Josie's bed. Josie didn't blame her. She'd sleep on the floor too if she thought it'd help.

Saturday morning Josie woke with a cough and a pain behind her eyes. She ignored it and carried on as normal.

Sunday morning she dragged herself out of bed, pulled muffin ingredients off the shelves then remembered it was Sunday and she didn't need to bake today. She let Molly out, crawled back into bed and pulled the covers over her head. Today she'd hibernate.

* * *

Kent woke at two o'clock in the morning to whining and scratching outside his bedroom window. Then Molly set up a howl. 'For Pete's sake!' He threw back the covers, muttering imprecations under his breath as he lurched to the front door and flung it open. Who'd ever heard of a dog afraid of the dark? 'C'mon, then,' he grumbled.

Molly didn't try to bowl him over with ecstatic wriggling and licks the way she normally did. She barked at him then turned her head in the direction of the cabins.

In the direction of Josie's cabin.

It might be two o'clock in the morning and he might be fuzzy-headed, but Kent didn't need a second signal. He jumped through the door, realised he was stark naked, raced back inside to pull on jeans and a shirt, dragged on his trainers and slammed out of the house to race after Molly.

Fear surged through him. His heart grew so large it pressed against his lungs, making him battle for every breath. Let her be OK. Let her be OK. The words pounded through him with each step.

Her cabin was all lit up and he didn't hesitate to catch his breath. He didn't hesitate for anything. He pounded on her door then tried it. Locked. He peered through the window but the curtains obscured his view. He pounded on the door again.

'Josie!' He rattled the handle. If she didn't answer he'd break the damn thing down. 'Josie!'

His shout should've woken the dead. From inside he heard a groan then a soft shuffling... The door opened. He took one look at her face and pity, tenderness and concern punched him. She looked terrible. She looked worse than terrible.

She blinked and clutched the doorframe, rested her head against it. 'What can I do for you?'

He could hardly make out the words as they rasped from her throat. Didn't she realise this wasn't a social call? That it was two o'clock in the morning? Another rush of tenderness took him off guard. 'Sweetheart, I think you'll find you're not well.'

She swayed and he leapt forward, slid an arm around her waist and moved her back to sit on the end of the sofa bed. She felt small and frail beneath his hands, her skin clammy and hot. She was burning up.

'Might be why I don't feel too good,' she slurred.

She went to lie back down but he stopped her, so she leaned into him instead. Even sick she still smelt good enough to eat. 'I promise to let you go back to sleep, as soon as you've answered a couple of questions.' She gave no indication she'd heard him, so he placed a finger beneath her chin and lifted her face towards him. 'Josie?'

'I'm wearing my silly, skimpy pyjamas.' Her mouth turned down. 'I should get my robe.'

He had a feeling she felt too tired and sick to care about the robe, but he wished she hadn't drawn attention to her nightwear. He'd done his best not to notice. Her pyjamas consisted of pale pink short shorts and a singlet top covered in fluffy white sheep jumping fences.

Corny. Cute. And in other circumstances down-right sexy. He fought the bolt of need that shot through him. 'I promise to tease you about them when you're well again.' Her lips twitched into what he guessed was meant to be a smile. 'Now, tell me where it hurts most.'

'Chest,' she wheezed. 'It's hard to breathe.'

'Are you an asthmatic?'

She shook her head and leaned further into him until her head rested fully against his shoulder. Her face lifted towards his, her eyes closed.

'Josie.' He cupped her face and felt her glands. Swollen. 'I want you to open your mouth and stick out your tongue.'

She opened one eye then lifted one hand and waggled a finger at him. 'Trust me, right? I'm a doctor.'

He smiled. He couldn't help it. He couldn't be-lieve she'd try and crack a joke when she obviously felt so bad. He fought the urge to kiss her forehead. 'That's the one.'

If only she knew.

None the less, she did as he asked. He angled her face to the light. He could smell the infection on her breath but a quick look at her throat confirmed it.

She had a throat and chest infection. And a fever. She needed antibiotics. She needed to keep hydrated. And she needed sleep. He helped her back under the covers. 'When did you last eat?'

But she'd drifted down under cover of sleep and he knew he wouldn't get any more from her tonight. He poured a glass of water, noticed the remains of a barely touched bowl of soup and drew his own conclusions. He made her drink several mouthfuls of the water.

'Stay,' he ordered Molly, who lay on a rug at the base of the sofa bed. Rug? He shook the thought away then strode back up to the house, seized a jar of broad-spectrum antibiotics from his bag, the night lamp from beside his bed then headed straight back down to the cabin.

He made her take two tablets and another couple of sips of water before cooling her forehead with a cold cloth. Then he set the lamp up on the table, flicked off the overhead light and settled down to keep vigil.

* * *

Josie had that dream again. That lovely dream where Kent leaned over her, his face softened in concern, his hands gentle on her face and beautifully cool. This time the room was bathed in a gentle light rather than the harsh light above her head. She tried to smile at him, tried to say she thought him wonderful…and sexy, but her body felt mired in thick mud and she couldn't manage it.

Then a jag of coughing shook through her entire frame and each breath felt like broken glass and it took all her concentration to breathe through it. For a moment she swore a pair of strong arms lifted her and supported her, but then everything went black as a deeper sleep claimed her.

The next time Kent entered her dreams she wanted him to get right back out of them again. Why couldn't she dream what she wanted to dream? Why couldn't they be floating down a wide, slow river on a beautiful, cushion-strewn pontoon, or lying in a field of wild flowers with the sky blue above them, listening to the lazy hum of the bees?

Sure, he was still as sexy as ever with a smile made for sin, and he smelt better than any man had a right to, but he was also annoying. She didn't want to take tablets and drink water. Why wouldn't he stop making her? She couldn't avoid him, though. He wouldn't let her. His big hands and superior strength mocked her efforts to elude him.

The dream was all the more annoying because in it she was as weak as a kitten and her brain was too fuzzy to bring into play her self-defence tactics. By the time she remembered the right move, she found herself lying back down on the pillow with a gentle hand soothing her forehead and she couldn't remember what she'd wanted to fight against.

Dreams were like that.

Josie opened one eye, noticed the soft light pouring in at the windows and realised she'd slept later than she'd meant to or, at least, later than she normally did. She pulled a tentative breath into her lungs. Her chest still hurt, but the sharp, broken-glass pains had dulled to an ache. A definite improvement.

She pulled herself slowly upright, pushed her hair off her face then froze. Kent sat half-slumped in one of the hard chairs at the kitchen table, fast asleep. What was he doing here? Then she remembered fragments from her dreams and wondered if they'd been dreams at all. She frowned. She had the faintest recollection of opening her door to him at some stage last night.

Molly lumbered to her feet from her rug on the floor, stretched and yawned. When she saw

Josie she gave a joyful bark. Kent was on his feet in seconds. Josie had never seen anyone move so fast in her life. Certainly not like that, from sleep to wakefulness in an instant.

He was at her side in seconds, his hand at her forehead, his eyes intent on her face. 'How do you feel?'

'Crappy,' she groaned.

He broke out into a huge grin.

'I'm glad you find it amusing,' she grumbled, throwing back the covers and reaching for her robe.

The smile slid right off his face. 'What do you think you're doing?'

'Gotta make the muffins,' she wheezed. Liz would be expecting them.

'No, you're not.'

He seized her feet and lifted them straight back into bed, and Josie found herself too weak to fight him. In fact, she found it took most of her energy just to breathe. He tucked the covers around her and sat on the edge of the bed. Luckily, she didn't have the energy to pull him down to kiss her either. She gripped her hands tightly in her lap all the same, just in case she found a sudden second wind.

'You're not getting out of bed at all today.'

'But—'

'Doctor's orders.'

She snapped her mouth shut. Then she frowned. 'The doctor's been to see me?'

He hesitated then nodded. 'Yep.'

She didn't remember that at all. 'Could you…?' She twisted her hands together. She hated putting him out like this. 'Could you ring Liz and explain that—?'

'Already taken care of.'

It was? She glanced at the light filtering through the curtains. 'But it can't even be eight o'clock yet.'

'Twenty to,' he confirmed with a glance at his watch.

'Heavens! What time did you call her?' A spurt of indignation shuffled through her. What right did he have to take matters into his own hands?

Then she remembered he was only following the doctor's orders. 'I… Thank you.'

A frown drew his brows low over the brilliant blue of his eyes, tightening then deepening the groove that ran from his nose to the side of his mouth. Her chest, already clenched, clenched up more until she realised he hadn't directed the frown at her, but at the wall behind her. 'What day of the week do you think it is?'

An awful premonition shook her. 'Monday, of course.' Though she suddenly realised there was no 'of course' about it. If she couldn't recall a visit from the doctor, then…

'You've been quite sick, Josie.'

'What kind of sick?'

He folded his arms and glared in the direction of the sink. As long as he didn't glare at her she didn't mind.

'You have a chest infection.'

Uh-huh. 'What day is it?'

He rubbed a hand across the back of his neck then glanced at her through the lock of hair that fell forward on his forehead. 'Thursday.'

'Thursday!' She surged upright, found it hard to breathe again and subsided back against the pillows. How could she have lost three days just like that? Another thought spiked through her. She didn't jump up and wring her hands, although she wanted to. Her mouth went dry. 'Have you been looking after me all that time?'

He nodded and she wanted to cover her face with her hands and curl up into a ball. 'I'm sorry.'

'No big deal.'

No big deal. He was joking, right? It was a huge deal.

Had he seen her naked? The thought spiked through her and she wanted to die. 'Serves you right for that crack you made last week about not being my nursemaid,' she suddenly snapped. 'You shouldn't tempt fate like that.'

He blinked then grinned. 'You'rc going to be one of those grumbling, sniping, griping patients, huh?'

She covered her mouth with her hand. 'I'm sorry.'

'Nah, it serves me right.'

It did?

She shook her head. 'I know how much you hate being... I mean, I'm sorry I've been such a nuisance. I wouldn't have put you to so much trouble for the world.'

He reached out and clasped her hand, his eyes gentle. 'I'm quite sure you'd have much preferred to stay healthy.'

He leaned back with that grin and her mouth watered. She suddenly found it hard to breathe leaning back against the pillows too.

'So, as penance, I have to spend the next three days playing chess with the worst chess player in the history of man.'

Josie stared then laughed. It ended in a fit of coughing. Kent's arms came around her and held her steady until it finished. Finally she drew back, just far enough to stare up into his face, to take in the lean, tempting line of his lips. He needed a shave and she wondered how it'd feel to run her palm along the length of his jaw.

Kent released her and shot to his feet, shoved his hands in his pockets. 'Time for you to rest.'

Then she remembered the way he'd raced away from her that day by the river, and how he'd avoided her ever since.

How he didn't want her on his mountain.

'Is that how long I have to stay in bed?' Is that what the doctor had ordered? 'Three days?'

'At the very least.'

She couldn't continue being such a drain on him for another three days, but she found it hard to focus that thought as her eyes fought against the sleep that suddenly wanted to claim her. 'I can't possibly stay here.'

'Sure you can.'

No, she couldn't. But her eyes closed and she found she didn't have the strength to push the words past her throat.

Fabulous. Wonderful.

Kent dragged a hand down his face. It'd been hard enough dealing with a Josie who was out of it. Having to touch her, hold her, whilst he administered antibiotics and made her sip water. Having to steel himself against the desire that coursed through him when he sponged her down, when he changed the sheets. Whenever he darn well looked at her. Having to fight the urge to kiss her when, in her delirium, she told him she dreamed of making love with him.

He despised himself for his weakness, for not being able to view her as just another patient. His lips twisted. So much for maintaining a professional distance.

He dragged a hand down his face. A sleeping Josie had strained all his reserves of self-control and discipline, but a waking one was that much more potent again. He didn't know how he'd get through the next few days.

'What about your cows?' Josie asked the next time he moved to sit on the edge of her bed.

'Steers,' he corrected. He hadn't realised she was awake. He hadn't wanted to wake her either, but it was time she ate something. She eased herself up into a sitting position. He propped the pillows behind her.

'Who's looking after them?'

He suppressed a grin. He should've known it wouldn't take her long to get around to that. 'Smiley McDonald. A neighbour. We have an arrangement.'

She eyed him doubtfully. 'You do?'

'Yep.' He slid a tray holding a bowl of soup and a couple of slices of toast onto her lap.

'Which is?'

When she didn't pick up her spoon and start eating, he put the spoon into her hand. 'Smiley hangs his head over our boundary fence and checks on my cattle. If there's a problem he takes care of it, or calls the vet, or lets me know. I'm returning the favour next month when he attends his sister's wedding in Adelaide.'

'Oh.'

She started to eat and he moved to the hard chair by the table. When she finished he cleared the tray and returned with a glass of water and a pill. 'Antibiotics,' he said when she hesitated.

'Thank you.' She took it without a murmur. 'Thank you for lunch and thank you for taking such good care of me.'

She smiled and in that instant he swore it was all worthwhile. 'Not a problem.' He retreated to the sink, out of temptation's way. Or at least out of its reach for the moment.

'Yes, it is. You said it's three days before I can get back up.'

He swung around sharply, not liking the tone of her voice. 'You won't be able to do too much all at once.' He didn't want her overdoing it. 'You'll need to take it pretty easy for a couple of weeks.'

'But—'

'There are no buts. Not if you don't want a relapse.'

She huddled back against the pillows and bit her lip. He wanted to pull her into his arms and tell her it'd all be OK. She just needed to take it easy, that was all. He bet she wasn't used to taking it easy. He had a feeling that over the last few months she'd taken care of her father at the expense of her own health. He didn't like that thought. Why hadn't her brothers looked out for her? He straddled the chair and tried not to scowl. He'd make sure she took it easy.

'I can't trespass on your kindness for that long.'

'Sure you can.'

'It's not fair on you. You have your work and other responsibilities.'

No, he didn't. Not real responsibilities like making a sick person well again. He'd forgotten what that felt like…and he missed it. He shrugged the thought aside. He'd chosen his path. 'Lots of things aren't fair.' It wasn't fair she was stuck halfway up a mountain on a holiday she didn't even want.

'I'll have to go home.'

Her voice was flat, matter-of-fact, and the words jarred through him. He leapt out of his chair, but then didn't know what he meant to do. Concern spiked through him when the colour drained from her face.

He closed the distance in an instant and felt her forehead—cool and dry. Her fever hadn't returned. Relief flooded him. 'Josie, you're not strong enough to drive home just yet.'

She met his gaze then glanced down to where her fingers pleated the blanket. 'I know, but if you rang Marty and Frank then they could come collect me.'

Marty and Frank wouldn't look after her as well as he could. If they were such good brothers, why had they sent her out to this God-forsaken spot in the first place, huh? He didn't want to let Josie out of his sight until he was one hundred per cent sure she was well again.

'Will they be able to look after you?' he fired at her.

'Of course.'

'Properly?'

'Yes.' She laughed but he caught the strain behind it. 'I think it'd be for the best, don't you?'

Her soft words speared through him and he wanted to say no. But damn it. What could he offer her other than a rustic cabin, huh?

And a hard bed.

And tinned soup.

She hadn't wanted to stay when she was well, why would she want to stay now she was sick? She deserved all the comforts of home and she wouldn't get those even if he moved her up into the house. She should be taken care of and made a fuss of by her family and friends, the people who loved her. A circle that didn't include him.

His hands clenched. If that was what she wanted he'd make sure it happened. 'I'll do whatever you need me to,' he promised. 'Are you sure you wouldn't rather stay?'

She smiled but it didn't reach her eyes. 'You're not my nursemaid, remember?'

She didn't say it in a mean way to make him eat his words or anything, and that only made it worse. 'But—'

'We both know I'm someone you just got lumped with.'

'Not true.' He wished he'd been friendlier in the first week of her stay. He shifted awkwardly. 'You'll be missed.'

She raised an eyebrow and he found himself shrugging. 'Liz enjoys her morning cuppa with you. And I haven't seen Clancy looking so dapper in a long time.'

'Oh.' She gave a wan smile.

'And I was looking forward to thrashing you some more at chess.'

She sent him an even thinner, sadder excuse for a smile. 'I don't believe you.'

If he kissed her she'd believe him.

For Pete's sake! She's sick, you jerk.

On second thoughts, it was probably a good idea if she went home. A scowl scuffed through him, but he kept his face bland and pleasant. No, not pleasant. He couldn't do pleasant if his life depended on it. He could just about manage polite if he concentrated really hard.

He concentrated really hard then seized a notepad and pen and thrust them at her. 'If you write down their phone numbers I'll get on to it.'

He swung away to lean in the doorway and stare out at the view. He wanted to get out of the close confines of the cabin. Now. He needed to stride out beneath a big sky and breathe in fresh air.

When he swung back, he found Josie pale and trembling. He was at her side in the space of a heartbeat, but she refused to relinquish the notepad when he tried to take it. 'Rest,' he ordered, cursing himself for not keeping a closer eye on her. 'We'll deal with this later.'

She scribbled down the numbers, tore off the top page and handed it to him. 'I'll rest while you get on to this.'

She hunkered back down under the covers and turned her back to him. He didn't even try to keep the scowl from his face as he strode from the cabin.

He glanced down at the scrap of paper. She'd scrawled four phone numbers—home and business for Marty, home and business for Frank. He wanted to scrunch it up into a ball and throw it away. When she woke he could tell her she'd dreamt the whole incident, and that she was staying put until she was well again.

But he knew it wouldn't work. Josie wasn't delirious any more. She knew fact from fiction. She knew what she wanted.

She wanted to go home.

He slammed into the house. It seemed strangely grey after the touches of colour Josie had added to her cabin. His scowl deepened. Without giving himself time to think, he pulled the phone towards him and punched in the first number—Marty, business.

Ten minutes later he slammed the phone down. The sound echoed in the sudden silence.

Of all the miserable low-lifes! Once he'd discovered she wasn't sick enough for hospital, Marty Peterson had claimed he couldn't possibly collect Josie before Tuesday next week at the earliest.

Tuesday. That was five days away.

And he was dreadfully sorry for the inconvenience, but he'd make sure Mr Black was amply reimbursed for all the bother.

Bother! Kent snorted. Josie didn't need some jerk throwing money around. She needed family and friends and some wildly overdue pampering. What she didn't need was a miserable excuse for a brother who couldn't come and collect her because he had *very important work* to do.

Kent would give him very important work. If he ever clapped eyes on Marty Peterson he'd knock him flat on his back.

He punched in the business number for the second brother, Frank. They couldn't both be low-life scum. Josie was a sweetheart. At least one of her brothers had to share some of the same personality traits, surely?

A busy signal greeted him. He gripped the receiver so hard by rights it should've cracked. He slammed it down and swore once, loudly. What was the bet crappy brother number one was on the phone warning crappy brother number two?

He paced. These were the guys whose feelings Josie had wanted to protect by staying here and not complaining?

It took him forty-seven minutes to get through, but he had no intention of giving up. Finally a secretary answered and informed him *regretfully* that Mr Peterson was away on a business trip, and would he like to leave a message?

The kind of message he wanted to leave would've blistered her ears and peeled the paint clean off the kitchen wall. He reminded himself not to shoot the messenger. With a curt, 'No,' he hung up.

What the heck was he going to tell Josie?

He had vivid, satisfying visions of beating both men to a pulp. Immature, he admitted, but still satisfying. He rubbed the back of his neck, his mind working overtime. He could drive Josie home himself. A round trip would take the best part of a day. No drama. He could drive her car then hire another for the return journey. At least he'd know she'd arrived safely. Three hours there, a couple of hours to see her settled, then three hours back again.

But what would she be going home to? He couldn't count on her brothers with their *very important work* to look after her. And she had that sick neighbour. He couldn't count on Josie looking after herself properly if she thought somebody needed her.

Nope, he wasn't taking her home. He might only be able to offer her a rustic cabin, but he could make sure she got the care she needed. That at least was something he could do. He reached for the phone and made another two calls, both far more satisfying than the earlier two. He actually found himself smiling at the end of them.

CHAPTER EIGHT

JOSIE MUST'VE DOZED because when she next opened her eyes the sun had moved across the sky and the shadows outside her cabin were lengthening. She reached for her watch.

'Nearly four o'clock,' Kent said.

She couldn't believe how much she'd slept. A thought that slid right out of her head when she sat up and gazed at him. He sat sprawled at the table with one of her crossword books and he looked so good her mouth started to water. It was pointless all this wistful sighing and mouth-watering, but she couldn't seem to stop it.

The sooner she left the better. For both their sakes. She gulped and tried to make herself believe it. 'Did you—?'

'What's a five-letter word for food seasoning? The fourth letter is M.'

She tried to visualise the word. 'A food seasoning? No other letters yet?'

'I think four down is "astonish", so that would give us H as the second letter.'

'Something—H—something—M—something? I don't like it.' She held her hand out for the book. 'I bet you've made a mistake.'

He handed it to her then stretched out along the foot of her bed and looked so darn sexy her eyes crossed, making it impossible to decipher the puzzle in front of her.

'Well?' He yawned.

'I can't make it out.' Wasn't that the truth?

He yawned again and guilt speared through her. She wondered how much sleep he'd managed in the last few days. Not much in those hard chairs, she'd bet.

She wanted to curl into a ball again and hide. The hairs on her arms lifted and her skin prickled whenever she thought about it. She opened her mouth to ask when Marty and Frank would be here, and something a whole lot greyer than guilt shuffled through her at the thought of leaving.

'Thyme,' she suddenly blurted out. 'T-H-Y-M-E. A food seasoning.'

Kent beamed at her and some of the greyness lifted. She'd ask about Marty and Frank right after she and Kent finished the crossword. But once they'd finished it, Kent stood and stretched, glanced around the cabin and she knew he was surveying the changes she'd made.

'Do you like it?'

He didn't pretend to misunderstand her. 'What's not to like? You've totally transformed the place.'

She snorted. 'Nonsense.'

'You have,' he insisted. 'The atmosphere in here is completely different.' He glanced around again, his brow furrowed. ' I can't even figure out what it is you've done exactly.'

'I've done nothing more than thrown a rug on the floor, a tablecloth on the table, and hung something cheerful at the windows.'

'What about that?' He pointed.

She shrugged. 'I hung a picture. Hardly an earth-shattering change.'

'And those?'

'They're just some candles I bought. They're supposed to smell like chocolate when you burn them.'

He was silent for a moment. 'You know, you might be right. Maybe I should do something… more with these cabins.'

Her jaw dropped. She wanted to throw her arms around him.

Bad, bad idea. What she should really be doing was asking him if he'd spoken to Marty.

But she couldn't seem to push the words out and

in the end it was Kent who raised the subject first. 'Are you close to your brothers, Josie?'

'Why?' Her chin shot up, her back stiffened and she slammed the crossword book closed. 'What makes you ask?'

He raised his hands and backed up. 'No reason.'

She ordered herself to act less defensive, less… touchy.

'But they sent you out here to the back of beyond, didn't they?'

His voice was light, teasing, as if trying to put her at ease, and it roused all of her suspicions. 'Why, what did they say? You have spoken to them, haven't you?'

He shrugged. 'Only Marty so far.'

'And what—?'

'Knock, knock.'

Clancy stood in the doorway, an enormous bunch of flowers in one hand, an assortment of odds and ends in the other.

'How are you feeling, lass?' He placed the flowers in her arms.

'Oh, Clancy, they're beautiful.'

'Knew you'd like them. They're a bribe.'

'A bribe?'

'If you can't come to me for lunch then I'll just have to come to you.' His dark eyes twinkled. 'If you can fit me into your schedule, that is.'

She didn't even know if she'd be here for lunch tomorrow. She could be on her way home. 'Oh, Clancy, I...'

Kent shook his head wildly behind Clancy's back and Josie swallowed the rest of her words and pasted on a smile. 'Why, that sounds lovely.'

Clancy beamed his delight and guilt trickled through her. And regret. She'd miss him when she left.

She made a silent promise to have lunch with him tomorrow, although Marty and Frank wouldn't like the delay if they were here by then. Her insides shrank. In fact, they'd hate it. She steeled herself against tomorrow's inevitable argument and forced her attention back to Clancy. 'Though you're a little late for lunch today.'

'Oh, aye,' he agreed, setting up a folding table by her bed then taking her flowers and handing them to Kent. 'Make yourself useful, lad. Put those in water.' He disappeared back outside. Kent looked so charmingly nonplussed Josie had to laugh. The flowers did nothing to take the edge off his masculinity, though.

'I wanted to get in early and make it a date for the rest of the week before someone else snapped you up,' Clancy said, trundling back into the cabin with her camp chair and setting it by the folding table. 'Those others,' he nodded to the wooden chairs by her table, 'are too hard for old bones like mine.'

He set about brewing a large pot of tea, as at home in her cabin as if born there. Kent managed to distribute the flowers between a single vase and a couple of jugs. Their fresh, clean scent filled the cabin. 'Clancy, you don't need to bribe me to have lunch with you.'

'They're not for lunch, lass, but for this.' He held up a pack of dominoes. 'Been feeling kind of dull over the last couple of days. Need a game or two to liven me up.'

Nonsense. He wanted to liven her up, keep her from being bored. His kindness touched her. But even she couldn't deny the enjoyment that coloured his cheeks and enlivened his eyes as he poured cups of tea, sliced a Boston bun and set out the dominoes.

He lifted his eyebrow at Kent, who hovered near by. 'I'm perfectly capable of looking after the patient. Don't you have work or something to do?' He held out the plate of Boston bun. 'Take a slice and be off with you.'

Josie choked back a laugh. Kent grinned. 'I can take a hint.'

Clancy's white hair danced. 'Smart man.'

A part of Josie followed Kent right out the door, wanting to dog his footsteps as he left. A bigger part of her wanted to throw her arms around Clancy and thank him. Kent probably needed a break. The less of a strain she proved to be the better.

Clancy stayed for just over an hour and left with promises to return for lunch tomorrow. He even left his folding table and dominoes. She stared at them and gulped. She had to find out what arrangements Kent had made with her brothers.

As if her thoughts had conjured him up, Kent stuck his head around the door. 'Worn out?'

'I'm fine.' She pulled in a deep breath. 'Kent, what—?'

'That was kindly done.'

She blinked. 'Oh, you mean it was kind of Clancy to come and visit?' Her face cleared. 'Of course it was and—'

'I meant exactly what I said.'

He folded his arms and the material of his T-shirt strained across his shoulders and the muscles of his upper arms. A great sigh rose up through her.

'He has one living relative. A nephew in Scotland. He's lonely. Visiting you made him feel needed.'

Josie didn't know what to say. 'I…I enjoy his company,' she finally managed.

'Exactly.'

'That's not kind, it's human.'

Kent took a step back and frustration pulsed through her, though she couldn't have said why. 'Look, Kent, what—?'

'Hello?' Footsteps sounded outside on the veranda and Liz appeared in the doorway, basket in hand.

'Come in,' Josie urged when she hovered there, staring from one to the other.

'Are you sure? Am I interrupting anything?'

Josie snorted though she wasn't sure why she did that either. She was aware of Kent's narrow-eyed gaze, though. 'You're not interrupting and visitors are always welcome.' She refused to look at him.

Liz bustled in. 'To be honest with you, I needed to get away from Bridget for a bit. You know what I mean?'

Josie wasn't sure if she should nod or not, but it didn't matter. Liz, with a roll of her eyes, took Josie's agreement for granted. Josie blinked when Liz pulled out a casserole from her basket and popped it in the oven.

'I told Bridge I was eating out tonight. I hope you don't mind.'

Josie shook her head. 'Not at all.'

Liz settled herself in Clancy's camp chair. 'No

offence, Kent, but my Hungarian beef stew is a whole lot tastier than your tinned soup.'

Kent straddled one of the hard chairs. 'None taken.'

As the rich aroma of the casserole filled the air, Josie's mouth started to water. From the furtive glances Kent sent towards the oven, she guessed his did too.

'It'll be ready in thirty to forty minutes.' Liz edged her chair closer to the bed. 'Just long enough for us to have a cosy, girly chat.'

Kent shot to his feet. 'I'll, umm, go do some stuff.'

Josie couldn't mistake the wistful glance he directed towards them, though. She remembered Clancy's comment the day of the fête, about how Kent wasn't cut out for all this solitude. She wanted to ask him what stuff he had to do.

She wanted to ask him to stay.

Then she remembered she was a millstone around his neck. It wasn't company he pined for. At least, not hers. It'd be the food. And it smelt so good she didn't blame him.

'I'll be serving up in forty minutes, so if you don't want to miss out...'

Kent grinned and it did the strangest things to Josie's insides. A grin like that should come with warning bells and flashing lights so a person had the chance to look away before it bammed them right between the eyes. So they had a chance to maintain at least a scrap of balance.

'I'll be back.' He settled his hat on his head, touched the brim in a farewell salute and swaggered out.

Josie couldn't help but admire the view as he left.

Liz leaned forward and touched Josie's arm. Josie could see the strain on her face. 'This is going to sound awful, but your getting sick is a godsend to me. Don't take it the wrong way, love.' She patted Josie's hand. 'I'm sorry you're feeling poorly.'

Josie didn't doubt it.

'But it does give me an excuse to get out of the house.'

Josie sat up a little straighter. 'Is it really that bad?'

Liz nodded. 'Your having breakfast with us helped me cope with her. Deflected her attention from me for a bit. She makes me feel like an invalid.' She paused. 'I loved Ted and I miss him terribly, but just because he's no longer here doesn't mean I can't look after myself.'

'Of course not.'

'But you try telling Bridge that.'

Bridget was pretty overbearing. 'She means well.'

'Oh, I know that, love. If she didn't I'd have turfed her out on her ear by now. But coming to see you not only gives me a break from her, but also makes me feel useful again.' She hitched herself up. 'I'm not ready to be put out to pasture just yet.'

Josie's throat started to thicken.

'I finally have a reason to cook dinner again if you know what I mean.'

Josie knew exactly what she meant. For the first week after her father had died, she hadn't seen much point in cooking for one. She hadn't felt much like eating either.

'So if you don't mind, I'd like to stretch your illness out for at least a week. Then I'll have to think of something else because I honestly don't know what I'm going to do once you leave.'

Josie gulped. A lie of omission was still a lie, and she couldn't do it. 'Liz, I might be going home as soon as tomorrow. I asked Kent,' insisted more like, 'to call my brothers to come and collect me.'

Liz stiffened. 'Get him to call them back and say you've changed your mind. You don't really want to cut your holiday short, do you?'

'I… But…I can't keep being such a burden on Kent.'

'Nonsense. You're good for him.'

She was? How?

Before she could ask, Liz had rushed on. 'How are you a burden? The worst is past. Kent doesn't need to sit up with you all night now, and you'll be right as rain after a bit of bed rest. What does he have to do? I'll cook you dinner in the evening and,' she folded her arms, 'I know how much Clancy is looking forward to taking care of your lunch. He dropped by the store as pleased as punch about it.'

Josie bit her lip.

'All Kent has to do is make you a piece of toast in the mornings and pop his head around the door a couple of times a day to check if you need anything.'

When it was put like that…

'In fact, he'll be gaining from the arrangement because he can have his dinner with us instead of cooking it for himself.'

That was true.

'And I need you to help me figure out what I'm going to do about Bridge.' Liz leaned across and clasped Josie's hand. 'Please?'

A great yearning opened up inside her. 'Well… if it's OK with Kent.'

Liz sat back and beamed. 'It'll be OK with Kent.'

'What'll be OK with me?' Kent said, sauntering into the cabin and pulling off his hat.

'If Josie changes her mind and stays on here after all.'

He swung around. 'Have you changed your mind?'

She nodded, unable for the moment to speak. But she kept her gaze on his face. She couldn't have watched him any closer if she'd put him under a microscope, but no scowls, not even a fraction of a frown, appeared. His eyes didn't narrow, his shoulders didn't freeze into place and his mouth didn't tighten. In fact, he literally beamed at her.

'It's more than OK. It's great.'

It was?

'That is smelling seriously good.' He nodded towards the oven. 'How long—?'

'Long enough for you to go ring Josie's brothers and tell them she's staying on after all.'

'No problem.'

With a nod and a grin he left, and Josie found she couldn't work Kent Black out at all. 'The tennis club,' she said, dragging her attention back to Liz. At least Liz made sense. 'Bridget needs something else to organise other than you. Does she like tennis?'

'Yes!' The word whistled out between Kent's teeth as he strode up to the house. He wanted to punch the air in victory. Josie was staying.

Not for good, he reminded himself. Just until the end of next week, but long enough for him to get her well and strong again. He wanted to celebrate. He pulled open the fridge and seized the neck of a bottle of chardonnay then remembered Josie couldn't drink while taking medication. He pushed it back in and pulled out several cans of lemonade instead. They'd celebrate properly when she was well.

Not him and Josie on their own, though. No. An image of candlelight and champagne and Josie in those cute little PJs of hers and—

He went tight and hard, his thickness straining against the denim of his jeans. He bit back an oath and tried to replace the image with a different one—he, Liz and Clancy holding a little party to send Josie off. That could be fun.

Not as fun as the first image, though.

He pulled his mind back, seized the phone and punched in Marty's business number. 'This is Kent Black,' he barked at the answering machine. 'Josie will be staying till the end of next week as planned.' Then he hung up.

He hadn't told Liz about his conversation with Marty, just that Josie had asked him to contact her brothers to come and collect her. The depth of Liz and Clancy's horror at the idea had surprised him. They'd done a sterling job at convincing her to stay, at convincing her she was needed. At convincing her she was no trouble at all. He'd never have managed that on his own.

And the way they'd marched into her cabin with its bright splashes of colour and its easy laughter, its comforting cosiness…all at ease and with that lazy kind of energy that spoke of goodwill and friendship, had made him realise everything his own life lacked. It gave him a glimpse of what life with a woman like Josie would be like.

Liz and Clancy would miss her when she left.

There was no denying it: so would he. But a man like him had no right messing with a woman like Josie.

He pushed that thought away and seized the lemonades. It was time to go and enjoy dinner with Josie. And Liz; he hadn't forgotten Liz.

When Liz left, Kent tidied up. He thought Josie had dozed off, but when he turned he found her watching him. He rolled his shoulders, shifted his weight from the balls of his feet to his heels and back again. He wondered if she sensed his reluctance to leave the cosiness of her cabin. 'Not tired?'

'I feel pleasantly lazy. I'm glad you wouldn't let me help clean up.'

Her honesty made him grin, put him at ease.

She readjusted a pillow at her back. 'Tell me about your sister.'

It took a moment for the words to hit him, and when they did they stabbed through him with a ferocity that took his breath. He took a step back and went to shout an unthinking 'No!' but clamped down on his lips until he'd brought the impulse under control. The night was cool but that didn't account for the coldness that rushed through him. 'Why?' The word sounded sharp in the silence of the cabin but Josie seemed oblivious to his reaction, to the difficulty he had breathing.

'Because I always wanted a sister.'

He thought of her brothers, took in her wistful expression, and understood why.

'What was her name? What things did she like to do?'

For Josie's sake he tried to think past the pain. 'Her name was Rebecca. I always called her Beck. Everyone else called her Becky.' His words came out short and halting as a picture of Beck's face turning to laugh at him in her sailing boat rose in his mind.

'I've always liked that name.' She shaded her eyes against the brightness of the overhead light. 'Would it be OK if we turned on the lamp?'

He switched on the lamp, turned off the overhead light and a warm glow suffused the room.

Josie patted the bed beside her, her lips curved in a soft smile he wanted to fall into. He sat in Clancy's camp chair instead. He couldn't trust himself any closer to her than that. Not when the dark beat at the windows, not when this room and this woman transported him away from his lonely mountain. If he was fanciful he'd say Josie's cabin was an Aladdin's cave where fairy tales came true.

Only he was too old to believe in fairy tales.

'Was Becky a girly girl or a tomboy?'

That made him laugh. 'In company butter wouldn't melt in her mouth. But when nobody was watching she'd try and out-rough and out-tumble me.'

Josie grinned. 'Did she succeed?'

'Not a chance.' He grinned too. 'She was two years younger and not much bigger than you.'

'What did she like to do?'

He told her about Beck's love of sailing, the job she'd had as a pathologist, her addiction to candied ginger, and about the time when she was fifteen and she'd dyed her hair such a deep purple they'd spent an entire Christmas calling her Miss Plum. And the more he talked the easier it became. Finally he stopped and he couldn't have said why, but he felt lighter.

'I envy you,' Josie sighed. 'Not losing Becky, of course. That's awful.'

Sadness swept through him, but the weight didn't press back down.

'But the relationship the two of you had… It was really lovely.'

He nodded. He'd been in danger of forgetting. He eyed Josie for a moment. 'It's not like that with you and your brothers?'

He waited for her to tense up, but she didn't. 'They're over ten years older than me. We didn't grow up together. They're the children of my father's first marriage.'

A wealth of meaning emerged from her words. Kent suddenly saw the picture clearly—along with what he suspected was Marty and Frank's resentment and jealousy of their younger half-sibling.

'Their lives have been harder than mine,' she added as if she read his mind. 'They grew up with their mother and she was a bitter woman, hard.'

'That's not your fault,' he pointed out gently.

'No, but I want to build whatever bridges with them that I can. I promised my father I'd try.' She fixed him with a look. 'What did Marty say when you spoke to him?'

'I left a message on his answering machine,' he hedged.

'Not tonight, but earlier when you spoke to him.'

He didn't want her upset, but he didn't want to lie to her either. He wanted her on her guard around this Marty and Frank. 'He said he was snowed under with work and would find it difficult to get away before next Tuesday.'

'Oh.'

At the look on her face he wanted to smash Marty all over again.

'They're always so busy,' she sighed. 'I think they hide behind their work.' She pleated the blanket between her fingers. 'I think they're afraid to love me.'

'What kind of nonsense is that?' he exploded.

She met his gaze head-on. 'I'd say it was your kind of nonsense, Kent.'

He shot to his feet, rubbed the back of his nape. 'It's getting late. It's time you got some rest.'

'Scaredy cat,' she murmured, but she settled back without demur as he pulled the covers up around her shoulders.

'Goodnight, Josie.'

'Goodnight, Kent.'

He hovered for a moment, wanting to kiss her forehead, but he pulled back at the last moment. Her taunt followed him all the way back to the house and plagued his sleep like a stray dog that fed on his dreams.

On Friday afternoon after Clancy left, Josie finally grew sick of staring at four walls. Actually, she'd grown sick of it yesterday, but today her inactivity really started to pall. This morning she'd argued with Kent about exchanging her pyjamas for real clothes, and lost. Pulling her wrap more firmly about her and tying it at her waist, Josie folded the camp chair, took it out to the veranda, unfolded it again and collapsed into it, breathing hard. She hated how the smallest thing wore her out.

She'd hated arguing with Kent too.

She cringed when she remembered the things she'd shouted at him. She'd called him a tyrant. And a voyeur. She still couldn't believe she'd said that.

He'd laughed at her, and she'd wanted to stamp her feet—a near impossible feat when confined to bed.

She doubted he even saw her as a woman now. She scowled. Oh, yes, he gave her friendly concern, teasingly derided her chess skills and praised the excellence of her crossword-solving skills.

She knew she was sinking low when she clung to praise about crosswords.

Somehow he'd purged his desire for her and she wanted to know how. Though maybe he hadn't had all that much to begin with. Her scowl deepened. She just wasn't his kind of woman, was she? That new sense of closeness that had developed between them since they'd talked about their siblings had disappeared too. In some imperceptible way Kent was withdrawing from her. And she didn't know how to stop him.

She made an impatient noise in the back of her throat. She hadn't come on this holiday to obsess about a man. If he wanted to withdraw that was his business. She'd come to formulate a plan for the rest of her life, remember? She was no closer to doing that than when she'd arrived.

And she only had a week left. Marty and Frank would be expecting an answer to that particular question at the end of all this. She could practically see their serious half-frowns, hear their foot-tapping impatience.

Oh, for heaven's sake! What business was it of theirs? It was not as if they had to financially support her or...

They were her brothers. She chided herself for her lack of charity. Of course they worried about her. And now that her father was gone she hoped they might forge closer ties.

She scowled again. She was all for promoting closer ties, but they needn't think they could bully her.

'Heck! Whose blood are you after?'

Josie started then drooled. Kent. She swiped a hand across her chin.

'Still imagining skinning me alive after our spat this morning?'

His grin told her he didn't harbour any hard feelings and she found herself smiling back at him. 'No, though I find myself cringing every time I remember calling you a voyeur.'

He eased himself down onto the single step, his grin widening. 'Nah, don't feel bad about that. You've got me pegged. I'm waiting with bated breath for those cute little shortie pyjamas to make a comeback. Those fluffy sheep did strange things to me.'

His teasing fired the blood through her veins, although she knew he didn't mean it. 'Funny things?' She tried to ignore the burn of desire. 'Like falling all over the place laughing, right?'

'More like getting me hot and bothered when I imagine peeling them off your body.'

Josie gulped and the blood pumped through her so hard and hot she thought her fever had returned. Kent jerked back as if he couldn't believe he'd uttered the words. And just like that the tension coiled around them.

With a muttered curse, he leapt up and strode several feet away. Josie expected him to plunge straight into the cover of the trees and keep walking. Without a backward glance. When he didn't, her eyes, greedy for the sight of him, memorised every hard, lean angle of his body.

He always wore jeans and either a T-shirt or a long-sleeved chambray shirt, and she couldn't decide which did him the greater justice. The jeans, whether low-slung, stretch or bootleg, did strange things to her pulse. They also left her in little doubt of his, uh, assets.

And she literally drooled at the sight of thin cotton stretched across his shoulders and arms in those fitted T-shirts. But the faded blue chambray intensified the blue of his eyes and caught her up in fantasies of making love with him on long, lazy summer afternoons.

Oh, who was she kidding? It didn't matter what he wore for her to get caught up in those kinds of fantasies.

He swung back to face her and she could see him trying to fight a scowl. 'Sorry.' The word snapped out of him. 'You'd better forget I said that.'

She didn't want to forget. She wanted—

'We already decided that wouldn't be sensible.'

Had they? When? 'I'm tired of sensible,' she muttered.

His eyes darkened, then he grinned. 'Either way, Josephine Peterson, you're not physically up for an athletic bout of lovemaking. Besides, it's against doctor's orders.'

She knew he was right. If a shower wore her out, then how on earth…?

Pictures rose in her mind. Pictures that didn't help. She tried to push them away, far far away where they couldn't torment her.

'So, in the meantime,' he took his seat on the step again, 'why don't you tell me why you were glaring at this glorious view as if you meant to do it physical harm?'

CHAPTER NINE

JOSIE'S LIPS TURNED down and her shoulders sagged.
Kent wanted to haul her into his lap, tuck her head
under his chin and wrap his arms around her slight
body until she stopped looking so glum.

Not a good idea.

He didn't do hugs. And he had no doubt that
if he hugged Josie she'd get the wrong idea. He
couldn't let that happen, couldn't let her rely on
him in the long term.

A scowl shrugged through him. He shouldn't let
her rely on him in the short term either.

If it wasn't for her darn brothers he wouldn't,
but she needed someone to look out for her. She'd
drawn the short straw in him, though maybe
Clancy and Liz made up for it.

'Did Marty say anything else when you spoke
to him? Has Frank called at all?'

Was she upset because of her brothers?

'Nope and nope.' He kept the snarl out of his
voice. Just.

Her lips turned down more. 'I mean,' he added quickly, 'he was concerned about your health, of course. Relieved when I told him you'd be OK.' Because then he wouldn't be dragged away from his *oh-so-important work*.

Not that he'd rung in the last couple of days to check on how she was doing. That knowledge hung in the silence between them. 'Why?'

She lifted one shoulder. 'No reason.'

'Are they why you looked fit to kill someone?' He understood that. In fact, he'd help her if she wanted.

'Oh, no.' She quickly shook her head and all the browns and russets and maples of her hair swished about her face before settling back around her shoulders. He wanted to reach out and touch it. He wanted to bury his face in it.

'But, you see, I haven't worked out what I'm going to do with the rest of my life yet and that's the reason for this holiday in the first place.'

The note of panic in her words hauled him back. He skewed around on the step to face her more fully. 'Let's back up a bit. Why can't you keep doing whatever it was you did before you came to Eagle Reach?' Had she been sacked or something?

She smiled, a sad smile that speared right through the centre of him. 'For the last two years

I looked after my father. That job doesn't exist any more.'

Bile rose in his throat. 'I'm sorry I—'

'It's not your fault.' She waved his apology away. 'My father had dementia and I didn't want to place him in a nursing home so I completed an Assistant in Nursing course. I don't regret it. I cherish the time I spent with him.'

'But you don't want to do that any more?'

'No, I don't want to do that any more.' A shadow passed across her face. 'No. No more.'

He understood. Watching someone die was the hardest thing in the world. Especially when it was someone you loved.

'What did you do, Kent? Before your sea change and you came out here?'

The question caught him off guard. He'd known she hadn't believed him when he'd said it before. He hadn't bothered trying to set her straight and now it reeked of deceit. He rubbed the back of his neck.

'Kent?'

'I was a doctor.' Dedicated to saving people's lives. He'd removed himself from society pretty quick-smart once he realised he had a greater talent for destruction, though.

If he had an ounce of decency in him he'd leave Josie alone too.

* * *

'You're a doctor?' Josie shot forward so quickly she'd have fallen out of her chair if Kent hadn't reached out and steadied her. His fingers wrapped around her arm, warm and vibrant. More than anything, she wanted to fall into him. He removed his hand before she could do anything so stupid.

His close-lipped silence spoke volumes. 'I was a GP.'

It shouldn't have made sense, but in a strange way it did. She wanted to cry. 'And why—?'

She gulped back her words at his glare.

'I found I was unsuited to the profession.'

She didn't believe that for a moment. She refused to risk another soul-crushing glare by saying so, though. 'So, the doctor's orders I've been following have been yours?'

'Yes.'

It explained his professional detachment.

A wave of dizziness shook her. He hadn't stopped practising because of his mother and sister, had he?

'You're free to consult a second opinion, of course. Dr Jenkins does house calls. If you want I'll ring him and—'

'No.' She stared at him, horrified. 'I trust your judgement.' The scowl left his face but not his eyes. 'You made Molly well again, didn't you?'

At her name, Molly lifted her head and thumped her tail. She'd hardly left Josie's side since she'd been let back in after the worst of her illness had passed.

'And she was in way worse shape than me.'

His lips twisted into the wryest of smiles. 'I hate to point this out to you, Josie, but Molly is just a dog.'

'Molly isn't *just* anything. She's lovely and you made her well again, like you're making me well again. I don't think you're unsuited to the profession at all.' But she didn't want him to start scowling again so she didn't pursue that line further. She collapsed against the back of her chair. 'Not that it's doing me much good.'

His eyebrows shot up and she laughed, realising what she'd just said. 'I meant inspiration-wise. It won't help me sort out what to do with the rest of my life.' Marty and Frank's faces rose in front of her and her quick surge of humour evaporated in a puff that berated her for her frivolity.

One week. She glanced out at the view spread before her and couldn't hold back a sigh. Her eyes drifted to the man seated on the step.

'What did you do before you took on the care of your father?'

'I was halfway through a teaching degree.' He raised an eyebrow but she shook her head. 'The thought of study doesn't fill me with a great deal of enthusiasm. Besides, I don't want to leave Buchanan's Point and there aren't many opportunities for teachers in the local area.' It'd take years before she was posted there.

'Why don't you want to leave?'

'It's home.' It was that simple. 'It's where I belong. And then there's the house. It's been in the family for generations. I couldn't just leave it.'

'Couldn't your brothers look after it?'

Marty and Frank again. The sky became a little greyer, although there wasn't a cloud in it. 'The house belonged to my mother. Her family have lived in it since it was built over a hundred years ago.' And she wasn't selling it.

Kent stared at her for a moment then grinned as if eminently satisfied with something. 'If you've a house, Josie, then at least you've a roof over your head.'

'I have a home,' she corrected, which was more than Kent could boast out here at Eagle Reach, for all his cows and cabins.

His eyes gentled. 'Tell me about it.'

She shrugged. Where to start? But as she imagined her home her lips curved into a smile. 'It's beautiful. It's called Geraldine's Gardens and it's the only house on the bluff and it looks out over the town and beach. A little path winds down to a private beach. It's only tiny, but it is lovely.'

He sat up straighter. 'And the house?'

'It's beautiful too. Federation style, return verandas, fancy fretwork.' All of which took an enormous amount of upkeep. 'It is a little large for one person,' she admitted, 'but…but who knows what'll happen down the track?' She hoped to fill it with a family of her own one day.

'Too big?' His eyes narrowed. 'How many bedrooms?'

She hesitated. 'Eight.'

'Eight!' Kent shot to his feet. 'I…'

'Yeah, it's big.' And it took a lot of cleaning, but it was worth it. And she wasn't selling.

'Josie?'

She pulled her thoughts back. 'Hmm?'

'Marty and Frank are OK about the house?'

'Oh, no, they want me to sell it. They think it's too much for me.'

Kent's eyebrows knitted together.

'But the house is like a family heirloom.' She smiled up at him. Instinctively, she knew he'd understand. 'I need to preserve it to pass on to the next generation.'

He brushed the backs of his fingers across her cheek. 'I envy you your home, Josephine Peterson.'

Her heart thumped like a mad thing. 'Then you

should come and visit some time. It's not like I don't have the room or anything. Next time you're passing through…' A pipedream, she knew. She also knew she was babbling.

He pulled his fingers back abruptly. 'Time you were back in bed.'

'But I'm not doing anything. I'm just sitting.'

Her argument died in her throat when he leaned down and picked her up. Her heart pounded so hard she swore there'd be bruises. 'I, umm…' Her tongue stuck to the roof of her mouth. She tried to unglue it. 'I can walk, you know?'

Not that she wanted to. She wanted to stay right here. She looped an arm around his shoulders, his broad, beautiful shoulders, and bit back a purr of pure pleasure.

His gaze met hers then flicked to her lips. She gulped. An insistent throb started up low, deep down in her abdomen. His lips opened and her breath stilled. Then he waggled those wicked eyebrows. 'I want you to conserve your energy. Doctor's orders.'

He made no move towards the door of the cabin, though. His hot male scent filled her nostrils, his hard body imprinted itself on hers and her heart continued to beat itself to a pulp.

'I, umm…' She wished she could speak properly. She gave a shaky laugh. 'I think I'd conserve a whole lot more energy if you put me down again.'

He grinned. 'Yeah?'

She loved his teasing. 'You do seriously wicked things to my pulse rate, Kent Black.'

He shook his head, mock serious. 'That's not good for conserving energy. You'll need to do something about that.'

Like what? All the images, ideas, suggestions flooding through her involved her expending a whole lot more energy, not conserving it. 'Doctor's orders, huh?'

'You bet.'

She trailed her fingers into the V of his shirt. Heat came off him in thick, drugging waves and she tugged gently at the hair there, revelling in its springiness, before tracing her hand back up his neck to his jaw. His breath caught when she ran her palm across the roughness of his half-day growth and hers quickened. The scrape of desire sparked from her palm to curl her toes.

His eyes turned a deep, dark navy. 'Josie.'

The single word growled out of his throat, but he made no move to set her down and a reckless triumph seized her. 'You know what?' She traced his lips with her fingers. 'I'm afraid of stray dogs and goannas and of the kind of solitude that means you don't clap eyes on another human being for three days straight, but I'm not afraid of this.'

She reached up and replaced her fingers with her lips. Kent's arms tightened around her and her whole body sang, but he held himself rigid, his lips refusing to respond as hers moved tentatively over his.

She'd never taken the initiative before. It part-appalled, part-thrilled her.

No, it wholly thrilled her. But Kent's lack of involvement sent a shock wave of frustration through her. Determination welled up, determination to draw out that response.

She traced the length of his bottom lip with her tongue, from left to right, slowly, savouring his taste and texture. 'Yum,' she murmured against the corner of his mouth when she reached it. Then she slipped her tongue inside to trace his inner lips, from right to left, and Kent jerked as if electrified.

Then he crushed her against him and his mouth devoured hers and she'd never known that so much feeling could go into a single kiss. She flung both her arms around his neck and kissed him back with everything inside her, a fury of need pulsing through her veins as his tongue teased and tangled with hers.

Both his arms went around her waist and the

lower half of her body slid down his until the tips of her toes touched the ground. Pulled flush against him, the most sensitive part of her pressed against the hard length straining through the denim of his jeans, teasing her until nothing made sense except her overwhelming need for him. With an inarticulate moan, her head dropped back and Josie lost herself in sensation.

Kent branded her neck with kisses. One hand curved around her bottom to keep her planted hard up against him, the other tangled in the hair at her nape to draw her mouth back to his. He claimed drugging kiss after drugging kiss until she was a trembling, sobbing mass of need.

Then a fit of coughing claimed her.

She leaned against him after it finished, trying to get her breath back, trying to draw strength into limbs that shook. His hands curved around her shoulders, steadying her, supporting her, but she sensed his withdrawal. Still…

What a kiss! She couldn't curb the exhilaration coursing through her body.

She wondered how soon they could do that again.

One look at Kent's face told her there'd be no repeat performances today. And from the look of that scowl, probably not tomorrow either.

Oh, well. It'd give her a chance to get her strength

back. With a sigh of regret she pushed away from him. 'Well,' she started brightly, 'that was…'

The words died in her throat for the second time when he swept her up in his arms and strode inside with her. Being held by Kent felt like coming home.

And she was homesick. Big time.

His face might be grim, but he laid her on the bed with a gentleness normally reserved for priceless artworks. She blinked furiously when he took a hasty step away, bit back a moan of loss.

He glared as she nestled down against the pillows. 'That was—'

'Heavenly,' she announced. 'When can we do it again?'

His jaw dropped then he swung away and stalked straight back out of the cabin.

'Kent Black,' she murmured, her eyes fluttering closed. 'You are one sexy man.'

She wondered if he'd ever stop running.

'Checkmate.'

Josie pushed the chessboard away with a sigh. 'I'm not improving.'

'You don't concentrate,' Kent chided.

How on earth was a girl supposed to concentrate when Kent's lips hovered just there across the chessboard and created all kinds of tempting fantasies inside her, huh?

Fantasies that were way more exciting than beating him at chess.

It was Sunday. Two whole days since their kiss. But for the past two days that kiss was all Josie could think about. She'd completed her three days of prescribed bed rest, but she could tell Kent didn't think her recovered enough for more kissing.

'What about catering?'

His words momentarily dragged her away from thoughts of kissing. 'Umm…' What had she missed?

'You could start up your own catering company.'

Oh, they were back to that. Still, it was better than nothing, she supposed. She'd expected him to bolt out of here as soon as he'd annihilated her at chess. As he had yesterday. As if afraid she'd try and kiss him again.

She wasn't going to kiss him again until she'd recovered her full strength. She had no intention of letting a little cough get in her way next time.

'I can't go into catering.' She'd already considered the idea and dismissed it.

'Why not?'

'Suzanna de Freits has the market cornered in

Buchanan's Point, not to mention the surrounding seaside villages of Crescent Beach and Diamond Head.'

'Afraid of a little competition?'

She grinned at the rallying note in his voice. He obviously thought she needed a pep talk. 'Her savouries are better than mine.'

'I bet her chocolate cake doesn't come close.'

Bless his heart. He actually looked as if he meant that. Thoughts of kissing rose up through her again. She shook her head. 'Suzanna is a single mother of three school-age children.' And a friend. 'She works hard. I'm not poaching her customers.'

'Not even to save your house…home?'

'People are more important than bricks and mortar.' Even when those bricks and mortar made up Geraldine's Gardens. 'I'd rather take on another dementia patient than do that.' Maybe it wouldn't be so bad if she wasn't nursing her father? Her stomach curdled at the thought all the same.

'Don't do that.'

She may not have any choice. Frustration shot through her. She should've spent the last two days searching for a solution to this particular problem rather than obsessing about kissing Kent.

'Ooh, humungous huntsman.' She shrank in her chair and pointed to the kitchen wall.

With an exaggerated sigh, Kent climbed to his

feet, rolled up yesterday's newspaper and advanced on the hapless spider. Josie scampered after him and snatched the paper out of his hands. 'What do you think you're doing?'

He stared at her. 'I'm going to squash it.'

Her eyes widened. 'But you're like a hundred million times bigger than it.' She whacked him on the arm with the rolled-up newspaper. 'It's only a spider.'

'You were the one that said—'

'I didn't say kill it!' She whacked him again. 'And just because I'm female doesn't mean I run yelling and screaming from a spider.'

'You do from dogs and goannas.'

'I'm going to pretend I didn't hear that.' She glared at him. 'Out of my way.'

Josie unrolled the newspaper, folded it in half then eased in under the spider's legs—slowly, slowly—until the spider sat on the end of the newspaper. Without taking her eyes off it, she walked across the room and outside.

She was halfway between her cabin and the nearest stand of trees when the spider rose up on all of its eight legs and raced the length of the newspaper towards her. She dropped the newspaper with a squeal and jumped back.

Kent laughed so hard from his vantage point

on the veranda he had to sit down. 'I didn't say I wanted it on me!'

She glared at him, but he only laughed harder. 'I've found your new career, Josie.'

'This should be good,' she muttered, but her lips started to twitch.

'Stand-up comedy.'

'Oh, ha-ha, very funny.' She rolled her eyes and collapsed onto the veranda beside him. Then glanced around warily. 'Where did it go?'

'Not scared of spiders, huh?'

She lifted her chin. 'Not scared enough to kill them.'

He grinned down at her, shook his head, went to turn away then swung back and kissed her, hard. Once.

Her eyes glazed over. When they finally cleared she could see him already regretting the impulsive act.

'Wow!' She swore she'd keep it light if it was the last thing she did. 'With that kind of positive reinforcement I'll never be afraid of spiders again. Though,' some imp made her add, 'I'll need another two or three sessions of that same therapy before I'm fully cured.'

His grin, when it came, was one of those long, slow, crooked ones that made her heart go boom. Desire slowly burned through her.

'You're impossible, you know that?'

She shrugged. 'If stand-up comedy is my thing then I'd best get in some practice.' But the stand-up comedy thing was just a joke. They both knew that. Her smile dipped as her original problem bore down on her again.

Kent nudged her shoulder. 'Earth to Josie.'

She shook herself. 'What are you up to for the next hour or so?'

His eyes narrowed. 'Why?'

She leaned back and raised an eyebrow. 'You know, that question just begs for a suggestive comeback.' She took pity on him when he dragged a hand down his face. 'I feel like making chocolate cake.'

She went to jump up but his hand on her arm stopped her. 'You're supposed to be taking it easy.'

'Don't worry.' She shot him a cheeky grin. 'You'll be the one doing all the hard work.'

Kent didn't know how Josie managed it, but she made baking a cake fun. He'd tried to tell himself he'd only hung around to prevent her from over-doing it, but that was a lie. He'd stayed because he couldn't stay away. In fact, if he could've eased her suffering and his own worry, Josie's illness was probably the highlight of the last year.

He cut that thought off, angry with himself.

But then Josie smiled and the tightness inside him eased. He enjoyed watching her deft hands measuring out ingredients. He enjoyed her teasing his ineptness with a wooden spoon. He enjoyed watching the colour bloom back into her cheeks.

Josie popped the cake in the oven then swiped a finger along the inside rim of the mixing bowl, gathering as much cake mix as she could, then popped the finger in her mouth and closed her eyes in bliss. He enjoyed that too.

'Yum.' As if aware of his gaze she opened her eyes and held out the wooden spoon for him. 'Go on,' she urged when he hesitated. 'I bet you and Becky fought over the wooden spoon when you were kids and your mum baked a cake.'

He jerked back, waiting for acid to fill his stomach at the mention of his family. It didn't come, so he reached for the spoon. 'She wasn't much of a one for baking cakes. Soup was her thing.' Big, rich pots of simmering goodness. In winter he'd rush home from school, his mouth watering with the knowledge of what awaited him when he got there.

He hadn't thought of that in a long time.

'Soup.' Josie stared at him in mock indignation. 'Your mum cooked the most scrumptious homemade soup ever, and don't tell me she didn't because I can tell from the expression on your face that she did. Yet you had the gall to feed me tinned stuff?'

He grinned, but he wished he had cooked her up a big pot of soup. 'To be honest, I didn't think you'd much notice…or care.'

'To be honest,' she leaned in close as if confiding a secret, 'you'd be right.'

He wanted to kiss her again, so he retreated to the table and set about licking the spoon clean. Josie had made this cabin the cosiest darn place on this side of the mountain. On second thoughts, probably the cosiest place on the whole mountain. He'd never set foot inside Smiley McDonald's house, but he'd bet Mrs Smiley McDonald didn't have the same knack Josie did. The knack of creating a home from nothing.

It'd started him thinking too. He could make improvements to all these cabins. The way Josie had done. And up at the house too. His mind fizzed with new possibilities.

Maybe she should go into interior decorating. He wondered if a person needed qualifications or whether they—

He jerked in his seat as the solution to Josie's problem slapped him on the head. 'How many bedrooms did you say you had at Geraldine's Gardens?'

'Eight.' She didn't turn from washing the dishes.

'And how many living areas?'

She tossed a glance over her shoulder then shrugged and went back to the dishes. 'There's the formal and informal lounge rooms, the family room, the sunroom, the breakfast room and the library. Oh, and there's a ballroom.'

How big was this place? 'Josie,' he tried to keep his tone measured, tried to keep the excitement out of his voice, 'why don't you turn Geraldine's Gardens into a bed and breakfast?'

She dropped the bowl she was washing and swung to face him. Soapsuds dripped to her bare toes. Her mouth formed a perfect O and Kent found himself wanting to kiss it.

Again.

Josie couldn't contain her excitement. She raced over to the table, plonked herself down and gripped his hands. 'Do you really think I could do that?'

'Sure you could.'

He squeezed her hands before gently detaching them and leaning back to survey her. She wanted to wriggle beneath his scrutiny, but she didn't. She stared back, held her breath and hoped he liked what he saw.

'I mean, look at what you've done with this place.'

She knew her grin must be ridiculously wide.

Kent had the kind of rugged good looks that could make her pulse perform a tango, but it was more than that. He possessed a kindness, a generosity, and, no matter how hard he tried to hide it, it always seemed to find a way to the surface.

She knew now what Clancy meant. Kent didn't suit this solitude any more than she did. Burying himself out here like this was a crime.

And none of your business, a voice intoned inside her.

Pooh. What did she care about that? She'd poke her nose in where it wasn't wanted if she thought it'd do any good. But it wouldn't. Kent wouldn't listen to her. He'd scowl and become a stranger and be glad to see the back of her.

'If you can manage all this here,' he continued, 'how much more could you achieve at Geraldine's Gardens?'

Excitement shifted through her.

'I bet there are plenty of local handicrafts in Buchanan's Point you could feature.'

She could theme the rooms. And she could get in tourist brochures for areas of local interest. Maybe even arrange the odd tour or two to the near by vineyards or the recreated colonial town less than an hour away.

'And you could showcase local produce.'

Ooh, yes. Suzanna made the most fabulous preserved fruit, and someone from the women's institute would be happy to provide her with pickles and jam.

Kent leaned forward. 'More to the point, you're great with people, Josie. You'd make a wonderful hostess.'

She found herself starting to choke up…then she sat back, her shoulders sagging. 'There are hundreds of little seaside towns all along the coast of New South Wales identical to Buchanan's Point. Not to mention the larger centres that offer nightlife and restaurants and attractions galore. How on earth do I compete with them? What can I offer except a stay in a lovely house?'

'You need a selling point.' Kent drummed his fingers against the table. 'How much did you hate the nursing aspects of looking after your father?'

She gazed at him blankly.

'I mean the bathing and feeding, making sure he took his medication et cetera?'

'Oh, I didn't mind that at all.' It was the watching him die that she'd hated.

'Then why don't you tailor your b & b for invalids and their carers? There's a rapidly expanding aged population in this country. There's a market out there, Josie, just waiting to be tapped into. Your qualifications are an added bonus, especially if you can offer the carers a couple of hours' free time for themselves each day.'

Her jaw dropped. There'd been days when she'd have killed for a couple of hours off. Not for anything special, just a haircut or to browse in the local library, or even just to sit over a cup of coffee she hadn't made herself. It would've helped. Marty and Frank had always been too busy to sit with their father much. And she wouldn't have dreamed of asking anyone else except in an emergency.

'Have you any savings?'

'Some. Why?'

'Because you'll need something to tide you over until the money starts coming in.'

Good point. She did a quick calculation in her head. If she was frugal she'd have enough for a few months.

'Advertising will be your major expense.'

Oops, she hadn't factored that in. She wondered if the bank would give her a loan.

'Let me invest in the project, Josie.'

Her jaw dropped.

'Don't worry, I'm not being altruistic.' His grin said otherwise. 'I have plenty of money stashed away, and I have a feeling I'll be seeing quite a return on that money.'

Did he really have that much faith in her? The blue of his eyes held such an earnest appeal Josie almost said yes. She dragged her eyes from his and forced herself to think the idea through.

Her heart sank. She tried to swallow the bile that rose in her throat. 'No,' she croaked.

He sat back as if she'd struck him. 'Why not?'

Because he'd made it clear he wasn't interested in any kind of personal commitment. If he invested in her project he'd be hovering in the background of her life for heaven only knew how long, kissing her then running away. She wouldn't be able to stop herself from building larger-scale fantasies around him.

She'd never move on.

She stared at the rugged, lean lines of his face and her mouth went dry. Some time over the last three weeks she'd gone and done the stupidest thing in the world. She'd fallen in love with Kent Black.

When? While he nursed her through the worst of her fever? Or earlier…when he rescued her from the goanna, perhaps, or the first time they'd played chess? Maybe it was the day of the church fête, or the time she'd caught him skinny-dipping down at the river or—

Enough already!

He'd never love her back. Panic pounded through her. She was afraid of dogs and goannas and ticks and spiders. She was even a bit afraid of

Bridget Anderson. He could never love a woman who was like that.

Numbness settled over the surface of her skin. Even if by some miracle he grew fond of her, she could never live out here with him in all his isolation. It went against everything she was.

And he would never give it up.

Stalemate.

Kent leaned across the table, took her chin in his hand and studied her face closely. 'You're pale. You need to rest. We'll talk about this later.'

Josie wanted to laugh, not because she found it funny but because her heart was breaking and Kent's concern over a mere chest infection seemed suddenly trivial.

Nevertheless, she made no murmur of protest, but climbed onto the sofa bed and buried her face in a pillow.

The minutes seemed like hours as she waited for Kent to finish washing the last of the dishes, to dry them then take the cake out of the oven when the timer rang. She could've groaned out loud when he started tidying the cabin. She sensed him hovering over her, but she refused to turn around, refused to unbury her face from the pillow.

Only when she heard him tiptoe out did she let the hot tears slide down her cheeks.

CHAPTER TEN

'WHY WON'T YOU let me invest in your b & b?'

It was Monday afternoon and Clancy had just left. Since yesterday, she and Kent had circled around each other very carefully—with the emphasis on the very. Super-polite. Extremely wary.

Josie didn't know how she'd get through the next week if things remained like this. She didn't know how she'd get through it if they didn't. The one thing she did know—she didn't want to have this conversation.

Kent straddled one of the hard chairs and folded his arms along its back. They bulged in his fitted T-shirt, each muscle clearly delineated in pale blue cotton. Josie curled herself into a corner of the sofa and tried not to drool. She might not want to have this conversation, but she didn't want to stop ogling him either.

That probably made her a female chauvinist pig. She cleared her throat and dragged her gaze away from his tempting arms, his tempting lips.

She doubted she could look at him and talk at the same time.

She hated confrontations. Wherever possible she avoided them. Kent's body language, though, told her she wasn't going to avoid this one. They could keep this pleasant and polite. She pulled in a breath. It didn't have to descend into an argument or a fight.

'Why are you refusing my money?'

'I really appreciate your offer, Kent, but I'm not going to risk your money when I don't know if I can pull this off.'

'You'll succeed. I know you will.'

His smile almost undid her. Of course they could keep this pleasant. They were adults, weren't they?

'If I invest in your project, I know I'll get a good return for my money.'

She couldn't let him go on thinking he could change her mind. 'What do you want with more money? It's not like you have anything to spend it on out here.'

His jaw dropped and she hated herself, but she ploughed on all the same. 'What kind of input would you expect to have at Geraldine's Gardens if you did invest, huh?'

'None. All the business decisions would be yours.'

He meant it too. She could see that. A lump

lodged in her throat and refused to budge. 'I don't want your charity,' she finally managed.

He leaned forward. 'Where will you get the money for the initial outlay, then?'

At least she could answer that. She'd lain awake last night pondering that exact same question. She forced her smile to widen. 'From Marty and Frank. This is just the kind of project designed to bring us closer.'

They were family. They'd help. This scheme was perfect. She crossed her fingers and prayed she was right, because she had a feeling she'd need their support when she returned home. In more ways than one.

Kent leapt up, his chair crashing to the floor. 'Marty and Frank!'

She hunched her shoulders up around her ears. What on earth…? They were supposed to be keeping this pleasant.

'Are you mad?'

No, but he was. Hopping mad. And she didn't get it. 'They're family. They're who I should turn to.' And if it all went to plan it'd be perfect.

Perfect except Kent wouldn't be in her life.

He wouldn't be in her life if he did invest in her b & b anyway, not in the way she wanted, so it was a moot point.

It didn't feel like a moot point.

'Do you seriously think they'll help you?'

He stared at her the same way she'd stared at that tick as it had burrowed into her flesh. Her chin shot up, though her shoulders stayed hunched. 'Why wouldn't they?'

They would. Of course they would.

'They sent you out here, didn't they?'

'Which just goes to show how thoughtful and—'

'Garbage. It just goes to show how little they know you.'

She hated the thread of truth that wove its way through his words. She resisted it. Her brothers had sent her on this holiday because they knew she'd needed it.

'For Pete's sake,' he glared at her, 'this is your idea of the holiday from hell.'

Had been—past tense. She'd come back. To visit Clancy and Liz. She wouldn't stay at Eagle Reach, though. She had a feeling she wouldn't be welcome. 'It's turned out all right,' she argued.

'You got sick!'

'That could've happened anywhere.'

He swung away, raked his hands through his hair then swung back. 'You can't trust them.'

She gaped at him. She couldn't believe he'd just said that, couldn't believe he'd try and dash all her hopes in one fell blow. They were the only hopes she had left.

She leapt up, trembling. 'You don't even know

my brothers. You've spoken to Marty on the phone for all of two minutes and...'

A horrible thought struck her. 'Unless you haven't told me everything. Is there something I should know?'

What on earth could Marty have said to make Kent react like this? Her mouth went dry. For one craven moment she wished she could call that question back.

Kent stared at her. He rolled his shoulders then shoved his hands in his pockets and glanced away. 'No.'

Her shoulders sagged until her thoughts caught up with her relief. *You can't trust them!* 'Then...' Her mouth worked but for a moment no sound would come out. 'Then you're basing your assumption on what you know of me. You think they'll take advantage of me, because I can't look after myself. You think I can be manipulated just like that.' She took two steps forward and clicked her fingers under his nose. 'You don't think I have a backbone.' Which was why he would never love her.

'You won't get any arguments from me on that score.'

She swallowed back her sudden nausea and wished she'd never seen herself through his eyes. Frustration rose up and engulfed her in a red mist. She'd give him backbone! 'Where on earth do you get off, lecturing me about backbone when you're the one who's burying himself out here in the back of beyond like some scared kid?'

The silence that echoed in the room after her hasty words made her take a step back. Oh, dear lord. She gulped. Then she hitched up her chin and held her ground. In for a penny… 'I don't care how responsible you think you are for your mother's and sister's deaths. You weren't.'

'Don't you…'

He didn't finish the sentence. He shoved a finger under her nose instead, but she batted it away. 'You weren't the one who lit the match and torched the house. You're doing penance for a crime that's not yours.'

His head snapped back. 'It was my job to keep them safe.'

But even as his eyes blazed their fury, Josie saw the desolation in their depths. She had to bite her lip to keep from crying out.

'I should've known what he'd do.' The words wrenched out of him, harsh and merciless.

Josie wanted to cry. And she wanted to drag his head down to her shoulder and hold him. Neither would help, so she gulped back the impulses and glared at him. 'Why?' she demanded. 'Why should you be gifted as a mind-reader when the rest of us aren't? Why should you have known what he'd do when neither your mother nor sister guessed either?'

He blinked.

'I know you'd have saved them if you could've. I know you'd swap places with them if you could. But you can't.'

The lines around his mouth tightened, stark in the tanned lines of his face, then that colour too seemed to leach away, leaving him grey. Her heart ached so hard her knees threatened to buckle.

'You blame yourself and hide out here because it's easier than risking all and learning how to live again.' Anger flashed in his eyes but, curiously, she wasn't afraid of it. 'So until you're prepared to rejoin the land of the living, Kent Black, don't lecture me about backbone.'

Then she had to sit.

His lip curled. 'You can do what you damn well please, but don't tell me how to live my life.'

The anger in his eyes chilled over with the iciness of his withdrawal and Josie hated it. 'What? That's a right you reserve for yourself, is it?' She wanted him angry again. 'Trust me, Josie, but don't trust your brothers?'

If possible, his eyes became colder. She gave a shaky laugh. 'You know as well as I do you should be out there being a doctor and saving what lives you can. It's what you want to do, what you were born to do.'

She watched him close himself up, become the stranger she'd met on her first day here at Eagle

Reach, and there wasn't anything she could do about it. She had no words left with which to reach him. Except childish words like 'Grow up', or 'Please love me'.

She couldn't tell him she loved him. He'd hate that worst of all. She glanced up and met his gaze. 'I'll accept your help for my b & b if you go back to being a doctor.'

The pulse at his jaw worked. 'No deal.'

Her heart slumped at his coldness. The last of her hope keeled over and died. She hadn't helped him at all. She'd just raked up painful memories and made him relive them.

He was right not to love her.

But before she could apologise, find some way to make amends, Kent spun around and stalked out of the cabin. Even though Josie recovered more of her strength every day, she knew she'd never keep up with him.

Molly whined and poked her head out from her hidey-hole behind the sofa. 'I screwed up, Molly,' Josie sighed. Molly crept out and rested her head on Josie's knee. 'Not only will he never love me, but he'll probably never speak to me again.'

So much for one final week of treasured memories. She had about as much hope of Kent kissing her again as she did of sprouting feathers and laying an egg.

* * *

Josie didn't see Kent for the rest of the day. Or the next. Or the day after that either. She and Molly took short forays down to the river, where Josie sat on the bank and lifted her face to the sun, but it never seemed to penetrate to the chill around her heart. She skimmed stones and prayed for a glimpse of Kent.

The stones sank. Kent stayed away.

She'd return in time to have lunch with Clancy. And a game of dominoes. She baked in the afternoons, or read. She did the crossword. Alone.

She ate dinner with Liz, and as soon as Liz left she climbed into bed and pulled the covers over her head.

Was this what the rest of her life entailed—missing Kent? She tried to harden herself to it. During the days it almost worked.

At night the pretence fell away.

She didn't notice the changing greens of the landscape any more, or the silver flash of the river. She didn't see the fat, ice-cream whiteness of the clouds in the bright blue of the sky. Each day dawned grey, no matter how hard the sun shone.

On Thursday she returned from her walk with Molly to find a note pinned to her door. She recognised Kent's strong, masculine scrawl and her stupid heart leapt. She snatched it up. Unfolded it.

'Jacob Pengilly rang. Asked if you'd return his call.'

That was it. No *Dear Josie*. No *Regards, Kent*. Nothing.

Her stupid heart kept leaping about in her chest though, because it knew that this was the perfect excuse to go and see him. Clutching the note, she set off towards his house. She didn't wait to pull in a breath before she knocked on his back screen door. She deliberately turned round to peer at the lush greenness of the forest beyond his back fence. Colour started to intrude itself on the periphery of her consciousness again.

She knew the exact moment he stood behind her because she could smell him. That unique combination of wood smoke and hot man. She closed her eyes and breathed him in before she turned. The screen door partially obscured him, thankfully. Her heart thump-thumped hard enough as it was.

'Hi.' She tried for a smile.

He didn't return her greeting.

She lifted the note. 'I got the message. Thank you.'

Still nothing. Not a word. Not even a flicker of recognition. Certainly no interest.

She blew a strand of hair out of her eyes. 'May I use your phone?'

She waited for him to tell her to go to blazes.

One…two…three fraught seconds went by. Just as she was about to give up and walk away, he pushed the screen door open. Josie, afraid he'd change his mind, squeezed past him in double-quick time then berated herself for not making more of it, for not slowing it down and relishing the brush of her breasts against his chest, her arm against his arm.

Kent, silent still, waved her towards the phone.

She made for it, stopped then spun back. 'Are you all right?' She marched back to peer up into his face. 'Are you sick or anything?'

'No, why?'

Because he was so darn silent, that was why. 'No reason.' She backed off towards the phone. It wasn't a good idea to get too close to Kent. Whenever she did she found she wanted to plaster herself against the hot lines of his body.

Could you imagine the look on his face if she did? If she'd had a sense of humour left she'd have laughed.

He continued to stare at her and she shrugged. 'I haven't seen you around for a few days. It suddenly occurred to me that you might've caught whatever I had.'

'Nope.'

'That's good.' She edged closer to the phone, but wondered what he'd do if he did get sick. How long would it be before someone found him? She wanted to ask if he had a plan in case that happened, but she knew if she did he really would tell her to go to blazes. So she didn't. She picked up the phone instead.

Then dropped the receiver back in the cradle. She'd so busily analysed the note for a clue to Kent she hadn't given a moment's thought to what it might mean.

More proof of an addled brain.

'Something wrong?'

'No.' She bit her lip and stared at the note. 'I just don't know why Jacob would call me.' Unless there was an emergency.

'Who is he?'

'A neighbour.' She shook her head. 'Actually he's my neighbour's son. The neighbour that fell ill, you remember?'

'I remember. You had to call her.' His lips lost some of their tightness. 'Once I got you out of the clothes-line.'

'He works in Brisbane now. Oh, I hope his mum is OK. I hope nothing has happened at Geraldine's Gardens. I hope…'

If there was an emergency Marty or Frank would ring her, surely. Unless the emergency was about Marty or Frank!

With a muttered oath, Kent strode over. 'There's only one way to find out.' He took the note and punched in the number scrawled along its base. 'Ask him.' He pushed the receiver into her hand.

His curt tone had the desired effect and, before she could go off into another disaster scenario,

Jacob had picked up the phone at the other end of the line. 'Hello?'

'Jacob, it's Josie Peterson. I got your message.' She abandoned pleasantries. 'Please tell me everyone is OK.'

'Sure they are. I didn't mean to worry you, Josie.'

She clutched her chest and sent Kent a smile. He shook his head, but his lips twitched. 'That's good news. Is your mum recovering?'

'Yes, she is. Look, Josie, I didn't know if I should call you or not, it's just…'

'Yes?'

'Marty and Frank have had a team of surveyors in at Geraldine's Gardens.'

She blinked. They had? She searched her mind for a plausible reason. Maybe there was some kind of mine subsidence in the area or… Her mind went blank.

'They've also had in a fancy property developer from the city.'

Her jaw dropped. She could feel Kent angle in on that straight away, so she hauled it back up. 'Uh-huh.' She couldn't manage much more for the moment.

'I don't know what they're up to, but I don't like it. I think you should come home and find out what's going on.'

So did she. 'I'll leave this afternoon.'

'Good.'

'Thanks for letting me know, Jacob.'

'It's the least I could do after everything you've done for Mum. If there's anything else we can do…'

'Thank you, but I'm sure it's nothing to worry about.'

Marty and Frank were her brothers. There'd be a perfectly logical explanation.

But then again…

You can't trust them. Kent's accusation pounded through her.

'Problem?'

After what he'd said about her and her brothers she had no intention of confiding in him. Not that he'd want her to, of course. 'Nothing I can't handle.' She pressed her hands tightly together. 'Though I'm afraid I have to cut my holiday short.'

'I heard.'

She swallowed. 'I guess it's only by three days.'

She wanted him to say something, anything. He shrugged and turned away. With a heart that flapped like a floundering fish, Josie stepped around him and left.

She was ready to leave in under two hours. That was, her bags were packed and she'd driven into Martin's Gully to say goodbye to Clancy and Liz. And Bridget. Bridget had been busy on tennis-club business but Liz had promised to pass on Josie's goodbyes.

They'd made her promise to ring and tell them she'd arrived home safely. They'd made her promise to return for a visit. Her heart ached, but she'd smiled brightly and promised on both counts.

Now all that was left was to take her bags out to the car, hand the cabin key back to Kent and hug Molly goodbye.

She didn't want to do any of those things. She wanted to unfold the sofa bed and dive beneath its covers. She didn't. If Jacob had spotted surveyors and property developers at Geraldine's Gardens then so had the rest of Buchanan's Point. And those who hadn't would've been filled in by those who had. Speculation would be rife. Not that she could blame them for that. Her own mind seethed with it too.

What on earth were Marty and Frank up to?

A property developer? She gulped. The townsfolk of Buchanan's Point wouldn't want their seaside village turned into the latest tourist destination, with all its associated high-rises and traffic. They were happy just to meet the passing trade from the nearby hotspots.

At least the deeds to Geraldine's Gardens were in her name, so Marty and Frank couldn't sell it out from under her. And they couldn't force her to sign anything against her will either.

Molly whined and pressed against her legs. Josie

dropped to her knees and buried her face in Molly's fur. 'At least you'll miss me,' she whispered. From the moment Josie had hauled out her suitcases, Molly had done her level best to get underfoot. Josie was grateful to her for it.

But she couldn't delay any longer. Not if she wanted to be home before dark.

Who cared about the dark?

Heaving a sigh, she pushed herself upright and shuffled over to her bags. She heaved them up then, dragging her feet, teetered to the door and dumped them outside. Kent jumped up from his seat at the end of the veranda.

How long had he been there? Josie gulped and gasped and coughed and found it near impossible to breathe. 'I, umm...'

He kind of half scowled, his nose curling up at one corner. He scuffed the toe of a work boot in a patch of dirt. 'Thought you might need a hand with your bags.'

Great. Was he escorting her off the premises? She bet he had his cleaning equipment out before her car reached the end of the driveway. She bet he couldn't wait to erase all evidence of her stay here. After her rant at him on Monday, she didn't much blame him. If she hadn't attacked him like some shrill fishwife then this goodbye scene might be a whole lot—

She slammed a halt to that thought.

Still, it didn't seem right for things to end like this.

'Thank you. I'd appreciate that.' She didn't smile. She couldn't. Not that it mattered. Kent didn't so much as glance at her as he seized both bags and strode off towards her car. Trademark Kent—no backward glances.

His lean denim-encased legs ate up the distance. She wished she could freeze-frame time and drink in her fill. Not just of him, but of Eagle Reach too. She wanted to feast her eyes on Eagle Reach, and Molly, but mostly on him. She wanted to feast her eyes on him, unimpeded, and fix him in her mind forever.

He's already there.

She spun away and stumbled back into the cabin, tripping over Molly in the process. 'Sorry, girl.' She patted Molly's head, drawing comfort from her warmth. She scanned the single room one final time. Her eyes stung. Resolutely ignoring them, she swung her handbag over her shoulder, shoved the key to the cabin in her pocket and picked up her box of groceries.

'C'mon, Molly.' She tried to do a Kent—no backward glances—but she couldn't quite manage it. She glanced longingly around the room once more before she shut the door behind her.

Kent's shadow fell across her as she turned away from the cabin. She stopped and stared at his chest and wished his physical body would follow, wrap around her completely. For one heart-stopping moment she thought it would, but he'd only moved in to take the box from her arms.

Swallowing, she headed for her car. He kept easy pace beside her. The scent of wood and smoke and man swirled around her. She wanted it to last forever.

It lasted until they reached her hatchback.

She didn't even try to avert her gaze when he bent down and placed the box on the back seat. He straightened and Molly started to bark and whine, circling around Josie's legs, pressing against them. It jolted her out of herself. Dropping to her knees, she hugged her, hard. Then drew back to scratch her ears. 'I'm going to miss you.' Molly licked her and tried to climb into her lap. Josie shot to her feet before she disgraced herself and began to cry.

Kent's eyes had darkened to that peculiar shade of navy. She could've groaned at the way it contrasted against the chambray of his shirt. She fished out the key from the pocket of her jeans and dropped it into his hand. 'Thank you.'

He stared at the key for a moment then his fingers closed round it, forming a fist. 'You're welcome.'

She held her breath and prayed he'd sweep her

up in his arms and kiss her until her blood sang. Hot, moist killer-kisses. She wasn't stupid enough to dream of a happy-ever-after. She just wanted a big, smoochy, full-body slam.

Wasn't going to happen. But her breath hitched at the thought all the same.

She jolted back to reality when he handed her a business card, his gaze not quite meeting hers. She glanced down at the line drawing of a quaint cottage on the front of the card overlaid with the name: The Station Café.

'"Drive. Revive. Survive."' He quoted a popular driver safety campaign and stared at a point above her head. 'You'll like this place. They do great cake and coffee. It's about halfway between here and Buchanan's Point. A good place to break your journey.'

She nodded and tried for a light, 'Doctor's orders, huh?' but it didn't quite come off. How glad would he be to see the back of her, huh?

His jaw tightened for a moment. 'Promise you'll stop. It's important not to overdo it.'

She tapped the card against her fingers and ordered herself not to cringe. 'I will. Thanks.'

So, this was it?

She dropped her handbag on the passenger seat and closed the door, wiped suddenly damp palms down the front of her jeans. There was still time for Kent to sweep her up…

He strode around the car and opened the driver's door for her and there was nothing for it but to follow him. Disappointment hit her so hard she felt she was wading through fast-drying concrete. Molly started up a long, mournful whine. Josie ducked into the car then got back out. 'This is horrible,' she blurted, motioning to Molly.

There was still time for a kiss. She'd settle for a solitary kiss with the car door between them. She'd—

'I'll look after her.'

Of course he would. She stared at the rigid set of his jaw and told herself to stop living in Cloud Cuckoo Land. It was just… 'I'm sorry we had a falling-out.' She reached up and kissed his cheek, breathed him in one last time. 'Goodbye, Kent.'

This time when she ducked into the car she didn't back out. He closed the door. She started the ignition. Without glancing at him, she wound down the window. He leaned in, brushed the backs of his fingers across her cheek. 'Have a safe journey, Josie.' Then he stepped away.

Josie gulped down the lump in her throat but another one replaced it. She nodded dumbly. When she set off down the drive, this time she didn't look back.

* * *

Kent ignored the kick in his stomach as Josie manoeuvred her car down the gravel drive. His chest gave an even bigger kick but he ignored that too. He did lift a hand, though, when she turned out of his driveway and onto the road, but she didn't wave back.

Or toot her horn.

Nothing.

Not that he deserved anything after the way he'd treated her since that ridiculous blow-up. Her sweet, fruity scent lingered around him. The touch of her lips still on his cheek. Bloody idiot to get up on his high horse like that and not come down until it was too damn late.

Too late for what?

Friends, he wanted to shout to the disbelieving voice in his head. They could've been friends.

What use did he have for friends?

He scowled. She was better off without him. And he was better off without her as a distraction. Tempting him with a life he'd promised never to return to.

He released Molly's collar and she bolted down to the end of the drive, but Josie's car had already disappeared. Molly whined then jumped up and down on the spot as if searching for one last glimpse of Josie. When that didn't work she turned and gazed at him, her head low, and he suddenly understood where the term 'hangdog' came from.

He understood exactly how she felt too. 'C'mon, Molly.' He patted his thigh but she ignored him and slunk off to Josie's cabin. He turned and headed back towards the house, then, with a bitten-off curse, swerved to followed her.

He found her laid across the doorway, head on paws and her big, liquid eyes downcast. 'She misses you too, Moll.'

Molly's tail didn't give even the tiniest of thumps. Kent had an unaccountable urge to lie down beside her.

Don't be such a bloody fool. He had cattle that needed attending to.

He didn't leave, though. He didn't lie down either. He pushed open Josie's door and stared at the room behind it.

The cabin was spotless. Its blankness reproached him. Not a scrap of litter, no accidentally abandoned socks, not even the newspaper. Nothing of Josie remained except the tang of her scent in the air.

Molly barrelled straight into the room and climbed up onto the sofa as if that would somehow connect her to Josie. He didn't have the heart to drag her off again. He sat down in the hard chair and pulled in great lungfuls of the sweet air.

CHAPTER ELEVEN

MARTY AND FRANK'S cars lined the circular drive when Josie finally turned in at the gates to Geraldine's Gardens. Her heart didn't lift at the sight of her home. The evening seemed grey, lacking colour, although light spilled from the house. As if expecting her, Marty and Frank burst out of the front door then came to startled halts.

At the same time.

Climbing out of her car, she felt herself moving through that quick-setting concrete again. Behind her a large van turned in at the drive, its headlights temporarily blinding her as it pulled in behind her hatchback.

Marty and Frank skulked on the veranda, shoulders slightly hunched. Neither came forward, so Josie found herself greeting the man who stepped down from the cabin of the truck. 'May I help you?' Her throat felt strangely dry.

'Ted O'Leary from O'Leary's Removals,' he said cheerfully, sticking out his hand.

Josie shook it. 'I think there's been some mistake.'

He consulted his clipboard. 'This Geraldine's Gardens?'

'It is.' She couldn't believe how normal her voice sounded.

'Then no mistake, miss. We have instructions from a Mr Marty Peterson to have the house cleared by morning.'

'With instructions to take it where?'

He checked his clipboard again. 'Into storage.'

Marty finally jogged down the steps to join them. He smiled brightly, but perspiration gleamed on his upper lip. 'It was going to be a surprise for you, Josie.'

His fake jovial tone had her bile rising. She swallowed it back. 'It's certainly that.' Again the calm, measured tone. 'I think you'd better tell Mr O'Leary you've wasted his time and that his services will not be required today.'

Without another word she turned and walked up the three tessellated-tile steps to the ornate wraparound veranda and started for the door. Frank stepped in front of her. 'There's no need to take on like this,' he blustered, though she noticed his hands shook. 'You need to at least hear—'

She stepped around him, ignoring the drone

of his voice. 'Tomorrow,' she said firmly, cutting across him. 'I'll speak to you both tomorrow.'

Then she closed the door in his startled face.

Molly refused to budge from Josie's cabin. Unless Kent wanted to physically pick her up, Molly was staying put.

He didn't want to physically pick her up. He didn't want to do much of anything.

Molly wouldn't touch her food either. Kent didn't have much of an appetite himself. In the end, neither one of them ate. In the end they both slept in Josie's cabin.

Kent pulled out the sofa bed, grabbed a blanket and he and Molly lay side by side...on Josie's bed. It wasn't even dark yet. He stared at the ceiling and wondered if she'd arrived home yet, if she'd got home safe.

Why hadn't he asked her to ring him?

Molly whined. He scratched her ears. The light behind the curtains had almost completely faded now, but there was still enough light for him to miss the colour Josie had created in here. And taken away with her when she left.

He wanted bright lengths of material draped at the windows. He wanted rag rugs on the floor. He wanted prints on the walls.

Tomorrow. He'd drive into Martin's Gully tomorrow and buy lengths of bright material at Liz's store. Maybe Liz would've heard from Josie. He'd order rag rugs from Thelma Gower; hopefully she'd have a couple to go. He'd stop by Rachel Stanton's studio and check out her water colours.

Then he'd lunch with Clancy. Josie would definitely have rung Clancy because Clancy would've made her promise to.

Kent scowled at the ceiling. Clancy was a smart man.

Josie opened the door. 'Heavens, that was quick. I'm really sorry to call you out like this, Steve.'

Having made it inside her house, Josie had found she was lucky to do so when she saw the shiny new locks in place. If she'd arrived when Marty and Frank weren't here she'd have been unable to get in.

'Not a problem, Josie.' He set his tools by the front door and sent her a shrewd glance. 'When it's a question of security and a woman at home alone then we locksmiths don't care what time of the day or night it is.'

She grinned. 'You guys take a professional vow in locksmith school or something? Like the doctors' Hippocratic oath?' She wished she hadn't said that, the doctor bit; it reminded her of Kent.

'You bet.' He glanced up. 'I'm glad you're home, Josie. The town's been worried.'

'I know. Jacob rang me.'

Steve wielded his screwdriver. 'Town took a vote and told him he had to.' He set about removing the lock.

That news didn't surprise her. Buchanan's Point was a close-knit community. Marty and Frank had never been a part of it. They were known as townies.

Steve was the only locksmith in Buchanan's Point. She'd gone to school with him. Had played spin the bottle in primary school. She could trust him. 'Did you change the locks at Marty and Frank's request?'

'Nope.'

Darn it. She wanted to know what excuse they'd given. She knew Steve would've asked for one. Which might be why they hadn't used him for the job.

'They hired a mate of mine from Diamond Head.' He winked. 'We went to locksmith school together. He told them I was closer and would be cheaper. But they insisted he do the job anyway. That made him suspicious, like, so he rang me.'

It made her suspicious too. She crouched down beside him. 'Did he find out why they wanted the locks changed?'

'The elder one, what's his name?'

'Marty.'

'He said he'd lost his spare key and rather than risk someone finding it and using it to break in, he thought he'd get the locks changed.'

She bit her lip again. 'He could be telling the truth.'

'Aye, he could be.'

But she could tell Steve didn't believe Marty's story. She didn't either. She jumped to her feet and started to pace. Kent had warned her about this.

She wondered if she rang him and told him he'd been right, if she apologised, if he'd hang up on her.

Josie glanced at the clock. One o'clock. She picked up the phone and hit redial.

'Mr Peterson's office.'

'Hi, Rita, it's Josie again.'

'I'm sorry, Josie.' Rita clicked her tongue in sympathy. 'He's still in a meeting with a client.'

'This is the fifth time I've called.' She'd rung on the hour, every hour, since nine o'clock this morning.

'I know. I'm sorry.'

She swallowed back her frustration. It wasn't Rita's fault Marty wouldn't return her calls.

'He swears he'll ring you tonight…or, at the very latest, tomorrow.'

Not satisfactory.

Josie didn't say that, though. She said, 'Thank you,' and rang off.

She drummed her fingers against the arm of her chair then picked up the phone and punched in a second number. 'I'm sorry,' a recorded voice started, 'this phone is temporarily out of range or—'

She hung up in disgust. She suspected Frank had turned his cell-phone off deliberately so she couldn't contact him. She massaged her temples. Perhaps if she'd slept better last night she'd feel more able to cope with this. But every time she'd closed her eyes Kent's image had risen up in front of her. Sleep had proven impossible.

She pleated the hem of her blouse with her fingers and wished Kent had asked her to ring him, as Clancy and Liz had done. A longing to hear his voice gripped her again. She'd lost count of the number of times she'd picked up the phone to call him and tell him she'd arrived safely, to tell him he'd been right about her brothers. At the last moment she'd chicken out. He'd have only given one of those derisive laughs and said, 'So what?'

In all fairness, he probably wouldn't, but she'd bet he'd want to. She didn't want that.

What she wanted was impossible.

Kent stepped back to admire his handiwork. Then swore. The material he'd twined around the curtain rods refused to hang in the same soft folds that Josie had created. He'd tossed a tablecloth across the table, he'd shoved flowers haphazardly in a vase and discovered the haphazard-flowers-in-a-vase-look required more skill than his fingers possessed. He'd scattered scatter cushions, he'd hung water colours, he'd thrown rag rugs across bare floorboards and yet it still wasn't working.

It didn't look cosy and inviting. It looked wrong.

Then he got mad. He shooed Molly off the sofa bed and folded it up with one hard shove. He shooed her right outside and slammed the door behind them. But Molly wouldn't budge further than the veranda. 'What's the point?' he shouted at her. 'She's gone.' And she wasn't coming back.

At least he knew she'd arrived home safely. She'd rung both Liz and Clancy. He scowled. And somewhere between yesterday and today the last trace of her fragrance had vanished. Gone. Just like that. He couldn't believe how much he missed it. That fact only fuelled his anger. He started to stride away then swung back to face his dog. 'And if you don't start eating again by tomorrow I'm taking you to the vet.'

At any mention of the vet, Molly usually bolted straight under the house. This time her ears didn't so much as twitch. With a snort of disgust, Kent strode off.

That evening, however, he carried Molly up to the house and tried to coax her to eat. She lapped at her water, a half-hearted effort, but she still refused to touch her food. At bedtime he carried her into his bedroom and laid her on her usual blanket. At least, it had been her usual blanket before Josie came to Eagle Reach.

Molly spent the night scratching at his door and howling. He wanted to join her. At midnight he relented and let her out. He wondered if a dog could die of a broken heart? Then he called himself an idiot.

By Saturday lunchtime he finally realised Molly was no longer his dog but Josie's. Josie and Molly had connected from the very first moment.

Almost the very first moment, he amended, grinning when he remembered Josie perched in his clothes-line.

With a strange sense of relief he packed an overnight case, made a quick call to Smiley McDonald then bundled Molly into his car and drove into Martin's Gully.

He leapt out at Liz's store. Clancy and Liz stood side by side at the cash register in close conference. Kent didn't waste any time. 'I'm heading for Josie's. Just wanted to let you two know.'

'Good.' Clancy pointed to a case on the floor. 'You can give me a lift.'

'Me too.' Liz hoisted her bag onto her shoulder.

He stared at them and his stomach clenched up so tight he found it hard to breathe. 'Why?' he barked. Had something happened? 'Is she OK?' He wanted to punch something.

'She's fine.' Liz walked around the counter and took his arm. 'We'll explain on the way.'

He didn't say anything more, just grabbed their cases and shot them in the back of his four-wheel-drive, his face grim as he waited for them to climb into the car.

Josie removed Mrs Pengilly's cup and saucer from the arm of her chair as the elderly woman's head began to nod. The doorbell sounded, twice in quick succession. She darted a glance at her guest then padded down the hallway in her bare feet. 'Shh.' She opened the door, finger to lips, then drew back and folded her arms.

Marty pointed a shaking finger at her, his face red. 'You…you had the locks changed.'

'Yes, I did. As neither of you,' she took in Frank with her glance, 'left me a spare key or would answer my calls yesterday, I had no choice.'

'No choice? Nonsense,' Frank snapped, pushing past her.

'I had errands to run. I can't leave a place like Geraldine's Gardens unlocked and unattended.'

'But...but...' Marty followed her down the hall.

'Yes?' She lifted an eyebrow, careful to keep a pleasant smile on her face.

He eyed her warily then pasted on a smile and pulled her to a stop, fake jovial again. 'We have great news.'

She couldn't help feeling he was getting cues over her shoulder from Frank.

She turned. Frank sent her a huge smile too.

'Good news?' she asked. They both nodded eagerly. 'Good.' She rubbed her hands together. 'I love good news. You'd best come into the formal lounge.' It was the room they preferred anyway. 'Mrs Pengilly is dozing in the family room.'

Marty's smile fled. 'What's she doing here?'

'She's my friend. That's what she's doing here.' She closed the door to the formal lounge and prayed Mrs Pengilly was a sound sleeper. 'Do you have a problem with that?'

'No, no.' He backed down and made straight for her father's chair.

'Damn Nosy Parker, though,' Frank muttered, throwing himself into the one opposite. The one she normally used.

She perched on the edge of the sofa. 'It's what I love about this place. Everyone looks out for everyone else.'

Marty and Frank exchanged glances and Josie's heart sank. She just knew she wasn't going to like their good news.

They wanted her to sell her house.

Oh, that news didn't surprise her. They'd been telling her for years that the place was too big for her, too much to keep up with. Part of her agreed, but it didn't mean…

Given time she'd fill it with people. Somehow.

But they had a buyer already lined up, a property developer. And they had a contract ready for her to sign.

Marty pushed his solid silver and gold plated pen, the one he normally guarded with his life, into her hand and pointed. 'Sign there and there.'

'But I want to think about it first.'

Both men started talking at her at once, gesturing wildly, pacing up and down in front of her. Panic spiked through her. Her shoulders edged up towards her ears as walls started to close in around her.

'This is a once-in-a-lifetime chance, Josie.' Marty slapped a hand to the contract. 'You'll never be offered such a good price again.'

He was probably right. The amount offered was obscene.

'And you won't have to work again either if you

don't want to,' Frank added. 'And you'll be helping the town.'

'Exactly.' Marty thumped another hand to the contract. 'At the moment it's dying a slow death.'

Her head shot up at that. 'Nonsense.'

'This will make sure it doesn't,' Frank rushed in with a warning glare at Marty.

She bit her lip. He might have a point. They weren't proposing to knock down Geraldine's Gardens and build a high-rise in its place. They were talking about a very exclusive, understated resort. Very swish, with the house and grounds of Geraldine's Gardens incorporated into the overall design. They'd shown her the projected plans. She couldn't deny the tastefulness of the enterprise. But…

'It'll be good for you, it'll be good for the community and it'll be good for us.'

'Good for you how?'

'For a start, we'll have peace of mind knowing you're taken care of. You deserve that after the way you looked after Dad.'

Frank's words hit the sore, needy part of her heart right at its very centre.

Marty patted her hand. 'You're our little sister. We want to see you settled.'

She gulped. She just needed to sign the contract and then… 'What was the moving van about?'

'The buyer wants to start work immediately. We wanted to clear the way for things to move as quickly as they could once you got back and signed the contract.' Marty spread out his hands. He still clutched the contract in one of them. 'We didn't think you'd have any objections. We're just looking out for you, Jose.'

The only person in the world to call her Jose had been her father. She leapt up and thrust Marty's pen at him. 'Mrs Pengilly is due for her medication.'

And she fled. She leaned against the wall outside the door of the room, fingers steepled over her nose as she drew in several breaths. All she had to do was sign then she, Marty and Frank would all be one big, happy family.

Somehow the picture didn't quite fit.

When had they arranged all this? Before her holiday?

For the hundredth time that day she wished Kent were here. Not for any other reason than to rest her eyes on him, to breathe in his wood-smoke scent.

Mrs Pengilly's medication. She roused herself, pasted on a bright smile and breezed into the family room to find Mrs Pengilly's chair empty. The doorbell rang.

'Hope you don't mind,' Mrs Pengilly called out

when Josie appeared at the end of the hallway, 'but I called for reinforcements.'

Mrs Pengilly opened the door and Josie's jaw dropped as she watched a substantial cross-section of the townsfolk of Buchanan's Point file past her and into the formal lounge. She followed in their wake, dazed.

'What the...? This is a private matter,' Marty shouted. 'What do you think you're doing?'

Jacob sent Josie an encouraging smile. 'We just want to make sure Josie has all the facts she needs to make an informed decision, that's all.'

'And it is our town,' Mr Piper called from the back of the group. 'Josie's decision will affect all of us.'

'Josie!' Marty hollered. 'You have to get rid—'

'They're my friends, Marty. I want them here.' She didn't wait for a reply but turned to the assembled crowd. 'Are you all aware of the proposal?'

Jacob nodded. 'Yes.'

It didn't surprise her. Someone's cousin's uncle would be on a board somewhere. 'It's not a high-rise,' she said anyway, just so they knew, 'but a very tasteful and exclusive resort.'

Jacob kind of shrugged. He didn't look very comfortable thrust into the role of town spokesperson. 'Town opinion is split. That's not the point.'

'Ooh, you should hear Josie's idea for a b & b,' Mrs Pengilly gushed. 'It's fabulous.'

'B & b?' Frank rounded on her.

'It was just an idea and—'

'We're getting off the track,' Jacob inserted quickly. 'What you decide to do with Geraldine's Gardens is up to you, Josie. It belongs to you. What we want is for you to know *all* the facts.'

That was the second time he'd said that. 'What facts?'

'That Marty's firm is guaranteed this buyer's business if the deal goes through. And Frank's firm will get the building contract.'

'That's not a secret.' Frank rounded on them. 'We were just telling Josie about all the advantages if the project goes ahead.'

Ha! She should've known. But she couldn't help wondering if Frank had meant to be as honest with her as he now claimed.

Marty swung to her. 'It guarantees Frank and I make partnerships with our firms.'

Weariness descended over her. For some reason she had never been able to fathom, Marty and Frank had always felt they'd lost out to her financially. They'd both worked hard to achieve partnerships. She couldn't deny that. Did she really have the heart to stand in their way now? If she signed the contract, would they finally feel she'd squared things up?

'Josie?' Jacob prompted.

'I…' She didn't know what to say.

'What do you want?' he persisted.

She didn't get a chance to answer. At that moment an excited dog burst through the door and knocked her off her feet.

'Molly!' She hugged the squirming bundle of fur. She glanced up and her weariness fled. 'Kent!'

'Sorry, she got away from me.' He stopped dead when he saw the crowd assembled in the room. Clancy and Liz peeped around from behind Kent's back and waved to her. Josie hugged Molly and grinned like an idiot.

'Who the hell is this?' Marty shouted in sudden frustration and Josie came back to herself, even though she couldn't seem to quite catch her breath.

She jumped up. 'Everyone, these are my friends from Martin's Gully. Kent, Clancy and Liz. Umm,' she waved her arm at the assembled crowd, 'this is everyone.'

Her mind whirled. Murmurs of greeting sounded around her, but she couldn't make sense of anything. One thing suddenly became crystal-clear. 'Marty and Frank,' she turned to her brothers, 'I can't make a decision on this tonight.'

Her brothers' jaws dropped. Marty's face went

so red she swore he'd burst a blood vessel. 'This is all because I wouldn't come and pick you up from that God-forsaken place, isn't it?' he yelled. 'It's some kind of payback.'

She didn't know how many volts of electricity it took to snap someone to full attention, but his words ensured he had hers.

Completely.

Her voice, though, was surprisingly calm. 'You knew it was a God-forsaken place?'

'Of course I knew,' he spat. 'What do you think I am? Stupid?'

No, but she was. Anger hit her then in thick red waves. Not only had they set all this up so that she was out of the way while they tried to seal their deal, but in their measly selfishness they hadn't even been able to provide her with a decent holiday.

'So you played me for a sucker?' Neither brother said anything. 'And you prettied it all up by feigning concern for me?'

Marty stared at the floor, Frank at the ceiling.

'Oh, and I fell for it, hook, line and sinker, didn't I? What an idiot you must think I am.'

She waited for them to protest, to tell her they really had appreciated the way she'd taken care of their father, that they really did love her.

Nothing.

'Out.' She picked up the contract and slapped it to Marty's chest. 'You too,' she shouted at Frank. 'Take your contracts and your measly, selfish minds and get out. I don't want to see either of you again.'

Marty blanched. 'You can't mean that.'

'But you're our sister,' Frank started, visibly shaken.

Marty took a step towards her, but to Josie's astonishment Molly bustled up between them, hackles raised. Then she drew back her lips to display every single one of her teeth as she growled. Josie pointed to the door. 'Go.'

Kent stared at Josie and couldn't remember being prouder of anyone than he was of her at that moment. He wanted to grab her up in his arms and swing her around. He wanted to kiss her. He wanted to drag her off to the bedroom and—

He wanted to stay!

The realisation slugged him straight in the gut. But it didn't knock him off his feet. Instead it surged through him and lent him a strange kind of strength. He wanted to stay and it had nothing to do with Molly, or Clancy and Liz, or sticking up for Josie against her brothers.

It had everything to do with him…and her. It was why he'd come, even if he had tried to hide behind all those other reasons.

He shoved his hands in his pockets and studied her as surreptitiously as was possible with a roomful of people studying him too. The sandalwood highlights of her hair gleamed beneath the overhead lights. Her lips, lush and inviting, hinted at exotic delights. Her eyes still blazed from her sudden flash of temper. He'd never seen anything more desirable in his life.

But what if she didn't want him here? His hands curled into fists. What if she didn't want him?

Then he'd become the kind of man she bloody well did want, that was what.

Josie shook herself, tried to unscramble her mind. She turned to Kent, Clancy and Liz. 'What are you all doing here?' She couldn't believe how good it was to see them.

She tried not to feast her eyes too obviously on Kent. Liz and Clancy both burst forward to hug her. She hugged them back. Kent stayed where he was—hands in pockets, glaring moodily at the floor—and her heart burned.

'We were worried what those no-good brothers of yours were up to, lass.'

Liz's eyes twinkled. 'But it appears you didn't need the cavalry after all.'

'No.' Josie gave a shaky laugh. Her audacity in telling her brothers exactly what she thought and sticking up for herself still shocked her. She glanced at Kent. Had he come riding to her rescue too?

He shuffled his feet, rolled his shoulders. 'Since you left, Molly has refused to eat. She's going to have to live with you.'

Her jaw dropped.

He scowled. 'She misses you.'

She hauled it back up. What wouldn't she give to hear him say those self-same words to her?

'We all miss you,' Liz said. 'And I was thinking, if you start up this b & b of yours you're going to need a hand. Since Ted died I've been looking for a change, and I'm a very good cook, you know.'

Clancy shuffled in closer. 'And I know I'm getting on in years, but I'm still handy in the garden.'

Liz folded her arms. 'You'll need a cook.'

Clancy set his jaw. 'You'll need a gardener.'

A huge lump blocked her throat. She glanced at Kent. He stared at Liz and Clancy as if they'd just lost their minds.

His scowl redirected itself to her. 'And you'll need a husband!'

His words knocked the lump clean out of her throat. All conversation in the room stopped.

'What?' She gaped at him.

His scowl deepened as he glanced around the now silent room, at all the avid, curious faces. He rolled his shoulders again. 'Need probably isn't the right word,' he muttered. 'You don't *need* a husband. You probably don't *need* anyone, but I...'

He glanced around the room again and bit back an oath. Grabbing her hand, he dragged her out of the room, out of the front door and around the side of the house. Then he let her go and continued to glare at her.

Josie shook her head. She couldn't have heard him right. He couldn't have said husband. It wasn't possible.

'Doctor,' she babbled. 'I need a doctor.'

'OK, I'll be that too.'

She wanted to throw herself into his arms. So she massaged her temples instead. 'Did you say I needed a husband?'

'Yes.'

'Is this all about me needing someone to look after me and stuff?'

'I took back the word need.'

Another surge of temper and hope shot through her. 'Did you have someone particular in mind?' She wanted to scratch his eyes out. She—

Then he did something she could never have imagined—he dropped to his knees, wrapped his arms around her waist and buried his face in her stomach with a groan. 'I love you, Josie. Me and Molly, we don't function without you.' His arms tightened. 'I miss your laugh. I miss your smell. I miss you.'

He lifted his head and stared deep into her eyes. 'I didn't see at first that there's more strength in your way. There's more strength in a community, in helping people, in building bridges. I want to build that community with you.'

She brushed the hair off his forehead in wonder, traced the strong planes of his face with her fingertips. This wonderful man loved her? Her vision blurred. 'You love me? Really?'

Everything inside her sang at his nod. 'And you can't function without me?'

He shook his head. 'No.'

Ooh, she knew how that felt. 'I'll let you in on a little secret: I can't function without you either.'

Kent surged to his feet with a whoop and swung her around. She wrapped her arms around his neck and laughed for the sheer joy of it. When he set her back on her feet she reached up and touched his face. 'I love you, Kent Black. I can't imagine anything more perfect than being your wife.'

He dropped a kiss to the corner of her mouth. 'Say that again.'

Heat started to pump through her. She wanted to melt into him and forget the rest of the world. 'I, umm…'

Her breath caught as he trailed a path of kisses

down her throat. He lazily trailed the kisses back up again to nuzzle her ear. 'You taste divine, Josie Peterson.'

If he didn't kiss her properly soon she'd die.

She drew back to catch her breath. 'I love you.' He'd doubted it. She could see it in his face. 'I love you,' she repeated. She'd never tire of saying it.

His hands came up to cradle her face. 'I thought I'd destroyed any chance I had with you. I thought I'd chased you so far away that… And by the time I realised I loved you so much I couldn't live without you I—'

She reached up and pressed her fingers against his lips, stemming the flood of words, needing to drive the demons from his eyes. 'I love you, Kent. Forever.'

'Forever.' He breathed the word against her fingers.

She nodded then removed her hand and as his lips descended she lifted hers and met him in a kiss that sealed their promise.

* * * * *

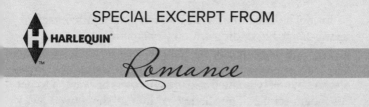

SPECIAL EXCERPT FROM

HARLEQUIN®

Romance

Have you ever dreamed of discovering that you're really a princess? That's exactly what happens to Amanda Carn in THE MAKING OF A PRINCESS by Teresa Carpenter!

"I MUST SAY good night." With obvious reluctance, Xavier saw her safely seated. And then he stepped back and raised his hand in farewell.

Amanda pressed her hand to the window and made herself drive away. Oh, boy. She was so lost. Absolutely gone. He made her feel alive, feminine, desirable.

She knew she was setting herself up for heartbreak. He'd be leaving in a few weeks and her life was here. There was no future to this relationship.

But better heartache than regret. She was tired of being afraid to trust. Tired of letting fear rule her. She felt safe with Xavier. And she longed to explore the chemistry that sizzled between them.

Xavier strolled back to the museum, his gaze locked on the vehicle carrying Amanda Carn into the night. When the car turned from his sight, he fixed his gaze forward and tried to calculate exactly how big a mistake he'd just made.

For the first time, man and soldier were at odds as desire warred with duty. He liked this woman, he wanted her physically, but if she was of the royal family, his duty was to protect her against all threats, including himself. With the addictive taste of her still on his lips, he recognized the challenge that represented.

Inside, he did a final walk-through of the entire museum, as was his habit, ending with the exhibit rooms.

He knew his duty, lived and breathed it day in and day out. Duty was what kept the soldier from kissing her when she so obviously wanted a kiss as much as he wanted to get his mouth on her. The shadow of hurt as she moved away drew the man in him forward as he sought to erase her pain.

And his.

Now may be the only time he had with her, this time of uncertainty while the DNA test was pending. Once her identity was confirmed, she'd be forever out of his reach....

If she's proved to be royalty, then Xavier will have to keep his distance, but he's been bound by royal command to protect Amanda until the truth is discovered. Keeping Amanda safe is his new mission—and where could be safer than in his own arms?

Available in June 2013 from Harlequin® Romance wherever books are sold.

LARGER-PRINT BOOKS!
GET 2 FREE LARGER-PRINT NOVELS PLUS
2 FREE GIFTS!

HARLEQUIN®

Romance

From the Heart, For the Heart

YES! Please send me 2 FREE LARGER-PRINT Harlequin® Romance novels and my 2 FREE gifts (gifts are worth about $10). After receiving them, if I don't wish to receive any more books, I can return the shipping statement marked "cancel." If I don't cancel, I will receive 4 brand-new novels every month and be billed just $4.84 per book in the U.S. or $5.24 per book in Canada. That's a savings of at least 19% off the cover price! It's quite a bargain! Shipping and handling is just 50¢ per book in the U.S. and 75¢ per book in Canada.* I understand that accepting the 2 free books and gifts places me under no obligation to buy anything. I can always return a shipment and cancel at any time. Even if I never buy another book, the two free books and gifts are mine to keep forever.

119/319 HDN F43Y

Name	(PLEASE PRINT)

Address	Apt. #

City	State/Prov.	Zip/Postal Code

Signature (if under 18, a parent or guardian must sign)

Mail to the **Harlequin® Reader Service:**
IN U.S.A.: P.O. Box 1867, Buffalo, NY 14240-1867
IN CANADA: P.O. Box 609, Fort Erie, Ontario L2A 5X3
Want to try two free books from another line?
Call 1-800-873-8635 or visit www.ReaderService.com.

* Terms and prices subject to change without notice. Prices do not include applicable taxes. Sales tax applicable in N.Y. Canadian residents will be charged applicable taxes. Offer not valid in Quebec. This offer is limited to one order per household. Not valid for current subscribers to Harlequin Romance Larger-Print books. All orders subject to credit approval. Credit or debit balances in a customer's account(s) may be offset by any other outstanding balance owed by or to the customer. Please allow 4 to 6 weeks for delivery. Offer available while quantities last.

Your Privacy—The Harlequin® Reader Service is committed to protecting your privacy. Our Privacy Policy is available online at www.ReaderService.com or upon request from the Harlequin Reader Service.

We make a portion of our mailing list available to reputable third parties that offer products we believe may interest you. If you prefer that we not exchange your name with third parties, or if you wish to clarify or modify your communication preferences, please visit us at www.ReaderService.com/consumerschoice or write to us at Harlequin Reader Service Preference Service, P.O. Box 9062, Buffalo, NY 14269. Include your complete name and address.